MIAMI REVISITED

DECADE OF DECEIT

BY JOAN HANSEN

PublishAmerica
Baltimore

© 2011 by Joan Hansen.
All rights reserved. No part of this book may be reproduced, stored in a retrieval system or transmitted in any form or by any means without the prior written permission of the publishers, except by a reviewer who may quote brief passages in a review to be printed in a newspaper, magazine or journal.

First printing

All characters in this book are fictitious, and any resemblance to real persons, living or dead, is coincidental.

PublishAmerica has allowed this work to remain exactly as the author intended, verbatim, without editorial input.

Photo used in cover art provided by Denise Pickett.

Softcover 9781451277302
PUBLISHED BY PUBLISHAMERICA, LLLP
www.publishamerica.com
Baltimore

Printed in the United States of America

DEDICATION

For you, my readers, who encouraged me to write a sequel to 100 Years in Miami, Betrayal under the Palms, my first historical novel about this magical city.

ACKNOWLEDGMENT

Thanks to the production and design team at Publish America for their support and patience and to photographer, Charlene Lane who captured the author photo on the back cover.

A particular thanks to my husband, Claude, who couldn't wait to read each new chapter as I wrote the novel. His critiques were always appreciated as well as his eagerness to know what happened next.

I would like to thank the wonderful women who inspired my writing about Miami, my great-grandmother, Eva Townsend and my grandmother, Margaret Waterbury who were early settlers in Miami in the early 1900's. And particularly my mother, Lyla Waterbury Haynes, who taught the first kindergarten class with 80 tiny students on Miami Beach. Their fascinating tales of early Miami and their eagerness for me to write about it started me on this journey.

PROLOGUE—
MIAMI-PRESENT DAY

Kaitlin stood by the gigantic window in her penthouse office and stared down at the white sails decorating the Biscayne Bay marina in Coconut Grove and her thoughts returned to that sad day in the past when she had strewn the ashes of her beloved father, Andrew Donegon, into the sea that he'd loved so much. Tears ran slowly down her cheeks as she remembered the heartache of waiting to find out the fate of her missing father and finally the tragedy of his suicide and learning the shocking reason behind it.

She rarely thought of the past, it was still too painful ten years later, but it all came back to her now with her premonition that someone was trying to sabotage the business that her great grandfather, Aidin, had started way back in early Miami in 1896. She couldn't let that happen. It was her life now, the heritage left in her hands when her father died. The huge and successful conglomerate of hotels which had now spread across the nation and to the far reaches of the globe was thriving, and now the new boutique hotels had sprouted up in Europe, Asia and Africa in addition to the brilliant success of the original colossal Grand Hotels, some of the first foreign ventures in London, Paris and Rome. Her grandfather, Calvin, had started up the first one in London which was a roaring success back in the 1940's and it had survived the bombings in World War II, even though her grandfather was shot down over Berlin when he later flew missions for the RAF. The world had never seen the elegance of such a hotel as the Grand London in those days, and she had tried to maintain those same standards with the loving creation of each new hotel. And now was it all to be destroyed, after all her efforts?

As her thoughts continued to wander, she didn't realize that her Senior Vice President and long-time partner had come up behind her and now enclosed her in his arms as he turned her away from the window. He took out his handkerchief and gently dried her tears as he tried to figure out what was going on. He was as stunned by Kaitlin's beauty as he had been ten years ago when he saw her for the first time. Her figure was as trim in her smartly tailored business suit as it was then and her lustrous blonde hair was arranged in a French knot and her brown eyes were still glistening but totally amazing as she moved her gaze to his loving eyes. John Martinez had seen Kaitlin through many traumatic events including the shock of her father's tragic death and couldn't imagine what could be causing her sadness now when she was at the height of her success.

"What is it Kaitlin?" he asked quietly as he pulled her over to the couch and then went to the bar and started mixing her a drink. As she started to refuse he continued, "I think you might need this, darling." He also poured himself a drink and then settled down next to Kaitlin. "Are those old ghosts of the past coming back to haunt you?" They sat there sipping their drinks until finally Kaitlin broke the silence.

"John, you may think that I am crazy, but I think someone is trying to takeover our hotel chain. Surely you must have noticed all the delays in new construction adding tremendous costs way above the original estimates," she paused waiting for his reaction. John was one of the sharpest persons in the hotel industry and one of the most perceptive.

"There have been rumors of a strike of the service personnel and in the last few months there have been several serious injuries in some of the construction crews," she sighed waiting for his reply.

"I agree with you, Kaitlin. There have been several suspicious incidents like the worker who fell off the scaffold at the site of the renovation of the Grand New York and was paralyzed. No one can understand what happened to him as he was young and in good health and considered one of the best workers. But, this is no reason to feel that there is some ominous plot afoot to steal your company away from you," he tried to reassure her.

Kaitlin paused wondering if she should go into this any deeper with John even though she completely trusted him, "During the time when you have been traveling on business trips, I have been getting some threatening phone calls, John." He looked alarmed but she continued, "If someone is trying to scare me, they are doing a good job! I have been getting phone calls in the wee hours warning me to get out of the business or face the consequences. Sometimes the caller just hangs up without saying anything." She started to cry again and John looked totally alarmed now.

"You need to be really careful, Kaitlin. It may just be crank calls but I think you need to notify the police and consider having a bodyguard if this continues," he said in a worried tone as he paced back and forth across the room. "Why do you think it only happens when I am away? How could anyone know my schedule?"

"I've hired a private investigator already. Do you have any idea who might be trying to harm me or the corporation?"

"No, but I can promise you that I will find out. I will leave no stone unturned until we get some answers," he said firmly. "I love you, Kaitlin and hope you will finally reconsider my marriage proposal. I will do anything I can to protect you." When Kaitlin had learned her father's tormenting secret, she had made up her mind that perhaps marriage and children weren't in the picture for her, and she had consistently put John's proposals of marriage on the back burner. After all, they had lived together for a number of years and their love for each other was solid and strong.

Kaitlin squeezed his hand and gently kissed him, "I'll think about it, John, but now I need to be alone with my thoughts." As he left the office, she made up her mind that she would not let fear grab a hold of her again. She had suffered enough with that anxiety when her father had disappeared without a trace. She would begin to check through personnel files herself and analyze each person who might have been involved in any company conflict. Although she owned the majority of stocks since the corporation went public, she needed to check to see if there had been any unusual action on the part of any other shareholder.

There was one thing she was sure of and that was her pride in the growth of a corporation that had started over 100 years ago in Miami when her great grandfather, Aidin, had turned his dream of Miami's potential into a reality, building his first hotel right here where she was now standing. She thought about how he had helped build Miami from a straggly infested jungle village to the flourishing, dynamic and exciting city it was today. There was no way she was or could let him down, or no one who would stand in her way of carrying on the Donegon tradition.

Over the past decade Kaitlin had been responsible for building some of the first Boutique Hotels, a group of smaller luxury hotels that cater to the guests' every need. They had started building in Miami, reminiscent of her great-grandfather, Aidin and her father, Andrew, who had changed the face of Miami in the early days. Kaitlin had inherited their courage and vision. Her first boutique hotel was a roaring success, and now they had constructed hotels in the larger cities of the United States and had continued the expansion in Europe and South Africa. She had recently received the prestigious Entrepreneur of the Year Award for the unique designs and innovation in her Boutique Hotels, and her picture had appeared on the cover of a leading financial magazine. This was not the time to retire!

Standing by the ocean at the Grand Miami Beach someone else was looking out at the water at the same time Kaitlin was gazing at the Bay in Coconut Grove. As the mysterious figure turned back to the magnificent hotel that Kaitlin's father had built years ago when he was a young man, the man was overcome by a feeling of strength and power. The Grand Miami Beach had been renovated several times over the years and still was one of the most outstanding hotels in the country with its spacious landscaped grounds along a long stretch of beautiful oceanfront with swimming pools with waterfalls pouring into lagoons surrounded by dazzling tropical blossoms.

"Soon this will be mine," he laughed, "along with all the hotels in the Donegon chain. Maybe old Aidin would have been a challenge, but not Kaitlin Donegon. She doesn't have a chance!"

CHAPTER 1—MIAMI IN 2000

Kaitlin had recently learned the devastating reason for her father's suicide. He had learned from his mother, Sarah Donegon, on her deathbed that he and his wife, Elizabeth, had the same father, Calvin Donegon. Sarah had kept the secret of Andrew's paternity for many years and she had been horrified when he chose to marry Elizabeth, Calvin's daughter. She told Andrew that she had prayed that he and Elizabeth would never have a child as in truth they were half-brother and sister. In fact, her protest of the marriage and later opposition to them having a child had caused an estrangement between them that had lasted for years until she called him to the hospital when she was dying. Andrew was the result of a one-night fling during the unexpected and tragic hurricane of 1926. Kaitlin's father was devastated and tried to protect his beloved wife and daughter from this unspeakable truth. He isolated himself in his study, drinking and reading a journal, written by his newly discovered grandfather, Aidin, who was his idol and mentor from the past, recounting the family history of "black sheep" dating way back to early Miami in 1896. Andrew practically worshiped Aidin as a young boy never dreaming that this tycoon who trained him in the hotel business was his grandfather.

Finally, in despair, he chose to go out to the ocean and went missing causing grief and pain to Elizabeth and Kaitlin as they waited for news. In time his body had washed up and remained hidden in the mangroves at the southern tip of the Everglades where the Atlantic meets the Gulf of Mexico. The sailboat had been originally found near Flamingo Point which is a diverse community of mangroves, hardwood hammocks and freshwater sloughs. Kaitlin hadn't believed that it could have been a suicide, until a courier delivered a package several weeks after the discovery of his body stating that her father was taking his life and that a shocking secret explaining it all would be revealed to her in Aidin's Journal which was enclosed in the package.

Her life had never been the same since her father had left them. She had no idea whether she should ever marry or have children under the circumstances even though she had fallen in love with John Martinez who had asked her to marry him. She and John worked closely at the corporate offices and she had grown accustomed to him as her right arm in business as well as her support during the difficult times. Her mother had suffered terribly and had just been released after an extended hospitalization and nervous breakdown. Elizabeth had always loved Andrew with all her heart and he had always returned that love. She felt lost without him and now worried about Kaitlin and her future since she had learned the truth behind Andrew's suicide.

On top of all this, Kaitlin had inherited the vast hotel network and as the top officer and Chairman of the Board, she suddenly had to cope with the full responsibility of operating a dynasty that started back in the early 1900's by Aidin in early Miami. Her father had trained her well, but had always been there by her side to help guide her through the tough times and there had been many. Now the responsibility of success or failure rested on her shoulders. She also wrestled with the decision of whether to confide in John about her father's secret. It would certainly affect their attitude toward marriage.

She remembered the first day she ran a Board meeting. Although she was nervous, she had inherited her father's strength as well as his business sense. John Martinez was also a member of the Board of Directors and was a powerful presence as he stood by her side when she entered the conference room. She looked at all the familiar faces of the people her father had worked with in the past and noticed most of the expressions were friendly, but a few of the men looked dubious, especially Robert Welch, the General Manager for International Development who didn't hide the fact that he had hoped to become the next CEO of the corporation.

She was quickly voted in as CEO as well as Chairman of the Board for she had inherited the major percentage of shares in the company. Also, she had earned an excellent reputation working at her father's side and she knew the business as well or better than anyone in the Board Room. Her mother also held a large percentage of the company as well as her father's sister, Emily, who had inherited about 10% of the business. Both Elizabeth and Emily were there at the meeting to support her.

After the election, she quickly steered the meeting into progress reports given by Robert Welch and David Wells, who was General Manager for Domestic Development.

Then John Martinez, who she introduced as her new Administrative Assistant, reported on future plans and the development of new concepts. Kaitlin noticed that Robert Welch and David Wells both frowned and eyed each other knowingly when she elevated John to the office of her personal assistant. It was common knowledge that they were living together.

After congratulations and handshakes were given, Emily hugged Kaitlin and asked, "How about we celebrate the success of your first board meeting at the Taurus Restaurant?" The Taurus was a favorite in Coconut Grove nearby where the corporate offices were located in the Grand Biscayne Hotel, Aidin's first hotel venture of many years ago.

Kaitlin laughed, "That couldn't be more perfect, Emily. According to Aidin's journal that location was called the Peacock Inn in the late 1800's and that was where he and his brother, Timothy, celebrated the election of Miami's first mayor. It was quite a revelation at that time with a bathing casino and a dance hall. In fact to share a little ancient gossip, it was at that party that Aidin started to fall in love with the girl that his brother planned to marry! He confesses that indiscretion in his journal."

Emily grinned, "Too much family intrigue for me at the moment so let's go to lunch before I starve!" Kaitlin was glad to see that Emily was so cheerful. She had suffered so much when her husband was captured during the Vietnam War, cruelly tortured and eventually died under unspeakable conditions. The only good outcome of the marriage was the birth of their daughter, Autumn, who Kaitlin considered not only her cousin but her best friend.

"Do you mind if John joins in the celebration?" Kaitlin asked as she saw John emerging from the conference room with a big smile on his face.

Emily gave her a knowing look," Bring him on! We could use a handsome escort like John." Kaitlin couldn't help but notice how attractive he was, tall and tanned in his tailored navy blue suit. It was hard for Emily to miss the electricity in their eyes as they gazed at one another. Emily was in her late sixties, but looked at least ten years younger and with a wonderful figure for a woman of her age. Her eyes were sparkling today and Kaitlin attributed it to her first successful board meeting.

After several toasts to the new CEO the conversation settled on the latest controversy in Miami which was spreading across the nation like wildfire. This was the case of Elian Gonzalez, a six-year old immigrant from Cuba, who was rescued off the coast of Miami. He had been raised by his Miami relatives as his mother died in the heartbreaking journey across the ocean as she tried to reach freedom from Castro's repression. His father still lived in Cuba and wanted him back.

Kaitlin gave John a loving glance, "John, please tell Emily about how you arrived in Miami."

John paused for a moment and then turned his deep brown eyes toward Emily, "I don't talk about it too much, Emily. It still hurts to have left my homeland. I was only ten years old when my mother and I came over from Cuba in a leaky shrimp boat. We landed in Key West where we boarded a bus to the Orange Bowl. Can you imagine living in a tent city in a football stadium at the Orange Bowl as a small, scared boy, and then fifteen years later publicizing the Miami Hurricane's games at the same Orange Bowl!"

"I can't imagine how traumatic that must have been," Emily said sympathetically. "And Kaitlin, just think that your mother, Elizabeth, was involved in social services that aided the Cuban refugees at that time. I remember how she talked about finding them housing, food and healthcare. I've heard how hoards of refugees, something like 125,000 arrived from Cuba during 1980!"

"I came over in the Mariel boatlift along with all the criminals and mental patients that Castro released and sent over to Miami with his blessings. Luckily, they were not all bad apples and a few turned out alright I hope," he sighed deeply. "As you know many of today's political giants here in Miami are from Cuba, and look at all the talented musicians and artists that came over on that pathetic boatlift. The film *Scarface* and then the TV series, *Miami Vice*, didn't help to glamorize us Marielitos portrayed as making the streets of Miami more dangerous, but it did help to lure tourists and to nourish the revitalization of South Beach."

John shook his head as the memories of his flight from Cuba came back to haunt him as they discussed the plight of Elian. Emily's daughter, Autumn, still worked as a reporter at the *Miami Herald* and had all the latest news on little Elian. Emily contributed, "You know the U.S. government and the Cuban government, and his father Juan Miguel Gonzalez, his Miami relatives and the whole Cuban-American community in Miami are all getting involved in this issue!"

John added, "Did you hear that the mayor, Alex Penelas has vowed that he will do nothing to assist the Bill Clinton administration and federal authorities in their bid to return Elian to Cuba. There have been tens of thousands of protesters enraged by the idea of sending Elian back to Cuba when he is with his loving family here in Miami. Rioters are blocking large sections of Little Havana." Little Havana was a section of Miami around S.W. 27 Ave. and 8th St. where Cubans originally settled after arriving in Miami. It brought a real taste of the homeland to displaced families. Here you could see the old men playing dominoes in Domino Park as it was now called or watch men rolling cigars or stop for a delicious tiny cup of strong and sweet Cuban coffee to enjoy with your Media Noche sandwich.

They were so engrossed in their conversation that no one noticed that Robert Welch and David Wells had entered the restaurant. They asked to be seated in a back corner where they could talk privately and still keep an eye on Kaitlin and her entourage.

After they had ordered drinks, Robert turned to his companion and sneered, "What do you think about our new CEO and her Administrative Assistant, Dave?"

Dave replied with a smirk on his aging face, "If you really want the truth, I think Andrew Donegon was not only crazy but a damn fool to put his faith in his daughter. She still isn't wet behind the ears. Both you and I have been with the company for years and look at the growth and expansion that we have brought about! And I'm sure that poor Andrew is turning over in his grave to see Kaitlin already making a poor decision in appointing her lover as her right arm!"

Kaitlin had a strange sense that she was being watched and as she turned to pick up her napkin she noticed the two men out of the corner of her eye. She saw enough to know they were glaring at her and obviously were unhappy about her elevation to CEO. "I think we have some unfriendly people watching our every move," she remarked.

Emily glanced back and saw the two men who realized they were spotted and quickly looked at their menus, "They're just jealous, Kaitlin. Actually, the company needs new blood with new ideas instead of the same old worn-out ideas from those two old codgers!"

Kaitlin looked at Emily's radiance again and asked her suspiciously, "Come on now, Emily, tell your favorite niece what is going on to make your eyes sparkle like Fourth of July? Surely it isn't because of my first Board meeting!"

Emily actually blushed, "Kaitlin and John, I can't hold it back any longer! I have met the most wonderful man and he is making me so happy. I haven't felt this way since I first fell in love with my dear Tom." She waited for their reaction, a little embarrassed at her age to be admitting to a love affair.

Both Kaitlin and John grinned from ear to ear and John called the waiter and ordered champagne. Kaitlin hugged Emily, "It's about time, Emily! We know how much you loved Tom and how you have grieved for him, but he died years ago and you are still so young in spirit. He would be very happy for you!"

"Even Autumn approves and you know how particular she is! He is Hispanic like you are John but of course older. He came over from Cuba in 1960 when the first influx of vocal, well-educated and financially secure Cubans left the island after Castro's takeover. Raul was 20 years old and his family was quite affluent in Cuba. He is now working in the financial district of Miami and we just happened to meet when I went into his company to do some estate planning," she explained. "I was stunned when he later called and asked me out to dinner. I haven't had a date since Tom died!" she said blushing again.

"I think it is absolutely fantastic, Emily," Kaitlin grinned as they raised their flutes of champagne. "I can't wait to meet him. Let's arrange a dinner including my mother and Autumn and of course John and your Raul."

Robert and David watched the happy group toasting with champagne and frowned at each other. "Isn't this disgusting! What a spectacle they are making of themselves. Getting drunk and calling attention to themselves! Poor Andrew would be so embarrassed if he saw his daughter's behavior. I give her about one year and God help the company during that time!" David Wells said as he downed his second drink with one swallow.

"Thank goodness, you and I will be there to watch over things," Robert Welch sighed as he miserably watched Kaitlin, John and Emily celebrating so many things.

CHAPTER 2—2000

Emily gazed at the mirror as she brushed her smartly coiffed gray hair noting that only a few dark strands remained. She had very few wrinkles for a woman who was fast approaching seventy, and her figure was still as slim as when she was a young girl. She carefully chose a becoming black dress and added a colorful scarf and then stepped back and turned as she gave her appearance a final approval.

Her heart was beating fast as she heard the buzzer and knew that Raul must be downstairs. Emily had moved to a high-rise condominium on exclusive Brickell Avenue after selling her beautiful home in Coral Gables after Tom had been dead for a number of years and her daughter, Autumn, had moved to her own place in the Grove. Brickell Avenue was named after William and Mary Brickell who were early settlers in Miami and had owned more than 2500 acres of land. They had a trading post on the Miami River located on what today is called Brickell Avenue. What had been a mosquito-infested jungle land in the 1800's was now the setting for expensive, innovatively designed condominiums facing Biscayne Bay.

She heard the elevator stop on her floor and opened the door to a smiling, distinguished looking Hispanic man carrying a bouquet of red roses. Handing her the roses he gave her an appraising look, "You look lovely tonight, Emily."

"Why thank you, Raul. Let me get a vase for these beautiful roses," she said picking out a sparkling Waterford crystal vase. While she was arranging the roses in the kitchen Raul walked out the wide expanse of glass doors and stood on the balcony overlooking Key Biscayne across the bay. In early Miami couples took boat rides over to Key Biscayne for picnics or to explore the lighthouse where the Seminole Indians had attacked and burned it down many years ago. Now as Raul looked out, cars were whizzing below on the wide causeway leading to the island, a trip that used to take two hours by boat in the 1800's.

Returning to the living room Elizabeth placed the roses on the coffee table and then offered Raul a drink. He surveyed the magnificent antiques and the stunning Oriental carpet and was convinced that Emily was a very affluent widow. He was well aware of the fact that her brother was the legendary Andrew Donegon who recently committed suicide and left his sister as well as his daughter a fortune. He felt that a gift had fallen into his hands when she came to his office for financial planning.

As they sipped their wine and walked out on the balcony to watch the sunset, he placed his arm around Emily and whispered, "I am so lucky that I found you, Emily. I have lived alone for many years and never dreamed that someday I would find someone like you."

"I have also been lonely, Raul, and had given up ever having a partner in my life again," she said softly as a tear rolled down her cheek.

Raul wiped away the tear and put his arms around her. What started as a gentle kiss soon became passionate as they clung together. She felt his maleness pressing against her and she didn't protest when he reached down her neckline and gently stroked her breasts. She hadn't had such feelings for so long and could hardly believe what was happening as they headed for the bedroom. In a moment, he had removed the black dress and was stepping out of his clothes and she gazed in amazement at the size of his erection.

They were both panting as the final clothes were removed and Raul stared at her youthful body, much more beautiful than he had dreamed for a woman her age, "You are so beautiful, my darling. I must make love to you before I die of passion!"

They clung together on the bed as he gently fondled her and heard her soft groaning. When he could no longer stand it, he entered her and heard her gasp his name. After only a few thrusts he heard her breathing increase to a rapid crescendo and then screaming his name over and over her whole body quivered in a gigantic spasm. He continued pounding as her tremors continued and he finally joined her and moaned in pleasure as she heard him say, "I love you, Emily." They never went out to dinner that night. Finally, in the wee hours they found their way to the kitchen and Emily made an omelet.

She was disappointed when Raul said that he couldn't spend the night. She felt like she never wanted to let him go. "I have an appointment in the early morning, sweetheart," he said as he finished dressing. "But this is just the beginning. I have a feeling this will last."

Emily went back to bed and dreamed of her future with Raul. She hoped that one day he would ask her to marry him. She knew she must share all this with her best friend, Elizabeth, Kaitlin's mother. She almost felt guilty though for having so much happiness when Elizabeth was still grieving for her husband's death. She couldn't wait to introduce Raul to Elizabeth and Kaitlin. She was so proud of him. He was so handsome and intelligent and only a few years younger than she was.

Raul Gonzalez grinned with satisfaction as he said to himself, "This could actually be quite pleasant. I knew the lady was rich but I never dreamed she would be so sexy. Now I need to find out just how much she is worth and learn a little more about her holdings in the hotel business. I've always wanted to be in that business and stay in all those luxury hotels all over the world. I need to talk again with my brother as soon as I can and see exactly what he has up his devious sleeve. He knows more about the Donegon dynasty than anyone else on earth. Personal experience pays off!"

After the luncheon at the Taurus, John and Kaitlin had discussed Emily's big news. Kaitlin couldn't wait to tell her mother. The next day she visited Elizabeth who seemed to be in better spirits than she had for some time. She hugged Kaitlin, "Congratulations to the new CEO of Donegon Enterprises!"

"Mother", Kaitlin grinned, "There is more exciting news than that! Aunt Emily has a boyfriend! Can you imagine after all these years?"

Elizabeth laughed, "No wonder Emily has been so cheerful lately. What does Autumn think? And when can we meet him? I hope he is good enough for Emily!"

"We'll find out soon as I am having a dinner party and she will introduce Raul to all of us. He is Hispanic like John and also came over from Cuba, but much earlier in the original influx in the sixties. Weren't you engaged to a Cuban man who came over about the same time before you fell in love with dad?"

"Don't remind me! He turned out to be a poor choice and as far as I know is still serving time in the federal prison in South Dade County for drug dealing and trafficking!"

"How in the world did you get engaged to someone like that?" Kaitlin exclaimed with a stunned expression on her face.

Elizabeth shook her head, "Let's just say he was a very good actor." She added, "but he forgot his lines and the curtain fell. Enough said! Let's hope Emily has better luck!"

After Kaitlin left, Elizabeth couldn't help but remember what a mistake she had made in trusting Carlos Gonzalez. He had stolen her heart in the beginning with his sparkling black eyes and his love of life. She had fallen in love with Andrew when she was a child and later had dated him off and on when he returned from the Korean War. He seemed to have so many girlfriends that Elizabeth doubted if he could ever settle down to one woman and make a serious commitment. Then Carlos came along and swept her off her feet. She thought that he was renewing his medical studies to become a doctor in Miami, but later she became suspicious when his personality hardened and he became secretive. When she pressed him about his strange new friends he yelled profanities and when she returned his engagement ring, he struck her on the face several times and threatened her.

It was then that Andrew who had become jealous when he learned of the engagement finally popped the question and she had never regretted marrying him and had loved him madly right through those devastating final days.

Although Andrew had warned her that Carlos was involved in some shady criminal business, she didn't really believe it until he was sent to prison after a sensational trial that made all the newspapers. She assumed that he was still at the federal prison in South Dade County along with some other major drug dealers like Noriega. She thought of

Emily finally meeting someone and fully realized that both Carlos and Andrew were out of her life but she wasn't alone. She still had Kaitlin, her beautiful and talented daughter.

CHAPTER 3—2000

Emily was so excited as she and Raul headed to Elizabeth's home for dinner. She had spent extra time dressing for the occasion and absolutely glowed especially when she looked into Raul's dark eyes. She just knew that he would make a big hit and she was so proud of him.

"Tell me a little about your family, Emily," Raul said. "I'd like to know something about the people I will be meeting." Actually, he had done quite a bit of research on the Donegon clan and the history of the family was mesmerizing.

She squeezed his hand, "Don't tell me you are nervous, darling? They will love you just as much as I do!"

"And I love you, too, but it never hurts to have a little background," he smiled at her with understanding.

"Well, Elizabeth is a few years younger than I am, but we have been friends since childhood. She married my brother, Andrew Donegon, who inherited the hotel chain from Aidin Donegon, one of the movers and shakers of early Miami." She paused and noticed how attentive Raul was to everything she said, "Actually, Aidin and his brother Timothy, came down to Miami in 1896 to help clear the land for Henry Flagler's extension of his railroad from Palm Beach. They also helped build the first luxury hotel, The Royal Palm, for Flagler and it was located right on the Miami River which is now downtown."

"That's amazing!" he said as they drove in Emily's BMW to Coral Gables where Elizabeth was living.

She continued, "Elizabeth was the daughter of Calvin Donegon, the World War II pilot hero who was shot down over Berlin on a bombing mission. Prior to being a pilot Calvin was also a mover and shaker in the hotel business which he had learned from Aidin. Calvin was Aidin's son and inherited part of the hotel dynasty which passed on to his wife, Kathleen when he died. Kathleen later remarried Frank Moss and they started the Silver Wings Flight School that eventually became a commuter airline. Frank passed away last year but Kathleen is still alive and happy living in a Retirement Village in South Dade County. Elizabeth or Liz as she was called was their only child.

Raul shook his head, "Too many Donegons! But the only one who is memorable to me is this Donegon or should I say Mrs. Pierce? Maybe I am confused, but were you always a Donegon before you married Tom Pierce?"

She laughed, "I guess I forgot to tell you my father and Andrew's was James Donegon, the son of Aidin's brother, Timothy. I never met my father, James, as he killed himself during the depression when he lost everything. He had put all his investments in the stock market, and totally fell apart when the crash came." She said sadly, "My mother was pregnant with me at the time but she hadn't told my father. She raised us as a single mother."

Emily had never learned the family secret, that Calvin was her brother's real father and that Aidin actually was his real grandfather. Elizabeth and Kaitlin had made a vow to never confide this secret of Andrew's true paternity to anyone, even to Emily who they dearly loved. The hurt was still too raw and the secret so shocking that it could only shake the family's foundation. Kaitlin still hadn't come to terms with the fact that her mother and father had been half-brother and sister even though they never knew it. It broke her heart and left a huge hole in it to know that her father took his own life because he couldn't bear to tell them the truth after his mother confessed.

Raul scratched his head, "I must be missing something. How did Aidin happen to make your brother his heir if he wasn't his grandson?"

"Well, that did make a few people angry but everyone who was honest knew he deserved it as Andy was mentored in the hotel business by Aidin since he was a young boy, and Aidin thought of him as the grandson he never had."

Raul thought to himself, "Something doesn't quite add up here but I'll figure it out in time." He turned to Emily, "Then what about the others I am to meet tonight?"

"Well, Kaitlin Donegon who you will meet tonight is Elizabeth's daughter and CEO of Donegon Enterprises. She and Elizabeth are major shareholders and then I guess you know my brother was kind enough to remember me. Am I totally confusing you, my darling?" she asked with concern.

Raul was silently calculating all the money involved with these Donegon women and he felt like he had found the treasure chest. "Is Kaitlin married or engaged," he asked?

"No, but you will meet her boyfriend tonight, John Martinez. He was just appointed her Administrative Assistant and they are very close, if you know what I mean," she blushed as she thought of Raul's ardent lovemaking. "You will like him as he also came over from Cuba and has stories to tell about that and it is fascinating to listen to him."

As they drove up to the huge estate in Coral Gables on the waterfront, Raul sized up the financial worth of the property and smiled as they parked on the circular drive, It was landscaped beautifully with tropical plantings and he could see a large yacht tied to the dock. A smiling Elizabeth opened the door and hugged Emily, and shook hands with Raul.

"We are so glad you could join us, Raul," she said cordially. "Emily is so special to us!"

"And very special to me I might add," he said as he gazed lovingly at Emily.

Just then, Kaitlin and John arrived and after everyone was introduced they went out on the terrace for cocktails. "You have a very fine view of the water, Mrs. Donegon, and I love the way your swimming pool looks like a tropical lagoon and who designed that waterfall?" Raul exclaimed as he observed the dynamics of the group. He quickly sized up Kaitlin. She was drop-dead gorgeous with that mane of beautiful honey blonde hair and almond-shaped brown eyes not to leave out a figure designed for a Goddess. He could hardly take his eyes off her, but noted that Emily was looking a bit distressed by his attentive glances at Kaitlin so he turned back to her. Elizabeth was also beautiful for her age and had the same blonde hair although he suspected it came from a bottle and the same haunting brown eyes. He didn't like John Martinez and hoped he wouldn't get too nosy about his Cuban background. There were a few too many skeletons in his closet.

John addressed Raul, "I hear you also came over to Miami from Cuba. Do you have family here or back on the island?"

Raul cleared his throat and said nervously, "I have a brother but he's still in Cuba." Then to quickly change the subject he asked, "What do you think about the federal government stealing that six-year old boy from his father?"

John said, "I think I hear Emily's daughter, Autumn, arriving. She's a reporter for the *Miami Herald* and usually knows all the latest." Raul noticed that she and Kaitlin were a stunning contrast, both beautiful but Autumn with her short, stylish dark hair and startling blue eyes was as breathtaking as her younger cousin.

Autumn breezed into the room, "Hi, everyone! Hi, Raul! I heard you talking about Elian Gonzalez and what a mess that is becoming! Since the Feds seized Elian, the Cuban-American community is going wild! As we speak rioters are protesting in a ten block area of little Havana. You can hear car horns blaring and demonstrators are overturning signs, trash cans, newspaper racks and even starting some small fires! I guess you know the seizure was directed by Janet Reno, the Attorney General, who actually hails from Miami."

John turned to Raul, "Elian is also a Gonzalez. Is he a relative of yours by any chance?"

Raul quickly answered, "Oh, no. You know there are literally thousands of us Gonzalez' here in Miami! A very popular name, as is yours, Martinez."

Autumn continued, "It will get even worse when they actually return him to Cuba. Fidel Castro is getting into the act and demanding the boy be sent back to his father."

The conversation ended when Liz called them into the house for dinner. They were served delicious conch chowder followed by grilled Florida lobster tails and avocado salad by the attractive housekeeper. Liz kept looking at Raul and for some reason he looked familiar but she had no idea where she might have seen him before. She had worked at

Freedom Tower in downtown Miami years ago helping newly arrived Cubans with immigration issues as well as providing food and shelter to those who needed it.

Since the overthrow of Batista, initially many Cubans rushed back to Cuba thinking things would be better, but after they discovered things were not as promised they began to trickle back to Miami and it soon became a flood of refugees. As Elizabeth had been a Spanish major at the University of Miami, she was in demand because they needed bilingual managers. The first wave of refugees brought their family wealth, jewels and bank accounts. They were able to purchase homes and resume their social life. Many of the transplants were professionals who had to take menial jobs to get by when they came over with only a few bucks in their pockets.

Finally the conversation changed to business over dessert and coffee. Kaitlin said, "We plan to present the concept of Boutique Hotels at the next board meeting, and I hope you, Mom, and Emily will support us. John has worked up a terrific presentation."

Emily and Liz said in unison, "Tell us more, John."

John sipped his coffee and reached into his briefcase which was laying on the coffee table, "It's a very exciting concept and I think it will catch fire! To simply state it my idea of a Boutique Hotel is an intimate, luxurious and smaller hotel than our Grand Hotels. It should provide personalized services and facilities. Although Boutique Hotels have been around now for about twenty years and are in primarily large city centers, I feel that the Grand Boutiques could be more individual than the ones I have studied, and I believe there is a whole new market waiting for Boutique Hotels in smaller towns in areas that attract tourists, especially in Europe. That's all I'll say for now as I plan to give a full presentation at the next board meeting."

Everyone seemed to agree that it was a great idea, especially Kaitlin who glowed with every word spoken. "No doubt," thought Raul, "those two are lovers." In his mind he was silently calculating how much more capital that would bring to the Donegon treasure trove.

It wasn't long before they were all preparing to leave and Raul was effusive in his praise of the dinner and the evening as he took Emily by the arm. Everyone couldn't miss the loving look they shared when their eyes met.

"I think my mother has fallen hook line and sinker for Raul," Autumn sighed after they had left. "I hope he doesn't get her hopes up too high as I don't feel that he is that serious about her. Did you notice how he kept staring at Kaitlin?"

"He did make me a little uncomfortable, but he seems nice enough," Kaitlin replied thoughtfully.

John chimed in, "No one asked for my opinion, but there was something wrong there. I just couldn't put my finger on it. I felt like he was playacting, and not letting us in to see his real personality. Also, he certainly changed the subject in a hurry when I tried to find out about his Cuban background."

"Oh, dear," sighed Elizabeth, "I hope for Emily's sake that you are wrong and that he was just a little nervous meeting Emily's family for the first time. Of course, you had met him before hadn't you, Autumn?"

"Only briefly, and I was glad he was making my mother happy," she answered. "I'll keep an eye on things. I wasn't made an investigative reporter for nothing!"

CHAPTER 4—2000

John was setting up his power point presentation for the Board of Directors. He was excited about the concept of smaller boutique hotels to be added to the chain of large and luxurious Grand Hotels. Kaitlin had seen the presentation and thoroughly approved of the idea and now to convince the other Board members.

As they filed in, John noticed that Robert Welch and David Wells were standing in one corner of the room whispering. Kaitlin quickly asked that they all be seated and started the meeting by introducing John, "We have a very important issue to present to you today and if it is approved, I believe it will put new life into the hotel business. The Grand Hotels are all doing well, but we think they can do even better." Smiling she nodded at John to begin. Emily, Elizabeth and several other Board members smiled back and seemed eager to learn more. Robert Welch and David Wells on the other hand were stone-faced, no expression at all.

John stood at the podium and explained the concept of Boutique Hotels, 'Boutique Hotels are nothing new, in fact they were first introduced in the 1980's. However, most of them were small and not connected with chain hotels like the Grand Hotels. We think it is the right time to add these smaller, more intimate hotels to our corporation."

Robert Welch frowned and interrupted, "If we are doing so well in our current concept, why invest in something new? It seems foolhardy to me!" David Wells nodded in agreement.

"Wait until you hear the whole presentation, Bob, before you try to nix it," John said emphatically. "To continue, the difference is in themes and specialized services. Sometimes a boutique hotel can be hip, another time historic. We would feature unique designs, and an unheard level of personalized service."

Again Robert Welch interrupted, "Isn't that what the Grand Hotels are already noted for, our degree of personalized services! What more can we offer our guests than what we are now doing. This is crazy!"

"Bob, I would appreciate it if you would hold your comments until the end of the presentation," Kaitlin admonished him in a firm voice. Robert Welch whispered something to David Wells she noted.

"We can offer many new services, Bob, such as signature restaurants with important chefs, destination spas and in-room spa services. I'd like to introduce an evening wine—hour in the lobby where guests can get to know each other," John added. "The target market will be ages 25-55, with high middle or upper incomes. We would cater to the corporate traveler who will give us repeat business during any season of the year. It's time for the Grand to catch up with the twenty-first century and I hope you will all see the need for constant change instead of resting on our laurels and letting others in the hotel business get ahead of us!"

Emily spoke with enthusiasm, "It sounds great to me. Where would we start?"

Kaitlin replied, "We would start in the big city markets like San Francisco, New York and of course Miami. Then I can see us branching out into smaller cities and villages, historic areas both in the United States and Europe. The corporation is solid financially and we are able to risk a new venture that may turn out to be extremely popular. John will distribute the figures for the opening investment and project future costs. We'll take the vote after you have had some time to study the projections. I'd like to vote on this issue when we convene after lunch."

Most of the board members appeared to be excited as they filed out of the conference room, but Robert Welch and David Wells grabbed the handout and hurried out of the room without further conversation with anyone. Kaitlin doubted if either man would vote in favor of the proposal.

William Petersen joined Kaitlin and John in the hotel's restaurant for lunch. He had been a friend of the family for years and an important financier and philanthropist. He donated large sums of his personal fortune to the development of museums and the Arts in Miami. Kaitlin noticed that he was slowing down due to his advanced age, but he still looked handsome and distinguished with his silver hair and alert blue eyes.

After ordering in the beautiful restaurant overlooking the sparkling Biscayne Bay, he looked at Kaitlin with a pensive expression, "I think you are going to have trouble with Bob and Dave. So far they haven't liked any suggestion you've made since you took over the Board. I think your father would have been very disappointed in their lack of support."

Kaitlin sighed, "I'm well aware of their hostility, Bill. Bob thought he would be made CEO when my father died and he makes his displeasure of my appointment very obvious. I can live with that, but it upsets me to think that he is putting his anger ahead of what is right for the corporation." She paused and then added, "And his cohort in crime, David Wells, follows his every lead."

John spoke decisively, "I think we have the majority vote, Kaitlin, even without their two votes. It would be a shame to vote down the growth of the business. They don't seem to listen to any proposals for change. I'd attribute it to their age, if I didn't know better. I trust you are in favor, Bill?"

"Absolutely! It is something your father would have loved. Andy was the great innovator since the time he first started in the hotel business. I know that the great founder, Aidin, took him under his wing when he was just a boy. Now he is lucky for he trained his own daughter, you, Kaitlin, to follow in his footsteps!"

After lunch, the proposal was quickly passed with Emily, Elizabeth and William Petersen as well as Edward Haynes, a wealthy banker and friend of Kaitlin's father, voting along with Kaitlin and John. As expected Bob and Dave voted against the measure and had grim expressions on their faces but they held their silence.

"We'll be starting the first Grand Boutique right here in Miami, so we can watch the progress every step of the way," John smiled.

"I want to be your first guest! Autumn will like it also, as she loves to be pampered! Wait until she hears about the in-room spa," Emily said. She was thinking to herself that it would be a wonderful place for a honeymoon if Raul ever popped the question. She colored when she thought about Raul and his high libido and hoped no one was aware of what she was thinking.

Kaitlin adjourned the meeting and she and John left in a hurry, eager to plan the next step in the Grand Miami Boutique Hotel. "Bob and Dave will have to help with this if they want to keep their jobs," Kaitlin remarked as she looked back and noticed their hostile expressions.

"Now you're talking like the real CEO, Kaitlin. No matter how much your father respected them, they are trying to put down every new suggestion. I think it's time we look at reorganization of the company if this continues," John added. "I'd like to help!"

Kaitlin paused and then said thoughtfully, "John, we need to hold back a bit and not make hasty changes to the present structure. Let's wait and see if Bob and Dave put genuine effort into the new project. I'd like to have projections of possible sites for the new boutique hotel, starting with Miami. Do we revamp some of our older properties and convert them to the new concept, or build from the ground? I'm going to assign that task to Dave, and Bob can explore possibilities in the international picture. I'll soon know if they are going to cooperate and we'll go from there. There may be some heads rolling in the future."

While Kaitlin and John continued to excitedly plan their first boutique hotel, Bob and Dave were huddled in Bob's office discussing in hushed tones their strategies for placing roadblocks in the new project. "We need to find some way to stop this insane idea, and also how to oust Kaitlin from the head office. She's a disaster and keeping her around will be catastrophic," Dave said as he sipped his coffee and flushed with anger.

"You're absolutely right, Dave. This can't continue. What's wrong with Haynes and Petersen to have voted in favor of this idiocy! It's up to us to save the corporation," Bob said emphatically as he reached for the whisky bottle in his desk drawer.

CHAPTER 5—2000

Several months after Elizabeth's dinner party where Emily introduced her new flame, Raul, the romance was heating up. They were not only sleeping together on a regular basis but Emily was beginning to hope that Raul might pop the question and she was more than ready to give him an affirmative answer. She felt like a new person, young and vital even though she was way past middle-age. Her hormones were raging like a teen-ager and she had to admit to herself that she had never enjoyed sex like this before, even with her beloved husband, Tom.

Raul let himself in to her apartment with the key she had given him, and before he had a chance to take off his coat, Emily was leading him to the bedroom.

"Wait a minute, darling, I need to relax a bit first and have a drink. It has been a hard day at the office!" Raul said with a tone of irritation.

Emily looked disappointed but then quickly poured him a drink and sat at his side, "I'm sorry, Raul." She paused and blushed much to her dismay, "I guess I was having some naughty thoughts and just couldn't wait until you got here. I didn't mean to rush things. It's just that I was feeling…"

"So horny," he completed her sentence. "Believe me, I love that about you, darling. You are always ready, but sometimes I need a moment when I have worked all day."

Emily sighed, "I'm a little embarrassed, Raul. You have become an important part of my life and I have gone for such a long time without male companionship." She said softly, "And I have fallen head over heels in love with you. And hope this can last forever."

Raul knew where this was heading and he was not at all ready to make a marriage commitment, especially when she had not fully revealed her financial status. He had his eye on her sister-in-law, Elizabeth, who was younger and more attractive, and probably a lot richer but he hadn't figured out how he could seduce her with Emily constantly pressing him for a permanent commitment. Also, Elizabeth's daughter, Kaitlin, really turned him on, but he figured Martinez had her all sewed up even though they weren't married.

Keeping those thoughts to himself, he tried to change the subject, "I love you, too, Emily, but now is not the time to talk about the future. Let's just enjoy the present," he whispered as he ran his hand inside her blouse and caressed her breast. That ended the touchy subject as her breathing reached a feverish pitch as she unzipped his fly, and they were soon on the floor making passionate love. Emily exploded in frantic waves of pleasure as soon as he entered her, and she knew that she could never get along without this man who made her feel like this. She must find a way to discuss marriage with him before too much more time passed.

Raul knew that it was time he discussed his plans with his brother who was serving a long prison sentence for drug trafficking and racketeering. He always hated to visit Carlos as he became more bitter as the years rolled by. He had ten more years to serve, that is if he behaved himself, before he could go before the parole board.

He knew the routine well. He was ushered into a visiting booth and they would converse through glass-encased tiny mesh, using phones and reading each other's thoughts. The guard led him in with handcuffs and they each picked up a receiver.

"Well, what's up in the real world, Raul?" Carlos asked. "Especially in the Donegon's world?" Raul noticed that he had a malicious smirk on his face.

"That Emily is one hot cookie. She's the sexiest old broad I ever met! You know how many times she wants to do it..."

Carlos frowned, "Spare me the details, hermano! Don't you remember I have been cooped up here for years without a woman! I don't need any more torture from you!"

"I finally met Elizabeth and she's quite a knock-out even at her age. I can see why you fell for her." He hesitated, "I'd really like to do her, too. What do you think?"

Carlos grabbed the phone in fury, "Don't you touch that Bitch! I am reserving that pleasure when I get out of here. She really screwed me, probably was the one who squealed on me and sent me here for years! I have big plans as to what I will do to her and it won't be pleasant!" He scowled at Raul, "Keep your hands off her, do you understand?"

Raul tried to calm him down, "I was just thinking, between Emily and Elizabeth we are talking big, big money. I have Emily's trust and I am getting close to knowing her financial picture. I have a what-if for you."

"Like what?" Carlos asked sarcastically.

"What if I marry Emily and when you get out instead of getting even with Elizabeth by force, what if you make her fall in love with you all over again by being the nice guy. She is a widow now and if she is as hot as her sister-in-law..."

Carlos interrupted, "I'm beginning to catch on, hermano. The two broads must be worth millions not to mention the hotel corporation. Believe me, it was my dream to get rid of her husband, Andrew Donegon, but he robbed me of it by bumping himself off!"

Raul looked at him with curiosity, "Didn't she marry that dude right after the two of you broke up?"

"Yea, in fact he might have been feeding her some of the bullshit about me. I think they both may have been the ones that put the feds on me," he said pounding his fist on the table. "But I will think about your idea. I have nothing much to think about around here and it might be interesting. I'll also be reading up on corporate takeovers in my spare time in the prison library."

Raul had always depended on his older brother even though he was in prison and looked at him thoughtfully, "Let me know if I should marry Emily the next time I come to visit. I could do worse. You deserve Elizabeth after all these years in the slammer."

Carlos at last smiled, "Deserve her? I will make her life one holy hell!"

Raul was grinning from ear to ear as they put down their receivers and he watched his brother being ushered through a heavy steel door at the side of the visiting room.

CHAPTER 6—
NOVEMBER, 2000

Florida was again in the national spotlight during the Presidential elections of 2000. No sooner had the roar settled down over the little Cuban boy being returned to his homeland where he received a welcome parade and personal affection from Fidel Castro than a new controversy focused attention on the state. This was the subject uppermost in conversation all over Miami and that included the Donegon family.

Kaitlin and Autumn were both working on the Al Gore campaign on the weekends by making phone calls and sending out materials as well as arranging rides for people to get to the polls. On the night of the election all the Donegons gathered together to watch the results. No one could have predicted what was to follow. Florida was a swing state and had a major recount dispute. The vote in Florida would determine who won the election as it became too close to call. The candidate who won Florida's electoral votes would be the new President of the United States.

They gathered at Elizabeth's house in the Gables and were toasting with champagne and cheering when the national television networks using information provided by the Voter News Service, an organization formed by the Associated Press to help determine the outcome of the election through early evening tallies and exit polling, announced that Al Gore had won the election.

Autumn screamed over the merrymaking, "Hey, hold it folks!" They all looked at her in astonishment.

As the newspaper reporter, she always looked at both sides of an issue and she continued, "The reports are only in from the eastern counties. The time zone up in the panhandle is on Central time and they are staunch Republicans so don't get your hopes up too high!"

Emily retorted, "You are a wet blanket, Autumn! They wouldn't have announced it if it weren't true. Do you always have to be so skeptical about everything?"

John Martinez said, "You may have a point there, Autumn. Maybe the announcement is premature. We need to wait until those northern counties report in before we celebrate."

The elated mood of the group dissipated quickly an hour later when the networks retracted their call for Gore and gave the win to George Bush. The group moaned until later in the evening when the networks retracted that call, too, and called it "too close to call."

Kaitlin frowned, "Bush only won the vote count in Florida by 2000 votes. I think they are going to have to recount the votes to make sure who the real winner is."

Autumn added, "You know that Florida state law provides for an automatic recount when elections are this close."

"Do you mean to say we won't know who our next President will be until a recount?" Elizabeth said incredulously.

Raul who was always at Emily's side these days piped in, "Well, at least you have a choice of candidates. A little different in my homeland in Cuba." Emily patted his hand in understanding and he gave her a quick kiss on the cheek.

This uncertainty was to grasp the whole nation and continued as a controversy in all circles especially in Miami-Dade County and Palm Beach. Emily, Autumn, Liz and Kaitlin were having lunch a few weeks later and their conversation centered on the election.

"What is the latest, Autumn, with the recount?" Liz asked.

"There are so many irregularities in the ballots that are favoring Bush like the 'butterfly ballots' in Palm Beach which produced an unusual number of votes for the third-party candidate Patrick Buchanan."

"But that's mainly a Democrat county," Liz exclaimed! "How could a Republican win all those votes?"

"That's the point, Liz. It was most irregular. Also, some 50,000 who they claimed were felons were not allowed to vote. Most of them were African-American voters and were not felons and should have been eligible to vote under Florida law," Autumn replied as she shook her head in disgust. "The worst thing to happen here in Miami is when the paid Republican protestors shut down the manual recount in Miami-Dade County by screaming and intimidating the vote counters. This whole thing is a nightmare!"

Emily sighed, "I'm afraid Florida is becoming the laughing stock for the whole nation."

Deadlines for vote recounts were also in dispute and also the manner in which each county would count undervotes or over votes. Numerous local court rulings went both ways, some ordering recounts and some saying a recount would be unfair.

"Well, Gore has won his appeal to the Florida Supreme Court ordering the recount to continue. Did you see all those trucks carrying ballots to Tallahassee?" Autumn asked.

Kaitlin laughed, "It was unbelievable! There must have been hundreds of trucks!"

Their joy at the recount quickly faded on December 9 when the United Supreme Court granted Bush's emergency plea for a stay of the Florida Supreme Court's recount ruling, stopping the count without all ballots counted.

Kaitlin called Autumn at the newspaper several days later, "I can't believe what I just heard on the television! Tell me it isn't true!"

Autumn knew just what Kaitlin was talking about. "Yes, it is true, the United States Supreme Court just ruled in favor of Bush, ending all recounting and legal review! What a great Christmas present they have given George W. Bush, our new president!"

Kaitlin moaned, "What about Al Gore? Can he do anything about it?"

"It's a done deal, Kaitlin. We may never learn who the true winner was thanks to stopping the recount. In the future Florida needs to rethink the voting process so that something like this never happens again. I need to get back to my desk, and I advise you to get back to your boutique hotels and build me one with an in-room spa. I will be your first guest!" Autumn teased Kaitlin.

Kaitlin and John had decided to renovate one of their own properties on Miami Beach for their first boutique hotel. The setting was beautiful, across the street from the ocean and in the popular South Beach area. The hotel would have only 70 rooms in contrast to their huge, Grand Hotels and they all would be suites. The décor would be Art Deco in the original pink and pastel colors and eclectic architectural design as well as interior design.

Kaitlin could hardly control her excitement and enthusiasm for the project, "I want to be sure our guests get a good night's sleep with the most comfortable mattresses available, 300-thread Belgian sheets and goose down pillows and comforters."

John laughed, "And don't forget the in-house masseuse that Autumn is waiting for!"

Kaitlin said with a grin, "She wouldn't let us forget that! I'd like to keep the price lower than our hotel chain to attract the traveler who is both style-conscious and watching his budget. We need to reach a hipper clientele who want cool design and local flavor."

"We have hired an architect who specializes in Art Deco design and we are bringing on board one of the top interior decorators. We should be ready to start reconstruction in a few months," John said looking at his planning calendar.

"Now comes the advertising campaign. We need to hire an advertising agency that will publicize the new Boutique Hotel concept for the Grand Hotels. And we need to think up a catchy name for the project," she said pondering potential names.

"How about UNIQUE BOUTIQUE?" John asked with a grin spread across his face.

Kaitlin laughed," I love it, John! How do you come up with ideas so fast?" She looked at him thoughtfully, "But how do we convey it is part of the Grand Hotels?"

John frowned, "That's a tough one, Kaitlin." He thought for a moment, "How about UNIQUE BOUTIQUE ala GRAND HOTEL?"

"Maybe we ought to let the advertising agency play with that one and see what they come up with," Kaitlin smiled. "I'm so excited, John! I can't wait to get the plan underway and I love the thought of the first one opening in Miami. I can just see my great-grandfather, Aidin looking down at me and saying, "Chip off the old block!"

CHAPTER 7—
DECEMBER, 2000

Raul visited his brother Carlos again shortly before Christmas. He hated to go into the prison as it always depressed him, but he desperately needed to speak to him about Emily's marriage demands. She was broadly hinting that she expected a ring for Christmas and Raul was getting cold feet about the relationship.

Carlos was led into the visitor's cubicle by an angry-looking guard. He glared at his brother, "You finally came to see me! Is this your way of wishing me Merry Christmas? You see how festive and merry this joint is!"

Raul frowned, "I've been busy, Carlos, working on our plan to get rich and spend the rest of our lives in luxury!"

"Great, Raul, that's really hard work fucking the sister while I sit here for another five years waiting to screw Elizabeth! I still have hopes of parole, but who knows what those bastards will say. My lawyer says I have a good chance of cutting off a few years but who knows," he shouted into the receiver in the glass booth and pounded his handcuffs against the table.

"Calm down, Hermano. I came to you for advice as well as to wish you Merry Christmas. Emily is driving me crazy with her hints of getting married! She gets all pouty when I try to change the subject and I know she expects a ring at Christmas. I found out that she's worth a fortune with her shares in the hotel business. Not as rich as her sister-in-law but you already told me Elizabeth is your property," Raul explained.

"I warned you, don't go sticking your dick into that one. She's all mine!"

Carlos said with a malicious smirk on his face. "Go ahead and marry the other one and I've given your idea some thought since you were here last time. I'll marry Elizabeth and get my revenge on that bitch later, after the two of us have grabbed their fortunes."

"I hate to mention this, Carlos, but didn't you tell me Elizabeth hates you. How do you intend to convince her to marry you? That daughter of hers, Kaitlin, is pretty damn smart and frankly she'd be my choice if she wasn't so hung up on another Cuban guy, John Martinez," Raul advised Carlos.

"Don't worry about Martinez, I still have plenty of friends on the outside that know how to make people disappear," he whispered into the receiver. "So happy wedding, Brother, and if you are smart you won't breathe a word about your brother in prison until after the marriage. And don't worry, I'll charm the hell out of Elizabeth and show her how I've reformed. I had her fooled once and I can do it again! Besides, I have plenty of spare time to think about it. Make sure she doesn't fall for some other dude while I'm in the pen."

"O.K. she'll get her ring for Christmas, and I'll get the dough," Raul laughed and was surprised when Carlos joined him. "Our future is looking brighter every day!"

Raul went to the best jewelry store in Coral Gables after leaving the prison and finally chose a beautiful 3-karet diamond ring. "She'll end up paying for it herself after we're married," he thought. He couldn't wait to give up his job and let her support him. He'd always wanted to travel, and now as he thought of the Grand Hotels all over the globe he couldn't wait to finalize the wedding plans. He'd prefer a younger woman, but what the heck, Emily wasn't all that bad and with all that money he could put up with her.

The next night Raul arrived at Emily's condo with the ring in his pocket. As usual she ran into his arms the moment he came through the door. He had to admit she looked stunning for an old broad and he felt his erection growing as he noticed the deep cleavage in her slinky black dress. Reaching down he fondled her exposed breasts and before they knew it he was removing the dress and unzipping his fly. Emily gasped as she saw his huge erection and soon was in heaven as he threw her down on the couch and without any foreplay entered her and pounded until she screamed in pleasure.

"Oh, Raul, I wish we could be like this forever. No man has made me feel like this before. I loved my husband, Tom, but I never felt the ecstasy that we have when we are together," she whispered as she nuzzled her head against his chest.

"I have a surprise for you, my darling," he replied. He started dressing much to her disappointment and said, "Now you put on that gorgeous dress and we'll go down to South Beach in Miami Beach and have an elegant dinner and then hit some of the hot clubs."

She looked like she was ready to cry, "Is that my surprise, Raul?"

Raul laughed as he reached in his pocket and fell to his knees, "No that is our celebration! I love you Emily and I want you to be my wife. Will you marry me?"

He gave her the small box and when she opened it and saw the huge diamond engagement ring she cried in joy and kissed Raul until she nearly smothered him.

"Yes, yes, yes! I love you so much, Raul and I will marry you as soon as it can be arranged." Emily was glowing with happiness as he placed the ring on her finger. She brought out a bottle of Don Perignon champagne and said, "I have been saving this and knew in my heart that one day my dreams would come true. You, Raul, are my dream and now we will be together forever!"

As he popped the cork and poured the champagne into the flutes he was thinking to himself, "We'll be together, but your money goes to me. I think I can get used to this lifestyle very quickly."

He raised his flute, "To my bride-to-be! The future Mrs. Raul Gonzalez!"

"Oh, Raul, I must call Elizabeth and tell her my wonderful news!" Emily said in an excited tone. "She'll be so happy for me!"

Raul frowned, "Don't forget we have big plans for tonight, Emily."

"It will only take a minute, darling," she said as she dialed Elizabeth's number. Elizabeth picked up right away, "How nice to hear from you Emily. I hope you and Raul will join us for Christmas dinner."

"That would be great, but Liz, I have the most fantastic news! Raul has proposed and has given me a beautiful ring. We plan to get married soon. Isn't that the most wonderful news!" she exclaimed breathlessly.

Elizabeth paused for a long moment, "I'm so glad you are happy, darling." Then she paused again, "Of course you will need a lawyer and a pre-nuptial agreement."

"I never had one with Tom, but I don't want to talk business, I'm too happy and excited!" she said while admiring her ring. "Talk to you later, as Raul and I are going out on the town to celebrate our happiness."

Raul frowned, "What was that all about? What kind of business was she talking about?"

"Oh, it was silly! She said I need a lawyer and a prenuptial agreement," Emily answered as she refreshed her makeup and combed her hair.

Raul stormed angrily, "That's ridiculous! We trust each other and don't want our love to be a business proposition. What an insult! Isn't she happy for us or is she just jealous because she can't get a man."

Emily hugged Raul, "Don't be angry, darling. Of course, I wouldn't want a prenuptial agreement. You are very financially secure so why worry. Our love and trust is what is important!"

"If she only knew! I'm up to my neck in gambling debts and my bank account is down to nothing. I have to pay for our great celebration evening, but soon all the bills go to my darling wife," he smirked as he escorted his enamored fiancé out the door.

CHAPTER 8—APRIL 2001

The opening of the Grand Miami Unique Boutique was a stupendous event. Crowds of the most important people and beautiful people flocked to the reception on South Beach. The Art Deco architecture with its pastel colors looked like a watercolor painting in contrast with the blue Atlantic. The circular bar wrapped around the swimming pool on the terrace facing the ocean. A huge buffet was set up and the champagne was flowing.

Kaitlin greeted the guests looking fabulous in her backless Versace gown in tribute to the murdered designer whose mansion was just a stone's throw from the Grand Boutique. It was here in July of 1997 that Gianni Versace, the famous fashion designer, was murdered after picking up an Italian newspaper at the News Café. On returning to his Oceanside mansion, he was accosted by a man named Andrew Cunanan and shot twice in the face, dying almost instantly. It was believed that Cunanan and Versace ran in the same social circles but it was never clear why he decided to murder him. Many recalled the old days when Al Capone also decided to make Miami Beach his home.

John Martinez stood next to Kaitlin in the receiving line, looking handsome and tanned in his white-jacketed tuxedo. Elizabeth attended the gala event and couldn't help but remember when she and Kaitlin's father, Andrew, also greeted guests at the opening of the fabulous Grand Miami Beach so many years ago, long before Andrew proposed marriage. Emily and Raul were there, Emily glowing from her marriage to Raul and Raul busy eyeing all the young, beautiful and glamorous women in transparent dresses and short skirts. While Emily and Elizabeth sipped their drinks, Raul circulated through the crowd stopping to engage the women in conversation without too much success.

Elizabeth noticed that Emily's former glow had disappeared and a look of sadness took its place, "Emily, it seems like Raul is a real party boy. He sure knows how to circulate!" Raul had his arm around a gorgeous twenty-something and was whispering in her ear.

She hesitated before she asked, "Emily, are you and Raul happy?" They had married quickly in December shortly after the engagement was announced. After a wedding and honeymoon in St. Lucia at a very exclusive resort which was listed at over $1000 a night, they returned to Miami as man and wife. Elizabeth had been disappointed that they weren't married in Miami and had offered to host the reception at the Grand Biscayne, but Emily insisted that Raul just couldn't wait that long to make her his wife.

Emily sighed, "I think I should have listened to you when you suggested the prenuptial agreement, but Raul was so against the idea and I was afraid he would back out of the marriage if I insisted."

"But I thought you said he was so financially secure that it was unnecessary," Liz said with concern as she looked into Emily's sad eyes.

Tears started to well up in her eyes as she said in a quivering voice, "Liz, I had to pay for the wedding and honeymoon. They wouldn't accept his credit card which apparently was maxed out."

Liz took her hand, "I'm so sorry, dear. But has the credit problem been resolved?"

"No, that's the worst thing, he hasn't straightened it out yet for some reason, and I am bearing all the expenses and he has very expensive tastes. He just bought a Jaguar car without even telling me," she was crying in earnest now.

"I can't believe this!" Liz exclaimed. "Do you want me to talk to him, or better still do you want Autumn to know about this? I'm sure she will be very concerned and know how to handle this discreetly."

"Oh, no, I'm sure it is only temporary. Raul has a good job and I have no reason to believe this will continue after he gets his affairs in order. I love him so much and I don't want to make him angry. I would just die if he ever left me, Liz!" she said drying her eyes.

Liz shook her head in sympathy and fear that her sister-in-law might have made a huge mistake. Without a prenuptial agreement Raul could take her for at least half of her wealth. She hoped it never came to that and she thanked her lucky stars that she wasn't involved with a man. Her memories of her beloved husband, Andy, would stay with her for a lifetime.

Kaitlin was the glowing star of the evening and many photographers snapped her picture with various celebrities and would certainly bring a lot of positive publicity to the new Grand Boutique concept. "We plan to go to France and Scotland to explore possibilities in building boutique hotels in the European market," she was telling a reporter from the *Miami Herald*. "We are fully booked for a number of months at this hotel which you know has many innovations. A booking includes an in-house massage and credits for some of the hottest South Beach clubs and restaurants. As the area attracts many young singles from all over the globe, we plan cocktail get-to-know you parties on a nightly basis. Plus this gorgeous setting!" She added with a grin, "That beautiful full moon over Miami is free of charge!"

"Where will your next Boutique Hotel be built?" the reporter asked.

"We are planning San Francisco next, then Chicago and New York and as I mentioned, we will be checking out possible European properties and locations."

Raul moved in hoping to be photographed with Kaitlin and appear in Sunday's paper in the VIP event section. He looked directly at the reporter, "My wife is the aunt of this beautiful creature. I guess that makes me her uncle!" He put his arm around Kaitlin in a possessive manner.

She eyed him coldly and backed away from him, "This is Raul Gonzalez who recently married my Aunt Emily." She looked around and saw Emily forlornly sitting alone, "She's over there," she said to the reporter, "and looks like she needs a drink, Raul." She had noticed that her mother was having a great time meeting the guests while Emily seemed lost in thought. Kaitlin walked away with the reporter and joined another group of guests for a photograph. John joined her and noticed that she had an angry expression on her face but thought better of asking her why until after the party.

That night after he and Kaitlin had made love and were glowing over both the success of the evening as well as their deep love for one another, "It looked like you were angry at one point tonight. Did Raul say something to disturb you?"

She replied angrily, "He tried to horn in on a photograph and told the reporter he was my uncle as if he was some way involved in the business. I also didn't like the way he put his arm around me, especially when I noticed poor Aunt Emily sitting by herself and close to tears!" She continued, "And did you notice how he was coming on to all the pretty young chicks? I was embarrassed for Emily and although I was too busy to spend much time with her, I thought Raul was behaving like a dirty old man, and they have only been married three months. Shouldn't he still be smitten on his bride?"

John sighed, "Maybe you ought to mention it to your mother. She and Emily are so close. Now that you mention it, Raul did seem overly interested in the cleavage and short skirts. I was too busy to really pay much attention, but at one point I saw a woman glaring at him as he came up behind her and put his arm around her waist."

"Mother told me that Emily refused a prenuptial agreement that she had suggested. I thought it was a little strange that they got married so fast and away from friends and family." She looked at John thoughtfully, "It also seems strange that the brother he mentioned has never showed up."

"But maybe he can't get out of Cuba. It does seem strange that we haven't met one relative or heard about his family," he added.

"Emily is such a sweet soul and suffered so when Tom died. I just hope that Raul is not more than she bargained for," she said sleepily. "We'll sleep on it."

Little did Kaitlin know how true that would be!

CHAPTER 9—MAY 2001

Elizabeth couldn't get the sight of Emily's sadness the night of the boutique hotel opening out of her mind. She didn't want to distress Emily further and hoped that the financial problem had been resolved. She hesitantly called Emily not knowing how to approach the issue.

"Hi, Emily, just checking to see how you are doing," Liz tried to appear cheerful.

"Hello, Liz," she answered slowly. "I'm sorry if I unloaded my troubles on you the other night. It was a fantastic opening and I know it is just the beginning for this new concept."

"You're so right, and I'm so happy for Kaitlin and John. What a success for her as the new CEO. Andy would be so proud of her and I hope he is looking down on us."

Emily sighed, "I guess I may as well tell you, Liz, Raul is still spending my money and so far he just keeps saying not to worry that he will straighten everything out. To just be patient and not nag him."

Liz was angry now as she responded, "You are his wife, Emily. Surely he owes you more of an explanation then he is giving you!"

She started to cry softly, "Liz, I don't know what to do. He won't talk to me!"

"Emily, I have an idea. Why don't you pay him a surprise visit at his office? Didn't you say that he was giving you some investment advice when you first met him?"

"I couldn't," she exclaimed! "He'd think I was checking up on him."

"Just tell him you dropped by to have lunch with him as you were in the area," Liz responded confidently.

Emily was silent for a long moment, "Well, maybe I will try that. How can it hurt? A lot of wives meet their husbands for lunch. I just hope he doesn't get suspicious."

"Good, Emily, and please let me know if you find out anything. I love you and want the best for you, and I have to tell you, something just isn't right!"

The next morning Emily dressed in a tailored suit and as she gazed at her image in the mirror, she looked like a business woman going to meet her husband for lunch. She was very nervous as she parked the car in a lot downtown and walked across the street to the finance building. It was a high rise, all glass and overlooking Biscayne Bay.

Her hands were shaking when she reached the door of the large investment bank. The receptionist looked up as she entered the lobby, "Oh, hello, Mrs. Pierce," she greeted her. Emily thought it was strange that she called her by her former name, but then she was Mrs. Pierce when she first came to the financial management division.

"I need to see Mr. Gonzalez," she said looking down at the briefcase she had brought with her and trying to appear like a client. She would settle with Raul later as to why he hadn't informed the staff about their marriage.

"Oh," the receptionist said, "didn't you get our notification that Mrs. Blum would be handling your account? I think she if available now if you would like to talk to her." She reached for the phone as Emily said, "No I didn't receive the notice. What happened to Mr. Gonzalez? I would like to remain with him instead of changing brokers."

"Mr. Gonzalez is no longer with us. Should I contact Mrs. Blum?"

Emily turned pale, "How long has Mr. Gonzalez been gone and what happened? Did he take another job?" She was afraid to hear the answer.

"I'm sorry, Mrs. Pierce, but I really don't know what happened. All I know is that he packed up his personal things and left several months ago."

Emily held on to the reception counter for support as she was feeling faint, "I don't feel well today, but I will call Mrs. Blum for an appointment next week. I'm afraid that I may be coming down with the flu."

The pretty young receptionist looked at her sympathetically and asked if she could get her some water.

Emily said, "No, thanks, I think I just need some rest." She hastily added, "I've been working such a heavy schedule that I must have gotten run down."

She left with her head reeling and asking questions she couldn't answer. "Where was Raul going each day when he supposedly left for work in a business suit and didn't come home sometimes until late at night? Why hadn't he told her he no longer had a job? Did he have any means of financial support other than herself?" She felt like she was losing her mind. The more she thought about it, the more betrayed she felt. She wondered what the best way to confront him was. She still loved him and didn't want to lose him, but being married to a liar and a user was more than she could tolerate.

As she planned what she would say to him, Raul came through the door, earlier than usual. She looked at him puzzled, "You got home early today. Aren't you feeling well?"

He poured himself a drink, "Oh, I had a couple of cancellations and you've been complaining so much about my late hours…"

She thought for a long moment and then asked, "Raul, I've been meaning to ask you whether you are still handling my account now that we are married?" Raul responded nervously, "What do you mean, am I handling your account? I have your file right here at home. Why should you have to go down to the brokerage to get financial advice when you are married to your financial advisor!"

"That's odd that you never mentioned that to me, Raul. I'd like to see how my investments are doing and how much the account balance has increased," she replied testily.

He appeared really angry now, "You sound like you don't trust me, Emily. This is my field and as your husband and financial advisor you don't have to be concerned."

She backed off a bit as she always feared his anger, "Well, I would like to see it anyway as it is my account and I should at least have some input like I did when I first started seeing you for financial advice."

"Emily," he crooned putting his arms around her, "we can go over that some time later. I didn't come home early for nothing," he said placing her hand over his huge bulge in his pants. Her eyes became huge and dilated as she felt the size of his erection. Before she knew it he was unbuttoning her blouse and fondling her breasts and much to dismay her heart started pounding in anticipation as he pulled down her panties and placed his hand on the wetness between her legs. She was actually panting as she waited for him to enter her. She gasped as he pushed inside her and pounded inside her over and over again causing her to experience an endless stream of orgasms. It was then that she knew that she would let him do anything he wanted as long as this would never end.

One thing she knew for certain was that she could not live without him regardless of what he did with her money. This was more important than money. She thought about Elizabeth living alone with no man in her life and she decided at that moment she wouldn't tell her about Raul leaving his job. After all, how could she explain to her the ecstasy she felt when Raul made love to her. Elizabeth could never understand how lonely she had been before he came into her life and how she was willing to put up with almost anything to keep him in her life. No, she would never understand.

CHAPTER 10—JULY 2001

As Emily continued to struggle with her marriage as more and more suspicious signs evolved in her husband's secret life, she still didn't know where he went each day and didn't ask, as long as he came home to her. Although she had been tempted on days when she was so upset, she was afraid to share her fears with Liz or Kaitlin. She knew they would try to get her to leave Raul if they knew the truth. She couldn't bear to think of that happening no matter how puzzled and anxious she was about Raul's behavior.

Liz was now busy preparing to take over the reins of CEO while Kaitlin and John were in Europe exploring possibilities for new boutique hotels. They planned to spend several months in France and Scotland. Elizabeth knew the business well after being married to one of the top movers and shakers of the hotel dynasty, her late husband Andy. Also, she had been active on the Board of Director's for many years except during the time she was grieving for her husband after Andy's suicide. Her mother, Kathleen, had at one time worked hand-in-hand with Aidin, her grandfather and founder of the first hotel and the innovator of the dynasty. She had a long history with the Grand Hotels and was the obvious choice to lead the corporation while Kaitlin was abroad.

Kaitlin had not considered Emily as her choice as poor Emily seemed rather unstable and insecure in her marriage. Neither she nor Elizabeth could figure it out, and Emily became mute when the subject was mentioned so they just didn't talk about it.

She and John were eager not only to investigate new sites for hotels, but to have some time together without worrying about family problems and keeping the staff happy and productive. Two of the top executives and Board members, Robert Welch and David Wells still were trying to be uncooperative, but Kaitlin had stopped that for now, by threatening to dismiss them if they failed to agree with company policy and work for the good of the corporation instead of constantly causing roadblocks. They had appeared to be rather shocked when Kaitlin laid down the law with them.

"Your father wouldn't approve of this, Kaitlin," Robert Welch said with a frown. "David and I have both been loyal employees for the over 25 years."

"I'll tell you what my father wouldn't approve of, Robert," she countered. "He wouldn't tolerate his top executives working on their own agenda instead of for the good of the company."

Robert sounded offended, "Just because I don't like the boutique hotel concept, doesn't mean I don't have the corporation's best interests in mind! I wasn't hired to be a "yes" man and I need to be able to disagree once in awhile if I don't go along with an idea."

"The Miami boutique has been fully booked for months, Bob. And people are trying to book in Chicago and San Francisco even before the new boutique hotels are fully completed. Your outlook is very old-fashioned and you need to be open to the changes in our culture since you first were hired," Kaitlin replied in an irritated tone.

Robert and David left her office red-faced with anger, but they also knew they better conform if they wanted to keep their jobs.

David grabbed Robert by the arm and pulled him into an empty office, "She doesn't know what in the hell she is doing! She's going to ruin and bankrupt the company if we don't do something about it."

"Let's think about it David," Robert said calmly, "you know she and her lover will be in Europe for several months and between the two of us, I am convinced we can influence Elizabeth and get her on our side. Kaitlin should have appointed one of us to run the company in her place. We know so much more than Elizabeth!"

While the two executives fretted over being passed over again, Kaitlin and John were planning their itinerary. They would stay at the Grand Hotel in Paris and take side trips to different parts of France scouting for new, exciting locations and meeting with architects and designers.

Kaitlin and John were warmly welcomed at the Grand Hotel when they arrived in the exciting city of Paris. They planned to spend at least a week exploring Paris before taking off for the smaller cities and villages in France that might be suitable for the boutique concept. After the pressures of taking over the business, they could hardly believe that they would have some time just for themselves. Their suite was magnificent with its oriental carpets and oil paintings and crystal chandeliers reflected in baroque mirrors. As they walked out on their balcony they gazed in awe at the Place Vendome.

"Let's try to shake off some of this jet lag and take an evening stroll after dinner," Kaitlin said trying to shake off the drowsiness from the long flight.

"Great idea, but I'm starved and can't wait to taste that French cooking," John said enthusiastically. "Let's save the fancy places for when we are more rested and go to a brasserie for the authentic Parisian experience," he laughed grabbing her arm and leading her out the door. "Let's take a taxi to the Ile St. Louis and see the illuminated Notre Dame Cathedral. Of course, this is after we've had a glass of wine and some good food," he hastily added as the doorman hailed a taxi.

They found a lively café filled with local Parisians and John ordered a bottle of red wine. "This takes me back to the early 1900's," Kaitlin said as she admired the stained glass and old-fashioned lights reflected in the beveled mirrors.

John was too busy looking at the menu to respond and as the waiter asked for their orders he was already ready and waiting, "I'll have the boeuf bourguignon. How about you, Kaitlin?"

"Let's make that deux," she smiled at the waiter adding, "I know that is a specialty here in France."

They were feeling very mellow by the time the delicious aroma of the beef stew dish wafted in their direction as the waiter set the dishes on the table. "This makes beef stew an art form," Kaitlin said. It had been stewed in a red Burgundy wine the waiter had told them proudly with sautéed mushrooms and braised onions. It was served with delicious noodles and French bread still warm from the oven.

"Dip chunks of this bread in your stew," John said savoring each bite.

After finishing their wine and wonderful meal, they walked out hand-in-hand and strolled along the Seine River. They kissed with the two bell towers of Notre Dame glowing on the horizon. Kaitlin could hardly believe the magic of this romantic moment and she couldn't wait to explore Paris the next day, but now she just needed a little sleep.

They had mouth-watering croissants along with their breakfast in their suite the next morning. Feeling fully rested, they left for their day in Paris with smiles on their faces and a guidebook in their hands. Although both Kaitlin and John had visited Paris many times, it was always primarily a business trip. This felt different as they were taking time to have fun and really explore fully some of their favorite places.

John said, "Let's make it a real adventure and take the Metro!" Kaitlin laughed, "You know you can get lost down there, but let's try it anyway!"

They found the nearest Metro station after a short ten-minute walk and on descending bought a carnet which they found was a set of 10 tickets. Their first destination was the Musee du Louvre. Although they knew from the guidebook which stop to get off, they wandered through underground tunnel after tunnel trying to find the right train.

Finally Kaitlin who was suffering a little claustrophobia by this time walked up to a group of laughing students. She had found in all her foreign travels that the young people in Europe usually spoke excellent English. She had some background in studying French but only remembered the basic words.

"Pardon me," she said to the students in a confused voice, "we are trying to get to the Louvre and I'm afraid we are hopelessly lost."

The students laughed and one rosy-cheeked girl pointed to the map up on the wall. "You aren't alone but it's really quite easy." She pointed to the end-of-the line and continued, "You look for your stop, then you check the station at the end of the line, same thing holds if you have to transfer. That will have a color like the red or blue line and the last stop will be listed as the route."

Kaitlin and John thanked them and then mapped out all their routes before heading back to the tunnel. Following the color code they finally arrived at the right platform and laughed at how easy it really was once you knew what the system was.

There was a long line at the entrance but finally it was their turn and they entered below the dramatic glass pyramid. "I hope you are wearing comfortable shoes, Kaitlin, as I have a feeling we are going to walk down the leather today," John said.

As they walked down the spacious, well-lit halls of the Louvre Kaitlin remarked, "This is a real history lesson, John. These masterpieces span all eras from 5,000 B.C. to the present day. I think we'll need the whole week just to cover half of this museum!"

They joined a crowd standing around a painting and Kaitlin excitedly nudged John, "I think we have found the Mona Lisa. Can you believe they allow you to take photos?" The crowd was pushing and people were trying to get to the front to take their photos. All of a sudden a flash appeared from one of the cameras and the guard promptly ushered the man out of the gallery room.

"Be sure you turn your flash off," John whispered. "I can see what they mean by that sweet, mysterious smile. I wonder what she and da Vinci were thinking about?"

Kaitlin grinned, "Not what you are thinking I bet! Now let's find Jan Vermeer's 'The Lace-Maker'. I loved the novel about his life in 'The Girl with the Pearl Earring'."

Although they had wandered through the ancient Greek and Roman works and the Italian collection with altarpieces, angels, saints and Madonnas where the Mona Lisa had been located, they were ready for now for the Impressionists, that period of French art in the 1800's so they headed for the Orsay Museum which houses paintings by the Masters of that era like Cezanne, Degas, van Gogh, Gauguin and Manet.

"My favorites are the Claude Monet's," Kaitlin said as she checked the floor layout. "I especially like the early rebels that paved the way for the Impressionists and the visionary young artists who bucked the system and changed the face of the art world."

John agreed, "I'm in awe at the almost photo detail of the old school of art that we just saw at the Louvre, but I think that true art is more than just painted reality. We can get that effect from our photographs."

"I hope you aren't saying your photos are better than the da Vinci's or Rembrandts," she teased him. "But I totally agree that I love how the

Impressionists capture the passing moment. I can just imagine them setting up their easels on hillsides or by the river, or by a pond like Monet's famous water lilies."

They spent many hours gazing at these magnificent paintings before going to the Orangerie to see Claude Monet's water lilies covering the circular walls of the museum.

Kaitlin exclaimed, "I must be in heaven," as she spun around 360 degrees completely surrounded by the amazing water lilies.

"This is truly unforgettable," John agreed totally immersed in the beauty of the all encompassing scene." He wearily added, "I think it's time for a nap, darling. Don't forget we can't see all of Paris in a day, and there still is the night ahead."

Kaitlin took his hand and glowed, "John, this has been one of the best days of my life!" Then she added with a wicked grin, "With the exception of the day I met you!"

CHAPTER 11—2001

It was a beautiful clear day in Paris as John and Kaitlin stretched their necks to see the top of the Eiffel Tower, "It looked so delicate and graceful from a distance, but now that we are close-by the size is a little scary! Are you sure you want to go to the top, John?"

"The only thing that daunts me is the length of the line. That looks like a two-hour wait!"

But they were busy taking photos, and the time passed faster than they thought. As John was exploring around while Kaitlin held their place in line, he found the stairs to the second level, "Let's give it a try, Kaitlin, and I have a surprise for you when we get up there!"

She looked at him dubiously, "You mean you want me to climb way up there? It better be a good surprise!"

He laughed and led her over to the stairs, "I think the second level is only about 400 feet. It's a good way to exercise after all these rich sauces we have been gorging ourselves on."

As Kaitlin climbed up through the metal beams she felt like she was inside a giant erector set. She also noticed that most people had chosen the elevators that took people to the three levels and that very few tourists were taking the stairs. "I think we would have been smarter to take the elevator up and walked down," she gasped as she caught her breath.

But it was all worth it when they finally reached the second level and saw the grand, sweeping view of the city below them. After taking numerous photos Kaitlin turned to John and asked, "Now, what is my surprise? I hope it isn't walking up to the third level!"

John grinned like a schoolboy, "No, my darling, it is much better. Just come this way."

As John led her into the entrance to the Jules Verne Restaurant her eyes sparkled as the waiter led them to their table next to the huge bay windows that looked out on an incredible view of Paris from their perch.

Kaitlin exclaimed, "You didn't even hint that you had made a reservation! My father brought me here years ago and I have never forgotten it. It's actually one of my favorite restaurants in the entire world!"

John ordered a bottle of champagne and they toasted each other as they gazed at the mind-blowing sight below. They finished the entire bottle before they ordered. Kaitlin had the pan-seared blue lobster with mustard and tarragon while John dined on the sautéed veal sweetbreads. After savoring the delicious food only topped by the view Kaitlin moaned, "I hope I have room for the toffee shortbread and an espresso. I hope you won't make me climb to the top level after this! I'll never make it."

They took the elevator to the top level and it was wild, windy and incredibly breath-taking. As they walked off the calories they headed for rue Cler, one of their favorite neighborhoods in Paris with its tidy village-like streets and open-air produce stands and colorful flower markets.

Kaitlin stopped in front of one of the pastry shops and gazed at all the delicious-looking baked goods designed with such creativity, "Why didn't we save room for this, John? I couldn't eat one bite but they are so unique and taste-tempting they are hard to resist."

"Control yourself, Kaitlin! I have another surprise in store for tonight," he grinned as he ushered her away from the pastry shops and delis.

"You mean there's more ahead? I simply can't believe we can work much more into this one day." She paused and looked at him searchingly, "What is it, John? My surprise?"

Let's stop at one of these outdoor cafes for a draft beer and discuss it."

"You mean une biere pression, I presume," she answered proud to be showing off her knowledge of the French language. "I'd like to see the Rodin Museum. It's not too far from here."

"That's fine with me, but then I suggest a nice long nap before we take our dinner cruise on the Seine River," he laughed and took a sip of beer.

Kaitlin's eyes sparkled, "Do you mean to say you have also booked a Bateaux-Mouche dinner cruise on top of lunch at the Jules Verne! I must be dreaming! Paris after dark must be magic by boat."

They soon found themselves immersed in the Rodin gardens ready for artistic reflection. "I want to see all of his great works, especially *The Thinker* and *Gates of Hell*", Kaitlin said excitedly.

"That's one of his greatest masterpieces, but he never finished it. I saw it several years ago and I've never forgotten it. There's a lesson in *Gates of Hell* for all of us. I guess we better behave!"

"I wonder if that had anything to do with his rocky relationship with his apprentice and lover, Camille Claudel?" Kaitlin teased. "I hear Rodin actually lived and worked in this mansion. He worked in so many materials. I think I like the chiseled marble sculptures the best but I notice he worked in modeled clay and cast bronze also."

They were ready for sleep when they finally lay down for a nap. Luckily they had requested a wake-up call or they would have slept right through the scheduled dinner cruise. Sitting by a huge expanse of windows on the Bateau Mouche they dined on a white linen tablecloth with gleaming candlelight.

"John," Kaitlin whispered, "you have made this day pure magic." He glowed as they looked out at Paris in the moonlight. As they passed the Eiffel Tower which was totally illuminated Kaitlin took his hand and said softly, "Now I know for sure that this city is truly magical, especially when I share it with you."

They knew that their time in Paris was ending but these memories of sharing Paris together for the first time would live in their memories forever.

CHAPTER 12—JULY 2001

Their final day was spent taking in a few of the sights they had missed including the magnificent Sainte-Chapelle, the triumph of Gothic church architecture created originally by Louis IX to house the supposed Crown of Thorns.

As Kaitlin climbed the spiral steps to the upper section, she caught her breath as she met the light shining on the 15 panels of stained glass. "Isn't this incredible, John?" she gasped as the vibrant colors depicting scenes from the Bible almost blinded her eyes after coming up from the darker ground floor.

"Look, Kaitlin, there's the altar at the end of the room. I guess that is supposed to be the Crown of Thorns relic," he said dubiously. As the sunlight streamed into the room he remarked, "The colors seem to sparkle like a million precious gems. I guess they allow photos, but how can you capture a sight like this? It has to be seen to be believed."

"I want to go back to Notre Dame next," Kaitlin said grasping John's arm as she looked at her guidebook for directions. "I didn't get to climb to the top last time I was here," she said as they strolled along the Seine and watched all the Bateau Mouches passing by crowded with passengers busily snapping photos of all the sights on both sides of the river.

"It might have as many steps as the Eiffel Tower, Kaitlin. Are you sure you want to do this? We still want to save time and energy to go to Montmarte and climb up to the Sacre-Coeur," John warned her but stopped after seeing the determined look on her face.

Some minutes later after they had paid the fee, they were climbing the 400 steps to the top along with a group of tourists. When they finally reached the top they were almost out of breath, but the grand view from the top of the South Tower made it all worthwhile.

Kaitlin put her arms around John, "Aren't you glad we did this? I wouldn't have missed this view for anything! Let's walk around to that park on the riverside in back of the Cathedral for a good photo of the flying buttresses and the gargoyles."

John laughed, "I am learning so many things about you, darling. I didn't know you had a thing for flying buttresses! Just don't try to fly over there from here!"

After spending the next hour admiring the amazing 700 year old cathedral which was packed with history and tourists, Kaitlin said, "I want to take a closer look at the rose window with Adam on one side and Eve on the other."

"O.K., but I'm ready for a riverside café and some lunch before I drop from hunger and exhaustion," he begged her.

After a glass of wine and a delicious quiche, they were ready to finish off their last day in Paris with a taxi ride to Montmarte and the top of the hill where the beautiful Roman-Byzantine basilica stands.

"Don't worry, Kaitlin, we will walk down and stroll through the neighborhood, but think of the steps we saved by taking the taxi," John remarked on seeing her frown. "If you think you are missing something you can always climb to the top of the dome. I read in the guidebook that it's a tight little spiral staircase all the way up."

Kaitlin grinned, "I think I can afford to miss that, John. The Eiffel Tower and the Notre Dame was enough for my bird's eye view of Paris!"

They watched all the mimes and the magicians and musicians on the first platform as they descended from the basilica with hordes of tourists. "Who says everyone leaves Paris in July?" John said as the crowd pressed in around them.

Finally reaching the bottom of the numerous steps, they looked up at the gleaming white basilica towering above them and they asked a passing tourist to take their picture in front of the impressive five-domed building dating back to 1875.

One block from the church they passed the place du Tertre. "I had to see this section, John. I've always loved the paintings of Toulouse-Lautrec, they so captured the bohemian lifestyle of this period."

John shook his head and said, "It looks more like a tourist trap these days, but I agree that his work was wonderful. I guess the cabaret life still exists if you consider the night spots like the Moulin Rouge."

"We must try to get tickets for the show tonight, John. I know it's our last night in Paris but it would be so much fun! I can't get the real feel of Lautrec in his old neighborhood as it has changed so much, but the color and the music and the dances of the cabaret would take us back to those days," Kaitlin persisted even though John didn't look too enthusiastic.

"Well," he relented, "I guess all those long legs doing the Cancan would be inspiring!"

So their last night in Paris was spent dining at the Moulin Rouge Restaurant which was part of the Moulin Rouge and included dinner and dancing before the show. John toasted Kaitlin with champagne as they enjoyed the Foie Gras with jelly and armagnac followed by lamb roasted with thyme, "Here's to only the beginning of our travels. From now on we will need to get down to the business of building new boutique hotels."

"But that will be fun, too, John! How can visiting the charming villages in France be work?" she asked as she savored the nougat glace with honey. The orchestra was playing and John led Kaitlin to the dance floor. She squeezed his hand as they started to dance, "Any place, any time with you is perfect."

John held her tightly and swung her around the dance floor, "That goes for both of us, Kaitlin. I love you, darling."

Before they knew it the show was starting and Kaitlin was glowing with pleasure as she watched the dancers in their glorious costumes sparkling with sequins and vibrant shining gemstones. "Look at all those feathers, John. There must be thousands of them!"

"I'm busy looking at the legs," he laughed, "can't be bothered with the costumes!"

Kaitlin didn't know if she was tipsy from the champagne or the music as it grew louder, but as the girls swirled and kicked and the beat got faster, she was transported back to the days of Henri Toulouse-Lautrec and the paintings of the cancan which were immortalized by the famous artist who spent his nights in the cabarets.

    The whole evening was unforgettable, but the best part they agreed, was the intimacy they had both felt on the dance floor. As they made love that night they again pledged their love for one another as they looked forward to their next adventure in France.

CHAPTER 13—JULY 2001

While Kaitlin and John were exploring French villages Raul was up to no good. It was time to visit his brother in prison and map out the next step in their plan to take over the Grand Hotel dynasty. He hated that wait before they led Carlos into the visitor's booth, handcuffed and shackled. As usual Carlos greeted him with a frown.

"How's marriage to the hot old broad," Carlos smirked?

Raul nodded not making eye contact with his belligerent brother, "It's ok so far and I have plenty of her money to spend, but she is getting nosy. She keeps asking me about my work and I'm running out of excuses about where I go every day." He paused, "I think she may have caught on that I got fired from my job but she doesn't come right out and say it."

"That's easy, Bro," Carlos shrugged, "I don't even have to ask, but how are things at the track these days? Any winners?"

Raul laughed, "You know me pretty well, don't you? Some days I pick winners, some days I pick losers, but at least I'm not losing my own money!"

Carlos reminisced, "Before I got put in the joint, and when I was making big bucks, I used to go the Hialeah Race Track a couple times a week. One time I won $100,000 in one race! You probably don't know it was started by Glenn Curtiss, that pilot who opened a flight school in Miami in the early days. It's too bad, I heard it closed down in May. So what do you do now, hermano, when you are supposed to be working?" He added sarcastically, "Do you go down there to Hialeah each day to watch the flocks of flamingos take off or what?"

"Don't you have any respect for anything," Raul said with disgust. "People come from all over the world to see that race track and some just to see those flocks of flamingos taking off!"

"Can't you take a joke no more?" Carlos asked. "Well, what do you do all day then?"

"I found a bunch of guys to play poker with. They play every day, sometimes for big stakes. Then I go to Jai Alai a couple times a month to lose some more of my wife's money." He sighed, "But she has so damn much of it she doesn't miss it."

"And how is Elizabeth? She hasn't found a guy yet, has she?" he asked with a degree of anxiety.

"God, no, she is such a frigid bitch! Now she's running the company while her daughter and boyfriend are lapping up wine in France! I don't think she's had a date since her husband died and worse I don't think she wants one! She gives me the cold shoulder every time I get close to her," he said with disgust as he lit up a cigarette.

Carlos thought for a moment before answering, "She sure didn't act cold in the old days when I was engaged to her. By the way, the parole board will be meeting sometime this year and if all goes well I might be out of here in a year or two. I can't wait to get her into bed. I bet that frigid babe will turn into one hot potato!"

Raul looked at him quizzically, "I still can't understand how you will manage that. After all you will be an ex-con, not exactly in her league!"

Carlos became incensed with anger, "Let me figure that one out. She loved me once and she can be made to love me again. Only my intentions are a little different this time. I am going to do my best to destroy her and show her what it means to cross me."

Raul looked away and then made eye contact with his brother, "I thought you just meant to take her money, like I intend to do with Emily. Do you mean you're going to hurt her?"

"I intend to take her money like you said, but I also plan to hurt her in every way possible including destroying her daughter. The Grand Hotels will be all mine, mark my words," he emphasized by pounding the counter in front of him and alarming the guard.

"Don't you mean that the Grand Hotels will be ours," Raul asked with alarm. "You seem to be leaving me out of the equation!"

"Of course, you are going to share everything with me. I don't want you to let on that I am your brother when I get out of this joint. That would spoil everything! There are thousands of Gonzalez' in Miami. If you want your half you better learn to keep your mouth shut or the whole scheme will fall through," he said in a threatening tone.

Raul pledged, "You have my word, Brother, and I keep my promises." He added thoughtfully, "Except for the ones I make to my wife."

CHAPTER 14—JULY 2001

John and Kaitlin took the train from Paris to the village of Amboise in the Loire River Valley area. They chose this for their first stop in their search for new locations to carry out their plans to establish Grand Boutique Hotels in Europe for two reasons. The location was perfect, not only a short distance by train or car from Paris but in close proximity to the important chateaux.

As they drove in their rental car through the carpeted green fertile fields, crisscrossed by the enchanting rivers and laced with rolling hills Kaitlin exclaimed, "Isn't this the most beautiful area, John! It still has the feel of the country and the small villages, yet it is a major draw for tourists with the wealth of castles, palaces and Chateaux!"

Practical John said, "Let's drop our bags off at our hotel before we do too much more exploring. By the way I have read that the locally produced food is delicious, especially the fresh trout from the rivers in the area so let's grab lunch before we decide where to go first. I'm starving!"

Kaitlin teased, "Why is it that food always comes first with you?"

"You can't catch me on that one Kaitlin," he laughed, "of course, you always come first!"

As they sipped a glass of wine on the terrace of a small restaurant Kaitlin mapped out their day. "First of all, I'd like to explore this village. It might be just what we are looking for. It's steeped with history you know," she said turning pages in their guidebook. "For one thing Leonardo da Vinci retired here. And if that isn't enough, a castle has overlooked the Loire from Amboise since Roman times."

"You mean the Chateau d'Amboise? It was designed by da Vinci to be a Royal Residence. Did you know that Charles VIII is noted for accidentally killing himself by walking into a doorjam during the building process?"

Kaitlin eyed him dubiously but he was adamant that it was a true story. After enjoying a delicious lunch and finishing it off with some of the region's fine goat cheese and tarte tatin, which they discovered was an upside-down caramel apple tart, they drove around the city discovering many possibilities for their new hotel in the hidden mansions with unimposing facades, but a treasure trove of history and ideas for renovation.

They explored a 750-year-old castle with hints of its Renaissance elegance. Kaitlin exclaimed with excitement, "Just think what we could do with this place, John and just look out here," she said walking out on the overgrown terrace. "It looks out over Amboise and forest trails over there."

He scratched his head, "It would take a heck of a lot of renovation to restore it, but I agree the view is spectacular and just think how near it is to the major chateaux that attract tourists from all over the world. I think we've found our first location and it is on the market for a reduced price."

"Let's make an offer and see what happens," Kaitlin said enthusiastically. "We could have our own castle garden and raise our own produce to serve in our restaurants and the rivers are full of fish. Remember hearing how my great-grandfather, Aidin, had his own garden and supplied the restaurant with fresh fish from the ocean when he built the first hotel in Coconut Grove where we now have our corporate offices. We can make this a showplace as well as provide gourmet dining." She measured off the great room by walking it off and counting as she continued, "The waitresses could be dressed in Renaissance costumes and background music of the period. What instruments did they play?"

"I suppose we could have a lyre or harp and a flute, the serving girls could sing madrigals at intervals. It has lots of potential. Actually, we could consider a madrigal operetta. We could plant a formal garden on the hillside in front of the entrance. We might have only glowing candlelight at dinner!" He was becoming more and more enthusiastic as ideas kept popping into his head. "As we tour Chateaux de Chenonceau and Chambord, let's look for decorating ideas for that period."

During the next week, they negotiated the price until finally their lawyer, Claude DuBois from Paris, closed the deal and this left the couple free to explore the beautiful scenery of the Loire River and the amazing chateaux.

"This is awesome," Kaitlin exclaimed as they toured the toast of the Loire, Chateaux de Chenonceau, 16th century Renaissance palace gracefully arching over the Cher River. They crossed three moats and two bridges before reaching the main building.

"Did you know this was considered a pleasure palace for the ladies, Kaitlin? In fact, I read that King Henry ll gave the chateau to his mistress, but his wife, Catherine de Medicis kicked her out," John said gazing at the arched bridge that the mistress had added to access the hunting grounds.

"My, my, John," Kaitlin laughed, "you do keep up with the tabloids don't you? We must have large wood-burning fireplaces in our Great Room like this one and somehow we have to decide on a Coat-of-Arms to make it more authentic. The use of tapestries on the walls depicting the history would be great! Certainly they won't be these priceless gems which took around 60 years to make!"

They visited several others of the major chateaux in the region and particularly enjoyed Chateau de Chambord surrounded by an enclosed forest park and a game preserve.

John gazed at the huge chateau in awe, "I hear this one has 440 rooms, a great place for hide-and-seek!"

"It was originally a hunting lodge for bored Blois counts according to the guidebook," John continued laughing and as an afterthought, "we should hold 'a hunt' on the grounds of our castle, you know."

Kaitlin retorted, "You are getting visions of grandeur, my friend. You know the point of having Boutique Hotels is to have a smaller, more intimate hotel with less rooms than the Grand Hotels. Our castle actually is a small mansion with only about 50 sleeping rooms, less if we make some into two or three room suites." She looked at him thoughtfully, "I bet there are some foxes living in the forest around our castle. Actually, offering a hunt might be just the trick to make it really unique!"

After finally getting their fill of palaces and chateaux, they jumped into their rental car and headed for the rolling hills of Burgundy. The scenery was incredible as they passed quiet farming villages crisscrossed with picturesque canals.

Kaitlin exclaimed enthusiastically, "This might be another perfect location for one of our hotels! It's easy to reach Paris from here by train or car or Alsace in the north where I want to go next, or east to the Alps or south to Provence!"

"Don't forget this is wine country! And the boeuf bourguignon," John said almost salivating. "This is the home of some of the greatest wines in the world, the great fruity reds and the dry whites. We definitely have to cover the vine route, and how about a boutique hotel in a restored winery?"

She laughed, "How about the escargot bourguinon served hot in garlic butter, and don't forget the coq au vin which also originated in the Burgundy area."

"Of course, lunch comes first! But then I'd like to make a stop at a castle in the making which I've read about. They are using materials, tools and techniques from the 13th century. The plan is the dream of only two people who based the idea on plans drafted way back in 1250. Using this primitive method they think it won't be completely finished for another 15 years."

Kaitlin looked at her map, "Oh, you mean. Guedelon. I have read about it and it sounds interesting, but I don't think we'll get any tips for our new hotel project. Hopefully, it will move faster with the modern approach."

They found a small café and just got in before they closed for lunch early in the afternoon. All the restaurants in France seem to adhere to specific hours for lunch and dinner and if you arrive a few minutes after lunch is over you will probably be turned away. Then following some scenic back roads they found Guedelon.

John and Kaitlin split up as their interests were different. He was amazed by the stonecutters who used the chisel and toothed hammer to finish a stone from the quarry. Then he watched the mason layers use mortar which they made themselves to bind the stones. Then he watched the tree cutters in the surrounding oak forest and the carpenters who worked the oak felled by the woodcutters. Like the stonecutters, John noted that the carpenters first drew on a tracing floor in their workshop. Then shaped and assembled the different parts of the wooden structure.

Kaitlin was intrigued by all the participants who were dressed in the costumes of the 13th century. She particularly was fascinated watching the women making bread in a wood-fired bake-oven. As she wandered, she visited the blacksmith shop and the basket maker. She discovered that the baskets were made for carrying mortar and small loads of stones.

She and John met up at the Dyer's Hut where they watched the sheep's wool being spun and dyed. "You have to see how they make rope, John," Kaitlin said leading him to where men took hemp and flax ropes and hooked them to a jack. The yarns were then twisted into strands and the rope maker then spliced the rope.

After spending three hours roaming the grounds and viewing all the various facets of life in the medieval days, they were exhausted and ready to find their next hotel in the little wine capital of Beaune in the heart of Burgundy. Medieval monks and powerful dukes of Burgundy laid the groundwork for the town's prosperity. The monks cultivated the wine and the dukes were responsible for the wealth.

As they settled into their hotel room it was fairly late and they decided to dine on cheese, pate and of course a fresh loaf of crusty French bread that they had picked up en route. John uncorked a bottle of Pinot Noirs which they finished off before falling into a deep sleep, arms entwined and dreaming of all the sights and sounds they had experienced during their trip that day over the scenic back roads of the wine country.

CHAPTER 15—JULY 2001

Elizabeth was looking forward to Kaitlin's return as she didn't think she was cut out for all the office politics that were going on around her. She had been a business woman for years and helped resettle Cuban refugees. However, she had never gotten embroiled in office politics. As Andrew's wife of course she had stayed current with the family corporation and enjoyed her service on the Board.

She laughed when she remembered when her mother, Kathleen, had told her stories of what it was like to work side-by-side in the hotel business with her famous great-grandfather, Aidin, and how she retired from that position when she knew she was pregnant with her. Kathleen had never gone back after she had been born. Her mother had remarried Frank Moss after Liz's father, Calvin, had died in World War II. They had started a flight school and Kathleen had earned her pilot's license. That had been her true love, not running hotels. Elizabeth now realized that it didn't feel right to her either.

She kept in touch with Kaitlin by email and was encouraged that they had found at least one location for the new hotel and that they were soon heading for the wine road in the Alsace region of France where they hoped to find a second property possibly in a winery that could be reconverted. She had asked Kaitlin to cancel the Scotland portion of their trip if they were successful in finding another property in France. She was more than ready to relinquish the reins to Kaitlin.

Bob Welch and Dave Wells were constantly badgering her about the foolishness of the Boutique Hotel concept. They were perfectly satisfied with the status quo as the Grand Hotels were still highly successful. Their theory was if you have a good thing, why break it.

They let her know in no uncertain terms that they thought Kaitlin's 'vacation' in Europe was nonsense and the cost of renovating some of these old mansions could exceed any profit they might make for many years.

Elizabeth had argued that the Miami Boutique was doing quite well and still remained fully booked but it fell on deaf ears. They also had broadly hinted that either one of them could do a much better job of running the corporation and that she should encourage Kaitlin's resignation before the Board of Directors voted for her removal.

Running it by Emily was impossible as she was transformed from the confident, assured, professional woman and former newspaper reporter that Elizabeth had always admired to an insecure woman drowning her sorrows about her marriage with alcohol and prescription drugs which she suspected that she abused. In the meantime, Raul was doing his disappearing act and Emily had no idea where he was and didn't have the nerve to confront him. Elizabeth thought she was a lovesick fool to not have insisted on a pre-nuptial agreement. Raul could walk off with all her money in a divorce issue. She might even end up having to pay him alimony in addition to half her wealth. It gave Elizabeth a headache to think about it. Autumn was terribly worried about her mother, but Emily refused to confide in her.

So Elizabeth called William Petersen, the trusted family friend and Board member, into the office to run it by him. "Good to see you, Bill, I think I need your advice on a few issues." She frowned as she told him about her problems with Robert Welch and David Wells.

He listened to all her complaints and then said, "I've been on the Board for over a decade, Elizabeth, and I probably knew your husband, Andy, better than almost anyone else connected with the hotels. Therefore, when I tell you that Andy had complete confidence in Kaitlin's ability to run the show, I am talking after having many conversations with him on the subject. I know I am old now, but both Bob and Dave are acting like dinosaurs. It's a new age and Kaitlin is perfect to lead us in that direction."

"I feel the same way, Bill, but then we are talking about my daughter so I may have a degree of prejudice in the matter."

He took her hand, "Try not to worry about it, Elizabeth. You are doing Kaitlin a great service by holding down the fort. She knows she can trust you and that makes her better able to research the new project in Europe. The other Board members think you are doing a great job, so try not to be too concerned with Bob and Dave. Kaitlin was considering firing them at one time, and when she hears this, I'm sure she'll take some action if they continue to try and undermine her. She's one smart gal! You can be proud of her!"

Before he left, he looked into her eyes directly and said with concern, "I was just wondering if anything is wrong with Emily. I know it is none of my business, but she is Andy's sister and she seems rather depressed."

"I've been worrying about her, too, Bill. I wish Andy were still alive so we could talk about it." She paused thoughtfully and then continued, "I don't think that her marriage is working out the way she had hoped. But she won't confide in her daughter, Autumn, or Kaitlin or me. In fact, she won't talk about it at all, and I think she's drinking too much."

"I'm sorry to hear that, Elizabeth. I remember how excited she was when she first announced her engagement to Raul. Well, let's hope that whatever it is, it will get better soon. She is such a lovely person and deserves the best. It was such a blow to her when her first husband, Tom, died in the prison camp during the Vietnam War. I remember she was badly depressed for a number of months. Who can blame her when she heard about all the torture Tom had to endure. I hope this marriage will have a happy ending for her."

In the meantime Kaitlin and John were exploring Beaune starting with the highlight, the colorful glazed tiles of the Hotel Dieu. They gazed in awe at the tiles in intricate designs glittering in the inner courtyard. Their guide explained, "This style is recognized as typically 'Burgundian' and the tiles last for 300 years or more. They are fired three times, once to harden, then to burn in the color and then for this beautiful glaze."

As everyone snapped photos of the glorious rooftop she continued, "This started as a medieval charity hospital at a time when almost all of Beaune was destitute after the Hundred Years' War and the Black Plague by an elderly chancellor of Burgundy who decided to help the people before he died."

The group moved into the huge Paupers' Ward for the poorest patients, "Every three hours the door of the chapel was opened at the end of the room and patients could experience Mass from their beds. The hospice was not a place of hope for people came here to die. Care was more for the soul than the body."

John edged Kaitlin toward the exit, "This is a bit depressing. Let's go across the street to the Marche aux Vins for a little wine sampling." They paid their fee for a wine-tasting cup and then plunged into the labyrinth of candlelit caves dotted with 15 barrels.

"Remember, we have to drive back to the hotel, "Kaitlin warned as they sampled the three Chardonnays and the twelve Pinot Noirs. "Let's grab some bikes and tour the countryside wineries. I need some fresh air and exercise after this!"

Within only minutes they were immersed in the lush countryside of the 'Cote d'Or'. They followed a loop wine road that laced together some renowned wine villages, Aloxe-Corton, Pernand Verelesses and Savigny-les-Beaune.

John had brought crackers to cleanse the palate and whispered to Kaitlin, "If you want to act professional, you have to spit out the wine instead of swallow it. I guess that is why they are able to sample so many without getting tipsy!"

As they pedaled back to Beaune over hills and vineyards they had views of castles and picturesque villages. "Let's get started for Alsace tomorrow," Kaitlin said. "I have a feeling that we will find our next location somewhere in that region and I'm ready to look at properties. We've had a great time, but Elizabeth emailed that she's having some problems back home so it's time we got down to serious business."

CHAPTER 16—JULY 2001

Emily had been pacing back and forth from the living room to the terrace where she had a view of the parking lot. It was almost midnight and Raul still hadn't appeared. She was used to warming up his dinner. They never sat down to a meal together anymore with Raul's irregular hours. She was on her fourth martini when she finally heard him open the front door. The alcohol had given her courage to at last speak to him about his erratic behavior.

Staggering over to him she slurred, "Where in the hell have you been all this time? It's past midnight and you left early this morning. I know you don't have a job to go to anymore. What do you do during all those hours?"

He pushed her out of the way, "Drunk again, I see! Where's my dinner?"

"You can eat your dinner wherever it is that you go," she said sarcastically spitting out the words. "I'm tired of fixing a big dinner and sitting down alone to eat it every night."

"Who would want to sit down and eat with a drunken old broad like you?" he screamed.

"I'm the drunken old broad who is supporting you so you better watch what you say to me," she shouted, "or I'll cut you off!"

Raul was red with fury as he slapped her in the face causing her to fall back and hit her head against the wall. As she then fell forward over the coffee table several glasses broke and cut her arm. She was sobbing hysterically by now and wrapped her scarf around her arm to stop the bleeding.

Raul smirked, "You better cut down on your drinking, Emily. You can't even walk straight anymore. No wonder you have accidents like this." With that he left her there on the floor sobbing as he slammed the door and left the apartment.

She finally staggered into the bedroom and fell into a drunken deep sleep. It wasn't until morning that she noticed that Raul had never returned that night. As she limped into the bathroom she cringed when she saw her reflection. Her face was swollen and bruised and she had a black eye. There was a nasty gash on her arm and she picked a glass shard out of it. The bleeding started up again but she was able to stop it. Walking into the living room she saw the overturned coffee table and all the broken glass.

She sat on the couch softly weeping as the events of the last evening marched through her thoughts. She moaned as she said aloud, "It wasn't only the glass that shattered last night, it was my heart."

CHAPTER 17—JULY 2001

John and Kaitlin drove into the Alsace province of France near the German border, with the Rhine River on the east and the Vosges Mountains on the west, they found the area in between to be a beautiful green region of picturesque tiny villages, stretches of vineyards and enchanting cities. Choosing Colmar as a base, they enjoyed the hybrid culture of the two countries. They learned that Alsace had changed hands several times between France and Germany. Locals usually spoke both languages and the food would be a delicious combination of the two cultures.

As they walked through historic Old Town Colmar John gazed up at the half-timbered buildings, "It was kind of the British and Americans not to bomb these wonderful old burghers' houses during World War II. Do you see how they have combined French shutters with the German half-timbered construction?"

They wandered down the cobbled lanes gazing up at the glittering red and green-tiled roofs until they reached the Venice of France. As they walked down the narrow canal lined by a collection of Colmar's most colorful houses Kaitlin said, "Isn't this quaint, John? Let's go to the bridge and see if a gondola may pass by."

"Are you kidding, Kaitlin? You must think we really are in Venice," John laughed as Kaitlin leaned over the rail on the picturesque bridge. Just then a flat-bottomed gondola glided under the bridge with tourists snapping pictures of all the historic half-timbered houses. Right next to the bridge were some of the houses with wooden beams that looked like 'a man' with the design of the upright, cross and angular supports.

"Look, Kaitlin," John exclaimed, "they are all trying to photograph 'the man' flanked by two half-men' on those half-timbered houses."

"I definitely must take a gondola ride, John," Kaitlin said in an excited tone. They checked the guidebook for more information and learned that the local river had been turned into canals during medieval times to provide water for tanners and allow farmers to barge their goods into town. The gondolas were used for this purpose in the old days, but now they were used for scenic tours along the canal.

It was starting to get dark and the canals made a very romantic setting with the sparkling lights on some of the waterside restaurants. They decided to order some Alsatian specialties, "I'll have the baeckeoffe and we'll have Muscat wine before dinner."

"What is that, John?" Kaitlin whispered. The waiter heard her and said, "That is a most delicious potato, meat and onion stew. Do you also wish to try it, Mademoiselle?"

"No, I think I'll try the rosti. Isn't that a baked potato and cheese dish?" she replied.

"Excellent choice," the waiter smiled. "I will get your wine right away. Don't you want to enjoy your meal outside on the terrace near the canal? I have a good table available now."

Over dessert which was tarte alsacienne, a delicious fruit tart, they discussed the plan for tomorrow. "Let's head up to Strasbourg on the Alsace's wine road. I have a feeling that our next property may be in that region. We will want to stop at some of the picturesque villages along the route and check to see what real estate is available," Kaitlin said sipping her espresso.

"Sounds like a plan! Let's do a little wine-tasting en route," John said eagerly. "But let's work in that gondola ride in the morning before we leave." Kaitlin smiled when she saw how John always tried to please her.

As they drove along the famous wine road, they stopped at picturesque villages and wineries galore. It was then that they found their favorite, the village of Riquewihr. Kaitlin immediately fell in love with it when she spotted storks nesting on the spires of the church and city hall. It had many stone houses testifying to its wealth centuries ago.

"This village has everything to attract a tourist, John," Kaitlin said as she took in the 16th century ramparts and the fascinating sign boards dating back hundreds of years and Dolder, the 13th Century belfry. The walled village was crammed with cafes, galleries, flowers and even cobblestones. Stopping in at a busy tourist shop they asked the owner about properties in the area and stated that they were looking for a good location for a boutique hotel.

The man beamed, "How about looking at our family winery on your way up north to Strasbourg. We have gone into the retail business here in town, and have closed the winery. Too much work and competition. Of course, I'll be honest with you, it will need some work if you want to restore it to the modern tourist's taste. It's been in our family for many generations."

Driving north toward Strasbourg through wooded fields along the slopes of the Vosges Mountains they passed acre after acre of green grapevines. At last they spotted the entrance to the old winery. After a long drive uphill they saw the magnificent building made of pink stones quarried from the Vosges Mountains according to the owner they had spoken to and surrounded by hundreds of acres of sad and unattended grapevines. When they reached the top of the hill in the Vosges Mountains they got out of the car and gasped at the magnificent view of the Alsace Valley with even a glimpse of the Rhine River in the distance.

"The scenery is postcard pretty," Kaitlin exclaimed! "It reminds me of Sleeping Beauty's castle with all the towers and turrets." As they opened the gigantic carved door, they saw a spiral staircase leading up to the living quarters. On the ground floor was the old tasting room with a long bar and tables and chairs.

"This room should be opened up with a large window and doors opening out to a terrace overlooking this spectacular view. We could put in an aerial tram to bring people up so they can enjoy the view and the parking lot could be below," John said excitedly.

They went down to the cellars and some of the equipment and oak casks were still there. Kaitlin smiled, "Do you think in time we could wake-up some of these grape-wines and actually produce wine here? It wouldn't have to be a large operation as we are in the hotel business, but similar to the Winstub in our hotel cellar in Riquewihr. We could have a gourmet chef and serve the traditional Alsatian specialties along with our own wine. A wine tour could be included in the hotel stay."

John raised an eyebrow, "Are you putting the cart before the horse? There's a lot of renovation needed and I don't know what kind of deal the owner is willing to make. If it has been on the market for a long time, we may be able to bargain."

"I'll get Claude DuBois down from Paris tomorrow to approach the owner. He's a master at the art of bargaining and he understands all the legal aspects and can take care of the closing," she said quickly. "I love the place and hope we can swing it!"

"It's a million dollar view, a historic building and do you know it's only about 40 minutes to drive to Baden-Baden on the German side of the Rhine River, plus you have the Alsace Wine Road! What a find! It should be an absolute magnet for tourists! I wonder if the owner realizes all the potential of the property," John said with enthusiasm and a little anxiety.

The debonair Claude DuBois arrived the next afternoon and by evening he had drummed out a deal with the owner to purchase the entire property including the old winery building for half the asking price.

As they toasted with champagne later that evening Claude explained, "I think we actually did Monsieur Derveau a favor. He has been trying to sell off his winery for five years and now that his shop is doing so well in Riquewihr he plans to expand to other villages on the wine route, and needs capital for the expansion."

They laughed as they set off for dinner, "Then we are all happy tonight," John said as he squeezed Kaitlin's hand.

She looked at him seriously, "We better make tracks back to Paris tomorrow. Elizabeth is having second thoughts about holding down the fort. We can do the Scotland search later this year when things calm down at home."

"Anything you say, Boss," John grinned. He didn't care where he went as long as Kaitlin was by his side.

CHAPTER 18—
SEPTEMBER 11, 2001

Kaitlin had returned to Miami to find a number of problems to deal with. One of her first duties was to have a conference for the record with the two troublemakers, Robert Welch and David Wells, as reported by Elizabeth. She gave them a timeline of six months to improve their attitude and competency. Robert Welch was to have the goal of overseeing the European boutique hotels which were to be under construction by the springtime in France. David Wells was to oversee the boutique hotels planned for Chicago and San Francisco. If they were unable to perform their assignments as prescribed, Kaitlin warned them to seek employment elsewhere.

She now had the habit of arriving at her office early each morning in an effort to catch up with issues that came up during her trip to France. It was while she was mulling over the expenses and profits on the new Miami Beach Grand Boutique that she heard a strange rumbling noise out in the office area. Rising to investigate she bumped into her secretary who was running toward Kaitlin's office.

"What in the world is going on?" Kaitlin asked as she noticed all her staff standing around a television set. Some of the women were crying and she saw fear on everyone's face as they watched the scene unfolding.

Her secretary, Janet, who was in her forties and very efficient had tears in her eyes, "Oh, Ms. Donegan, an American Airlines passenger airplane just crashed into the World Trade Center's North Tower! They think it may be a terror attack but no one knows for sure. Think of all those passengers and the people inside the Tower!"

It was just then that Kaitlin heard a scream from the employees and she just got to the set in time to see the second plane, a United Airlines aircraft, crash into the South Tower. Reports were starting to come in that some of the doomed passengers who were able to access airplane service or mobile phones had called loved ones to tell them that hijackers were aboard each plane and that some kind of chemical spray had been used and that some passengers were stabbed.

A call came through from John Martinez who had remained in France until both of the hotel sales were completed and architects had been hired. "Have you seen the television report, Kaitlin? I can't believe what I just saw!"

"Hold it a minute, John," Kaitlin said in panic, "my God another American Airlines plane just crashed into the Pentagon in Arlington, Virginia, just outside of Washington D.C. carrying passengers. There must be lots of workers in that building that are also trapped." She was crying now and the others were weeping. "Try to get back to Miami as soon as possible, John. I don't know what is happening! Oh, no, there are people jumping from the top of the towers! The buildings are crumbling right before my eyes on television. People are trapped inside!"

"How horrible, Kaitlin! I don't know when I can get back. I have already heard that aviation is coming to a stop all over the globe. There may be more planes with terrorists in the air. This has to be stopped!" he shouted.

As they watched the scenes in disbelief, it was announced that a fourth plane had crashed in Pennsylvania after the passengers on board had fought the hijackers after learning from phone calls that they were able to secretly make that other aircraft had been crashed into buildings that morning. That plane was headed for the United States Capitol and the White House. The passengers who risked their lives and died in that crash were real heroes and brave beyond belief.

Kaitlin looked in stunned silence at her grieving employees and then said gently, "Go home to your loved ones. Your children will need you more than ever. Give yourselves a chance to heal from this tragedy."

Slowly each employee walked out of the office with a dazed expression. The world would never be the same again.

The attacks caused widespread confusion among air traffic controllers across the United States. All international civilian air traffic was banned from landing on U.S. soil for three days. Aircraft already in flight were either turned back or redirected to airports in Canada and Mexico.

Kaitlin had little time to heal herself in the aftermath of the tragedy for the impact on the hotel business was staggering. People occupying rooms in their hotels in the U.S. and abroad were unable to fly as all aviation had come to a standstill. There was such a demand for rental cars to substitute for flight plans that no more were available. In most places, the Grand Hotels were able to accommodate most guests as the new arrivals had to cancel their reservations and that left rooms for those who had to stay over.

She had advised all the hotel branch managers to make exceptions and either relocate persons who couldn't return home, or set up sleeping cots in the ballrooms as a last resort. She also offered a free accommodation for those who were held over through no fault of their own. After the first three days she discounted all the rooms by half. She ordered the manager at the Grand New York to try to help accommodate guests at hotels in the immediate proximity of the Twin Towers.

Several months later after John had finally returned the grim statistics were announced to the shocked nation. Nearly 3,000 victims and 19 hijackers died in the attacks including 343 firefighters and 60 police officers from New York City and the Port Authority who were the first responders and died trying to rescue persons from the burning and collapsing buildings.

Kaitlin spoke to the Board of Directors in a sad and serious tone of voice, "I am sorry to announce that we have stopped all construction on our new hotels. The terrorist attacks on September 11 have had a negative impact on hotel values in the United States and throughout the world. This tragedy will go down in history as the most immediate and profound decline in all types of travel which has led to massive drop-offs in our hotels' occupancies in the days following the attacks."

Robert Welch sighed, "How long do you think this will last?"

"I'm not a psychic, Bob. But I would estimate at least 6 months to a year before things start to move upward. Travelers need to become more confident in security issues before they start returning to the air on aircraft. The fear factor is tremendous and the aviation business is suffering even more than the hotel industry."

After the meeting Kaitlin asked Emily to come into her office. She was pleased to see her looking so much better and more confident, "You look great, Emily. I was worried about you for awhile."

"Thanks, Kaitlin," she said. "Sometimes it takes a tragedy like 9/11 to make you reevaluate your life and your goals. I now have a new outlook on life and am thankful to be alive. I feel like I have been dead for a long time."

"You're so right, Emily. We all have so much to be thankful for. They say 'live each day as if it is your last.' It's time to smell the roses and get our priorities straight," Kaitlin said squeezing Emily's hand. She noticed Emily did not mention Raul.

That evening when Raul came in around midnight Emily was waiting for him along with his suitcase which she had already packed. She looked beautiful in her royal blue silk pantsuit and her eyes were sparkling.

Raul stopped dead in his tracks as he noticed the changes in Emily's appearance. He hadn't even noticed that she was no longer drinking or taking prescription narcotics. "What's going on here, Emily? Why is my suitcase sitting here in the living room?" he asked with more respect than usual as her new self-confidence was intimidating.

"Because you are leaving tonight," she said with self-assurance. Raul looked at her in shock as he started to pace.

"What are you talking about? Just because I missed your dinner you don't have the right to kick me out!"

"Yes, I do, Raul," she said firmly. "I own this property. Your name is not on the deed. If you refuse to leave, I am calling security. I have already informed them it might be necessary. Now, GET OUT!"

Raul tried to put his arms around her, "Oh, baby, I need you so bad! Right now!"

Emily struggled out of his reach and picked up the phone as he grabbed the suitcase and started out the door before she could make the call downstairs. As he went out she said, "And by the way don't try to withdraw any money. I have changed all my accounts to my name only. I have also cancelled all the credit cards and have new ones in my name only."

He looked so shocked that she couldn't resist saying, "You'll have to use your own money for a hotel as the old credit cards will no longer work!" With that she slammed the door in his face and shouted, "Good riddance!" She was amazed at how peaceful she felt knowing that Raul wouldn't be coming back. She had seen a lawyer after he attacked her and photos were taken of her black eye and swollen face and other bruises on her body. She didn't think she would have much trouble with the divorce.

The tragic 9/11 had made her realize that there was much more to life than Raul's clumsy love-making or waiting for the next time he hit her. The tragedy had made her realize herself again and she no longer would tolerate abuse from a man she no longer loved.

CHAPTER 19—OCTOBER 2001

Shortly after the attacks, the FBI was able to determine the personal details of the hijackers. Mohamed Atta from Egypt was the ringleader. He died in the attack but later his luggage was recovered on another flight and revealed the identity of all 19 hijackers.

Autumn, who was on top of the news, told Emily and Elizabeth, "Fifteen of the hijackers were from Saudi Arabia, two from the United Arab Emirates and one from Lebanon in addition to Atta. But the real culprit is Osama bin Laden who declared what he called 'a holy war' against the United States."

Emily who was looking better and better every day since Raul's departure asked, "Is it true that Bin Laden and his henchmen are hiding out in the caves in Afghanistan?"

"Yes, that is why President Bush has launched his War on Terror in Afghanistan which according to all reports is the training ground for Al Qaeda terrorists. They also intend to remove the Taliban regime from power and create a viable state," she explained.

Emily said hesitantly as she thought of her husband and Autumn's father who had died in the Vietnam War, "Don't you have a good friend who is going over there, Autumn?"

Autumn sighed, "Yes, I am sorry to say that Bill Harden, my best friend and the photographer that goes with me on my assignments from the newspaper has decided to serve in the Marines and will be leaving for Afghanistan within a week or two. I tried to talk him out of it but all he can talk about is helping our country after the terrorist attack."

"You have to admire his patriotism but I have had a feeling that he might be that special man you have been waiting for," Emily said not wanting to push Autumn to confide the status of the relationship before she was ready. She hoped history wouldn't be repeating itself as she remembered the grief she felt when her husband died in a POW concentration camp after being badly tortured.

Autumn smiled, "You always can read my mind, Mom. Yes, Bill could be the one. He has hinted about marriage, but we have kind of put that conversation on hold because of his deployment."

Elizabeth was ecstatic with the thought of Autumn's consideration of marriage. She was still hoping that one of these years Kaitlin and John would finally tie the knot and marry. They were so in love but she realized that Kaitlin was still dealing with the revelation that her mother and her father had been half-sister and brother. That terrible secret had destroyed her beloved husband and she wasn't sure whether she was ready to deal with it herself.

"Will we get a chance to meet him, Autumn? Before he leaves, I mean?" Elizabeth asked.

"Yes, of course. Kaitlin and I are already planning a going-away bash for him and we mean to include everyone. Kaitlin has offered us the restaurant at the Grand Biscayne for our private party. She plans to close it down for other guests that night," Autumn said excitedly.

Bill's going-away bash actually took place a few weeks after their conversation. Emily couldn't help but recall the party that was held for her former husband, Tom Pierce, who worked as a newspaper reporter as did she, who later died in Vietnam. Like that gathering, the gang from the newspaper were all there to send off Bill with their good wishes. Emily feared for Bill's life remembering all the pain of losing Tom.

It was at that party that Bill and Autumn announced their engagement even though definite wedding plans were on hold. They made a handsome couple. Bill was well over six feet tall with sandy hair and steel blue eyes set off by his golden tan and beautifully tailored navy blue suit. It wasn't often that Bill wore a suit, for as a photographer he usually could be found in jeans and a t-shirt. Autumn was a striking contrast with her chestnut brown dark hair stylishly cut and her sparkling blue eyes. Slender and tanned, she glowed in her off-white cocktail suit trimmed with gemstones. She was almost as tall as Bill in her four-inch silver stiletto heels.

Bill quieted down the crowd and holding Autumn's hand said, "This party tonight is more than seeing old friends and co-workers before I am deployed. I am proud to announce that this lovely lady, my Autumn, has agreed to marry me and we want you to share our happiness."

The crowd loudly applauded and John Martinez and Kaitlin directed the waiters to pass out champagne to all. John raised his flute, "Here is our congratulations to Bill and Autumn on their engagement," and he added laughing, "and we hope we'll all be invited to the wedding." Everyone applauded wildly and guests hugged the happy couple.

Then Bill brought Emily into the inner circle and announced, "And here is my wonderful new mother-in-law who has generously given me her permission to marry her daughter." Tears welled up in Emily's eyes as she looked into her daughter's eyes sparkling with happiness and excitement and love.

Emily prayed silently, "Please, God, keep Bill safe. Watch over Autumn so that she will never suffer the pain I endured when I learned that my beloved Tom would never be coming back to us. Autumn has already lost a father that she never had a chance to really know so give her your divine protection as her fiancé leaves for war."

Even though she was fearful for the future, Emily was radiantly happy to see her daughter so in love with a man who worshipped her. She thanked God silently, "Thank you for giving me to strength to send Raul out of my life. Thank goodness he is not here at this happy occasion to ruin it for me and my loved ones."

While Emily was thanking God for being released from her obsession, Raul was confiding in his brother at the prison, "I guess I blew it for good, Carlos!"

Carlos glared at him and shouted into the receiver, "You mean the broad actually kicked you out without any money! How did you manage that, you idiot? I thought you had her all sewed up!"

Raul moaned, "So I made a mistake! I misjudged her badly. I thought I had her hooked on sex and I am pretty hot in bed. I thought I could do anything I wanted and she would accept it. Also, I made sure she had plenty of drugs and booze around. The old broad was drunk most of the time."

Carlos snarled sarcastically, "Apparently, she sobered up and you were too dumb to realize it! You have just made it harder for me to seduce her sister-in-law when I get out of here. Now, I can't claim to have any connection to you or the game is over! Shit!!!!!!!"

"Hold it, Bro, I didn't say it was hopeless! I'll give it some time. Maybe get a job so I look more reliable. She fell for me once, and maybe if I play my cards right, she'll take me back on the gravy train," Raul whined desperately.

Carlos stared at him, "How are you supporting yourself now that she has cut you off? You're married. Aren't you entitled to half her fortune in a divorce?"

Raul flushed, "Well, there's something I forgot to tell you."

Carlos shouted impatiently, "What the fuck are you up to now? You mean to tell me you screwed up further?"

Raul looked away from Carlos' icy gaze, "So, she made me angry! When I'd get home late she'd nag me about where I had been and what I was doing. She was drunk and looked like an old slut so I might have hit her around a bit."

"You, what?" Carlos asked incredulously. "Most dames deserve it once in awhile anyway. What's so bad about that?"

"Well," he hesitated, "when I hit her she fell backwards against the wall and cracked her head and then fell forward and hit some glass on the coffee table. She might have cut herself."

"What do you mean, might have? Are you saying you left her that way and didn't call a doctor or anything," Carlos screamed.

Raul now was getting angry, "She was drunk. You can't hurt a drunk!" He pushed his hair off his forehead and Carlos noticed he was sweating. "It's just that she went to a damn lawyer and he took photos of her cuts and bruises. I guess she also had a mild concussion. So it looks kind of bad for any kind of settlement."

Carlos was really disgusted now, "Is she charging you with assault?"

"No, but worse, I won't be getting any more dough until the divorce goes through." He whined, "You have a lot of dinero stashed away from all your drug deals. Can I have a little to hold me over?"

Carlos was furious, "Shut your damn mouth!" He furtively looked at the guard to see if he had heard Raul's remark. "You're not getting your hands on any of my money. I've served so much time in this joint, I deserve every cent of it. Now get the hell out of here before I kill you!"

Raul couldn't wait to get out of there. As far as he was concerned he didn't ever want to see his brother again, especially now that he found out that Carlos was so selfish he didn't want to share any of his millions. Raul knew that he had plenty of cash in an off-shore bank. After all, he was one of the major drug dealers in Miami when he was arrested. He was a rich man behind bars. Why couldn't he give him some?

He frowned as he realized that Carlos was his last resort. He owed over $100,000 in gambling debts and they wouldn't even let him back in the poker group to make it up. Also, a couple goons were threatening him if he didn't pay off soon.

"I have to get Emily back," he panicked. "She loved me once and I can make her love me again. But how? I know I'll think of a way."

CHAPTER 20—PRESENT DAY

Kaitlin needed to call a Board Meeting as the situation was getting more threatening with every day that passed. She now was certain that a plot to take over the company was immerging. The corporation lawyer, Byron Harrell, sat at her side. He was a formidable person with his full head of dark hair touched with gray and his commanding appearance. He reeked of sex appeal enhanced by his sharp intellect.

The corporation had gone public several years ago with Kaitlin as CEO and president, her significant other, John Martinez, and her mother, Elizabeth Donegan as Vice-Presidents, her sister-in-law, Emily, as Managing Director of Operations along with Robert Welch and David Wells, Directors of International and Domestic Operations respectively. William Petersen had retired several years earlier, but Edward Haynes, the wealthy banker still remained on the Board.

She spoke in a serious tone of voice, "There have been too many interruptions and one serious accident which is unexplained at our renovation of the Grand New York Hotel. I am afraid our image is being tarnished by all the bad publicity surrounding the construction worker who fell from the scaffold and is now paralyzed. The Grand Hotels have never had any scandal connected with them, and we need to work together to see where the threat is coming from. I would appreciate any suggestions or insights any of you might have in this most serious matter." She turned to the handsome lawyer, "I will let Byron describe some of the issues we are facing."

Byron Harrell stood up in his perfectly tailored suit and said with authority, "I am afraid I have some bad news to deliver. A personal injury lawsuit has been filed by Peter McInerny, the injured worker, and the suit has named the Grand Hotel Corporation as the responsible party. Kaitlin Donegon, as Chief Executive Officer has also been named in the suit."

Everyone exchanged pained glances as he continued, "As you know the Department of Buildings has shut down construction for the past month while they snoop around. Now they have issued multiple safety violations, something we have never seen in past constructions."

Elizabeth asked, "Does anyone know the cause of the accident? What caused the scaffold to fall?"

John Martinez answered, "No one knows for sure what happened up there on the 32nd floor, but we are starting to suspect sabotage. It's just too suspicious to be completely accidental or negligent. McInerny is on full Workman's Compensation and is a patient in the Spinal Injury section of Bellevue Hospital. He's unable to do anything, paralyzed from the neck down and on a breathing tube. It's a real tragedy. He's only 28 years old and has a wife and two small children."

"They are subpoenaing all our records relating to the building," the lawyer informed the distressed group.

"Our hearts go out to that devastated family. We have nothing to hide. Let them take the records. We have always been above-board with our contractors. If anyone of you knows anything about the contractors' cutting corners or using cheaper materials than we have specified please see me privately after our meeting today. I have also heard rumors that the laborers are planning a strike to regain pay for the time the project has been closed down. The problems related to this construction are multiplying as we speak," Kaitlin said in a worried tone.

That evening as John and Kaitlin were having dinner she reported to him that she was still getting hang-up calls late at night even though she had changed her phone number and had it unlisted. "I can't imagine how anyone would know when you were out of town and call me during those times."

"You certainly don't think that I'm making the calls? In fact, this makes me even more determined to marry you, Kaitlin. This has gone on too long, and we need to make it official," he said handing her a little velvet box.

Kaitlin opened it to find a beautiful sparkling diamond ring. With tears in her eyes she said, "Pour us another glass of wine, darling. There's something we need to talk about before I accept this ring."

"I don't care what it is, Kaitlin. I love you and want to marry you, especially now when you could use the support of a husband with all you are facing," John said pouring her a glass of wine.

"It's time for the secrets of the past to be revealed," she thought and she took John's hand in hers and started to explain.

CHAPTER 21—PRESENT DAY

As they sipped their wine Kaitlin said gently, "There is something I have chosen not to share with you over the years, John, even though we have always tried to be completely honest with each other. I guess as years passed by it was easier to try to forget than to broach the subject and perhaps destroy our relationship."

John looked confused, "I don't understand, Kaitlin. What could you say that I wouldn't accept? I have loved you since the day I first met you. Nothing can destroy that."

"Maybe you are right, but in all fairness to you, I didn't feel like I should marry you or anyone else for that matter. We have been happy living together, being partners in both work and love. I thought it would always stay that way, and I would never have to tell you the family secret."

John sighed, "Please go ahead, Kaitlin. Nothing you tell me will change my mind. I want you to be my wife, to be in my life forever."

She continued speaking softly, "My mother and father were half-brother and sister. They both had the same father, Calvin Donegon. My father committed suicide when he found out the truth from his mother, Sarah, in a death-bed confession. It seems that Calvin, my grandfather, had a short affair with Sarah before he married my grandmother. Apparently Sarah never told him that she was pregnant and kept my father's paternity a secret all those years until finally out of guilt revealed the truth to my father as she was dying from cancer. He couldn't bear to tell my mother and me. He thought he had ruined my life and my chances to marry and have children." She started to weep and was unable to continue speaking. She looked at John sadly with those big eyes wet with tears.

She finally composed herself and continued, "That is where you came into the picture as we waited for days to find out what happened to my father when he disappeared. After his death, I received a package delivered by courier from my father directing me to the stilt house on Biscayne Bay where I would find my great-grandfather, Aidin's journals. After reading those accounts of Aidin's amazing life, I finally learned the truth. I also realized that marriage would be out of the question for me."

John hugged Kaitlin, "Do you mean to say that you have kept this to yourself all the years we have been together. Why?"

"My mother and I decided that we should keep it to ourselves. There were others that it might harm. For instance, Emily still thinks that my father was her brother. She was brought up to believe that. Sarah never confided in her daughter. My mother has told me how Sarah tried to discourage dad from marrying my mother and later told him that mother was too old to have children. This caused an estrangement between my father and his mother that lasted for many years. After her confession, he understood why she had tried to keep them from having children. She knew all along they were brother and sister!"

John held her as she started to weep again, "Kaitlin, did you think any of this would stop me from loving you and wanting to marry you? Children are not that important to me and as a matter of fact, you are talking about half-brother and sister so genetically everything could be alright. Children can always be adopted if you really are worried and want to have them. Listen, Lady, I want to marry you, with or without children!"

Kaitlin gazed at the sparkling diamond ring, "John, don't you want to think about this for a few days and then decide if you really want to make that kind of commitment to me? I think of myself as damaged goods."

John placed the ring on her trembling finger, "Are you kidding me? I have been thinking about this for a decade! Ten years is long enough to wait!"

He got down on one knee and said the magic words, "Will you marry me, darling Kaitlin?"

She now was crying for joy as she said, "Yes, yes, yes! I love you John with all my heart and soul. Thank you for understanding. From now on no secrets between us. That I promise you."

CHAPTER 22—
NOVEMBER 2001

Autumn was trying hard not to worry about Bill who was fighting in Afghanistan but she had to admit that she had many sleepless nights. He was able to email her and that helped some but she knew that he and thousands of U.S. troops were in danger daily while at home their loved ones had to learn to live with their worry.

Kaitlin and Autumn met over drinks one evening at an oceanside restaurant and after they had caught up on the family news Kaitlin turned to her friend and said, "Autumn, I know how worried you must be about Bill. What have you heard about the progress of the war?"

Autumn sighed, "Well, you know that the Bush administration launched this war, Operation Enduring Freedom, to defeat Al-Qaeda and end the use of Afghanistan as a base for terrorist operations. They also are trying to remove the Taliban regime from power and create a democratic state."

"Tall order I would say," Kaitlin frowned. "Their history shows that they are not easily conquered. And how actively is Bill involved in the fighting?"

"It's the worst kind of fighting partly because of the mountainous terrain. Bill, along with several thousand U.S. troops began entering the country this month mainly to search the caves in the mountains for bin Laden who has admitted responsibility for the attack on 9/11 and the Taliban leader Muhammad Omar. He can't talk about it by email, top secret you know, but I gather that sometimes it is difficult to tell a terrorist from an Afghan soldier and his life is constantly in danger."

Kaitlin nodded sympathetically, "That must be exhausting carrying all that equipment on his back in that rough mountain country. Is there an end in sight?"

"It looks like by December the opposition forces will have ousted the Taliban and Al-Quaeda forces from the major urban areas and they are even being aided by the defection of forces allied with the Taliban. The women of Afghanistan are so controlled by the Taliban that they have virtually no freedom at all. I'm sure they would welcome a U.S. victory," she added as she watched the vibrant sunset over the ocean.

Kaitlin hesitated but then decided to broach the question, "Any plans to set a wedding date in the future? I think you and Bill make a beautiful couple and you have so many interests in common."

"Actually, we are talking about it when Bill comes home on leave around Christmas time. We just want to go to the courthouse and not have a huge church wedding even though it would please mom. We might plan a small reception for only family and a few of our closest friends. Bill won't have a lot of time at home and we want to spend every minute of it honeymooning," she laughed. "I'd like you to be my maid-of-honor, Kaitlin."

"I would love to do it, Autumn. In fact, I'm so honored that you asked me," she said squeezing her friend's hand.

Now Autumn turned to Kaitlin with a smile, "And should we make it a double wedding? Don't you think it's about time for John to make you an honest woman?"

Kaitlin raised her cocktail glass for a toast, "I like to keep them guessing, but who knows what the future has in store. As they clinked their glasses, each woman was thinking how lucky to have a lasting friendship like theirs.

It seemed like an eternity until Bill's leave came around at the end of December. They were married the day before Christmas at the Miami-Dade County Courthouse. Autumn's mother, Emily, and Kaitlin's mother, Liz, were the only family present. Kaitlin and John stood at their sides during the ceremony and afterwards they took the glowing couple to the restaurant on the ocean where the two women had toasted to the upcoming wedding. It was Christmas Eve and the colored lights reflected on the ocean waves. They were also blessed by a gigantic full moon over Miami. A huge Christmas tree decorated with silver angels was in the center of the room and there was a small orchestra for dancing.

Bill and Autumn fell into each others' arms on the dance floor as the orchestra played, 'When I Fall in Love' and 'I've Got You under My Skin'. People at the tables couldn't keep their eyes off them. They were such a beautiful young couple and their eyes were sparkling brighter than the Christmas lights. They noticed that the man was in dress uniform and they guessed he was home from Afghanistan. As they were leaving the dance floor everyone applauded and Bill planted a tender kiss on Autumn's lips to the delight of the crowd.

Kaitlin and John took them to Miami International Airport for their flight to Jamaica for their honeymoon. As they started through security, Autumn removed her orchid corsage and threw it to Kaitlin, "I don't have a bouquet but this will do. You're next, Kaitlin!'

John grinned, "Now it's official, Kaitlin. You have to marry me! My only question is when?" Kaitlin gave him a mysterious Mona Lisa smile as they left the airport.

CHAPTER 23—AUGUST 2002

It had been almost a year since the terrorist attack on the Twin Towers in New York City and the lagging hotel business was starting to pick up now that people were not so afraid to travel. David Wells was in San Francisco overseeing construction of the new boutique hotel and Robert Welch was in France where construction had already commenced in their first international boutique hotel in Amboise, France.

John stepped into Kaitlin's office and remarked, "It certainly is more peaceful around here without Bob and Dave! They always cast a pessimistic gloom over everything but Bob actually looked excited about his trip to France!"

Kaitlin laughed, "I certainly know what you mean. I hate the way the two of them are always whispering together as if they are designing some dubious plot. Actually, I'm kind of fed up with their behavior and if they don't make good on this current assignment I will have to let them go. They are both nearing retirement age and I think we need new blood to generate some enthusiasm about the boutique concept."

"The Grand Miami Beach Boutique is certainly a success story. It is fully booked for the coming year including the off-season months. Now that South Beach has such a cosmopolitan flavor with all the international tourists there actually is no off-season on South Beach."

"I can remember hearing stories of the old days when hotels actually closed most of the year and then opened during the winter months when tourists flocked from the cold north to the balmy breezes of Miami," Kaitlin reminisced. "When I read my great-grandfather, Aidin's journal he wrote about the cost of refurbishing the hotels after they had been closed for so many months. He pioneered keeping his hotels open all year long and maintained it saved money in the long run."

"He was quite a business man, way ahead of his time from what I have heard," John remarked. "No wonder you are such a success coming from that line of entrepreneurs."

She laughed as she pulled out a map of Scotland, "Speaking of entrepreneurs isn't it time we embarked on our trip to Scotland that we postponed? I have finally convinced my mother to take responsibility for the operations while we are away. Actually, I think it is good for her. It helped that Robert Welch and David Wells are working on projects away from Miami. She certainly hated working with them when we were gone before."

"Great idea, Kaitlin," John exclaimed! We can route our flight through Paris and double check on the progress in Amboise. Kind of let Bob know that we are looking over his shoulder. That area has so much potential to attract tourists. I'm sure it will be a winner!"

"I loved how the architect preserved the historic castle design. Tourists seem to be hooked on actually staying in a castle so I feel sure that it will attract a lot of attention especially in that scenic location," Kaitlin said as she marked key locations on the map of Scotland where their next search for prime locations would take place.

It wasn't long before Kaitlin and John had landed at Edinburgh airport and after they rented a car they tried to find the Bed and Breakfast that they had booked but got hopelessly lost. Finally, they saw a group of people standing outside a pub and Kaitlin got out to ask directions. The people couldn't have been friendlier as they all tried to give directions, even drawing a map. By the time they had found out where Kaitlin was from and asked many questions they even offered to buy them a 'Pint' before they left.

Kaitlin laughed, "If we ever want to find our Bed and Breakfast I don't think we better have that pint. But thanks anyway for all your kindness."

"Any time, Lassie. Come back and see us. We're usually here at the pub most nights," one heavy-set woman said as she sipped her pint.

They later discovered this was not a unique experience and that even seasoned travelers got lost in Edinburgh where streets changed names frequently. They also found the Scottish people to be warm and friendly and particularly interested in U.S. visitors and quick to engage you in conversation.

They were greeted by their charming host at the Dunedin House which turned out to be a delightful surprise. As they climbed the staircase Kaitlin exclaimed, "Look, John at the beautiful ceilings complete with angels!"

Their room was large and airy and the furnishings were elegantly Scottish. The friendly host explained the interesting background of the house and gave them tips for getting around the city. He suggested that they take to bus to go downtown because of parking problems and the chance of getting lost on the confusing streets.

After sleeping off their jet-lag, they went to the breakfast room the next morning for the full Scottish breakfast. "I don't think we'll need to eat again today after this," Kaitlin whispered as they set her plate in front of her.

"Let's see," John counted, "eggs, bacon, sausage, black pudding, mushrooms, tomatoes, baked beans, potato scones and toast! And if that isn't enough, I see cereal and fruit on the breakfast buffet!"

As they hadn't eaten much on the plane, it all tasted delicious. After their third cup of coffee, Kaitlin moaned, "Do we need to go back to the room for a nap or go sightseeing?"

Their first stop was Edinburgh Castle, home to Scottish treasures. "Take my picture, John, next to the guards in their kilts." He obliged and snapped her picture in spite of the fact the guard never changed his serious expression or acknowledged Kaitlin's presence.

"The castle certainly has a strategic location sitting on this rock high above the city. But then I read that it has been both a fort and a royal residence since the 11th century, but used as a military garrison in more recent years," John said as they gazed over the wall and looked down at the city far below.

"I want to see the famous Crown Jewels," Kaitlin said as she read her guidebook. "Do you know that they were hidden over 100 years after the Act of Union which dissolved Scotland's parliament into England's to create the United Kingdom? It wasn't until 1818 that Walter Scott rediscovered the jewels intact!"

After gazing at the gold, diamonds and precious gems they headed down the Royal Mile which led them to the other end from the castle to the new Parliament Building with its controversial modern lines across from the Holyrood Palace, the royal residence most known for love and murder of Mary Queen of Scots.

"I don't think this modern Parliament Building fits into the history and period of the castle across the road. It seems out of place in my opinion," Kaitlin sighed as she gazed up at the streamlined architecture.

John laughed, "Don't worry, Kaitlin! Even after that breakfast, I feel the need for a pint and a pub meal. I noticed a quaint pub half-way along the Royal Mile so let's walk back a few blocks and see if we can get a seat. It looked crowded."

They gazed at the beautiful and ornate ceiling and the murals on the walls. "I can't believe this is a pub," Kaitlin said as she read the history of the Deacon Brodie's Tavern. "Listen to this, John, some say the Deacon was the inspiration for Dr. Jekyll and Mr. Hyde as it says he was both a humanitarian and a scoundrel!" She continued as they sipped their icy cold beers and nibbled on the delicious fish and chips, "He was hanged in 1788 on gallows that he had built for the town!"

John grinned, "All I know about him was that he serves a mighty fine pub meal for 10 pounds and the pints are 2.90 pounds so he can't have been all bad!"

They returned that evening exhausted from the jet lag and their busy first day. "Let's wait until tomorrow to map out our itinerary. I know that we will be lucky and find a few great locations for our next boutique hotels. The scenery should be incredible as we head through the Loch country and the highlands. I can't wait to explore the Isle of Skye! But tonight I just want to explore this comfortable bed and soft pillows," Kaitlin said as she kissed John goodnight and promptly fell asleep.

CHAPTER 24—AUGUST 2002

Their itinerary was a circle route that made it possible for them to explore many regions in their quest for the perfect boutique hotel location. Kaitlin had already decided that John could do all the driving.

"I still can't get the hang of driving on the opposite side of the road, especially driving in what I still think of as the passenger side," she apologized. "I hope you don't mind doing all the driving but I am sure we would crash the first time we go around a rotary circle if I were at the wheel."

John grinned, "I've already noticed you keep hopping into the driver's side and I know it isn't because you want to drive."

"I just can't get used to it," she sighed, "but I will be glad to be the map-watcher and navigator and also guide you into the right spoke when we come to a rotary circle."

"Sounds like a plan!" John looked over at Kaitlin who was studying the map, "Where to my fair lady?"

"To the Bonnie Bonnie Banks of Loch Lomond, and then we will drive further north to Loch Leven passing through the Glencoe region where we can expect the arresting impact of Scotland's mountains. Let me clue you in on the famous Glencoe Massacre of 1692," she said looking out the corner of her eye at John's reaction.

"Are you sure it's safe?" he laughed.

"Now be serious, John. It was one of those clan disputes between the Campbell and MacDonald clans. Men, women and children were massacred by the Scottish troops aided by the despised Campbell's," she reprimanded him.

"I've changed my mind about searching for a MacDonald's for a hamburger and fries!" he quipped.

Kaitlin didn't have time to fret as they were entering the amazing Loch country. They stopped in Balloch for a cruise on Loch Lomond, one of Scotland's most beautiful lochs. They sipped a glass of wine as the glorious scenery passed by.

They noticed a series of stately homes and castles as well as a fantastic view of the mountain named Ben Lomond. "How about a hotel on one of the Lochs?" Kaitlin said with enthusiasm. "This area is certainly popular with tourists. Do you think we might find a lovely castle for sale?" she asked.

"With your eye for beauty and marketing, I'm sure we'll find something worth considering. Just beware of the Loch Ness monster when we reach that loch!"

That evening they stayed at a hostel on the east side of the loch that accommodated hikers and decided to take a short hike the next day. As they sipped their single malt whiskey distilled at a local distillery in the hostel's dining room, they got some tips from veteran hikers who had all the equipment for long walks. The next day they borrowed walking sticks at the hostel before they set out for their trip on one of the shorter hiking trails. It was a remote area that was incredibly beautiful with its hills, forests and the stunning shoreline. They hiked farther than they had planned they were so entranced by the magical setting. They returned late that afternoon thoroughly exhausted.

"I admire all these older people who do these long hikes." They had met some hikers in their seventies and even one in her eighties on the trail. "They must be very physically fit," she said as she huffed and puffed the last one hundred yards back to the hostel.

After a delicious Scottish meal of mussels and prawns they were more than ready to go to bed early and fell asleep as soon as their heads touched the pillows.

The next morning with aching muscles from the long hike the day before, they drove through Glencoe on their way to Lock Linnhe. Glencoe offered them a grand vista of nature in the raw. As a mist descended over the mountains Kaitlin said, "I feel like this glen is haunted by ghosts."

Just then the sun broke through and the beautiful mountains and gushing waterfalls appeared. The colors seemed to glisten and change as the clouds rolled by. They noticed hikers up on the heathery crags. John shook his head, "No, Kaitlin, no hikes today!"

They stayed that night at a small hotel on the banks of Lock Linnhe near Fort William, a city with Ben Nevis, the highest mountain in Scotland towering over it. As they approached the city of Inverness in the north and the capital of the highlands they started to see more castles especially on the banks of Loch Ness.

As they pulled over on a layaway to take a photo of the gleaming water and a castle in the distance another driver motioned them over frantically. His family was all staring out at the ripples in the water through binoculars.

"We've found Nessie, the Loch Ness monster. Look at those ripples! My daughter saw the monster's tail!"

Kaitlin and John exchanged furtive glances and not wanting to discourage the excited man, she said, "What a find! You should notify the newspapers of your sighting." He looked at them proudly as the children continued staring into the binoculars.

They laughed as they drove away, "I think he must have had a few too many single malt whiskies!"

All of a sudden Kaitlin spotted a castle with spectacular views over the loch. "Let's investigate that one," she said as she noticed a small sign announcing it was 'FOR SALE'. As they drove up the narrow road they passed waterfalls and gorges and beautiful woodland. The castle seemed to be in good repair although the gardens surrounding it needed work.

As they got out of the car, the owner rushed out to meet them. "I don't get many visitors these days," the frail old man said in a quaking voice. "Even though this was the home of the Earls of Glasgow in the olden days, most buyers think it's too big for a house and too small for a hotel. I'm too old and can't afford a gardener anymore and my beautiful gardens have gone to pot!"

Kaitlin and John asked to see the interior and he led them through the gigantic front door without hesitation. The rooms were spacious but quite dark and the furniture was old and rugs threadbare. He looked embarrassed and said to Kaitlin, "My eyesight is poor these days and I can't afford help so I'm afraid I'm not much of a housekeeper these days. When I sell this property I plan to move into a retirement home on the loch where they do everything for you."

After negotiating the price he finally shook his head, "I guess at this point I could lower the price considerably as long as I get enough to have lifetime care at the retirement home."

"We'll think about it," Kaitlin said. "It's only fair to tell you we will be considering other locations for our boutique hotel. If we decide to make a bid, you will hear from our lawyer, Robert MacTavish in a few weeks."

"I'm willing to make a deal at this point," he said. "I'm unable to keep up this place much longer."

After John and Kaitlin drove away they discussed the possibilities. "The place needs a lot of work, but the location is sure to draw in tourists who want to explore Inverness and The Highlands," Kaitlin said pensively.

"And they could watch for the Loch Ness Monster right from the front terrace," he laughed. "But all kidding aside, it is an awesome property and has its own history. The owner is very anxious to sell and we probably would be doing the old guy a favor to take it off his hands. He's obviously overwhelmed by keeping things up. I felt sorry for him as he probably is in pain as he had a hard time walking. I think he deserves to spend his last days gazing at the loch and having someone take care of him."

"It sits on about 30 acres of land and that has all kinds of possibilities and the scenery is incredible. There's plenty of room for hiking trails and gardens. We want to maintain the authentic castle architecture, but it can be opened up with large windows overlooking the loch as it is much too dark as is. Some of the rooms are small but could be turned into two and three room suites. We could always have a welcoming fire burning in the Great Room and perhaps a grand piano and pianist to play during cocktail hour," Kaitlin said as she took notes on her ideas.

"How about a billiard room and an indoor swimming pool?" John asked enthusiastically. "And a telescope on the broad terrace to watch for Nessie!"

"We'll send for MacTavish from Edinburgh to negotiate and close the deal. If all works out the way I hope, we have found our first boutique castle hotel in Scotland!" Kaitlin beamed with her eyes sparkling.

"Have I told you today that I love you," John said planting a passionate kiss on her lips. He grinned in a suggestive manner, "My hiking aches are better and I have urgent business to conduct with you at the hotel. He placed her hand over the large bulge in his pants.

"I get your message, John. Don't exceed the speed level on these narrow roads. I think we can come to a quick agreement on the business you are proposing," Kaitlin said kissing him back.

CHAPTER 25—
SEPTEMBER 2002

While the negotiations were taking place on the Loch Ness property, they decided to swing over to the western side and cross over to the Isle of Skye. They immediately fell in love with the island where stark jagged mountains drop to gentle, white sandy beaches. inlets, bays and islands and created a complex lacework pattern with the sea.

"Let's cross by the Skye Bridge," Kaitlin said excitedly, "and we can explore the northern part of the island and then head to the southern end and take the ferry back to the mainland."

They found a small hotel right on the harbor across from the bridge where the hostess was so pleasant and helpful in planning day trips on the island. John was soon behind the wheel again driving on the precarious single lane roads on the island where they not only had to look for oncoming vehicles, but also herds of sheep crossing over the road after you have turned a curve.

"This must be the 'rush hour' for sheep," John quipped as they constantly slowed down to let the sheep cross over. As they continued on their route they passed tiny villages and historic keeps.

All of a sudden Kaitlin shouted, "Oh, stop, John. I see the 'Old Man of Storr' ahead in the mist." John was glad to find a layaway where he could let other cars pass him and get a little breather. The layaways were small scallops at the side of the narrow road enabling the oncoming car to pass or pull over and let you pass. Grabbing her camera, Kaitlin stood below the great pillar of rock.

"This area below the cliffs is called the Sanctuary," she said as she studied the guidebook. "It is possible to climb up to the pinnacles but I'm happy to just gaze up at the cliffs of The Storr," Kaitlin said snapping photos as fast as she could since the mist had lifted.

"Thank goodness for that," John sighed looking up at the towering pinnacle, "It does look like an old man with a very big nose! Cyrano had nothing on The Old Man of Storr."

Kaitlin laughed, "I doubt if he's ever been compared to Cyrano before."

"Maybe Pinocchio?" Tom asked with a wide grin on his face.

But there were many magnificent sights ahead as they stopped at Lealt Gorge to see a spectacular waterfall. As they walked up to the top of the cliff for the best view they passed many mountain sheep with their black faces grazing on the mountainside. Further on they made another stop at the Kilt Rock cliffs plunging down hundreds of feet to the sea.

They gasped at the beauty of the scenery but Kaitlin remarked, "As gorgeous as Skye is, I'm not sure it would be the best site for our hotel. It is so remote, but then that adds to the beauty."

"I agree with you Kaitlin," John nodded adding, "and some tourists would be too intimidated to drive these single lane roads, especially Americans who are used to driving on the opposite side of the road."

They decided to drive to the most northern point on Skye mainly due to Kaitlin's interest in the outdoor museum. She had highlighted the museum information in her guidebook.

John said wearily, "Are you sure you want to see this, Kaitlin? Don't forget that we have to drive back to the bed and breakfast on this same road or else change the scene by rounding the top of the island and going down the western route which is also a single lane road from what I can see."

She replied firmly, "It's a collection of traditional blackhouses which show how islanders used to live in the past. Not only that, the guidebook says there is a monument to Flora MacDonald near the outdoor museum!"

John looked confused, "Who did you say?"

"Flora MacDonald, the brave lady who helped Bonnie Prince Charlie escape from his enemies! Don't you remember that when we were in Inverness near Loch Ness, I read you about the Culloden Battlefield where Bonnie Prince Charlie who hoped to claim the throne for the Stuarts was defeated and escaped to Skye after pretending to be the maid of Flora MacDonald who was later imprisoned for her part in the drama."

John laughed, "That must have slipped my mind. I'm so glad to have a walking and talking guidebook with me."

On their return after an hour of touring the blackhouses with all their relics of the old days and stopping to see Flora's monument with the Celtic cross, they headed back to the hotel tired and hungry. However, they weren't too tired to stop in the village of Broadford for their fresh, local mussels steamed open in white wine, butter and garlic.

Next John who was regaining his strength ordered the house specialty, "We'll have two orders of your main dish, the hand-dived Isle of Skye King Scallops."

The rotund waiter smiled, "Perfect choice! We pan-sauté them with dry vermouth and cream. They are unforgettable I assure you!"

After finishing off the splendid feast and downing a full bottle of excellent white wine, they finally arrived back at their hotel.

As they walked up the stairs to their room Kaitlin grinned, "Wait until you hear about the day trip I have planned for tomorrow!"

John groaned and fell into bed and was soundly snoring in another minute.

CHAPTER 26—PRESENT DAY

Raul prepared to pick up his brother at the South Dade Federal Correctional prison. The big day was here at last. Carlos had served more than thirty years for his drug dealing and racketeering when he was a young man. Sometimes it was hard for him to imagine how his good fortune had turned away from him. When he first arrived in Miami from Cuba he had studied to be a doctor and had been in love and engaged to the beautiful Elizabeth who came from a prominent Miami family.

Then the lure of easy drug money had roped him in, and before he knew it he was a kingpin with the Cuban Mafia. As his personality changed along with his new career in crime, Elizabeth grew to distrust him and in the end feared him when he became secretive and abusive.

About that time her former love, Andrew Donegon entered into the picture, got the goods on Carlos and persuaded Elizabeth to marry him. She had loved Andy since she was a young girl and confessed she loved him in letters to him while he was in the Korean War. When he finally returned he saw her occasionally but was wrapped up in running and building new hotels for the family chain. They had made love several times, but there was no serious commitment on Andy's side and when fun-loving Carlos came her way it was love at first sight.

Carlos was still a handsome man in spite of his age. He thought that those touches of gray in his dark hair actually improved his appearance. He had worked out all the years of imprisonment and was slim and muscular. Now dressed in a new suit provided by his brother, Raul, he knew that he made a dashing figure. He had bitterly resented the news that his former fiancé was marrying Andrew Donegon, the wealthy hotel dynasty heir, after he was convicted and sent to prison. In fact, he suspected that Andrew might have been the one to turn him in. He had planned to kill Andrew after his release, but Andy had committed suicide and robbed him of the pleasure. Now he had a score to settle with Elizabeth and her daughter, Kaitlin, who was running the hotel operation and was worth a fortune.

Raul hugged his brother, "Congratulations, Hermano! You look like a million bucks in that silk suit I brought you!"

"Too bad I don't have that million bucks," Carlos laughed and then added, "actually I have to figure a way to get it, and I already have hatched a plan."

Raul grinned, "I always knew you had it stashed away somewhere, you Diablo!"

"I didn't serve all those years for nothin'" he continued. "Give me an update on Elizabeth. That's the first order of business."

"She's still a pretty good-looking dame for her age and still unmarried. I don't think she has dated since her husband died. Her daughter, Kaitlin, is a knockout and I read in the paper that she and her lover, John Martinez, another Cuban dude, are getting married. He runs the corporation with her and I don't know if it's love, or if he'd like to take over the company," Raul explained.

"Let's talk it over at Joe's Stone Crabs. My mouth has been watering for them since they locked me up. Unfortunately, they don't serve them at the 'luxury resort' I have been staying in, even though it was 'all inclusive' with three square meals a day," he quipped.

After a few double scotches and a plate of super jumbo stone crabs, Carlos ordered some Cuban coffee and a cigar and sat back contentedly, "First I need a fake passport. I still have connections with some old compatriots that will do that for me. Then I plan to get my money out of my Swiss bank and have some plastic surgery done. I plan to assume a new identity and then I will charm the pants off Elizabeth."

"I have no doubt you can pull it off. I never let Emily know that I had a brother in prison although I told her my brother lived in Cuba," Raul said as he sipped his coffee.

"How is the Emily thing going? Any chance she might take you back if you behave yourself?" Carlos asked with a frown on his face.

"I doubt that will happen, but I finally got a pretty good judgment out of the divorce and on the sly I have been buying some of her shares in the company under a phony corporation shield as I know that she is short of money. Of course, she is high maintenance and wants the best of everything even if she can no longer afford it," Raul said in a conspiratory whisper.

Carlos roared with laughter, "You got some brains after all! Keep getting those shares and hopefully with my new look after surgery, Elizabeth's shares will fall into my hands. Then I can start making her life miserable. Mark my words, she will pay for having me locked up for thirty years!"

"When are you leaving the country?" Raul asked

"I have a friend working on my new identity as we speak. As soon as that is ready, the old Carlos Gonzalez will disappear from the face of the earth and the parole board," he sneered. The two brothers hugged each other as they looked forward to their new life.

CHAPTER 27—PRESENT DAY

There was a somber atmosphere as the officers entered the Board Room. Things had gone from bad to worse. Although the Grand Hotel Corporation had millions invested in their hotels it had little liquidity and coming up with a few hundred million on their own would be a problem and they all knew it.

Robert Welsh and David Wells were frowning and whispering to each other in low tones. Robert was the first to speak, "I knew this would happen when we invested so much capital in the boutique hotels all over the globe! No one would follow my advice and now look at the mess we are facing! We'll probably have to sell a hotel and with the country in recession and the market shaky, we'll probably only get a fraction of what it is worth!"

Kaitlin cut him off curtly, "We're not here to cast blame on anyone but to find solutions to the problems we are facing! We're here today to discuss the wrongful death suit and the District Attorney's subpoena." She pointed to the boxes and bundles containing hundreds of company records for their attorney to sort through.

Their lawyer, Bryon Harrell, then addressed the distressed group, "As you all know the injured worker, Peter McInerny, has filed a personal injury lawsuit. It now appears that he will be paralyzed for life according to the latest hospital records." He waited until the group absorbed the bad news. "My team of lawyers will be sorting through all these records to see if we can find any documents that would exonerate the Grand Hotels from any knowledge of safety shortcuts or to show no documents existed to explain the cause of the accident. If the plaintiffs make the Grand Hotels liable for the accident, they'd have to show how someone had put pressure on the general contractor to cut corners."

Robert Welsh interrupted, "This could drag on for years and cost us millions of dollars in legal fees! I can't see that the case has any merit, but yet it will take every cent we have to fight it!"

"That's enough, Bob," Kaitlin said glowering, "you can leave right now if you persist in making negative remarks instead of positive suggestions."

The lawyer continued, "The Rackets Bureau handles all incidents involving New York's construction industry. Unfortunately, 'the mob' has weaseled their way into this industry. I've invited the New York D.A., Arthur Gimenez, to address us today." He went to the door and ushered in the tall, well-dressed man in his early fifties.

"Good morning," he said as his gaze swept the room to see which important citizens might be present. "We are still reviewing the papers you have turned over, but we are grossly understaffed and it will take time. I have been told that you will be sending additional documents in the future."

Bryon Harrell responded, "I don't think any of these documents are going to help with your investigation."

The D.A. sniped, "How do you know what we are investigating?"

Kaitlin snapped, "I thought you were looking for negligent or deliberate failures in construction or safety issues!"

"The invoices tell me another story, Ms Donegon," he retorted. "It looks like there were some materials bought and paid for and never delivered. It looks to me like a couple million dollars spent for labor and concrete that never happened. I'm sure you are conducting your own investigation. We will wait until we see all your documents before we proceed." Pointing to the boxes of records he said, "It looks like you have some work ahead for you. My office will be waiting for the additional pertinent records." With that he nodded to the group after gathering up his papers and left the unhappy group around the conference table.

John stole a glance at Kaitlin and saw that she registered shock and surprise at this latest bombshell.

"We'll leave this in your hands, Bryon. The news keeps getting worse. I have hired a team of investigators to get to the bottom of the accident. If inferior materials were used in the concrete foundations it could have been the cause of the accident if a section had collapsed when Peter McInerny was working on the scaffold. Another piece of bad news is the workers who have been laid off because of the halt in construction because of this investigation are demanding that they be paid for the time-off. They plan a strike if they are not compensated," Kaitlin groaned.

John Martinez spoke nervously to the group, "If anyone is concealing knowledge about the missing materials they will be dismissed unless they come forward with the information. It looks suspiciously like someone might have been substituting inferior materials for the more expensive ones that were never delivered. That would be a nice profit on the side for someone. Unfortunately, inferior materials make for shoddy work and yes, accidents."

Robert Welsh shouted, "I don't like your implications, Martinez! Do you think that one of us is responsible for this mess?"

Kaitlin responded icily, "John was not implying that, Bob. But someone may be trying to sabotage our corporation in an effort to take over the company. We all need to pool our resources and give this our best thinking instead of blaming one another."

Emily and Elizabeth left the Board Room with Kaitlin trying to offer their love and support in this difficult time. Emily took Kaitlin aside, "I probably should tell you, Kaitlin. I have had to sell some of my shares in the past six months. I had to give Raul a pretty big payoff to get out of my life and I have been somewhat strapped financially."

"Why didn't you tell me?" Kaitlin asked confused. "We would have helped. We want to keep the majority interest in the family."

"I know, Kaitlin, and I'm sorry, but I'm sure it won't hurt us. You and Elizabeth have most of the shares," she said looking distressed.

"Who did you sell the shares to?" Kaitlin continued.

"Some company I have never heard of that approached me when I had quite a few debts to settle related to my divorce," she said meekly.

Kaitlin frowned, "Please give me the details of the sale, Emily, and information on the company you sold to."

"I'll check my sales documents and let you know as soon as possible," she said without hesitation and feeling very guilty for not consulting Kaitlin first.

As Kaitlin walked away despondently she thought to herself, "I'm more certain now that someone is trying to steal my company. I can't let that happen."

CHAPTER 28—PRESENT DAY

The man looked furtively in both directions before entering the offices of the Rivera Cement Company. He was shaky and couldn't be too careful when it came to contacting the owner, Johnnie Rivera. His perfect plan was ripping apart at the seams and it looked like his gravy-train was coming to a painful end, Rivera roughly pushed him inside his office and locked the door, "I've told you to never come here to my office. You must be crazy!" he shouted angrily.

The man cringed. He had always been afraid of Johnnie. He was well aware of his connection to the mob. "I had to see you right away," he explained. "I found out that the DA's office has gotten hold of some of the invoices for the job in New York. He's also found out that the good materials were never delivered even though the company paid for them."

The mobster stared at him red-faced and ready to explode, "So what am I supposed to do, you fuck-up? You got paid off plenty and now you come crying to me? Were you stupid enough to leave a paper trail and not get rid of the invoices? You were supposed to fix those old records so they showed that the cement was actually delivered and the labor done. Did you bother to do that, you fuck-up! What if we cut a few corners and sent inferior materials! You were supposed to cover that up, asshole. So what if the foundation wasn't as solid as it should have been?"

The man was trembling now, "I'll tell you what is wrong! You didn't tell me that the shoddy stuff your outlet delivered in New York would develop fatal cracks! Now we've got a wrongful injury suit against the company, thanks to part of the building collapsing with this guy out on the scaffolding 32 stories high. Now he is paralyzed for life and the company is under investigation."

Rivera laughed, "You didn't worry much about that when you collected your pay-off! Some of the boys saw you driving your new Mercedes the other day, and we hear you bought a huge estate in the Caribbean. I hope you were smart enough to buy under a fake company shell so these expenditures won't come back to haunt you."

"I have an account in the Cayman Islands where I bought my villa. I have set up a dummy company front that can't be traced to me. I'm not as stupid as you think. But I don't like this investigation and thought you should be aware of it. You probably will have to give a deposition. After all you own the cement company!" he said testily.

Rivera grabbed him by the neck and shook him until he was blue in the face, "Just keep your damn mouth shut or the cops will be finding your body floating in Biscayne Bay. As far as I know those materials were delivered and I've got plenty of loyal friends who will back me up in New York City. And if you know what's good for you, never, I said never come near my office again!"

With that he opened the door and motioned to his big burly bodyguard, "Lenny, throw this asshole out before I do it myself."

The terrified man landed on his face on the pavement in front of the building and slowly rose to his feet and limped over to the next block where he had parked his brand new Mercedes. His pleasure at owning such a vehicle was gone and he wished to hell he had never gotten mixed up in this crazy scheme.

As he nursed his wounds, Kaitlin was answering a phone call from Emily. She asked, "Emily, did you check who you sold your stocks to? I have been talking to John about it and we are both very curious."

"Yes, I went to my safety deposit box and found the paperwork. The company is called G.S. Chalmers, Inc. and there is no address. Only a post office box here in Miami. They didn't want to pay broker's fees, so I dealt directly with one of the officers."

Kaitlin paused, "That seems strange. What was the name of the person that finalized the deal and do you have an address or phone number for him?"

Emily seemed flustered, "I know how this sounds and I'm so embarrassed. I really needed the money at the time and I probably should have talked to you first."

Kaitlin replied impatiently, "What was his name Emily?"

"That's the funny thing, I can't read his signature. I think it was some common name like Smith or Adams. I really can't remember. He seemed very nice so I didn't really pay that much attention. He had a business card with the G.S. Chalmers logo on it, but I can't find the card. I have looked everywhere. Do you think there was something wrong with the company?" she asked meekly.

"Frankly, I won't know until our investigator looks into this. I am fearful that someone is trying to buy up our stocks for a takeover. Please let me know if these people contact you again about selling your shares," Kaitlin said in a worried tone.

"I am so sorry, Kaitlin. You must know that if I had suspected anything like that I would have never sold my shares, regardless of how broke I was."

Kaitlin sighed, "I know that Emily. But you must remember there are a lot of evil persons out there in the corporate world that are just waiting until a company is in a weakened position to make a hostile takeover. We are vulnerable now with the personal injury suit and now the charge that we may have used inferior materials and that someone in our company was taking a payoff. I could never live with myself if I felt that we were compromised and that we were responsible for the terrible injury Peter McInerny suffered."

After she hung up, Kaitlin moaned and as if her father were there in the room with her and said, "Oh, dad, I have let you down. I have ruined everything you and Grandpa Cal and Great Grandfather, Aidin, built up through the years. Why did you leave me with this terrible responsibility?" She didn't notice that John had come into the room. He took her in his arms and gently rocked her.

"Darling, it will all work out. You have done a fantastic job. You are not responsible for any of these problems. No one has been more concerned with safety and workers' rights than you have been. The company has an outstanding safety record and in all the hotels we have built there has never been any kind of negligence charge. We have some clues now and a focus for our hunt for the bastard that is trying to ruin us. We'll find him and then let the D.A. handle the punishment. I love you, Kaitlin," he whispered.

"We have to find him, John. We owe it to Aidin and all the Donegons that had a part in the creation of our hotel masterpiece." She had a faraway look on her face as she relived Aidin's journal and the history of how it all began.

CHAPTER 29—
SEPTEMBER 2002

"I'd like to find one more ideal location in Scotland," Kaitlin said as they headed for the south end of the Isle of Skye. "Although we didn't find Skye the right place even though I loved it, I'd like to visit Armadale Castle before we get on the ferry for the mainland. I hear that their gardens are spectacular and even though the castle is in ruins, apparently they have a museum on the grounds that offers a well-presented picture of its history."

"It sounds good to me as long as we leave early enough to get a spot on the ferry," John agreed.

"The ferry port is supposed to be near the castle so it should work. The castle is right on the sea and belonged to the clan MacDonald."

"Oh, no, not the MacDonalds again!" John teased Kaitlin. But after spending several hours looking at the fantastic displays in the museum he had to agree that the stop was well worth the time spent.

Their wanderings next took them on the trail of poet Robert Burns and Sir Walter Scott, a best-selling author in his time, to the border villages in southern Scotland. Ayr, Dumfries and Kirkcudbright were charming towns in the southern region of rolling hills, lush forests, crystal-clear lochs and tumbling rivers, towering mountains and an extensive coastline.

Kaitlin was very excited about the southern region and said, "I think this has real potential for our second hotel site. What a contrast in landscapes! Let's spend a few days in Kirkcurbright. I'm particularly attracted to that village."

John replied with enthusiasm, "A few days off the road sounds good to me! It's a working artists' colony and what a location it has on the Dee estuary where it meets Kirkcudbright Bay. There's something about harbor towns that really appeals to me!"

The picturesque town was surrounded by a unique landscape of rolling hills, bluebell woods and fields of bright yellow gorse. As they walked down the streets they noted the medieval layout of the town and that many of the artists made their homes and studios in its elegant 18th century buildings.

They stopped in numerous art galleries and in one called the Harbor Cottage Gallery where they spoke to the very attractive manager of the colorful exhibition. She explained, "This village has attracted artists for the last century but it wasn't until 1957 that our gallery opened. Now there are 15 galleries in our little village and there's now talk of a gallery of national significance here."

Kaitlin and John exchanged glances which meant they recognized the future for attracting tourists to the region. She asked, "Do you have any major art festivals or other events here in Kirkcudbright?"

The woman beamed proudly, "Oh, yes, there are special art exhibits all year long but in the summer there is the spectacular exhibition 'The Glasgow Girls' which attracts crowds from all over Scotland and beyond. We also have a major jazz festival with top artists every year including some of the finest bands in the world. It kicks off with a parade and they perform in various venues around town, including a Jazz Church Service at the Parish Church on Sunday." She continued in an excited voice, "I am a jazz fan, and you can also book a table in local restaurants during Jazz Week and enjoy smaller groups and solo performers in a more intimate setting while you enjoy a fine meal!"

Kaitlin asked, "We are touring Scotland looking for good sites for boutique hotels. We represent a major hotel chain, but are branching out into the smaller, boutique concept. Do you know of any interesting property available in the area?"

She thought for a moment and then replied, "I guess you must be looking for something unique and I might have a suggestion. There is a castle on a small island in the River Dee. You have to be ferried over as there are no bridges to the island. I always thought that would be a most romantic place for a hotel."

John asked, "Is it occupied now, and do you know if the owners are interested in a sale?"

"I think it's possible as the owners inherited the castle and rarely visit it from what I hear. There is a caretaker that takes people over in a small boat. Check with the realtor on High Street and perhaps they will take you out to see it," she replied turning to new clients who had entered the gallery.

After a short discussion with the realtor they were driven to the site. Kaitlin immediately fell in love with the setting, the lone castle standing on the tiny island was surrounded by water.

The realtor said, "The owners are ready to sell. They live in Spain and have no interest in moving here at this time. This area has quite a history. In the year 1200 Kirkcudbright was an important center for the Lords of Galloway. They used the excellent natural harbor provided by the River Dee for their fleets of warships."

"How far is this from Edinburgh?" John inquired.

"That's the best part! If you are interested in attracting guests to your hotel there is a scenic road between the two points that gets you away from most of the tourist traps and you see Scotland at its finest! The scenic road is called the Roman Road and many Iron Age hill forts can be seen along the route. The drive is only a little over 100 miles from Edinburgh and ideal for people coming in at the airport."

Kaitlin said as they toured the small island and visited the castle, "Our lawyer will be in touch with you if we are interested." Although she tried not to show her enthusiasm, the happy realtor could sense that she was in love with the place.

That night after talking to their lawyer Kaitlin said, "John, I think we've accomplished what we've set out to do. I love both of the sites and can't wait to talk to the architects if both deals go through."

John hugged her, "It's time to go home, my Bonnie Lass. It's been a great vacation and to be honest, I will be glad to be driving again in Miami in spite of the traffic!"

CHAPTER 30—2003

Autumn called Kaitlin to tell her the good news. "I just heard from Bill and he will be coming home from Afghanistan next week! I am so excited I can hardly stand it! I don't know what shape he will be in but just to have him back home will be wonderful!"

The couple had had little time to enjoy married life with Bill's two deployments to Afghanistan. The internet had helped them maintain contact and being a newspaper reporter Autumn was privy to all the latest news and worries.

Kaitlin smiled, "That's wonderful, Autumn! I am so happy for you. Bill is a real hero and we all are so proud of him!"

Autumn replied, "He loves our country and he loves what he does to defend our country. 9/11 changed his thinking after the terrorists attack. He wants to make a difference."

"Let us know when we can throw a party for him, Autumn. All the family and his friends will want to see him."

Autumn couldn't forget the day she received a call from an official from the Department of the Army informing her that her husband had been injured but was breathing and intact. The call lasted for only a minute but the fear raged within her. She sat numb for hours not taking any calls from family or friends for fear she would miss Bill's call when it flashed on the caller ID. In the back of her mind she remembered her father and how he had died in a prison camp during the war. Even though she was a baby at the time the scars remained as she remembered the years when her mother, Emily, was depressed and just not able to be a real mother to her because of her grief.

These kinds of situations are an extreme challenge to the resiliency of a family because outcomes are not known, and Autumn felt like she was left hanging. When she finally heard Bill's voice he tried to reassure her that he was o.k. but she had seen the pictures a friend in the Pentagon had sent when he was awarded the Purple Heart in the hospital ceremony. She thought that he looked terrible and his face was so pale.

She was standing there waiting when he finally stepped off the plane in Miami. He was limping and walked with a cane. As they hugged and kissed one another Autumn felt his trembling even though he had a brave smile on his face.

It wasn't until he was actually home that she learned the full story. He had sprinted about 300 yards under fire to gain higher ground in a cemetery. An explosive had detonated near him creating a blast so powerful it blew off the roof of a nearby tomb.

Shrapnel had hit Bill's left side, making a golf ball size hole in his hip.

"I really can't discuss the reason for the mission," he told Autumn who was crying as she could almost feel his pain.

But he didn't really need to tell her all the details as she saw them firsthand as she cleaned, packed and bandaged the holes in his hip. The stark conditions of living on a combat outpost outside of Kabul were evident in the filthiness of his gear.

The party Kaitlin planned was beautiful but Bill constantly searched the room for enemies. When Autumn saw him flush and sweat beaded on his forehead she sneaked him out on the terrace for a breath of fresh air. Things were so different now from the engagement party where there had been so much happiness and hope. Even with the warmth and love of his family all around him, Bill kept his back to the wall and his nervousness was evident. Autumn then decided that big family gatherings would have to wait until the war was over.

Autumn stood watching Bill's 6-foot frame lying on the couch and was so thankful that he was home and alive. All the family and his friends had such good intentions in planning the party to celebrate his life, but she realized that the hours-long affair had taken a physical and emotional toll on Bill. Two deployments in Afghanistan in the war zones had taken their toll and had left invisible scars she had not only seen but bathed.

The reality of almost losing her husband was mindboggling and she was so thankful he was home and alive with no limbs missing. Yet war had robbed her in other ways. She felt like she was walking on eggshells and was afraid to drive with him in traffic in case it might rattle him. She was unable to shake the anxiety because she knew Bill would return to war.

After Bill had been home for several weeks he began checking in with his squad in the days leading to his departure for his next deployment. He was anxious about the men in his command. Who was looking out for their safety?

He explained to Autumn, "Family now includes my team, my squad, my platoon. When you've gone through life and death situations with these guys and had to rely on one another for your life, you form a lifelong bond."

Autumn put her arms around her husband, "I can understand that, Bill. I love you so much and I wish you could stay here with me out of harm's way."

Bill kissed her fervently, "We will have a lifetime together when I come home for good." They retired to the bedroom where they made love passionately as if it was their last time.

When Bill was judged well enough for another deployment, this time it was to Iraq or Operation Iraqi Freedom as it was called. President Bush had diverted attention from Afghanistan where it was suspected that Al Qaeda terrorists were hiding, to a new front because he announced to the nation that Iraq was harboring weapons of mass destruction that were a threat to the United States. This turned out to be untrue in the long run as no weapons were discovered. Violence against coalition forces and among various sectarian groups soon led to the Iraqi insurgency, which caused strife between the Sunni and Shia groups and bred a new faction of Al Qaeda in Iraq.

Bill was in the midst of the fighting which was unlike anything known before, many times involving house to house skirmishes and danger of being taken out by an IED explosive device at every turn.

Autumn lived with the anxiety of waiting for another phone call notifying her that Bill had been wounded or worse. She had been feeling emotionally vulnerable and nauseated for several weeks.

There was only one note of cheer and hope when her doctor smiled and told her, "You're going to have a baby, Autumn. In about 7 months."

She called her best friend brimming with excitement, "Kaitlin, guess what? Bill and I are going to have a baby!"

CHAPTER 31—PRESENT DAY

Carlos had no trouble getting a new identity. His friends in the Cuban Mafia had been waiting many years to greet him and couldn't do enough to oblige. He had been a little worried about his new passport with the security regulations since 9/11 at the airport but he breezed through with no trouble at all.

He settled himself in a comfortable seat in first class and before the plane took off the sexy flight attendant was asking if he wanted champagne.

"Here you are, Mr. Gersbach," she smiled as she handed him the bubbly. "Let me know if I can do anything else for you."

Carlos was thinking to himself, "How about a fuck in that tiny can when we are 35,000 feet up?" He couldn't help laughing. He was used to small places.

When the plane landed in Geneva, Switzerland Carlos took a taxi immediately to the Swiss bank where he had his account listed under a shell company. He was pleased to see that the interest and investments after thirty years had accumulated until his balance reached the 60 million dollar level. After taking out what he needed for his plastic surgery, he still had enough to last a lifetime.

He had changed his name and now he needed to change his appearance so Elizabeth wouldn't recognize him. He realized that all people read faces to a certain degree. They make judgments about personalities just by the way a person's face looks. He was tired of looking like the bad guy. He realized that changing his appearance so radically could change the course of his life and bring Elizabeth back to his arms. She adored him once and he believed he could charm her a second time with his new face. He sadistically dreamed of how many ways he could punish her for her defection when they were young and at one time in love.

He had investigated plastic surgery clinics in Switzerland and had settled on one in the city of Montreux on the Swiss Riviera with fantastic views of Lake Geneva and the mountains. The clinic advertised their anti-aging revitalization, a magnificent spa and an advanced dentistry center in addition to all types of reconstructive surgery.

As his eyes swept over the luxurious surroundings he couldn't help but smile when he remembered his accommodations at the federal prison in south Miami-Dade County. He planned to make his reappearance as Bruno Gersbach, Swiss banker. He would bear no resemblance to his former self.

He entered the consultation room and after a few moments the surgeon entered and shook his hand. Carlos noticed he was very young looking and handsome for his age which was supposed to be 60. "Probably a product of his own work," Carlos thought.

"What did you have in mind, Mr. Gersbach? I am curious. You have a Swiss name but your facial characteristics tell me you are Hispanic," Dr. Kaser remarked.

"That's why I am here," he said sarcastically wanting to add 'asshole'. He added, "Money is not a factor as long as you do what I say."

The doctor frowned, "Yes, I see. But I must warn you it is important that you know that aesthetic surgery that alters your face can have consequences both positive and negative. Are you trying to save a marriage or career, Mr. Gersbach?"

Carlos thought, "What the fuck, I'm trying to change 30 years in the can!" However he didn't say that out loud. "No, doctor, I have Swiss heritage and I turned out looking like a damn Hispanic. So can you change me or not? There are other clinics here in Montreux that I am considering."

"Of course, we can do it here, but your motivation is important. We find that if your motivation is external, in other words if not to save a marriage or a career, it would be to please others. This rarely works. However, if your motivation is internal and you have negative feelings about personal deficiencies and a corresponding desire to effect change it can be highly successful," he explained in a patronizing tone.

Carlos had heard enough, "Cut the bullshit, Doc. Can you make me look like a Swiss dude or not?"

The doctor sighed, "I see you have a number of wrinkles and very dry skin. You could profit from our anti-aging revitalization process. We also offer hair transplant surgery using our exclusive Microscopic Follicular Hair transportation which involves the use of high powered microscopes to divide the donor strip into natural hair growth units."

"Speak English, Doc! I want blond hair and blue eyes," he shouted. "Can you do it or not?"

The doctor was sure that he wasn't going to like this patient very much, "We can give you blue contacts that are so real that it looks like your natural eye color. I also notice you need extensive dental work. We will need to give you almost a complete set of implants to correct it. Also, you are developing some loose skin under your chin and you have circles under your eyes. I will have to do a face lift including a chin implant and eye surgery to eliminate the bags and circles under your eyes." He paused as his new patient looked stunned, "This will cost a great deal of money for this amount of work. I know you said money was no objective, but I hope you realize the cost as none of this is covered by health insurance."

Carlos thought to himself, "Hey, all my health expenses were covered when I was in prison. Maybe it was a better deal than I thought."

"How much are we talking about?" he asked.

"Close to a million dollars for this big a job," the doctor replied.

Carlos thought for a moment and then said, "When can you get started and how long will it take?"

"You can check in today if it is convenient. We have beautiful suites for our patients overlooking the lake. You will start with x-rays today and then you may want to spend the day in our Spa and have a nice massage and swim before your treatments start. We serve three gourmet meals a day as part of the program. We carefully monitor your diet so that you don't gain weight. In fact, I am putting you on a low-calorie diet for the first month as you really need to lose about 10 pounds if you really want to change your appearance."

"Between surgeries you will have an exercise program in our fitness center although you seem to be quite physically fit, it still will help in your final appearance. You are free to accept visitors if you would like although some of our patients want privacy. We are very discreet and answer no questions as far as who are patients are and what treatment they are receiving. That's why our clinic is so highly regarded," he stated proudly.

Carlos smiled to himself, "Yes, privacy would be nice. Just what the doctor ordered!"

CHAPTER 32—2003

Autumn met Kaitlin for lunch on Miami Beach to share the good news. She was still able to hold down her investigative reporter job at the *Miami Herald* in spite of her pregnancy. They found an outdoor café on South Beach in the art deco section. As usual both women observed the continuing renovation of the original hotels, now gleaming in glass and fresh pastel colors.

Kaitlin hugged her cousin and looked at her with admiration, "You're positively glowing, Autumn. Can I guess what you have to tell me?" she smiled.

Autumn laughed, "I guess you noticed my bulge and yes, Bill and I are expecting a baby and we are both so happy and excited. And guess what, I know its sex? It's going to be a boy! I'd love a girl also, but Bill seems ecstatic about having a son!"

"That is so wonderful, Autumn! Will Bill get home for the delivery?" Kaitlin asked.

"We're hoping by then he will be home. Things are really rough in Iraq. It is like no other war. It's guerrilla warfare and Bill feels like it is more a civil war between the Sunni's and the Shia factions and the U.S. soldiers are caught between."

Kaitlin frowned, "I thought the whole purpose of these wars was to find the terrorists responsible for 9/11! None of them were from Iraq so why did we leave Afghanistan where they are supposed to be hiding?"

"You're right, Kaitlin. And I suppose you read the op-ed in the New York Times written by Ambassador Joe Wilson who was sent to investigate the administration's claim that Iraq was trying to obtain yellowcake uranium from Niger and found it to be untrue, yet the Bush administration continued to claim that it justified our military action in Iraq."

"And no weapons of mass destruction either! Now I read that Wilson's wife, Valerie Plame was outed as a CIA agent thanks to a columnist spilling the beans. Do you think it was retribution for her husband's report?"

"I'm sure of it, Kaitlin, and I still think it was a huge mistake to leave Afghanistan and transfer the majority of our troops to Iraq. It was a lousy move to remove the cover of a very effective CIA operative. Now, she'll be out of job!"

As they ordered salads the topic switched back to the new baby. "I want to give a baby shower for you, Autumn. After all, you never gave us time to give you a wedding shower."

"That will be wonderful! I'm sure my mother will want to be involved."

"By the way, Autumn, how is Emily getting along since the divorce? She seems much happier and content since she pushed Raul out of her life," Kaitlin remarked.

"She's so much better, Kaitlin. I was really worried about her for awhile but now she is so excited about the baby that she doesn't have time to worry about the divorce even though it is pretty nasty. Raul is demanding alimony and also half of her fortune. He doesn't work so supposedly she has to support him! Disgusting, isn't it!"

"Makes you think twice about marriage. I'm glad I'm still single even though John would like to get married. I'm scared off when I hear what some of these scoundrels are getting away with!"

"Come on, Kaitlin! Is that why you are keeping John on the string? He has wanted to marry you for years," Autumn teased Kaitlin. "Remember, you caught my bouquet!"

"No, I don't doubt John in the least. He is a perfect partner and I intend to keep the relationship that way. We had a wonderful time choosing locations for the European boutique hotels and they are all under construction as we speak. We have two wonderful properties in

France and another two in Scotland. The hotel business was flat for a long time after 9/11, but people are now travelling again and looking for unique places to visit."

"You've done a fantastic job developing your great-grandfather, Aidin's original concept for hotel building. I sometimes wonder if he is looking down on you and is amazed at your accomplishments."

Kaitlin laughed, "I sometimes think all three of them are looking down on me and cheering me on, my father Andy, my grandfather Calvin and finally my great-grandfather Aidin. I wonder what they would think of the boutique hotel development? The European boutiques are going to be so unique and different from our original Grand Hotels. I just hope that my forbearers don't think I am investing foolishly like Bob Welch and Dave Wells. Sometimes I would like to throttle them!"

"Make them walk the straight and narrow, Kaitlin. You've got what it takes to run a big corporation so never look back with regrets."

"Thanks, Autumn, and again congratulations! You and Bill will make wonderful parents," Kaitlin said as she picked up the check and hugged her cousin. The girls called for their cars as it was time to get back to their respective jobs.

CHAPTER 33—PRESENT DAY

John Martinez was in New York evaluating the operation of the boutique hotel. It hadn't caught on quite as fast as the hotels in Chicago, San Francisco and Europe. Kaitlin had sent him there to find out why. She wondered if the bad publicity surrounding the renovation of the Grand New York had rubbed off on the business of the smaller boutique hotel. Since the news of the investigation, the serious injury and the implication of safety concerns had broken in the newspapers, they had been receiving droves of cancellations in contrast to its popularity since the day it opened.

To top this worry off, Bryon Harrell, the company lawyer had dropped another bomb on her when he dropped by that afternoon.

"Kaitlin," he said in a nervous tone of voice, "I thought I'd better deliver this news personally." He paced the floor as he continued, "I heard from the DA's office today that the testing on the concrete used in the building where the collapse occurred is inferior material. They sent the samples to an independent lab and the samples did not pass any of the nine separate stability tests."

She gasped, "That can't be true, Bryon! We have always demanded the highest quality of cement in all our construction even though the cost was higher. And our records have shown that we paid for it! How can this be?"

"Obviously someone ordered the inferior grade and substituted it for the high quality grade that we paid for. Apparently the lead investigator has submitted a letter to the commission today that makes it clear that if the cement had done its job there would have not been an accident. To make it even worse they have sent a gallon of the actual cement mixture used to be held as evidence in a criminal and civil investigation."

Kaitlin was appalled, "Can't we prove that we were not responsible, that we had ordered and paid for the high quality cement?"

Bryon frowned, "You see, Kaitlin, it most probably was an inside job. Naturally, I know you would never scrimp or cut corners. I have worked with you for years and you are as honest and above-board as anyone I have ever worked with. However, it is very possible that someone else who is connected or working for the corporation is guilty of planning this and probably becoming very rich in the process."

"We've got to find that person, Bryon, before the company is destroyed. I am heartbroken that someone in my employ might have caused that poor man to fall and to be paralyzed for life, and all for greed. How in the world will we find that person or do we leave it to the investigators?"

Bryon paused for a moment and then lit up a cigarette, something she had never seen him do before, "Kaitlin, have you noticed anyone in your employ suddenly buying new houses, boats, cars, and the like?"

Kaitlin glanced down at her huge diamond engagement ring which surely was at least 2 carets and was surrounded by smaller diamonds. The only one she knew that had talked about buying a house was John. He had looked at a huge house overlooking the bay on Old Cutler Road and said that after years of living in her hotel apartment it was time she had a real house of her own. She had argued that being in the same building that housed the executive offices was very convenient. After all, it all started with that first hotel in Coconut Grove built by her great-grandfather Aidin.

She flushed as her mind quickly discounted her most loyal friend and fiancé as a possible suspect, "Well, just about all the board members drive luxury cars and I think that Edward Haynes mentioned buying a yacht recently and said that he and his wife would be sailing in the Virgin Islands for a week or two."

"It's hard to imagine that Haynes would be our culprit. He's loaded with money of his own without having to steal from the company! But keep your ears open in personal conversations or note if someone has recently struck it rich and report back to me. We can then send out investigators out to see what they can dig up. We can only hope that the contractor was cutting corners and had no connection with the good intentions of our company to continue the high quality construction we are noted for," he said as he rose to leave the office. He added, "After all, we did pay for the higher grade cement even though it was never delivered." He couldn't help being dazzled by Kaitlin's beauty even in her despair. He held her hands for a long moment before he departed.

Kaitlin had a hard time falling asleep after her conversation with the lawyer. Her mind reeled as she tried to figure out who might have a motive to ruin the company. As she tossed and turned the telephone rang in the wee hours.

Startled she grabbed the receiver and demanded, "Who is this? Why are you calling? Tell me if you just dialed the wrong number?" There was silence at the end of the line but she could tell that no one had hung up. "Whoever you are, stop calling!" she shouted into the phone. After she hung up she was shaking.

After about an hour the phone rang again. This time she heard a muffled voice at the other end of the line. "It's time for you to retire or you will be sorry. What's happened so far is only the beginning. If you don't retire, we will retire you and it won't be pleasant."

Kaitlin screamed, "Who are you, you coward? Can't you identify yourself or are you just going to make threats incognito?"

"You don't want to find out who I am. Believe me. That would be your worst mistake," the muffled voice answered as Kaitlin slammed down the receiver.

She took the phone off the hook and poured herself a glass of wine to settle her nerves. She doubted if she could get back to sleep. She thought to herself, "Why does this always happen when John is out of town?" As she twisted her engagement ring she had a startling thought, "It just couldn't be John. He would never betray me. He loves me and I trust him."

So why did the nagging thought remain? It was true, John was never home when she received the threatening calls.

CHAPTER 34—2003

It was now November and Autumn's baby was expected any moment. As Bill was unable to get a leave to come home and be with her the whole family was alerted. Emily was practically living on Autumn's doorstep and couldn't wait to have her first grandbaby.

The ladies of the family hosted a baby shower at Elizabeth's home and everyone was excited.

Autumn had reached gigantic proportions and they knew the shower had come just in time. She had prepared a delightful nursery in wait for her first child, and had proudly painted and wallpapered the walls, added colorful pictures and numerous baby toys were purchased.

After opening the brightly colored packages, the grand finale was rolled out. It was a stroller and Autumn was thrilled. "This is the final touch," she said thanking them. "Little Bill will also be the best dressed baby in the nation thanks to all of you!"

As the afternoon rolled on the topic turned to Miami's latest news. Autumn had left on maternity leave two weeks before, but she still had an inside line on everything the newspaper reported that was going on in Miami.

Emily asked, "What is this big protest going on with the free trade meeting here in Miami? I read that the police had to use tear gas to disperse protesters."

"Yes, that's true," Autumn explained. "The meeting is between the Americas and is being held at the InterContinental downtown. Sporadic scuffles broke out as protesters discussed the future of trade in a region of almost 800 million."

Kaitlin said thoughtfully, "When I read my great-grandfather's history of early Miami, I remember him quoting Miami pioneer Julia Tuttle who claimed that in the future Miami would be the hub for all Latin American trade. The fact that Miami is the site for this important trade meeting certainly proves her theory. What are they protesting?"

Autumn replied, "That is fascinating when you imagine that this would be around 1896 when Julia Tuttle made that prediction. What an amazing woman! And wasn't she the one that talked Henry Flagler into bringing his railroad down to Miami?"

"Yes, she sent him an orange blossom after the citrus crop was lost up in north Florida due to freezing weather one winter, to show him that southern Florida was the place to invest. Miami was just a straggly village at that time if you can believe it as you face the traffic on the roads today," Kaitlin added.

"To get back to your question, the protesters that are opposed to the movement range from labor unionists to environmentalists. One woman came all the way from San Francisco and was dressed as a tomato to support organic food and small farmers. Large papier mache puppets derided the International Monetary Fund and privatization and called it similar to war."

Elizabeth said, "What's the progress of this Americas-wide free trade pact?"

Autumn explained, "The United States and Brazil are chairing the event and seemed to have overcome some of their disagreements on how comprehensive the pact should be. I've heard that a draft declaration has been crafted in the past three days by regional deputy trade ministers that would require all countries in the Americas to agree on a common set of commitments."

"Leave it to Miami to be right in the center of things! But don't remind me of the presidential elections where Floridians held the country hostage on the vote issue," Emily sighed. "Al Gore won the popular vote and should have won the election in my opinion if it weren't for all the shenanigans about butterfly ballots!"

The group then got on to pleasanter topics and all offered their help to Autumn when the baby got ready to arrive. No one had mentioned the fact that Bill would still be in Iraq when his first child was born. It was a topic that brought too many frustrations and worry to Autumn and they loved her and wanted the birth to be a happy event.

Two days later Autumn called her mother in the wee hours of the night, "Mom, I think Baby Bill is about to arrive." Emily was so excited that she sped to Autumn's house and soon deposited her at Mercy Hospital. She paced the floor like an expectant father and about 6 a.m. the doctor called her and smiled, "You have a beautiful, healthy grandson and your daughter is doing just fine." Emily couldn't remember ever being as happy as she was as she peeked into the nursery and the nurse pointed out her new grandson.

It was then that she thought of her husband, Tom Pierce, and said to him as if he were standing there next to her at the hospital nursery, "Oh, Tom, our first grandson. How you would have loved this moment! I feel like you are here with us, my darling." There were tears of joy in her eyes but sadness at the realization that neither little Bill's father or grandfather were there to greet him.

CHAPTER 35—2004

It was January of 2004 and Bill was coming home on leave and his first chance to meet his infant son. Things were not going well in Iraq. Kaitlin had dropped by to see her tiny cousin and to help Autumn by babysitting while she went out to shop for Bill's arrival. She planned to have all his favorite foods on hand and was buying a few new things to decorate the house in anticipation of his arrival.

Autumn discussed the latest news with Kaitlin, "Do you realize that Condolezza Rice, President Bush's 'right hand' and a strong advocate of the invasion of Iraq has now admitted that the intelligence that they had weapons of mass destruction was wrong. They now say that Saddam Hussein had no chemical weapons either!"

Kaitlin grimaced, "Then why in the heck are Bill and all those other brave troops fighting over there? I thought all the perpetrators of 9/11 came from other countries."

"From the tone of Bill's emails lately I get the impression that he is also asking why. So many of his buddies have lost their lives to roadside bombs. Apparently, suicide bombers are everywhere, not caring if they blow themselves up as long as they can take a lot of Americans with them."

"We should have never left Afghanistan where the real terrorists were hiding out and invaded another country!" Kaitlin exclaimed angrily. "Thank goodness Bill is coming home and has not been wounded this time around like his injuries in Afghanistan!"

Autumn reached for little Billy as she had warmed his bottle and continued, "I'll be a nervous wreck until he really steps through the doorway safe and sound. I remember when your mother worked to settle Cuban refugees when they arrived in Miami. What does she think of the embargo and the restrictions on travel to Cuba?" "I just found out recently that the Treasury Department entrusted with blocking the financial resources of terrorists has assigned five times as many agents to investigate Cuban embargo violations as it has to track down Osama bin Laden and Saddam Hussein's money!"

"As you might expect, my mother is against the embargo for she feels that a lot of innocent people who are still living in Cuba will suffer for it," Kaitlin said. "Did you know that she nearly married a Cuban refugee when she was a young girl?"

"Yes, I remember stories about how he got caught up in the drug trade and is now serving time in a federal prison. Knowing your mother's hatred of the drug scene here in Miami, he must have been quite a disappointment to her."

Autumn shook her head and frowned, "I'm not at all surprised that she broke up with him. When does he get out of prison?"

"I think he still has many years to serve. Mother never mentions him. She refers to him as her 'personal nightmare'."

A week later Autumn met Bill at Miami International Airport. She was carrying little Billy who was soundly sleeping. She hardly recognized Bill as he came through the Gate. He had lost a lot of weight and was very pale, but as his eyes lit on Autumn and Billy a wide smile crossed his face. As he wrapped his arms around them for the first time in months he felt secure and safe. His arrival was bittersweet as both Autumn and Bill realized that he would be deployed again to Iraq after their short time together.

CHAPTER 36—PRESENT DAY

Carlos stepped out on his balcony overlooking the lake and mountains in Switzerland. He took a deep breath of the cool, crisp air and thought how wonderful it was to be free. He had already had the dental implants completed and now when he smiled he saw sparkling, straight white teeth. The hair transplants were in process and he was scheduled for the facial surgery next week. When that was healed he would look like a new man.

As he enjoyed daily messages and swam laps in the pool, he had lost that extra weight and was slim and trim. On top of that he was beginning to get used to the new nutritious diet and it made him feel great and full of energy.

So far no one except Raul knew where he was staying. He opened the package he had received from Raul the preceding day and to his surprise saw a pile of newspaper and magazine clippings. They were all relative to the lawsuit pending against the Grand Hotels and Kaitlin Donegon regarding an accident involving a construction worker. One tabloid had a spread on the cover with the headline, 'Grand Hotel Cuts Corners on New York Hotel Renovation'. As Carlos read further he noted that poor quality cement was believed behind the tragic injury.

He telephoned his brother, "I got your newspaper clips. Who did the cement job?"

Raul answered, "Guess who? Rivera Cement Company."

"I might have known Rivera would have his hand in the till. He has been taking payoffs for years but has never gotten caught at it. As you know a lot of construction in New York is mob-connected and I'm not surprised that Rivera got into the act. But he must have had some help. He's too savvy to be caught red-handed."

"Yea, that's what I think. The papers suggested that some payoffs were going to someone in the Grand Hotel Company. In other words, an inside job. I'm trying to figure out who might have mob connections in that straight-laced bunch of assholes at the Grand Hotel Board of Directors," Raul said scratching his head. "I know Emily has been hurting for money, but she doesn't have the smarts to carry something like this out. The paper said that it may become a criminal case and the New York DA is investigating."

Carlos paused, "What about that Cuban lover of Kaitlin's? Do you think he could be involved? Do you think he has connections with the Cuban Mafia? You still keep in touch with the mob don't you?"

"Yea, but I'm not in very good standing as I haven't paid off all my debt. I don't trust that Martinez. I'll nose around a little bit and see what I can find out from the boys. I remember Emily telling me that a couple of men on the Board were always giving Kaitlin a hard time and wanted the CEO post for themselves. In fact, I think she said that they wanted Kaitlin to resign in the worst way."

"This is all most interesting, Bro. Find out what you can." After thinking for a moment a thought occurred to him, "I bet Kaitlin and Elizabeth are hurting for capital if they are being sued. They might consider a loan from a wealthy Swiss banker."

"Whose name is Carlos," Raul laughed.

"Watch it, Raul! I am now Bruno and be careful to never let my old name slip out even when you are drunk!"

After the phone call ended Carlos sat quietly starring at the water and thinking how Elizabeth's bad luck might fit into his plans. He thought to himself, "Maybe all that bullshit from the doctor was right about a new appearance changing your personality. I'm beginning to doubt that Elizabeth was the one who turned me in. Even though she was through with me I don't think she is capable of doing that. She would never betray me to the cops no matter how much she hated me. It was Andy. I remember how devastated he looked when Liz told him about our engagement and introduced me as her fiancé when we happened to be sitting at the next table at Joe's Stone Crab restaurant."

He looked into the mirror then and liked the transformation. Next week there would be surgery and more changes. He had lost all traces of his Hispanic accent in prison and now was achieving a slight Swiss accent. Soon he would not be recognized by anyone. He smiled as he got ready for his massage. He thought, "This cost a hell of a lot of money, but from the way I feel it is worth every cent of it."

Back in Miami, John had returned from New York and Kaitlin met him at Miami International Airport. Kaitlin was still upset over the anonymous telephone calls she received while he was in New York but she didn't quite know how to approach him on the subject.

"What did you find out about the lack of bookings at our Grand New York Boutique?" she asked as he climbed in the car.

He asked, "What business before a hug and kiss?"

She reached over and gave him a quick peck on the cheek, "The security police are coming my way and will order me to move on, so don't be hurt if you didn't get a hug. Later, my dear," she smiled driving away.

"You were right about the bad publicity causing cancellations. The New York papers have been full of the story and I'm afraid that it has really hurt business in that area. However, luckily, it doesn't seem to be having much effect on reservations elsewhere. While I was there, I worked with an advertising agency on a TV commercial to boost business," he explained.

Kaitlin frowned, "John, I didn't authorize you hiring an ad agency. We need to preserve what working capital we have until this lawsuit is settled one way or the other."

John apologized, "Sorry, honey, I should have checked with you but you asked me to try and promote more business. The boutique hotel was extremely popular until we hit the tabloids."

Kaitlin waited until John had unpacked and had made a drink before she told him about the phone calls. "John," she said, "something happened while you were gone that really upset me in addition to all the company problems I am facing."

He regarded her seriously, "What now, Kaitlin?"

"I received two phone calls in the wee hours while you were gone. The first one the caller didn't say anything and I thought it might be a wrong number. But then a second call came in and it was very threatening. The voice was muffled and the caller threatened that if I didn't resign, they would resign me. I couldn't sleep all night after that call I was so upset."

John held her in his arms, "How terrible for you, Kaitlin! I suggest that you notify the police and have the phone line tapped. They must have a way to trace these calls. "

"I already have, John, and they are going to try and find out who the caller is," she said as she stared at the telephone. "I have changed to an unlisted number and I hope that will help." She paused, "They asked about you, John, as I mentioned that the calls always came when I was alone and you were out of town."

He looked shocked, "Why did you tell them that? Are they regarding me as a suspect, your fiancé?"

"No, of course not, John. But the fact remains I always get the calls when I am here alone and I had to tell them that. After all, it is no secret that you were in New York. All the Board members were aware of it as well as many other people we work with on a regular basis. No one suspects you would do such a thing, but it kind of narrows the suspects to someone who knew you were going out of town."

"I'm tired after the flight, Kaitlin," John said abruptly. "I think I'll turn in early," he said without even giving her a kiss goodnight. Kaitlin stood there wishing she hadn't brought up the subject. The atmosphere in the room had quickly changed for the worse with her honest revelation.

CHAPTER 37—PRESENT DAY

Bryon Harrell asked to see Kaitlin immediately. He had told her secretary that he had some urgent business to discuss with her. Jan Summer's, Kaitlin's attractive and efficient secretary notified her boss immediately and she agreed to cancel her other appointments in order to see him.

"What is it, Bryon?" she asked nervously as she offered him a cup of coffee which Jan Summers promptly brought to him.

"Joe Evans, the primary investigator for the Department of Buildings, has given his findings for the cause of the accident and it looks like the construction company must have known more than they were reporting to us at the time."

"That sounds impossible. What did they say they found?" Kaitlin questioned.

The lawyer cleared his throat, "He's saying that the reinforcing steel that was supposed to support the floor wasn't anchored according to regulations and they didn't give what he called the inferior quality of cement time to set. This caused the cement to crack and some of the workers reported it to their boss and nothing was done about it even though there was that evidence that there was risk of collapse. He called it willful negligence and has given this information to the criminal investigation. He's claiming that this probably caused the wall to crumble and the scaffold to fall carrying McInerny from the 32nd floor to the 10th floor when the ropes stopped his plunge to the bottom and broke his neck. He was lucky he didn't hit the ground or he would have been killed instantly."

Kaitlin saw the irony, "Lucky he didn't die but paralyzed for life, Bryon," she said sarcastically. "What else did the inspector say or don't I want to know?"

"That this would lead to huge fines and a referral to the DA for criminal prosecution," he frowned.

Kaitlin glared at the lawyer, "Bryon, did the investigator believe that Grand Hotels played any role in this? You know that we paid for the higher quality of cement and the labor costs and it was never delivered. Surely, they don't have any possible proof that we were aware of the substitution?"

Bryon shuffled some of his papers nervously, "Yes, they have those invoices in their possession and they are going to depose Johnny Rivera of the Rivera Cement Company that supplied the cement." He paused as he considered his next words, "I have heard rumors that Rivera may have some mob connections, especially in the New York branch of his company. However, I get the feeling that the DA still thinks that someone connected with the Grand Hotels was skimming money off the top."

"Well, while this investigation is dragging all construction has been halted and now the workers are actually suing for their lost wages which is impacting the Grand Hotel's financial status," she said with disgust. "Someone out there is trying to ruin us, Bryon, and doing a pretty good job of it. Even if we are completely exonerated in the end, we may go bankrupt. I can't face losing this company after all the years my family has been involved in the hotel business. I just can't be the one who causes it to fail."

"I've asked the DA to drop the charges against the Grand Hotels but so far he just says the investigation is not over," the lawyer informed her knowing it would cause her pain.

"In the meantime we 'go for broke' while he drags his heels!" she replied angrily. "We don't have the working capital to support all these legal fees and potential fines. And to make it worse, I as CEO, had absolutely no knowledge of this supposed negligence. In all the hotels we have built all over the globe we have never been accused of willful negligence and our record has been spotless as far as construction workers being injured on any of our projects."

He said patiently, "In the end, I feel confident that our records will prove that your company had no connection. Even if one of your employees was involved in the payoff you are not liable for something you had no knowledge of. That person will have to face criminal charges if this caused the horrible accident."

She said bitterly, "Even if you prove we are innocent, our company will be open for any hostile take-over. I guess I need to start looking for an 'angel' to give me a loan if things don't improve."

The lawyer closed his briefcase and wished that he had brought this beautiful, conscientious woman better news. He was well aware of her heartache.

After he left Kaitlin sat at her desk with a stunned expression on her face. She was reliving her great-grandfather's journals and his courage as he faced hardships in the early days of Miami's development.

She reached for the phone but not to call John, but to talk to her mother, Elizabeth, who had lived in the times when her father, Calvin, her grandfather, Aidin and Kaitlin's father, Andy, had developed the early and the later hotels before she inherited the business.

"Mom," she said in a sad voice when Liz answered, "I'm afraid I've failed the family. I'm almost certain I will be the one responsible for us losing the Grand Hotels."

Her mother realized immediately from the tone in her daughter's voice that she was serious and asked, "Kaitlin, what are you talking about? You have been a wonderful, courageous leader and you have caused the corporation to expand with your very successful boutique hotel projects. Aidin would be so proud of you and so would my father and your father who knew he was leaving it in good hands."

"No, they wouldn't, Mom. You see we are going broke, and every day of this investigation and the continuing scandal we are digging ourselves into a deeper grave. I wonder what Aidin would have done?" she sighed close to tears.

Liz paused for a moment and then said with authority, "He'd start looking for a loan to tide things over until it was settled. He would never consider losing his hotels."

"Who is going to take a chance on loaning us money with all this bad publicity and lawsuits pending?" Kaitlin asked her mother in a discouraged tone.

"Let's put our heads together, dear. I'm sure we can come up with some possibilities. Come over right now and we will have a cocktail on the terrace and watch the beautiful Miami sunset and then I'll fix your favorites for dinner," Liz said lovingly.

"Thanks, Mom," Kaitlin said, "you always know the right thing to say when I am down in the dumps."

As she drove over to Coral Gables it suddenly occurred to her that she hadn't shared the latest news with John. She'd let him know she wouldn't be home for dinner.

CHAPTER 38—2005

Autumn was back at the *Miami Herald* working as a star reporter while Emily looked after little Billy, a job she really enjoyed. The beginning of the year had brought about George Bush again being inaugurated for President of the United States. He ran against the Democrat, John Kerry. Although this election had less controversy than his election in 2000 when vote-counting was the issue in Florida and held the whole country in suspense for days, this time doubt was cast at the vote in Ohio. Both John Kerry and Democratic National Committee Chairman Howard Dean had stated that in their opinion that voting in Ohio did not proceed fairly and that had it done so, the Democratic ticket might have won the state and the election. However, there was far less controversy about this election than the Florida vote in 2000 when vote-counting in Miami was an issue.

Autumn had written an article about the excessive expenditures connected with the inauguration festivities. Some congressmen had accused the President of extravagance and using money that should have been sent to the troops in Iraq. Autumn was sensitive to that issue as Bill was still in the midst of fighting the insurgency and often complained about not having the proper equipment to protect the men. She hoped that he would be coming home soon.

In July there was excitement at the newspaper when suspended Miami Commissioner Art Teele fatally shot himself in the head in the lobby of the *Miami Herald* building downtown. That evening she shared the story with her mother when she got home excited and upset over the day's event.

"Sorry I'm so late for dinner, but the most horrible thing happened tonight. I was just getting ready to leave when I heard that someone had shot themselves downstairs. It was Arthur Teele and he was taken to Jackson Memorial Hospital by the City of Miami Fire and Rescue but he died several hours later," she explained.

Emily took little Billy out of the highchair and put him in the playpen before asking, "Oh, my goodness, why would the poor man do such a thing? I know he was in some sort of trouble but that was really extreme!"

"He was up to his neck in legal problems including federal charges for money laundering and mail and wire fraud. He also was accused of helping a minority company with more than $20 million worth of electrical contracts at Miami International Airport when the work ended up actually being done by a much larger, non-minority company," Autumn continued.

Emily nodded her head in disapproval, "But taking his life didn't solve anything did it?"

"No, but it kept him from a possible 20 year prison sentence on the federal charges if he had been convicted. He was convicted in March for threatening a Miami-Dade police officer and he was also awaiting fraud charges in state court," Autumn added.

"It's no wonder he was suspended from the Miami Commission. How did he get such a responsible job in the first place?" Emily frowned as she served Autumn the warmed up pot roast dinner.

"I guess this all happened after he was elected. Regardless, he certainly made sure he would make the front page killing himself in the lobby of Miami's largest newspaper! I remember how Kaitlin told us of another sensational killing in Miami right in Bayfront Park written up in Aidin's journals. In 1933, while shaking hands with President-elect Franklin Roosevelt, Mayor Cermak of Chicago was shot in the lung and seriously wounded. I think the assassin was trying to shoot Roosevelt and hit Mayor Cermak instead."

"Oh, my," Emily sighed, "That was tragic for the mayor, but just think if President Roosevelt had been killed. He led us through the depression and in my opinion was one of our greatest presidents. I'm sure he didn't throw fancy inauguration parties like Mr. Bush."

"Well, the assassin may have really been gunning for Cermak according to rumors at that time. As I recall Mayor Cermak had vowed to clean up Chicago's rampant lawlessness and posed a threat to Al Capone and the Chicago organized crime syndicate. The gunner also hit four or five innocent bystanders in the crowd who had come to hear Roosevelt in Bayfront Park."

Emily asked, "Didn't Al Capone later decide to make Miami his home?"

Autumn laughed, "Yes, one of our most famous residents! I believe he had a gorgeous mansion on Star Island between Miami and Miami Beach. I bet he was very unpopular with his prominent neighbors!"

"Not to change this fascinating subject, but the two boutique hotels in France are opening this month and Liz told me they are fabulous. One is a reconverted castle and the other was once a winery. I saw the brochures and they both should be very popular," Emily said in a very excited voice as she handed Autumn the brochures. "The Scotland properties should be ready early next year."

Autumn smiled, "Leave it to Kaitlin! She's an entrepreneur like her great-grandfather, Aidin. He must be looking down on her and smiling."

There was no new excitement in Miami until hurricane season. In August and October two major hurricanes descended on Miami, Hurricane Katrina and Wilma. Contrary to the Hurricane of 1926 that Aidin wrote about that caught everyone off guard, now the National Hurricane Center was in Miami and there were constant bulletins alerting people to get prepared days before a hurricane made landfall.

Miamians were ultra-anxious ever since Hurricane Andrew in 1992 that was one of the country's worst natural disasters. Miami took a direct hit and the South Dade neighborhoods were virtually wiped out. It took several years to restore the Grand Biscayne in Coconut Grove and the Grand Miami Beach Hotel had major damages. Both hotels were near the water so water surge was also a problem. Kaitlin's father, Andy, was the CEO at that time, but Kaitlin still suffered through some of the renovation problems. Everyone was without electricity for a number of months and phone service was limited also.

If you were in the hotel business an approaching hurricane was always bad news. Should you evacuate guests, provide a community shelter, cancel incoming reservations? And then the aftermath of making repairs, restoring the grounds and finally getting back to business after utilities had been restored and property renovated.

After Hurricane Andrew many small insurance companies failed due to the tremendous damages incurred by the terrible storm. Some of the larger insurance companies then refused to insure houses and buildings in Miami-Dade County as the risk of another Hurricane Andrew hung over the city. People were forced to buy the only insurance available from the State of Florida at very high premiums and high deductibles.

Also, new windstorm building codes went into effect to try to protect the homes and commercial buildings from damage caused by future storms. Andrew proved that most current hurricane shutters were useless and new requirements were instituted.

Warnings for the impending Hurricane Katrina had been sounded and Emily and Liz rushed to the store to load up on supplies along with all the worried residents. The shelves at the grocery stores and hardware stores were soon empty. People remembered Hurricane Andrew and standing in lines a mile long in the heat of August to get a jug of water.

The women filled their grocery cart with canned food, juices and non-perishable packaged food as well as infant food for Baby Bill. They were lucky and got the last two cases of bottled water. Loading up on batteries, candles and flashlights they next added non-electric can openers and duct tape to their basket.

Next they went to the gas station to fill their tanks with fuel. It was almost impossible to get gas after Hurricane Andrew as most stations were completely destroyed.

When they got home they filled their bathtubs with water and let down the level of the water in their swimming pools to half-full level.

They heard the radio broadcast on the way home, "Tropical storm Katrina has now become a hurricane and is expected to make landfall in Miami on August 25 so be prepared. Fasten those storm shutters and keep tuned to this station for future advisories."

Liz sighed, "I guess we're going to get this one. Why don't you and Autumn and the baby come over to my house to sit out the storm? Emily had sold her condominium on Biscayne Bay after the baby was born and Autumn had asked her to stay with her in Coconut Grove. She planned to return to work at that time and felt Emily would be the best person to look after Billy. Emily was very lonely and delighted over the offer.

LIz added, "I'll also ask Kaitlin and John to join us. We can have a hurricane party!"

Both women knew that a hurricane is far from a party but it made them laugh to think about it.

Katrina was kinder to Florida than it was to Louisiana although four people died and over 1,000,000 were left without any electricity. The hurricane crossed the panhandle of Florida and into the Gulf of Mexico where the storm which was now a monster storm then hit New Orleans with all its power and might, literally destroying the city.

Miamians breathed a sigh of relief but just when they thought hurricane season was over, Hurricane Wilma descended on them toward the end of October causing a mandatory evacuation of residents in the Florida Keys. Evacuees were housed at Florida International University in Miami. County offices, schools and courts were closed in anticipation of the storm. This was a wet storm. Several feet of water drenched low-lying areas and flooded homes in the lower Keys. As it approached Miami it pushed water across the Keys from north to south.

"Oh my God," Liz screamed, "the pool is overflowing into the house. I almost emptied it before the storm. I have never seen so much driving rain in a hurricane before."

John managed to push himself out on the patio and in spite of the wind and rain made an opening that let the ponding water out. However, it had entered the house and ruined the carpeting and cabinets and major appliances. Luckily, there was no electricity so the danger of electrocution was avoided. Miamians had learned though to be cautious as many live wires threatened residents who walked out right after the storm. Kaitlin and John found some water damage at the Grand Biscayne where their corporate offices and apartment were located. The guests had been evacuated due to the hotel's proximity to the Bay and the Atlantic Ocean. Only the maintenance staff had remained to respond to emergencies during the storm.

Autumn was relieved to see that her house in Coconut Grove had withstood the storm with very few damages other than several fallen trees. They had a generator which had been purchased after Hurricane Andrew that produced enough electricity to cook and have lights instead of candles and lanterns until the electricity was restored. They considered themselves lucky.

Shortly after telephone service was restored, Autumn received one of those terrible phone calls from the Armed Services informing her that Bill had been exposed to a roadside bomb or an IED as they called it. He was recovering in a hospital in Germany and would be coming home for good when he had made sufficient progress to make the trip.

Autumn had covered enough Iraq stories to know what that meant. According to a recent 2005 report from Walter Reed Army Medical Center, two-thirds of all soldiers wounded in Iraq who don't immediately return to duty have traumatic brain injuries. Furthermore, the grim facts were frightening. She had learned that IED's carry hidden danger. The detonation of a powerful explosive generates a blast of high pressure that spreads out at 1,600 feet per second from the point of explosion and travels hundreds of yards. The lethal blast wave rattles the brain against the skull.

According to what the official told Autumn, Bill had suffered a loss of consciousness after the blast and although he quickly regained consciousness, they feared that it had caused some neurological deficits. He would be transferred from Germany to Walter Reed Hospital when it was feasible for further diagnosis.

Emily tried to comfort her daughter and spoke softly, "Autumn, I know it is hard, but Bill will recover in time and will be coming home to you and Billy. I only wish your father had been able to return to us. You would have loved him, Autumn. He was so bright and so much fun, and he loved you very much in the short time he had with you. Try to visualize Bill as regaining his good health and coming back to the love and support of his family."

Autumn was paralyzed by fear. She didn't know the extent of his brain injury or how it would affect their future, but she knew how much she loved him and was thankful that he was coming home.

CHAPTER 39—PRESENT DAY

Bryon Harrell visited Kaitlin again, but this time it was to inform her that he would be sitting in at the deposition of Johnny Rivera, the owner of the concrete company. Rivera had his own team of lawyers and Bryon would only be an observer to see if anything was said that would harm the status of the Grand Hotel's case.

He noticed again how damn attractive she was even in her distress. He had to restrain himself from holding her in his arms and telling her everything would be alright. He knew that she was an engaged woman but he had noticed some coolness between her and her fiancé lately. "Wishful thinking," he told himself.

When Bryon entered the conference room he immediately noticed a strained atmosphere. Rivera looked surly and glared at his own lawyers as well as Harrell who realized this was probably a key deposition. As far as he was concerned Rivera was guilty as hell, but if his testimony would take down the Grand Hotel it was another matter. He needed to find out.

Rivera under intense questioning angrily admitted that the cement pouring was behind schedule and the steel bar had not been properly seated and the concrete formed cracks and eventually collapsed. As his lawyer pressed on, Rivera sweating profusely admitted, after the invoices were exhibited, that they had billed for work never done. He vehemently denied that he had personal knowledge of any corners being cut or hearing about any concerns from the general contractor. He claimed to have no knowledge of an inferior grade of cement being substituted for the higher quality ordered and paid for.

Harrell felt somewhat pleased knowing that there was no liability for Grand Hotels if the general contractor didn't know about the problem and had never reported it in updates to the company.

After the deposition Rivera pulled Harrell aside and said, "You tell that asshole that I held up my end of the deal!"

Harrell looked confused, "What are you talking about?"

Rivera flushed, "That creep that got me into this mess."

"Really, Rivera, don't talk in mysteries. I have no idea who you are referring to," Bryon answered curious if there was a new twist coming to the case.

"You are full of bullshit, Harrell. Don't you think I know why you are here?"

"I honestly have no idea. My clients, the Grand Hotel, are being sued and accused of negligence. Why shouldn't I have an interest in your deposition?" he asked with some degree of disgust in his voice.

"Maybe you are ignorant of what's really going on. The answer to that lies with your own people," he snarled.

Now the lawyer was really confused. Rivera was broadly hinting that it was an inside job. Now he needed to check again with Kaitlin to see if she remembered anything about the bidding process and why Rivera's firm had been selected in the first place. Certainly there were more reliable persons in the concrete business.

Kaitlin was nervously awaiting Bryon's report. "There's good news and bad news. Apparently Rivera had no knowledge of the faulty concrete setting so that exonerates our position on that score, but the bad news is that he spoke to me privately after the deposition and made it clear that someone from Grand Hotels was involved in the deal and he seemed to think I knew all about it," the lawyer said. "What do you make of this?

Have you ever seen any direct communication between Rivera and any of your employees?"

Kaitlin looked distressed, "I don't think anyone at Grand Hotels was actually dealing with the sub-contractors. We relied on the general contractor for that."

"Well, keep your eyes open. Try mentioning his name at your next Board meeting and both of us will watch for reactions from the members. Sometimes body language or eye contact or the lack of it are good clues. In my profession, I need to get a feel for who is telling the truth or lying."

"I hope and pray it was not one of our people taking payoffs at the expense of safety," she said sadly. "Bryon how do you think this will all end?'

It was like a shock of electricity when he looked into her eyes and took hold of both of her hands and said, "Things may seem black now, but never lose hope. Just remember that anyone who really knows you also knows you would never compromise on safety."

She had also felt a jolt when they had touched and as she looked down at her ring she had to admit that ever since the last frightening batch of anonymous calls had made her suspicious of her lover, things between them just hadn't been the same. They had been avoiding each other at work and at home.

"What next?" she asked herself not really wanting to know the answer.

CHAPTER 40—PRESENT DAY

Kaitlin called an emergency Board Meeting and everyone was in attendance as she addressed the curious group. John Martinez looked a little upset feeling that he had somehow been left out of the loop. Kaitlin's accusing tone when she told him about the anonymous phone calls had left a bad taste in his mouth and now this affront.

She called on Robert Welsh to report on the status of the European boutique hotels before breaking the news about the investigation.

He addressed the group proudly and full of himself as usual, "I am glad to report that both the hotels in France have caused a sensation. Not only are foreign travelers booking far in advance, but it is also most popular with the French people. All the newspapers have carried large feature spreads in their Travel sections. The castle in Amboise has been completely restored and is a gem! The gardens are beautiful and the view is spectacular. The guests who are outdoor types love the forest trails. Guests seem to love the thought of staying in a 750 year old castle, especially with all the two room suites with spa bathrooms. We also offer tours to the amazing chateaux in the area and specialize in serving gourmet meals using all fresh produce from the castle garden."

After accepting praise for his part in overseeing the project he continued, "The other property in Alsace is equally popular. The view of the Rhine River and the valley is sensational. The vineyards have been restored and guests love the novelty of staying in a restored winery. There is an aerial tram that brings people up to the hotel and affords a breathtaking view of all the vineyards in the area. A different wine is selected for each course of the dinner and of course guests can meet for a glass of wine and to socialize in the restored tasting room with its long bar and tables and chairs with the view of the vineyards to gaze at."

After everyone applauded Kaitlin asked him about the Scotland properties. He took the floor again, "Two winners also, in a great part due to the superb locations. The one by Loch Ness not only offers a spectacular view of the lake, but 'Nessie watching' from the terrace is a great sport. After consuming enough wine you'd be amazed at how many guests claim to have spotted the Loch Ness monster in the lake below." The group laughed at his description and he now was in his glory.

"The other boutique hotel is booked for the next year. Who would have dreamed that staying in a castle on a small island only reached by boat would be so popular? A lot of celebrities and wealthy people are booking it for weddings because of the romantic setting. The profits coming in should more than cover the cost of buying the properties and the cost of the renovations," he bragged evidently forgetting how opposed he was to the boutique project when it was first presented.

Kaitlin thanked him for his presentation and asked Dave Wells to pass out updates on the status of the U.S. boutiques. He made a brief statement, "You will see that the hotels in Miami Beach, San Francisco, and Chicago are doing well. However, our boutique in New York City has been going downhill for the past six months. It was very successful when it first opened but now there have been many cancellations and it's going in the hole."

Kaitlin interrupted him at this point and said grimly, "This is one reason I called the emergency meeting today. What we have to share with you will explain why business has dropped in the New York boutique hotel, Dave. I will let Bryon update our position and then I will ask you for information. We need everyone's help and cooperation."

The lawyer stood and addressed the crowd updating them on the current lawsuits and the status of the criminal investigation. The shocked group slowly absorbed the seriousness of the matter.

He paused and then swept the room with his eyes, "In a recent deposition, the owner of the cement company admitted faulty construction caused the accident, but denied that he knew or had been informed that there were any safety issues. After the meeting he pulled me aside and told me that someone inside this company was involved in causing the accident. If this is true, someone has been getting a great deal of money for cutting corners and not delivering the high quality materials that we ordered for the construction. If you know who might be responsible, please report it to me. Any suggestions at this time?"

Kaitlin and Bryon were warily looking around the room. Robert Welsh and David Wells were whispering. John Martinez seemed to be avoiding Kaitlin's stare and was looking down at some papers in front of him. The rest of the board sat in stunned silence.

After the meeting, one of the men rushed into his private office and nervously dialed a number. After a few rings Johnny Rivera answered and when he realized who was calling him he shouted into the receiver, "I told you never to call here, you fuckup. They may have my phone bugged!"

"I don't care! I want to know why you told Bryon Harrell it was an inside job," the man demanded.

Rivera snorted, "Who knows better than you? You're the asshole that got the big payoff! If it makes you feel better I didn't mention your name. That's for them to find out. The DA is really going after this case, my friend, and you are in deep shit! Now don't bother me again, but you might think of taking a little trip before they put you behind bars." With that Johnny Rivera hung up the phone leaving the man pale and frightened.

Kaitlin and Bryon met behind closed doors to plan their future strategy. They both felt that someone on that board knew something. But how to find out.

It was then that John Martinez came through the door without knocking, "We need to talk, Kaitlin," he demanded. He gave Bryon Harrell an icy look.

"Why didn't you inform me about the latest findings before the board meeting, Kaitlin? We have always discussed company issues before presenting them to the group. What is all this secrecy?" he asked looking suspiciously at the lawyer.

Bryon responded curtly, "You seem to be overreacting. We have been quite upfront about the whole investigation. What is upsetting you?"

"Because I don't understand. Why is Rivera being held responsible?" he asked angrily. "Didn't we pay him for doing the job?"

"It's the safety issue. He should have been responsible for the safety work and failed to do it. He has admitted that. It's pretty obvious that he was overbilling but not performing the work," Bryon replied. "You oversee all the finances. Didn't you notice that this job was costing you more than for normal construction?"

"So it's my fault, you are implying? Kaitlin, are you going to stand there and let him get away with these insults," he exploded. He turned on his heels and slammed the door.

Raul in the meantime was doing his own detective work for his brother. He was greeted suspiciously by Johnny Rivera at the Cement Company. "What's up with you Raul? I hear your brother skipped town and that the parole board is on his tail. Where is Carlos?"

Raul laughed, "He's taking a little vacation. You know, a little rest and relaxation after his recent incarceration."

"So how do I have the honor of your visit? Are you here to pay off the rest of your gambling debts, asshole?"

"Hey, I only owe another couple thousand and I'm good for that and more if you cooperate. There can be big money in my proposition for you if you work with us," he said smugly to the mobster. "You see my brother has just fallen into an unexpected inheritance and we're willing to pay for information," he added.

Johnny was very curious now as Carlos' whereabouts had been widely discussed in mob circles. "What's your proposition? And does this come directly from Carlos or is it your idea?" He didn't trust Raul for a moment and thought he was a complete sleaze even though he had been married to a prominent member of the Donegon family.

Raul boasted, "Let's say it is a shared idea. You see the proposition is this. We hear you are on the hook for the Grand Hotel accident, overbilling and all that crap. We know that this is nothing new for you. But the word is out that the DA's office might indict you for deliberate negligence that caused a serious accident."

Johnny interrupted, "Where in the hell did you hear that? I just had my deposition a few days ago! What are you trying to prove, Raul and why do you care?"

"Carlos has his tentacles out even though he is 'on vacation'. He still has his New York connections. He heard by the grapevine that they have a paper trail leading right to your door. But Carlos says that you must be protecting someone who is part of the Grand Hotel group and probably was reaping in the payola. He wants to know who that person is," Raul said as he lit a cigarette and stared at Johnny.

"Fuck," Johnny shouted, "how much is it worth to him and why are you asking me? John Martinez runs the Grand Hotels' financial affairs so why aren't you asking him?"

"Carlos will transfer a great deal of money into your bank account if you agree to tell us who is involved. Your answer will be kept top secret Carlos assures you," Raul added taking a deep drag on his cigarette.

Johnny only thought a few minutes, "I'll consider it, especially if he can help me with his connections in New York." He stood up, "But tell him I only deal with Carlos not you, you fuckup." With that he rang for Lenny to escort Raul out the door.

CHAPTER 41—2006

Autumn took a leave from her newspaper job and she and Billy moved to Washington D.C. temporarily while Bill was receiving treatment for brain trauma. She had learned that Bill was near a vehicle where an IED exploded, knocking him unconscious to the ground. It was determined that he would need further treatment for a number of months after he was sent to a hospital in Germany, and now at last was at Walter Reed Medical Center where they specialized in this kind of injury.

Emily flew to Washington D.C. with Autumn in order to watch over little Billy while she was visiting Bill at the hospital. They had a suite in a long-term residential hotel which was comfortable but nothing like home. The change was upsetting to Billy who normally was a happy child and now cried a great deal.

Autumn couldn't wait to see Bill but when it actually came time for their reunion, she was shocked to see his condition. His head was bandaged and although he seemed to recognize her, he was unable to talk to her. She sat there in stunned silence squeezing his hand but getting no response. When the nurse came by Autumn pleaded, "I need to speak to my husband's doctor as soon as possible."

The nurse had seen this kind of panic and anxiety many times before when the relative saw the patient for the first time. Unfortunately, there were too many patients who were returning from Iraq with this kind of injury instead of the chest and abdominal wounds typical of past wars. The 'improvised explosive devices' or IED's were the signature weapon of the war in Iraq. Even though some top level commanders at

Walter Reed had been fired, she knew that the military was ill-equipped to handle the large number of these brain injury cases they were seeing at the hospital. She was not about to share that with this poor woman who obviously had not been prepared for what she was facing in her husband's recovery.

She said gently, "Mrs. Harden, I am Becky Johnston, your husband's nurse. I know you are upset but perhaps after talking to the neurologist you will have a better understanding of your husband's treatment and condition. His life is not being threatened. The swelling in the brain has gone down and now the doctor will advise you on steps that will be taken to help him recover."

Autumn wiped away the tears that were rolling down her cheek, "It's just that I didn't really understand the scope of his injury until I walked through the door to his ward this morning. I have received little information about his injury and condition."

"I'll see that you are able to meet with the doctor sometime today. He is extremely busy as we are treating many soldiers for brain injuries here at Walter Reed, but Dr. Miller, the neurologist in charge of your husband's case always makes it a point to speak to the families of returning troops," she said as she made Bill more comfortable in his bed.

Autumn looked at her with gratitude, "Thank you Ms. Johnston. I'll be staying here by my husband's side until the doctor can see me. I don't care how long it is, but it is important that I talk to him."

She never let go of Bill's hand as she waited several hours for the doctor. She rose to her feet and shook hands with the doctor, "I'm Mrs. Harden and I need to learn what is going on and if my husband will ever recover and go back to the life he once had."

The doctor looked at her with compassion and said, "Sit down, Mrs. Harden. "Your husband has what we call a TBI or traumatic brain injury caused by being in proximity to an explosive device. These explosions lead to significant neurological injury. In your husband's case we suspect memory loss and a loss of brain function in the speaking part of the brain."

"Oh, my God, doctor!" she exclaimed. "Are you saying that he won't be able to speak again?"

"I didn't say that. We don't know what he will be able to do, but plan on a long period of rehabilitation. He will be getting physical therapy to help him learn to walk again and therapists will help him relearn words. Some soldiers have been quite successfully treated in cases like your husband's and have returned to fairly normal lives," he explained.

"How long are we talking about?" she asked with a shaky voice fearing to hear his answer.

"Luckily your husband was wearing body armor and that dramatically saved him from wounds to the chest and upper abdomen. As far as the brain injury, there is no way of telling how long recovery will take or in what degree he can be rehabilitated. But don't lose hope as there are plenty of success stories around here," he said as he examined Bill. "I plan to start him on physical therapy next week and assign therapists to help him regain his speech. Now don't give up hope! I have to see my other patients but I look in on Captain Harden every day and he is in good hands here at Walter Reed."

That evening she returned home weary and frightened. Emily hugged her daughter and sat down to listen to her heartbreaking description of her husband. As Autumn wept Emily brought her a glass of wine and warmed up her dinner.

After Autumn calmed down her mother gently reminded her, "Thank goodness Bill came home alive. He has a chance to recover. I only wish your father had been given that chance. Let's try to be thankful that he has come back to you and little Billy."

Autumn hugged her mom, "I am so thankful that you are here with me. I don't know what I would do without you. I'll tell you something, Mom. I will always miss my father. I missed really knowing him. I'll always have a little hole. I would have loved to debate politics with him and I would have liked to go to the movies with him and walk down the aisle with him when I married Bill. Even though I was only a baby, I remember him calling me his 'little princess'. I don't want Billy to grow up without really knowing his father. All I have is a picture of dad. Billy will have his father when he recovers."

Emily shed a few tears as she remembered the long years of depression she had suffered after Autumn's father, Tom, had died in the concentration camp, and how she had neglected her daughter while she was in that black hole of severe depression. She still remembered how her life collapsed the day the telegram arrived announcing that Tom would never be coming home. "Maybe," she thought, "I can make up for abandoning her emotionally when she was a baby. Just maybe I can rid myself of the guilt I have felt all these years."

CHAPTER 42—PRESENT DAY

Carlos was ready to be dismissed from the plastic surgery center in Switzerland. He looked at himself in the full-length mirror and smiled at what he saw. He saw a tall, slim man with sandy-colored hair and deep blue eyes staring back at him. He laughed, "Not even my brother will recognize me now." The only thing that could give him away was his fingerprints he thought.

The doctor had a final consultation with him and shook his hand, "Much success to you, Mr. Gersbach. I hope that your new appearance will bring you much happiness and will help you achieve your goals."

Carlos shook his hand, "It was worth all the dough I paid. You sure know what you are doing. No one can accuse me of being Hispanic again thanks to you."

The doctor was actually glad to see him leave. "A most difficult and unusual personality," he thought. He wondered what the real reason for the change was, but then he wasn't a psychologist. However, he suspected there was more to the story than his patient had revealed to him.

Back in Miami, John and Kaitlin faced each other in their own hostile confrontation. After he had left her office angrily, he waited until they met that evening at home. He glared at her, "What in the hell is going on between you and Harrell? I used to be the one you came to with problems. It seems like your new confidant is Bryon."

Kaitlin glared at him, "It sounds to me like you are jealous, John, and you have no reason to be. Bryon is deeply involved in helping us out of this mess. Why shouldn't I listen to his advice? That's what we are paying him for!"

"I saw how he looked at you. Like he worships you! And it seems like since you got the last batch of phone calls while I was out of town that you don't trust me anymore!" he shouted as he paced back and forth.

Kaitlin started to cry, "I'm sorry, John. I don't doubt you. It's just that I am so afraid that I will be responsible for losing the company that I'm insecure, and confused. Forgive me if I am taking it out on you."

John held her in his arms, "I guess I was jealous, Kaitlin. I love you and I guess I haven't been sensitive enough to what you are going through. Please forgive me. I would never call you and upset you. I don't know who is making those calls when I am out of town but if I ever find out, I will kill the bastard!"

He led her to the bedroom where they made desperate love, so happy to have resolved their differences. There were too many problems to face without having a lover's quarrel and Kaitlin felt guilty for ever doubting John who had always been there through thick and thin. He had proven his love time and time again.

The next morning as they had their coffee in the kitchen Kaitlin said thoughtfully, "Last night was wonderful, darling, but now we must get back to reality. We are looking at a hostile takeover of our company. Now what are your ideas about how we can defend ourselves, especially when we don't know who is behind this?"

"Well, I have one idea that might work," he replied. "We could formulate a poison pill the hostile buyer won't want to swallow."

"And just what is in that pill?" she asked.

"We can make a takeover prohibitively expensive by granting our current stockholders the right to purchase newly issued stock at a greatly reduced price."

Kaitlin thought that one over before answering, "That sounds good but that could become a suicide pill if we take on so much debt that it sends the company into bankruptcy!"

"Well, we could seek out a more acceptable buyer than the mysterious stalker we are dealing with. Perhaps consider a merger with the right kind of investor," he continued. "I believe in the business they call the right buyer 'the white knight'."

Kaitlin frowned, "I hope we never have to resort to that. Aidin would never have approved of relinquishing even a part of the company to an outsider!"

"It's a different world now, Kaitlin, than in Aidin's day. If it meant saving the company I bet he would have considered it."

Little did they know 'the white knight' was ready to enter the picture as wealthy and now distinguished Bruno Gersbach stepped off his international flight at Miami International Airport. His new passport reflected his change in appearance and the Customs agent hardly gave him a second look.

He walked right by Raul and who didn't even recognize him. Carlos laughed, "Hey, hermano, aren't you even going to greet your brother?"

Raul was completely shocked, "Holy Fuck, Carlos, I never would have spotted you!"

"It's Bruno. Remember Carlos has disappeared from the face of the globe, and enter Bruno Gersbach. I better not hear you slip up. You could blow my cover!" Carlos ordered him. He trusted his brother but wasn't too sure he had the brains to keep his mouth shut.

Bruno said, "I have made a reservation at the Grand Miami Beach and want to go there to rest and maybe have a swim in the ocean before we meet for dinner. Then I want to buy a car and start looking for a suitable estate in Coral Gables. Preferably not too far from Elizabeth's home. I want to hear about what you found out from Rivera about the company snitch but that can wait until later tonight."

Raul dropped him off at the luxurious Grand Miami Beach and said, "Just think Car…I mean Bruno, someday if we play our cards right this will be ours!"

Bruno thought to himself, "You mean this will be mine, little brother. I don't plan to cut you into the deal. Maybe a little payoff to keep you quiet. But I want it all, Elizabeth, the hotels…all of it." As he walked into the lobby and checked in he couldn't help but notice the respect he was given both from the porter and the manager who personally greeted him.

"Welcome to the Grand Miami Beach Hotel, Mr. Gersbach. I think you will be happy with your suite. It overlooks the ocean of course and has a wide balcony. I will be sending up a bottle of our finest champagne and hope you will enjoy it. May I make dinner reservations for you in our Ocean Dining Room?" he asked.

Bruno affecting a slight Swiss accent which he had acquired during his long stay at the clinic, "Thank you, but I have plans with a business associate and we will be dining elsewhere this evening."

"Well, please let me know if there is any service that you need. I will personally attend to it," the manager said. "Will you need a car and driver during your stay?"

By now Bruno was losing his patience and said curtly, "I'll let you know if I need anything. Right now I need to get rid of this jet lag."

As he entered his penthouse suite it opened to a breathtaking view of the Atlantic Ocean. The porter opened the wide French doors leading out to the balcony and he could hear the crash of the waves. The tropical setting was lush and beautiful.

"This is the life," he said gazing around the elegant suite as the waiter rolled in a cart and opened his champagne. Taking a flute of the bubbly, he stepped out on the balcony.

He raised his flute in a toast, "Here's to you, Bruno Gersbach. Life is good!"

CHAPTER 43—PRESENT DAY

Bruno met with his brother that evening and after a few drinks and dinner at a restaurant facing the ocean he sat back and lit a cigar and got down to business. "What's the scoop from Rivera? Did you find out who the mole was from the Grand Hotel?"

"He wants you to pay for that information and said he would only deal with you. However, he implied that Kaitlin Donegon had nothing to do with it. He said John Martinez, that Cuban dude, is the chief financial officer and oversees all the money. "

Bruno laughed loudly, "I'll be damned if Martinez isn't embezzling from the Grand Hotel construction through Rivera! I don't need to pay Rivera for information. That's all I need to hear. And this Martinez guy is also sleeping with the boss, not a bad deal!"

He sipped his espresso and thought for a moment, "What about the Grand Jury? Is the DA looking into John Martinez or only Rivera?"

"I've heard that Rivera is the only one on the hook, but that could change I guess," Raul answered thoughtfully.

This sounded all too familiar to Bruno who was well-schooled in crime, "There had to be a go-between Rivera and Martinez unless Martinez is dumb enough to take the payoff himself, and he sounds like a pretty smart dude the way he has weaseled into the boss's panties. Who do you think was the bagman?"

"I don't have a clue and Rivera ain't spilling his guts until he gets paid for it," Raul frowned.

"Rivera can't be trusted and I want no direct contact with him. He's famous for double billing and skimming, all the ways the mob likes to rip off the construction industry! If he knew I was in town, the next thing I'd be hearing from the parole board and be back in the slammer. I think I can find the answers myself once I work myself into the inner circle. I'm starting tomorrow to find a house in Coral Gables near Elizabeth and a way to be introduced back into her life," he said picking up the check and leaving a big tip for the happy waiter.

As the two brothers waited for the valet to bring Raul's car Carlos turned to him and said, "I'm getting used to the Grand Miami Beach Hotel and the lifestyle. If I play my cards right, someday it will be mine."

Raul noted that his brother hadn't said, "It will be ours," but decided it was not the time nor place to discuss it. His brother was in a good mood and he didn't want to change it. Carlos could be vicious when he was angry.

The next morning Raul picked up Carlos early in the morning. Carlos was again in a good mood for he had taken an early morning swim in the ocean and then had his breakfast delivered to his balcony overlooking the crashing rollers of the Atlantic Ocean. First on his agenda was to buy a new car. Luckily his new identification package included a current driver's license. He liked the sleek lines of the Jaguar and he wanted to impress Liz with his wealth, but he decided on the Mercedes-Benz roadster with the retractable sunroof. The salesman was delighted when Carlos offered cash for the car. He didn't see that very much in the hard economic times in Miami and throughout the nation. Many customers had taken out loans that they were not able to repay during the recession and the number of repossession rates had dramatically increased. Also, many homes were being taken back by the banks and it definitely was a buyer's market.

Carlos bid Raul goodbye as he drove off in his brand new vehicle and headed for a realtor in Coral Gables. He knew the location where Liz had her home. It was in a group of mansions that faced Biscayne Bay. He asked to be taken to that area much to the delight of the realtor.

"Yes, that is a lovely area of Coral Gables. Would you want to be on a canal that accesses the ocean so that you will have docking for your yacht? We have several estates that we can show you that have been on the market for quite a long time. Unfortunately, property has been losing its value due to the times and this should work favorably for a buyer like yourself," she told him as they got into the realtor's car.

As they drove along Old Cutler Road Carlos gazed at the huge estates that had been built during the years he had been in prison. The size of the newer houses amazed him. They looked like hotels instead of houses. Obviously they had a fleet of gardeners as all the lawns were beautifully manicured and the landscape was lush and tropical. He remembered Liz telling him about how her grandfather Aidin and her father, Calvin, had been the pioneer builders in Coral Gables and had helped set the building requirements even in those early days of its development.

"Do you have anything on Alameda Way?" he asked knowing Liz's house had that address. "I am from Lucerne, Switzerland, but I will be relocating to Miami and my business partner lives somewhere in that area"

The realtor gushed knowing this could mean big bucks, "Oh, Mr. Gersbach, that is one of the loveliest neighborhoods in all of Miami-Dade County. Would you like to drive past your associate's estate and we can see what else might be available nearby?"

"Sure, let's check it out," Carlos said happily and anxious to see the kind of place Liz was living in. He gave the realtor the address and several minutes later she drove up to a beautiful estate set back from the road. "Here it is! Lovely, isn't it? This is one of the original estates built in the Gables. You will notice that there are older mansions interspersed with the newer estates. Because of the strict building codes, these older homes really established the codes that are in place today."

Carlos was hoping to get a glimpse of Elizabeth, but after looking at the elegant landscaping he guessed she never came out to pull a weed.

The realtor continued, "Do you want to see your partner while we are here? I know that all these places have a terrific view of the Bay and waterways for the boats."

"No, I don't have time for social calls. What do have to show me in this area?"

"There's a beautiful estate for sale about two blocks from here. The owner has been transferred to another state and has already left. Of course, he is anxious to sell and has reduced the price several times. It has five bedrooms and five bathrooms and faces the bay. It has a lovely swimming pool and a terrace overlooking the sea. It was built about five years ago so everything is the latest including a sensational kitchen. There is a gym and outdoor spa. Oh yes, a pier is built and a boathouse."

"What's he asking for it?" Carlos asked the realtor who was starting to annoy him with all her gushing.

"He's asking two million five, but I have the feeling he will listen to lower offers." She looked at him nervously afraid she might be losing the sale and that the asking price was out of her client's range, "It was listed at 5 million only six months ago."

The realtor found the key box and extracted the key. She and Carlos entered the spacious house. The floors were white marble and the wide foyer opened to a great room that overlooked the sea. A wide terrace fanned out from the house and the pool was incredible, sparkling water surrounded by waterfalls and tropical plantings. In the distance he saw the pier just waiting for a yacht to occupy the space. The interior was gorgeous with a spiral staircase leading to the bedrooms. There was a huge recreation room and an adjoining gym with the equipment there in place. Everything about the estate was perfect.

Carlos was thinking to himself, "It sure beats my last accommodations at South-Dade Correctional." The realtor kept raving on and on about how lucky he was that this prize property was available making Carlos nervous and irritable.

"Let's cut to the chase, Miss Fernandez," he snapped. "I'll offer one million five."

She looked somewhat shocked, "That is a 50% reduction from the asking price which I told you was already reduced. Would you like to see some more properties that are less expensive? And of course you would need to get approval for the mortgage."

Carlos replied sarcastically, "I don't need approval. This will be a cash transaction and I want immediate occupancy. Present this offer to the buyer and let me know. I don't want to look at any more houses today. He can take it or leave it and so can you!"

She immediately changed her tone. Not many buyers could pay cash in this day of economic turmoil. Maybe only a drug dealer. She quickly dismissed that idea. Obviously this was an important business man with endless resources. "I'll call him tonight and let you know. Perhaps he will make a counter offer. Of course, an all cash sale might really appeal to him."

Carlos who was a master of negotiation with fellow inmates from his prison base felt like saying, "Cut the bullshit," but this would not fit in with his new image. "I'm staying at the Grand Miami Beach and you can call me there. If the seller isn't interested I'll be checking with another realtor."

They drove back in silence. Finally she said fearing she might lose the sale, "I think we can work something out, Mr. Gersbach." As he walked to his car she noticed it was a top-of-the line Mercedes-Benz. This was too good a prospect to lose.

CHAPTER 44—2007

Autumn and Billy had been visiting Bill for months during his rehabilitation and recovery period due to the traumatic brain injury he received while in combat in Iraq. Finally the day was coming when they would bring him home from Walter Reid where he had been receiving treatment.

Bill was now walking with the support of a cane and he was sleeping better which gave him more energy. His depression had improved especially when Billy visited. They had developed an immediate bond even though Bill could only speak a few words. He had been given intensive therapy and could now sometimes form sentences. As Billy was starting to talk sometimes Autumn thought they communicated so well because both had such a limited vocabulary.

The doctor met with Autumn before Bill was released and said kindly, "Mrs. Harden, we feel that Captain Harden has made remarkable progress. I have arranged for him to get outpatient therapy at the Veteran's Hospital in Miami. They will continue to work on him regaining complete control of his muscles and in time we think he will be able to walk without a cane or walker. In fact the more exercise he gets the better it will be for him both physically and psychologically. He tends to have depression but we have given him medication for that as well as for pain control. He is still experiencing headaches but not as frequently as before. This sometimes causes him to be irritable or angry so be prepared for this."

Autumn looked at him fearfully, "You are scaring me, doctor. Do you think our family will ever have a normal life again?"

"You have every reason to be encouraged. He is really motivated to learn to talk again and is making amazing progress even though it may not appear that way to you. You will have to be patient and not demand too much in the beginning. Remember, this all takes time. He had a very serious injury. But it could have been a lot worse and he is way ahead of many of my patients who are suffering the same type of injury," he told her.

She sighed, "Thank you, doctor, for all you have done to heal my husband. I pray that the progress will continue when he gets to Miami."

"Their VA program is excellent so stop worrying and be happy that your husband is coming home. By the way, I've been hearing about your son Billy. This will be a tremendous positive relationship for Captain Harden. Sometimes our patients feel more comfortable with the children in the family than adults who are more task-oriented and demanding."

After Bill bid goodbye to his hospital buddies and the nursing staff, they picked up Emily and drove back to Miami with Autumn at the wheel. Billy couldn't have been more happy and excited that they were going home and insisted that his father sit in the back seat with him. The women smiled and looked at each other when they heard them laughing together like two kids.

Autumn had hoped to return to her job at the newspaper but she soon realized that that would be impossible. Bill still needed a lot of care and was still screaming out in the night when he had frequent nightmares. This pattern caused sleep deprivation which in turn caused him to be angry and impulsive. He spent many hours just sitting on the couch staring into space. Autumn was thankful for the days when he was picked up by Rehabilitation Services for his therapy sessions. Then she would get together with Kaitlin who always was willing to listen to her vent.

She offered Kaitlin a glass of lemonade and they sat out by the above ground swimming pool and watched Billy happily splashing in the water and playing with his toy boats.

"How are things going with Bill?" Kaitlin asked not sure that she wanted the answer. She could see that Autumn was nervous and upset.

"Some things have improved, but sometimes it feels like I am taking care of two children. I want my husband to come back and be the man I married," she said shedding a few tears.

Kaitlin hugged her cousin and said, "This won't last forever, Autumn. Is he able to get out and take walks now? Exercise is a great morale booster."

"Yes, he is able to walk now without the walker. He still uses the cane for support. But frankly, he is too depressed to want to do much of anything. He watches TV but doesn't really seem to be paying attention to what is happening but merely stares at the picture. Then he doesn't sleep well at night and I never know when he will have one of his flashback nightmares. I'm a bundle of nerves!"

"Does he express any anger about the war and what happened to him?" Kaitlin asked.

"Now that he is able to express himself and the good news is he is forming sentences now and able to communicate much better. The bad news is that he thinks his service in Iraq meant nothing and the war was unnecessary. He calls himself a fool for volunteering," she added.

Kaitlin sighed, "Well, he's not alone. Did you hear what happened at Miami-Dade Community College yesterday?"

"Believe it or not, I don't keep up with the news now that my days are so filled with taking care of Bill. What happened?"

"It seems that President George Bush gave a speech at the Kendall campus and protestors celebrating 'National Impeachment Day' held a peaceful march while Miami police looked on. There were pictures of them in the newspaper holding signs saying 'Out of Iraq' and 'No Blood for Oil'. People are beginning to realize this was a useless war and the administration went to war using faulty intelligence. Worst of all, we transferred most of our resources from Afghanistan where there really were terrorists and started a war with a country that at that time was not connected with Al Qaeda! "

"And look at the victims like my husband that thought they were revenging September 11th and ended up fighting in a Civil War between the Sunni's and the Shia's! I do realize that I am one of the lucky ones whose husband returned in one piece even if his recovery seems to drag," Autumn said as she pulled little Billy out of the water and put him in the sandbox.

Kaitlin sat for a moment thinking, "You know Autumn, I was thinking, isn't it time you considered going back to work? I bet Emily would be glad to be a caretaker again and she and Bill seem to hit it off. It might do you both good."

Autumn grinned, "You know I have been thinking about that. My mother doesn't hover around Bill like I do, and it might do him good to be a little more independent. They have been encouraging me to come back to work, and I also heard that as soon as Bill has recovered his job at the newspaper will be waiting for him. He was one of the best photographers they have ever had. I hope someday we can work together on stories like we used to in the past!"

"I just had another idea! Why don't you get out his camera equipment and encourage him to start taking photos again. You might suggest a photo essay of Billy's growth and development. That should motivate him as they are very close," Kaitlin said in an excited tone.

Autumn hugged her cousin, "You always have the greatest ideas! This may be the one thing that could get his mind off the war and open a new window of hope!" She was glad that her mother lived with them and she would talk to Emily as soon as Kaitlin left and see if she would go along with the plan. Both Billy and Bill loved Emily and she felt that she would feel at ease going back to work knowing her mother was there to care for her loved ones. For the first time in months Autumn felt pure happiness as she envisioned her life returning to normal.

CHAPTER 45—PRESENT DAY

Carlos wasn't surprised at all when the charming Ms. Fernandez called that very evening after he had looked at the property in Coral Gables. She said breathlessly, "I have the best news for you! The homeowner has agreed to accept your bid and says you can have occupancy as soon as you want. If you want to continue with the same pool service and gardening companies, I can set that up for you. We can also recommend several housekeepers that are reliable if you will need that kind of service."

"I'd like to close the deal immediately and move in next week. You can keep the same service people. They are familiar with the pool and grounds. I don't want a contract though, as if I'm not satisfied I will want to change," he said in a demanding tone.

The realtor was a little disappointed as she thought he'd be more pleased at the deal she had cut. Regardless, there was a huge commission waiting for her so she couldn't complain. She hadn't been able to move many houses in the past year, especially in this price range.

"I forgot to mention that there is a homeowner's association in that community. A very prominent group of Miamians I might add! There will be some dues connected with it but I think you'll find it a great way to get acquainted with your neighbors. I checked on it for you, and found that they will be holding a cocktail party next Friday and as a new owner you are automatically on the guest list!"

Carlos replied, "I am not much for social gatherings, but I would like to meet the neighbors. I don't know many people in Miami as I have lived in Europe most of my life."

"I will give you the information at the closing then, and congratulations on being a new homeowner in one of the finest neighborhoods in Miami-Dade County!" He was afraid she was going to explode, she was so excited. He wondered what she would think if she knew the last housing he had had in Miami-Dade County was courtesy of the federal government.

Carlos moved in the next week. He hired a decorator from one of the best furniture stores in Coral Gables and she had already designed furnishings fit for Architectural Digest. He particularly liked the white grand piano in the great room. It looked great on the white marble floors. After the dark days in the drab prison the all-white theme really grabbed him. Then the huge windows opened up to the sparkling blue sea beyond. He would take his time choosing the rest of the furniture and paintings, but at least the master bedroom was furnished in addition to the elegant white leather furniture imported from Italy in the entertainment center which overlooked the bay and the swimming pool. After he saw the huge kitchen with the granite counters and streamlined appliances he considered hiring a cook. Frozen dinners didn't quite fit in with such elegance.

The following Friday he drove up to a neighboring estate where the cocktail party was being held. You couldn't even see the house from the road, and as he entered the gate and drove down the long driveway, the mansion came into view. He whistled to himself as he admired the spectacular estate facing the water. "My kind of people," he thought. "Wonder if this crowd is mixed up in drugs with all this dough? It would be interesting if some of my old buddies are now living high on the hog in this kind of neighborhood. A good test of my new image!" He was a little worried that someone might recognize him but was confident that he bore no resemblance now to the old Carlos Gonzalez.

Actually the whole reason for Carlos' introduction to Miami society was to get a glimpse of Elizabeth and maybe even talk to her. He was quite nervous at the thought and hoped his surgery was really as good as the mirror told him. Seeing her would be the real test. As he thought of her the bitterness welled up as he thought about the years he had spent in prison while she enjoyed the lifestyle of a wealthy woman with an adoring husband. "I wish that bastard husband of hers hadn't bumped himself off before I got my hands on him," he thought growing angrier by the minute. He knew he had to keep his emotions in check as he appeared as the distinguished Swiss banker, Bruno Gersbach.

Carlos was dressed like a successful businessman and he was surprised to see many of the male guests in more casual dress without neckties and jackets although they reeked of money. Most of the women were more elegantly dressed with cocktail dresses that didn't leave much to the imagination and stiletto heels. He noticed a great number of trophy wives with older men. His host was a Hispanic man named Alfredo Griego who greeted the newcomer warmly and made a great effort to introduce him to the other guests who Carlos noticed were lapping up the booze in large quantities. Carlos suspected that Griego was from Cuba and wondered what his racket was to be able to buy a mansion like this.

"What business are you in, Bruno?" he asked noting the expensive clothes Carlos was wearing.

"I am a banker from Lucerne, Switzerland and I am opening an investment branch of my business here in Miami. When I asked where the best neighborhood was, I was told it is this community so here I am!" Bruno said pleasantly as his host handed him a flute of champagne. "What business are you in Mr. Griego?"

He laughed, "Please call me Al. We aren't formal around here. I guess you might say I'm in the money business. I run a hedge fund."

Carlos thought to himself, "Probably money laundering." He looked at his host intently, "I want to talk to you further about this, but tonight is not the right time. Give me your card and I will be in touch in the future."

All the time he was talking he was sweeping the crowd with his eyes hoping to get a glimpse of Elizabeth. By now several of the single ladies had discovered that there was a rich, eligible man in the crowd and were vying for his attention.

He was just deciding that the evening was a bust and he might as well get drunk when out of the corner of his eye he spotted Elizabeth. Age had treated her well and he thought that she still was as beautiful as she had been as a young girl when he had first fallen in love with her. She was still slender and he guessed that she worked out. Her hair was still blonde and arranged in a French twist. He suspected that she got a little help from her hairdresser as he didn't see any gray. She was wearing a beautiful turquoise colored cocktail dress and stiletto sandals in the same shade.

He excused himself from the aggressive lady who had already invited him to her house for dinner and worked his way over to Elizabeth. As he approached her she showed no sign of recognition when she turned to him and said, "I don't believe we have met, Mr. Gersbach, but I have been alerted that we have a new neighbor and I want to welcome you to our neighborhood." She smiled a million dollar smile and he noticed that her eyes still sparkled like a young girl's. "I'm Elizabeth Donegan although feel free to call me Liz. I have lived in this area for years and know most people by now. I'm sort of the Hospitality person I guess you could say."

"Just call me Bruno, no need to be formal," he said as he affected his slight Swiss accent. "Then you must tell me all about Miami. I have been here on short business trips but have never really had time to see the sights. You see, I am from Switzerland. Have you ever been to Lucerne, Liz?" he asked.

"Oh, yes, in my younger days I did a lot of skiing and loved Switzerland. And Lucerne was perfectly charming. I particularly loved the covered bridge in the center of town. It was so picturesque. I'll never forget it. How did you happen to move to Miami? Did you get tired of those cold winters?" she laughed as he handed her a flute of champagne from the passing waiter's tray.

"On the contrary, I found it a good business opportunity. I run a large bank in Switzerland and I have decided to open an investment subsidiary here in Miami," he explained. He said in a conspirator's tone, "A lot of Miamians have money in my bank. They like the safety and privacy we offer." Unspoken was, "They like the tax breaks, too, as well as hiding their money."

He was annoyed when several women who he had talked to previously interrupted their conversation, "Oh, Liz, I see you have met our new Mr.

Gersbach. But you can't monopolize him for the whole evening," the overweight blonde cooed as she grabbed his arm and started to lead him away.

He pulled back and said rather curtly, "Another time. I'm busy learning all about Miami from your Hospitality chairman." The woman walked away looking disgruntled and Liz laughed, "You have already made a hit I see. A new single man is always popular here as we have many widows and divorcee's living in our community."

"I don't see a ring on your finger, Liz. May I hope that you are single also?"

"I am in the widow group I'm afraid. My husband died a number of years ago. But contrary to some of the other eager ladies, I don't date so you are safe, Mr. Gersbach," she teased having noticed how abruptly he brushed off the woman who had interrupted them.

"Seriously, I would appreciate it if we could get together and maybe you wouldn't mind showing me around town, or does that go beyond the duties of the Hospitality lady? We won't call it a date if that makes you feel better. Unless you are too busy? Are you also a business woman?"

"It would take too long to discuss the whole family history dating back to 1896 when my grandfather was one of the early pioneers that helped develop Miami. He started one of the first hotels here in Coconut Grove. Now we have a large chain of hotels all over Europe and America. We don't have a Grand Hotel in Switzerland but a business man like yourself has probably stayed in some of our hotels. Lately, my daughter, who now heads the corporation, has started developing boutique hotels," she said proudly. "I serve on the Board of Directors and pinch hit for Kaitlin when she is out of town."

Carlos laughed, "I was staying at the Grand Miami Beach Hotel while I looked for a house. I have stayed in your hotels often." He was thinking of his years at the 'grand correctional hotel' in South Miami Dade and had to control the anger that was welling up in him. The wasted years because this woman or her husband squealed on him.

Elizabeth looked at this very attractive man who somehow seemed familiar even though that was impossible and replied, "No, Bruno, I would really enjoy showing you around and welcome to the neighborhood!"

Carlos thought to himself, "This was much easier than I thought it would be. You don't know what you are in for, Miss Hospitality Lady!" An evil plan was already hatching in his mind. This was the moment he had waited for in all those long years behind bars.

CHAPTER 46—2008

Getting back to work had really raised Autumn's spirits and instead of it hurting Bill's recovery as she had feared, it had the opposite result. He was now able to work part-time at the newspaper. He and Autumn had worked together on several stories and he still was able to capture the realism of the moment in his photographs. Not only that, but his book of photo essays on Billy's childhood and the child's positive influence on a returning veteran with traumatic brain injury had been snapped up by a major publisher and would be released shortly.

Although he still had some nightmares and flashbacks they were coming less frequently. He was more organized and less likely to be impulsive and have fits of rage and anger like in the early days after his return home. Billy was a constant joy for him and Autumn thanked God for the strong bond that had developed between them.

Kaitlin was totally involved in her boutique project but they were also starting some renovations of their older hotels that were still popular but definitely needed updating. They planned to start renovations on the Grand New York Hotel and John had been overseeing the project. It would be a massive restoration job. As the hotel was located near the vicinity of the twin tower terrorism tragedy, the hotel had sustained some damages from flying debris and dust and smoke. David Wells who directed domestic operations was doing a lot of the leg work and taking bids and talking to contractors.

Wells had recently run into some financial problems. His wife of 25 years was divorcing him and demanding a big settlement and he had huge mortgages on both his home in Miami Beach and his summer place in the mountains of North Carolina where his wife spent several months each summer when Miami was steaming hot and humid. His wife had developed expensive tastes over the years and they had bought estates priced well above their income level. Also, for the last few years he had been renting an apartment in North Miami for his mistress who was strictly high maintenance. Carmen was a stunning Hispanic girl, 20 years younger than he was and dynamite in bed. She did things to him that he never dreamed of in contrast to his frigid wife who lay on the bed like a corpse on the rare occasions that they had made love. The more he saw Carmen, the more totally obsessed he was. Since he and his wife were separated he and Carmen were now living together in the apartment and she was pushing him to buy a house for the two of them.

When Carmen didn't get what she was asking for she threatened to leave him. Then he would promise her the moon and she would unzip his pants and take him in her mouth until he exploded in pleasure. He knew that he had to find a way to buy her the things she wanted. He couldn't bear to give her up. He thought how boring and mundane his life had been before he met Carmen. She was a waitress at the restaurant where he frequently had lunch and he couldn't keep his eyes off her. She had voluptuous curves and beautiful shiny black hair and sparkling brown eyes with endless eyelashes. She flirted outrageously with him and he could hardly believe it when she accepted a dinner date with him. They had gone to her small room after dinner and when they made love it was a life-altering experience for him.

He was frantic with worry when he called at the Rivera Concrete Company to get their bid for the work at the Grand New York renovation. They had branches in New York and Chicago, but the boss, Johnny Rivera, preferred to keep his main office in Miami where he could go sailing on his 52-foot yacht as often as he wanted.

After being greeted by Rivera he asked for his spec sheets and reviewed the charges on the bid. He could hardly keep his mind on business as he kept worrying about Carmen and if she would still be there when he came home to their apartment. Rivera who was nobody's fool recognized a patsy when he saw one. Something was bothering this dude big time and it wasn't his figures on the cement job.

He noticed David Well's hands were shaking as he shuffled through the papers. Rivera needed to know what his weak point was. He was thinking, "If it's money, I may be able to make big bucks on this." Instead he said, "Hey David, man, you look a little strung out. I have just the thing for you. He went over to his bar and poured them each a few fingers of whiskey.

Wells gulped it down and said sheepishly, "I usually don't drink on the job. But I'm having a few personal problems today and it's hard to concentrate."

Rivera refilled his glass and reached in his drawer and rolled a joint for both of them. "Here take a few puffs of this and I'm sure you will forget your troubles." After Wells took a few hits of the pot and finished off his second drink Rivera said in a compassionate voice, "Perhaps I can help you. What is your problem?"

Wells was feeling very relaxed and mellow by now and said, "It's woman trouble. My wife is divorcing me and asking for big bucks and my girlfriend wants me to buy a house. I'm running out of money and I don't know who will give me a loan. I already owe two banks for mortgages that I can hardly afford to pay each month. My wife is asking for both houses plus alimony."

Rivera smiled thinking, "I've found myself a real idiot. Now to tempt him to make a deal."

"Well, if you need money I think I could help." He paused for effect and watched while Wells took another hit of pot. "It's not exactly dishonest, but we would have to keep the deal quiet, just between the two of us."

"What kind of deal are you talking about?" Wells asked looking hopeful.

"Well, you see we could overbill Grand Hotel Company and we could pass on the skimmed money to you. Of course, I would expect a cut you understand. It's a foolproof plan and no one will be the wiser and you'll be able to buy your dame that house," Rivera said confidently. "It's nothing new, mind you. People in construction do it all the time. No risk at all for you."

David Wells was sobering up, "It sounds illegal to me. Could I be sent to jail for this?"

Rivera laughed, "No way, I've been doing it for years and never served a day in my life!"

Wells thought for only a few moments as he thought of how Carmen would reward him for the good news that she could start looking for a house, "OK, Mr. Rivera, you win the bid. I'll pass on my authorization to John Martinez, the Chief Financial Officer." He waited while Rivera adjusted the figures to reflect the overbilling.

"You should clear about a million before I take my cut," Rivera told the nervous man.

"Remember, part of the deal is you don't tell anyone, especially that dame you are screwing. Do you understand? Also, I don't want you to come to my office again. I don't want them to connect us in any way. Do you understand?" he threatened grabbing Well's arm.

Wells was beginning to regret his decision already, but then when he thought what a million dollars would buy he felt he had no choice. He was already envisioning a villa in the Caribbean where he and Carmen could make love day and night. He shook Johnny Rivera's hand and said, "How will I get my money?"

"As soon as the company pays the invoice a courier will deliver your money, or we could transfer it to an off-shore bank account if you have one," he answered. He patted him on the back and said confidently, "You see we don't sign a written contract for this, partner. But if you don't follow through I assure you that you will regret it."

David Wells sat in his car for at least a half hour before driving off. As the alcohol and pot wore off he suddenly realized what he had done. He started to shake uncontrollably as he thought of the consequences if his part in the affair was discovered. He was in over his head wishing he could run this by someone who knew how to deal with it, but knowing his life and future depended on him keeping it to himself. He could always back out but then he thought of Carmen and knew that wasn't an option.

While David Wells was filled with guilt over his decision, Autumn and Bill were discussing the presidential election. The primary race had been a tough battle between the first woman candidate, Hillary Clinton, and the first African-American, Barack Obama.

"Just think, Bill, Obama has won the primary and I never believed I would see an African-American as a presidential candidate. I covered the Republican candidate, John McCain's visit today in the streets of Little Havana and the Cubans were saying that Obama's call for change reminded them of everything Fidel Castro said. Some even called Obama's change communism," Autumn said thinking it was so wonderful to be able to discuss politics with her husband again.

Bill said, "That all goes back to 'Joe the Plumber" the guy that confronted Obama about his plan to "spread wealth around". McCain has tried for weeks to tap into fears that Obama would raise taxes for business owners using the story of Joe the Plumber. Of course, nowhere in the nation has McCain found a more willing audience than South Florida, the heartland of Cuban exiles."

Autumn nodded her agreement, "You're so right, Bill. Cuban support is crucial to McCain if he is to hold Florida in Tuesday's presidential elections, and block Obama from winning the White House."

"I'm afraid that here in Little Havana in Miami even the faintest whiff of socialism revives memories of exile from Castro and McCain is currently playing up these fears," Bill frowned.

In the small, tidy homes of Little Havana in Miami lawn campaign signs warned that an Obama presidency would be the first step in communism. Spanish language radio stations and there were many in Miami, berated Obama for saying he would negotiate with Castro, Chavez from Venezuela and Iran's Mahmoud Ahmedinejad.

Autumn continued, "The Cuban vote is crucial if McCain is to counter the surge of support for Obama in South Florida. However, Obama's camp says he has won over many of the younger Cuban voters and that Cuban Americans under the age of 30 are defecting from the Republicans."

Bill said, "I was doing photos of Obama when he spoke at Bicentennial Park in Miami. He drew a crowd of about 30,000 and ridiculed McCain's 'Joe the Plumber' act and made the point that McCain was trying to win by attacking him rather than by new ideas. But frankly, I will vote for Obama because he was against the war in Iraq. My buddies are still being killed for this needless war."

As he was starting to lose his temper Autumn changed the subject. "Why don't you take Billy for a little swim in the pool? I hear him waking up from his nap."

As the election drew near the polls showed the race deadlocked in Florida. It was amazing when the underdog, Barack Obama became the first African-American to sit in the Oval Office as President of the United States.

Florida was won by Obama who ended up winning the state with 51% of the votes despite the fact that polls showed McCain in the lead for most of 2008. Bill and some of the other veterans of the Iraq War had cause to break out a bottle of champagne. Maybe the war would be ended at last and no more brave warriors would be returning home with traumatic brain injury.

As most of Miami was focused on the election results, David Wells could only think of the seriousness of what he had agreed to do. He was fearful that someone would find out and send him to jail even though Rivera had said it was impossible. Even Carmen's lovemaking didn't help at this point. He had had no trouble submitting the bid to John Martinez who said, "I have great confidence in you, David. Frankly, I prefer to stay out of the construction end of the business. I trust your judgment. I notice there were several lower bids. What is the reason you chose the highest bid?"

Now David was really worried and replied quickly, "If we're concerned with safety of our workers, it's best to take a more reliable company with a good reputation like Rivera Concrete. Some of these low bidders cut corners I am told, and I know Kaitlin always insists on a high quality product."

John agreed, "Yes, we don't want to compromise the high standards we are known for. I might know that you would always put the company first, Wells."

John sat there thinking over the enormous amount of the bid. Finally, he picked up the phone and called the number on the bid. When Rivera answered, John said, "I hear that you are interested in doing the cement work on our New York project. As you have sent in the most expensive bid, I feel like the two of us should sit down and talk."

CHAPTER 47—PRESENT DAY

Kaitlin stopped by her mother's house to share her latest tale of woe. The bottom line was they were running out of money due to the slowdown in construction at the Grand New York Hotel.

"This is a nightmare, and it just keeps getting worse. After the stop-down during the investigation we started to make progress in continuing the renovation, but now they have reopened the investigation and work is bogged down again. The delay is costing us more money every day. With this recession our country is going through the commercial real estate markets are down and selling one of our other hotels is not feasible and the banks refuse to listen to reason and offer a loan when the work has been slowed down. Where is that 'white knight' that you talked about?" Kaitlin moaned.

Elizabeth hated to see Kaitlin so disturbed. She was usually so upbeat and confident that things would work out. But now Liz began to suspect that her daughter was on the brink of disaster. The hotels meant everything to her and Liz knew that it would break her heart to sell off hotels or file bankruptcy. She knew that she would think she was disappointing her father who had so much faith in her.

A light suddenly flashed in Elizabeth's brain as she thought of the charming Swiss banker that she had met a few nights ago at the neighborhood gathering. "Kaitlin," she said, "by coincidence I have just met a man who has moved into the neighborhood and he told me he ran a large Swiss Bank and was opening an investment branch here in Miami."

Kaitlin eyed her mother, "Are you saying that he might take a chance on us as an investment?"

"I really don't know, but he asked me to show him around Miami," she blushed much to her dismay. "It's not a date! I made that clear to him. You know, I am the hospitality chairman of the group and it's my job to welcome newcomers."

Kaitlin sensed that after all these years her mother might actually be interested in another man. Her father, Andy, had been her mother's life and she had never considered dating even though she was stunning for a woman her age and had had many offers which she had refused.

Kaitlin encouraged the meeting, "It can't do any harm to take him around the city. Maybe you can get some insight into whether he might be interested in an investment in the hotel industry."

Liz smiled in response, "Well, he did mention he was staying at the Grand Miami Beach Hotel before buying his house and that he liked it very much. He also said he has stayed at Grand Hotels all over the globe on his business trips." She thought for a moment, "Kaitlin, he bought the Bryant estate so he must be loaded. Al Griego, the president of our community group told me that he had heard that he paid cash. It was originally listed for 5 million but he may have gotten it for less because I know the Bryants didn't want to leave it empty for long after they moved."

Kaitlin said, "I'm going to call the manager at the Grand Miami Beach and get his impression of your new neighbor. Let's see what kind of accommodation he had and how he paid his charges. In the meantime, when you see him on your tour of Miami try to find out everything you can about his business."

"He did say something about many American businesses having accounts at his bank. I thought he implied they were off-shore customers looking for tax breaks."

"Well, Switzerland is certainly known for a good place to hide money," Kaitlin said. "Let me know what you find out and if it is plausible I will ask John to approach him for a loan. I don't think Grand Hotels will be held liable nor will I in the accident lawsuit as we had no knowledge of the cement company cutting corners. Our invoices show that we paid for the best even though it wasn't delivered. However, our legal fees are enormous and it still isn't settled. They have indicted Johnny Rivera who ran the cement company but that trial needs to be completed before the lawsuit is heard."

Liz said gently as she hugged Kaitlin, "At least that part is good, and we'll work on Mr. Bruno Gersbach about the financing."

After Liz got back to the office she phoned Paul Navarro, the manager of the Grand Miami Beach. "Hey, Paul," she asked, "do you remember a guest named Bruno Gersbach staying at the hotel recently?"

"How could I forget him, Kaitlin," he said, "for he stayed in our most expensive penthouse suite and paid the entire bill in cash. I understand that he is a very important business man from Switzerland and he was most generous with his tips according to the staff that waited on him. Any particular reason you asked, Kaitlin?"

"He moved into my mother's neighborhood and I was just curious, Paul. Glad to hear that he was a reliable guest on his visit with you," she said not wanting to reveal the real reason for her inquiry. After she hung up the phone she called her mother, "He got a good report from the Grand Miami Beach. Maybe we have found our 'white knight'."

That evening she received a call from Mr. Gersbach, "Elizabeth, are you still willing to give me the grand tour of Miami? Do you have a day this week where you would be available for the whole day and evening? I'd like to take you out to dinner as a reward for your tour. You can choose your favorite restaurant in Miami or Miami Beach." Before she could answer he laughed, "And mind you this is not a date!"

She grinned, "How would tomorrow be? I'll plan our itinerary tonight. What time do you want to start out and do you have any special places you would like to visit?"

"Tomorrow would be great. Let's start early and end late! I'll pick you up at 9 a.m. and anything you plan will be fine with me." He thought to himself, "This is working out a lot easier than I thought. Elizabeth, you don't know what you are getting into."

That night Carlos dreamed of taking over the Grand Hotel dynasty and at last getting even with the woman who had caused him so much pain and grief and years behind bars.

CHAPTER 48—PRESENT DAY

Bruno arrived at Liz's doorstep exactly at 9 a.m. He had dressed carefully with white slacks and a well-tailored navy-blue sports coat. Liz also found herself taking extra care in choosing a becoming outfit and she looked slim and beautiful in her white designer pant suit. She had to admit that she was a little nervous about touring the city with this handsome and distinguished man who she barely knew.

She offered him coffee on the terrace but he was anxious to leave and quickly escorted her out to his gleaming Mercedes-Benz. She suggested that perhaps she should drive as she knew the city so well, but he insisted on doing it.

"You should be free to be the tour guide and not have to worry about driving," he insisted as she pulled out her suggested itinerary.

"I thought we would start out with sights in the vicinity. If you are interested in gardens we are very close to Fairchild Gardens and they are magnificent. Also, the Viscaya mansion and gardens are close by," she said as they drove along Old Cutler Road.

"I'm a stranger in these parts, Liz, so I'm going to leave the day up to you. Anything you think is worth seeing is alright with me," he said agreeably as they pulled into the Gardens.

"My ancestors were early pioneers here in Miami, Bruno. My grandfather, Aidin Donegon came down here in 1896 to clear the land for the first railroad and the first luxury hotel. My father, Calvin Donegon not only helped to build our hotel business but also had a stint as a pilot with the original Pan-American Airways which started in Miami. Unfortunately, he was also killed flying a bomber over Berlin in World War II. So you see the history of early Miami has always been part of my life."

As they boarded the tram at the entrance she continued her narrative, "Fairchild Garden goes way back to 1938 and as you see is in a beautiful location, right on the Bay. You will see every kind of tropical plant imaginable and when we are in the rain forest you will think we are in the jungles of South America."

Bruno thought to himself, "The last thing I need to see is a bunch of plants unless of course it is a field of marijuana." Instead he feigned an interest in everything the tram guide had to say as she pointed out each plant and imparted too much information on each one in Bruno's opinion. But he could see that Elizabeth was enthralled even though she had probably toured the gardens a million times.

Next they stopped off at Viscaya and Bruno found the opulent Italian Renaissance-style villa more to his liking. "Who built this mansion, Liz?" he asked with curiosity. He had never taken time to see it when he first arrived from Cuba and made Miami his home.

Liz smiled, "It was built for the industrialist James Deering in 1916. Wait until you see the formal gardens. They are magnificent!" They toured the house with a docent who explained the 15th to 19th century furniture, tapestries, paintings and decorative arts.

Bruno only half heard what she was saying as he looked out at the villa's location on Biscayne Bay with what looked like a stone boat docking area which he thought would be perfect for smuggling drugs. A cigarette boat could come in from the sea and be hidden from the sight of the Coast Guard. The cigarette boats were streamlined speed boats commonly used by drug smugglers because of their intense speed. They literally flew through the water sometimes with the Coast Guard in hot pursuit.

Liz smiled noting his concentration and thought, "Mr. Gersbach really seems interested in the seaside grounds."

"Let me show you the secret garden," she teased.

"That sounds promising," he said as he took her arm. She looked a little surprised but tried not to show it.

They passed beautiful fountains, sculptures, elegant pools, a Florentine gazebo and finally arrived at the secret garden. They sat for a few moments in seclusion and Bruno put his arm around her shoulder, "How am I so lucky to get such a beautiful and intelligent tour guide?" he asked.

Liz was flustered. It had been a long time since she had been in the company of such an attractive man. She still missed her husband Andy who she had loved passionately during all the years of their marriage, and she had never even considered that one day another man might appeal to her. The thought had never entered her mind. But there was something about Bruno that seemed familiar, like she had known him all her life even though they had only met a few days before.

She hated herself for blushing but this attention was making her nervous. She had planned to make their day all business and she was beginning to have other thoughts that embarrassed her. Trying to hide these new unexpected feelings she said briskly, "Oh, I am sure that there are much more professional tour guides. But I do have the love of Miami's history and for me it's such fun to introduce it to someone new, especially a foreigner like yourself. I know you said you had been here on business trips but perhaps with my family background I will be able to provide you with more insights."

"What's next on the agenda, lovely lady?" he asked as they drove out of the spacious grounds of the estate.

"I don't know how much you know about the great Cuban exodus after Castro took over the Island, but here in Miami it has had a profound effect on our culture," she explained.

Bruno aka Carlos nearly smashed into a car he was so startled by her statement. Surely she hadn't seen through his disguise so soon. That would ruin everything!

"Oh, be careful, Bruno. These Miami drivers are a little wild. You really have to drive defensively. When my grandfather first came to Miami it was only a straggly village and now look at the traffic! But the reason I mentioned it is that there is a neighborhood called 'Little Havana" where many of the Cuban exiles settled. I thought you might find it interesting to stroll through that area and seeing it's getting on toward lunch time,

I can suggest a very good Cuban restaurant that serves excellent Cuban dishes and delicious Sangria."

"Dios mios!" Carlos thought. "That was where I lived when I first came to Miami and I wonder if she is taking me to the same restaurant that the two of us used to go to when we were engaged! This was not good!"

Liz continued her history lesson as she directed him to Calle Ocho. "When I graduated from the University of Miami, I had majored in Spanish and soon was hired to resettle Cuban immigrants. We processed them at Freedom Tower which I will point out to you when we get into downtown Miami. There was an early influx in the 60ties when Castro overthrew Batista in Cuba. There was a flood of immigrants, enough children to fill 52 new schools in Miami. Of course, what it meant was overcrowded classrooms as schools are not built that fast. We gave each family one hundred dollars and food stamps from the U.S. government."

Carlos was decidedly nervous seeing he was one of the recipients of the early handout and actually first laid eyes on Liz when he was being processed. This subject was too close for comfort. "I speak several languages but never learned Spanish," he said trying to change the subject as it was making him very uncomfortable.

"The first wave of refugees brought their family wealth, jewels and bank accounts. But many of the transplants were professionals and arrived with only a few dollars in their pockets and had to take on menial jobs to support their families. I was engaged to a Cuban man before I met my husband. He was trying to regain his medical license in the U.S. and taking classes at the University of Miami. Many of the exiles advanced in their fields as time went on and became influential in the community," she explained wondering why Bruno seemed to be squirming in his seat.

"I take it you didn't marry the Cuban man you were engaged to. Am I being too nosy? If so, you don't need to answer my question," he said starting to panic.

"I'd rather not get into that subject, Bruno. It is highly personal. All I will say is the relationship changed and after we broke up, I reconnected with my husband, Andy, who I had known since I was a small child," she sighed not wanting to recall unpleasant memories of the failed and painful relationship with her Cuban fiancé.

Carlos couldn't help it, he wanted to know more. Especially whether she was seeing Andy before she broke their engagement so he asked, "I don't need all the details, but was the fact that the man you were engaged to was Cuban that caused you to change your mind?"

"Oh, no! I love the Cuban people. Don't forget I worked with getting them settled, introducing them to the new community." She paused, "You may remember the failed 'Bay of Pigs' invasion in Cuba. Kennedy was president of the United States at that time and made his first major mistake. He was secretly planning an attack which was named 'the Bay of Pigs'. The Cubans suspected an invasion was coming and were well-prepared. 200 soldiers were killed and over one thousand captured and put in prison. My fiancé lost several close friends and family members and I'm afraid he became a changed personality after that. Very bitter outlook on life."

Carlos pulled into the Little Havana area, "Now where do we park? We can talk more about this over a coffee. Tell me how the Cuban coffee differs from the espresso that we so love in Europe?" He recognized all the landmarks of his former life and hoped he wasn't giving away anything.

Liz smiled, "We'll try some at the restaurant. I have become addicted to it unfortunately for it's very strong and sweet-flavored and gives you a caffeine and sugar rush. However, it is worth it as Cuban coffee is wonderful. I hope you will enjoy it!"

They pulled into the parking lot of a restaurant and Carlos did a double take for it was the restaurant that he used to take Liz to, "That sounds like a French restaurant. Versailles? Are you sure it is still a Cuban restaurant?"

Liz laughed, "Oh, yes, but the name is misleading!"

Carlos wasn't sure he was ready to walk down memory lane with his former fiancé so he said, "I'm not hungry yet. Let's walk around a bit and work up an appetite."

Liz agreed and she continued her narrative about Cuba as they strolled down the streets of 'Little Havana'. A vibrant Hispanic culture permeates everything and Carlos felt right at home. They passed colorful murals and monuments to Cuban heroes past and present. They passed by a small park where elderly men were playing dominos in the bright sunshine. "This is aptly named 'Domino Park'," Liz explained while Carlos stopped to watch the moves the men were making with the dominoes.

They next stopped to watch the cigar rollers deeply at work amidst the aroma of Cuban Coffee which permeated the streets of 'Little Havana'. They stopped at an outdoor vendor and Liz ordered two Cuban coffees for them. Carlos had a hard time pretending that it was a new experience for him. He loved his Cuban coffee but instead said, "I'm afraid it's a little too sweet for my liking but thanks anyway."

Liz looked a little disappointed at his reaction as she savored her coffee in the small cup. They found a bench and she continued, "In the 80ties there was a new influx of refugees from Cuba from Mariel. Unfortunately, Castro emptied the mental institutions and prisons and sent his most undesirable citizens to Miami in boatloads. But they were not all bad apples. My daughter's fiancé, John Martinez who is the CFO of the company was one of them. My sister-in-law, Emily, also married a Cuban man, but sadly the marriage failed." Carlos knew she was talking about his brother, Raul, and thought it wise not to explore that further.

"You told me that your daughter is CEO of the company and you now tell me that this Cuban man is also her CFO. How is that working out? Sometimes relationships with a business partner don't work out too well," he added. "At least that has been my experience."

"She and John have worked together for years and he was very supportive when my husband died." She paused for a moment wondering if now was the time to say anything, "Bruno, I'm afraid we are in a little financial trouble at the moment but it has nothing to do with John. A worker was injured seriously in one of our hotel renovations in New York and the District Attorney is investigating safety violations. We have always used top quality materials and labor so it seems there might have been some underhanded stuff going on without our knowledge. But unfortunately, construction has halted due to the investigation and costs are mounting."

Carlos was quick to note her worry and frustration and knew that Rivera and his mob-connections were involved but he didn't show a sign of understanding any of it, "That must be difficult to deal with. According to what you told me the company has been run by several generations of your family."

Liz frowned, "Yes, and now it appears that someone may be trying to takeover our company. At least my daughter strongly suspects foul play."

Carlos feigned surprise, "Do you mean a hostile takeover?"

"I'm afraid that is just what she suspects and it looks like bankruptcy might be just around the corner if our expenses keep mounting," she sighed. "But let's not ruin our day, Bruno, as there is something I want to show you."

They continued walking silently both engrossed in their own thoughts when they came to SW 13 St. where Carlos saw the series of monuments of Cuban patriots and freedom fighters. He was speechless as all the memories of those days came flooding into his mind. Finally, he took Liz's arm and said, "Enough of the serious matters for today. Let me try that Cuban food that you've been telling me about."

After they had perused the menu Carlos' mouth was watering. Not thinking he started to order in Spanish, "Puerco asado, frijoles negroes...", he stopped noting Liz's stunned face. He laughed, "We Europeans know all the romance languages and we have a branch of the bank in Spain. I don't really speak Spanish, but I do know some of the restaurant items."

"But your accent seemed so authentic, Bruno. You certainly are a man of many talents!" she commented.

After a pitcher of Sangria Liz found herself laughing at Bruno's dry wit and enjoying his appreciation of the Cuban food. She was having a wonderful time, so when he suggested a trip over the causeway to Miami Beach and the Art Deco section of South Beach that he had heard so much about, she found herself joyfully anticipating spending the afternoon and evening with him. She thought to herself as he left a huge tip on the table and paid the bill, "Kaitlin, perhaps I have found someone to rescue the company, our 'white knight'."

CHAPTER 49—PRESENT DAY

As they drove over the causeway they passed some cruise ships waiting to depart for the Caribbean. Liz turned to Bruno and said, "My grandfather was here when they dredged Government Cut which is the passage way from Miami to the Atlantic Ocean. You wouldn't see all these beautiful big cruise ships if that hadn't happened. As you know Miami Beach is on an island and before these causeways were constructed people had to reach it by boat. Oh, Bruno, look at that island to the left! That is where the house of the gangster, Al Capone, once lived. My grandfather said the rich neighbors were not too pleased with the new resident."

Carlos had always admired Capone, but kept his feelings to himself. As they continued he pointed out an island to the right of the causeway, "Is that another enclave of the very rich?"

Liz responded, "Well, you might say so. That is Fisher Island and the residents have to reach it by boat or ferry. From time to time my family has stayed in a villa there and it is a spectacular setting with perfectly manicured lawns, exotic birds walking all around, white sandy beaches and a stunning harbor. They have a 9-hole golf course in case you like golf, Bruno. It's actually a golf cart community. You never see a car. We joined a croquet party there once and everyone wore white."

"Maybe I should have bought a place there," he said. "How much are the condos?"

"They are millions of dollars, maybe some are less now because of the recession but as far as I have heard that is one place where real estate has kept its value." She gave him a questioning look, "Would you really prefer a condo over the beautiful estates in our lovely area on Biscayne Bay?"

"Probably not. I think that the realtor mentioned it. Wasn't it once the home of the Vanderbilts?"

"Yes, the main house on the islands belonged to the Vanderbilts and later several other millionaires. It was sold to developers in the 1960s. It has remained a wealthy and exclusive community. But I love the area we live in and wouldn't trade my place for ten of these condos!" she exclaimed.

They had a hard time finding a parking place in the Art Deco section of Miami Beach, so finally Carlos who was exasperated chose valet parking in front of a lively beachfront outdoor café. They stopped to sip a cold drink before strolling down the interesting and vibrant street.

Liz explained, "Tourists have been coming to Miami Beach since the 1920's to escape from ordinary lives and to share the sand with millionaires, bathing beauties, movie stars and presidents. My ancestors built many of the original Art Deco Hotels along Ocean Drive. In fact, you may have heard of my daughter's phenomenal success in building boutique hotels. Her first one was on Miami Beach and we will stop there for you to see it. She has been written up in many magazines and newspapers and won an award for Entrepreneur of the Year. Sorry if I sound like I am bragging!"

"You have every right to brag. But tell me, how with such a successful business is it in trouble? It doesn't sound like one construction accident should bring down the whole company," he asked with curiosity.

"Well, my daughter has used a lot of capital to build these new boutique hotels all over the country and globe, and now with the delays and large legal fees and money not being fluid right now, she is possibly looking for an investor," Liz said glumly. "She hates to sell off any of our existing hotels in this poor market for commercial real estate. Also, as I explained some mysterious things have happened to cause her to fear a hostile takeover."

Bruno took some time sipping his drink and thinking so Liz finally broke the silence, "Penny for your thoughts, Bruno. I'm sorry to have brought up unpleasant subjects on our beautiful day. I hope I haven't ruined it!"

"I have been thinking, Liz. As you know I am establishing an investment branch of my Swiss bank here in Miami. The Grand Hotels have a wonderful reputation globally and when I get more information and see your annual reports, I might consider investing in your company. When there is a hostile takeover like you hint at, sometimes another 'White Knight' investor comes along to help a firm get out of the hole.' The Knight' investor comes in as a friendly partner in contrast to your hostile suspect and rebuilds the firm and integrates it into itself. Possibly our investment company could serve as a friendly 'white knight' partner," he explained.

"That's awfully kind of you, Bruno. If you like I can put you in touch with John Martinez, our Chief Financial Officer," she said smiling and liking what she had heard from Bruno.

Carlos was thinking to himself, "I can't wait to meet that Cuban dude. He must be taking a cut from Rivera Cement and who knows how many other projects. There has to be someone high up in the company skimming accounts." Instead he replied, "Yes, I will talk to him and see if an investment is feasible for us at this time. But for now, let's look around a bit. It looks like a lively place to stay." He surprised Liz by taking her hand as they walked.

They walked past the pastel Art Deco hotels and sidewalk cafes enjoying the ocean breezes off the Atlantic. Carlos noticed all the bikini-clad beauties gathered around the hotel swimming pools and just about every location had a photo shoot with glamorous models. They could hear all the European languages as South Beach was a tourist Mecca and drew an international crowd from around the globe. The glamorous beautiful people were sipping drinks and laughing. For atmosphere Carlos noticed vintage cars of the old days in mint condition parked along the curb in front of the resorts. He thought how the area had changed since he went to prison. It was like a new, sophisticated, swinging world. He had missed half his life due to this woman and her husband. He tried hard to hide his bitterness as it was there constantly waiting to creep out.

"The movie star Clark Gable was here in service during World War II. They used these Art Deco hotels to house the military. Can you imagine an assignment like that!" she laughed. "In the 50's it was Frank Sinatra and the Rat Pack, in the 60's Jackie Gleason and the Beatles. In the 80's the TV series *Miami Vice* put the area in the limelight. Then Madonna and Stallone bought mansions in Miami and Versace, the designer who was murdered, lived right here on Ocean Drive in this mansion we are passing. And then the supermodels arrived who you see posing all around, movies being filmed with this as a background and celebrities rubbing elbows with the tourists!"

They briefly stopped at the Grand Miami Beach Boutique Hotel and Bruno raved about the innovations. "I really am getting intrigued with investing in your project. If this is an example of your Boutique Hotel line, I'm sold! You know there have been many of these friendly mergers in the past few years. Bayer acted as a white knight to Schering Pharmaceuticals in 2006, JPMorgan Chase acquired Bear Stearns allowing Stearns to avoid insolvency in 2008. Last year Fiat took over Chrysler to save them from liquidation."

"I'm afraid I don't understand the financial end of the business but I know Kaitlin and John will be interested in what you are proposing. I'm so happy you like the Boutique Hotel, Bruno. I am sure that John will give you a complimentary suite for a visit if you would like a closer look at what we are offering here." Carlos glanced at the curvy blonde with her voluptuous breasts fully exposed sitting by the pool and thought he might just enjoy that. He thought of all the years he had been celibate living in the prison and felt the anger rising in him again. The prospect of taking over the Grand Hotels tempered his anger and bitterness. Now it looked even more promising.

"Where would you like to have dinner, Liz? You know the area and the good places and I'm sure there are plenty of good ones in the area," Carlos said as the valet brought the car to the curb.

Liz thought for a moment, "Have you ever tried stone crabs, Bruno? There is a restaurant that specializes in them that is not too far away."

Carlos could have predicted that it would be another restaurant that was a favorite of theirs during their courtship. First the Versailles and now he guessed Joe's Stone Crabs. He answered, "It sounds good to me, Liz. Yes, I tried stone crabs on one of my previous business trips to Miami and I liked them very much. Let's try your favorite restaurant that specializes in them. How do we get there?" Of course he didn't need driving directions but pretended that it was all new territory to him. He also knew that there were specific seating times at the restaurant because it was always crowded. He hated to wait but thought maybe he could talk their way in.

When they were finally seated at a table after downing a few drinks while they were waiting Liz continued her Cuban narrative while they munched on the succulent jumbo stone crabs which they dipped in a special mustard sauce, "I'm glad you like the stone crabs, Bruno. The hash browns and Cole slaw are delicious too, aren't they? I didn't finish giving you the history of Miami's relationship with Cuba. You seemed so interested in the monuments to the Freedom Fighters in 'Little Havana'."

"Yes, do carry on, Liz. Do you mind if I light up one of the Cuban hand-rolled cigars I bought?" They were in the smoking section so she nodded that it was alright with her.

"Way back in my grandfather's pioneer days in Miami he was asked to form a military company during the Spanish-American War. Are you familiar with that, Bruno?" she asked. He looked blank so she continued. "The Spanish weren't treating the Cubans fairly and they revolted. The conflict went on for a long time and over a quarter of the Cuban population died and parts of the island were destroyed. The United States sent a battleship to protect any Americans who might be living there but the ship blew up in the Havana Harbor killing several hundred people on board."

"I remember the slogan, 'remember the *Maine*'," Bruno said.

"Yes President McKinley demanded full independence for Cuba and Congress authorized the military to force the Spanish to leave the island. Miamians fully expected a Spanish warship to fire on their city and a near panic existed when all the able-bodied men became the Miami Minute Men under the leadership of my grandfather, Aidin. They trained on the grounds of the Royal Palm Hotel, the first luxury hotel in Miami."

"What happened? Were they ever attacked?" Bruno asked.

"Luckily no shots were ever fired from Miami. A few years later a Cuban sailor brought the Yellow Fever Plague to Miami which really decimated the population. They actually had a quarantine and people were not allowed out of the city!" Carlos frowned. It seemed to him that Liz was blaming his homeland for a lot of Miami's problems.

"I guess in the old days you could reach Cuba in about 30 minutes by plane from Key West." He felt the anger and the color rising in his face, "The embargo your President Bush placed on the Cuban people is very unfair. I'm sure many of their people are suffering. And the same policy continues with your President Obama. Also, it is ridiculous not to let people travel from the United States to Cuba by plane. We could travel there from Europe but not from Miami!"

"You can always leave from Mexico or Canada. Some people who have very good reasons can get permission from the government, but it's impossible for a tourist to get permission to leave from the U.S.," she sighed. "I hope you aren't getting bored, Bruno, but it was our proximity to Cuba that caused all the anxiety here in Miami during the Cuban Missile Crisis. After all Cuba is only 90 miles from the U.S. and when the people of Miami learned that Soviet offensive missiles were being installed in Cuba in the 60ties they became very nervous! But they responded like they had learned in the past to prepare for a hurricane by laying in extra food, supplies and drinking water. Some Miamians just packed up and left the fear was so great!"

"We Swiss people try to stay neutral in conflicts and I think that is the best policy. I certainly do remember your President Kennedy announcing that your country was on wartime alert. Everyone in Europe was afraid it would start World War III." Little did Liz know that she and Bruno aka Carlos had joined thirty thousand cheering Cubans in the Miami Orange Bowl Stadium after the Russians agreed to remove their missiles if the United States would never invade Cuba. That had not made Carlos happy! He had been hoping they would retake the island and oust Castro once and for all. The cheering was not for the promise not to invade, but because a prisoner exchange had been made and the President had come to Miami to pay his respect to the men of the Brigade that participated in the failed invasion of Cuba in the 'Bay of Pigs' attack. The memories of the heartache of his exile friends whose hopes were dashed that they might never be able to return to the homeland while Castro ruled the island with an iron fist overwhelmed Carlos' mind and he suddenly seemed pensive and silent to Elizabeth.

"I'm sorry, Bruno. Surely you have learned more about Cuba today than you needed. Because of my job where I was so closely attached to the Cuban community, I tend to dwell on some of those experiences and I am sure you've heard enough by now."

Carlos paid the bill and ushered her out. He was glum and depressed and had a hard time being civil. "I think I am too tired now to try out some of those hot South Beach Clubs that I have read about. If it's alright with you, Liz, I would like to call it a day."

Liz was aware of the change in atmosphere and couldn't imagine what she had done to cause the change. "I'm tired, too, Bruno, so let's head for home."

They hardly spoke on the drive back over the causeway to Miami. As he walked to the door with Elizabeth he said, "Thank you for the day. It has been most enjoyable. And, I would like to meet with John Martinez and hear more about the Grand Hotels and how I can help with your current problem."

"I'll tell John that you might be interested and I'm sure you will hear from him. I enjoyed our day, Bruno," she said politely, then added, "and I hope you will allow me to show you more of Miami. I promise not to dwell on Cuban history the next time we meet."

Carlos was trying very hard to control his anger. As he walked back to his car after shaking her hand formally, his hatred started to boil over. It had been held at bay all day and he needed to vent. He screeched out on Old Cutler and sped to Matheson's Hammock, a marina on the bay before heading home. He parked in an empty space and bowed his head, hitting it several times on the steering wheel. He thought of stealing a boat and going for a joy ride, but then he didn't want the Coast Guard on his tail. He reached in the glove compartment and took out a joint and took a few hits.

The moon shone down on him as he started to relax. He took a few more hits on the joint and felt a sudden euphoria. The sea and moon and tropical plants reminded him of Havana, his homeland.

As he walked along the shore in the moonlight he thought to himself, "As painful as it was to be with Elizabeth again, I am getting closer to my goal. Revenge is so sweet. And I intend to savor every moment of pain I can inflict on her."

CHAPTER 50—PRESENT DAY

John Martinez was very worried as he assessed the current financial position of the Grand Hotels. He was worried also about his own personal finances. He had gone way out on the limb buying Kaitlin that expensive diamond ring and he had made an offer on a house on Old Cutler Road thinking that he was soon due for a huge bonus.

Now this mess with the unions demanding pay for all the weeks the damn Building Department had shut the Grand New York reconstruction down in addition to skyrocketing legal bills. They had expected the hotel to be ready for business a long time ago and here this investigation stretched on endlessly.

He had taken out some short term construction loans thinking that all the new business at the Grand New York would cover them. And now to compound it, the credit market was collapsing and the banks were hollering for repayment of their loans. The thought of an extension back in the days before the country's financial downfall was now out of the question. On paper it looked like the company had plenty of money, but actually the assets were all in the hotels and with the current real estate market nobody was looking to buy a hotel for the true value.

To make it worse, he had taken some money from the construction of the European boutique hotels so that he could keep up with the lifestyle he had gotten used to. It was fairly easy at first finding contractors who would overbill. So what if they skimmed some off the top for being given the contract. He deserved a little extra for all his hard work. Nothing had ever happened in the past until the Rivera concrete fiasco.

It looked like a perfect deal and he needed a huge down payment on the new house. Rivera's offer came at just the right time. He had suggested using David Wells as a middle man and to his knowledge he was sure that Wells was not aware of his involvement. Rivera had assured him of that. But now, Rivera was indicted and was going to trial unless he could make a deal with the DA. He was worried sick that Rivera would squeal on him when he got to the witness stand.

He loved Kaitlin and had tried to please her with the ring and the new estate. But now she could possibly lose a business that dated back to the 1900's if the company went bankrupt and insolvent due to lack of funds. Investors would smell blood if they put up some hotels for sale way below market value and they would be fair game for a hostile takeover. Kaitlin and her family would lose everything and so would he. He'd never get a decent job again. This would be viewed as his failure by the world of finance.

John poured himself a drink and phoned Rivera in a panic, "Hey, it's John. I just want your reassurance that you will not involve me in your testimony. That's what you promised."

Rivera paused then let fly a series of expletives, "You dumb jerk, if revealing your involvement will get me a reduced sentence or a plea bargain I won't hesitate. John, admit it, this mess is as much your fault as it is mine. You agreed to the overbilling and wanted a payoff and you certainly profited from the deal so stop whining like a kid who got caught with his fingers in the cookie jar!"

"But you never told me you were going to cut corners and bring about a safety issue. I would never have agreed to the deal if I knew you were risking the safety of the workers!" he said angrily.

"You asshole, don't you think I know you have been in this payola game for a long time. Word gets around. Why do you think I approached you in the first place? I knew you were a greedy son-of-a-bitch and would jump at my offer!" Rivera shouted.

"Listen, I'm warning you, Rivera, not to involve me in your problem. You caused the accident by cutting corners," John threatened.

Rivera laughed, "Oh, I'm so scared, Johnny Boy. By the way, I am informing you that this conversation is all on tape. If I get convicted and have to serve time, you are going down with me!"

John sat there stunned. This whole thing had snowballed and was getting worse by the moment. At that moment his phone rang and his secretary said, "A Mr. Bruno Gersbach is on the line and wants to talk to you about a possible investment to help your company. Do you want to talk to him?"

He was still shaking as he replied, "Set up an appointment with him. I can't take any calls right now." He sat there painfully thinking of seeing Kaitlin that night. How long could he hide this from her? How do you tell someone they are losing their company and that he had been responsible for the financial catastrophe that was bringing it down.

CHAPTER 51—2009

Bill was improving by leaps and bounds and his efforts to reach recovery from his traumatic brain injury had really paid off. After starting to learn to speak again he had patiently practiced saying words and reading sentences to little Billy from his children's books. Now he had almost returned to his old pre-war persona and was increasing his time at work from part-time to full-time at the newspaper and his eye for the good photograph was just as keen as in the past.

When he had a chance he loved to do free-lance photography and he was continuing to work on the second edition of his photo essay of his son to document each stage of his growth in touching photographs. He and Billy had developed a deep bond and even though he still had occasional flashbacks of the painful combat experiences, they happened less frequently. Autumn was such a loving, supportive wife and he wondered how he could have gotten through this painful aftermath of his wartime service without the loving support of his family.

Unfortunately, the nation wasn't doing as well. When the economy had slowed in early 2008 President George W. Bush and Congress had agreed on a plan consisting mostly of tax cuts. When it teetered at the brink in late 2008 even after the Fed cut rates to practically zero, pressure grew for a large-scale stimulus, and Mr. Obama began working on one even before taking office. In February, 2009 the Democratic Congress passed a $787 billion dollar stimulus bill requested by the now President Obama to shore up the failing economy and stave off a depression.

Autumn and Bill were sitting at Kaitlin and John's having after-dinner coffee when Kaitlin moaned, "Business has really fallen off during this recession. People who formerly took vacations every year are postponing their plans waiting for better times. We have had to lay off some employees to keep up with our dwindling profits."

Bill piped in, "The unemployment rate is up to almost 10 percent. The property values here in Miami have dropped drastically. The worst part is so many families are losing their homes to foreclosure. I have been given an assignment to photograph the new Miami homeless people who formerly had jobs, homes and a decent life and are now living in cars, in outdoor encampments or trying to get a space in a shelter for the night. Whole families have been affected and it's bad enough seeing the despair of the parents, but the newly homeless children are completely stunned. They have not only been uprooted from their homes but their schools and their friends. It is heartbreaking for me to see so many suffering."

"What about the Rescue Missions for the homeless? Can't they help these poor people?" John asked.

"They are trying, but the numbers are staggering. I'm afraid we are about to see the return of the Soup Kitchens of the Great Depression where people lined up for a bowl of soup when they were hungry," Bill answered shaking his head sadly.

"Let's pray that the stimulus package helps," Autumn sighed.

"Just how can that help when things are going downhill so fast?" Kaitlin asked.

Autumn explained, "It's supposed to replace money not being paid by businesses or consumers. It's meant to put a floor under a recession and pave the way for a return to growth of the economy."

"Sadly, the Republicans and the Tea Party conservatives are bitterly attacking the idea of the stimulus and it has become a radioactive word," John said frowning as he sipped his coffee. "President Obama has his plate full with the big deficit and two wars which he inherited from the Bush administration."

"It looks like we will have to hold back our plans for expansion by stopping the construction of new boutique hotels if this continues. Unless business improves soon and people start traveling again we will be in deep financial trouble," Kaitlin said with a worried expression on her pretty face.

Little did she realize the problems that lay ahead of her in the year to come. Earthshaking revelations that would turn her world upside down. She didn't realize that evening that the lack of people traveling would only be a small fraction of the trials she would be forced to face. Pandora's box was opening and heartache was at her doorstep.

But that evening ended on a warm, happy note as she hugged Autumn and Bill as they left.

She and John watched the couple walk toward the elevator at their penthouse hand in hand. They could hear them laughing and things were finally back to normal after Bill's long and painful recovery.

Kaitlin smiled, "Isn't it wonderful to see them so happy? Bill's recovery has been remarkable!"

John looked at Kaitlin, "Are we o.k.? Are you happy, Kaitlin?"

"Divinely happy with you, John, even though the business side of my life is on a downslide," she said hugging him. "Do you want me to prove it?" she asked pushing John toward the bedroom.

The decade mark since her beloved father's death and Kaitlin's advance to head of the Grand Hotels was coming to a close. So far her rise to power had been brilliant. Her beautiful face had graced the cover of many of the major magazines as "Woman Entrepreneur of the Year". She was known all over the globe for her business acumen and forward-thinking projects.

But for such a young woman to rise so quickly to the top of her field there was no place left but down. The forces of evil had set their sights on her success and she would have to wage the hardest battle of her young life in the year to come. The Decade of Deceit was rearing its ugly face and her life would never be the same.

PART TWO
2010
THE DECADE OF DECEIT (2000-2010)

CHAPTER 52—2010

Carlos had requested a meeting with both John and Kaitlin. "Two birds with one stone," he mused. He thought he looked the picture of a wealthy, distinguished business man as he was escorted into Kaitlin's gigantic office overlooking Biscayne Bay. He quickly took note of how attractive she was and how John Martinez stood next to her like a protective guard dog. It was obvious that John was Hispanic from his dark, handsome good looks. Carlos already suspected that he was somehow in on the take with Rivera since his conversation with Raul who had told him Rivera hinted at Martinez' involvement. He was quite sure Kaitlin was not aware of it.

He shook hands with both of them and explained that he was starting an investment branch of his Swiss bank in Miami and that he had moved into the same neighborhood as Kaitlin's mother.

"Your charming mother, Elizabeth, gave me the Grand Tour of Miami the other day. Of course, it wasn't my first visit but the others were business trips and I didn't see much of the city. She mentioned that you were experiencing some financial problems due to delays in your renovation of your New York Hotel and that there was some sort of investigation going on that was costing you a pile of money. Is that correct?" he said noticing the gigantic diamond ring on her left hand. "That must have cost Martinez a fortune," he thought suspiciously.

John and Kaitlin glanced at each other with a look that said, "Maybe mother had done too much talking". John replied rather curtly, "Yes, that is essentially the picture, but we have many assets as you can imagine with hotels all over the world."

Bruno quickly responded, "Yes, but in this current economy, selling a hotel in this market is out of the question, isn't it? If you offer it for a lower price than its value, it's a true tip-off to the market that you're in big trouble."

"What are you proposing then?" John said quickly getting to the point.

"I would like to look over your current financial picture and study your annual reports for the past 10 years. If everything is in order, I might be prepared to be your 'White Knight' and invest a sizable cash infusion to help your company," he offered noting the look of dismay on Kaitlin's face.

"I don't think you understand, Mr Gersbach. This corporation was started way back in the 1900's by my great-grandfather, Aidin Donegon, who was one of the first builders in Miami. My grandfather, Calvin, continued the legacy followed by my father, Andrew, who passed away about 10 years ago. At that time, I carried the family banner and I'm proud to say the business has expanded under my leadership," she said rather huffily.

"No one doubts your success, Miss Donegon. The company would retain the Grand Hotel name and you would remain as CEO. Naturally, I would expect to be on the Board of Directors to oversee my financial investment in the company. You must bear in mind that once the vultures get wind of your current financial problems you will be vulnerable to a hostile takeover as I'm sure you know. You should take seriously the choice of a friendly investor like myself who will try to bolster the company rather than tear it down," he said patiently as he glanced around her office and imagined himself sitting in the chair behind the huge desk.

"You have a point worth considering, Mr. Gersbach, but of course as you peruse our records, we must also peruse your credentials." She turned to John, "Please make the information available for Mr. Gersbach. We both need to check each other out before the proceedings can continue further. We do thank you for your interest in our company and let's talk again in about a week. Please leave the information on your investment bank with Mr. Martinez. He is our Chief Financial Officer and should be able to answer any of your questions and I am sure he will have some questions for you."

Bruno had already set up a shell company in anticipation of their questions. Everything was already in place to establish himself in the business community. He had rented a "front" office in Coral Gables and had placed an ad in the newspaper for potential employees. He also was an excellent con man and very convincing in his approach to business. The first step had been taken and he had sized up John Martinez as a crook and opportunist even though it was fairly obvious that Kaitlin adored him.

After John gave the materials to Mr. Gersbach he was having second thoughts, "Was Gersbach smart enough to figure out the overbilling that he had allowed contractors with the pay back to him it involved?" The endless aftermath of the accident at the Grand New York had spiraled out of control and the cover-up was worse than the original crime. He was still very wary of Rivera taking him down with him. His conversation with Rivera had been really threatening and had shaken him up.

Then he would rationalize that Rivera was the guy responsible for the accident by switching the bad concrete to the job so he could make a little more on the deal. Just because he took a little reward for himself for giving bidders the contracts wasn't a crime. Almost everyone did it he told himself. He was certain Kaitlin wouldn't look at it this way and it might end their relationship if she ever found out the truth. That would kill him. He couldn't let that happen.

As soon as Carlos left the executive offices loaded down with annual reports and other financial graphs of the company's growth, he headed for his lunch date with Raul. After greeting his brother he asked, "What is going down with Rivera? Have you checked into the status of the case?"

"I hear through the grapevine that Rivera is going to claim Chapter 11 before the plaintiffs in the accident suit come for their dough for the settlement. His business is no longer worth shit and I guess his insurance company won't pay off because of his negligence in causing the accident. He's between a rock and a hard place," Raul reported.

"Hell, he's facing jail time anyway. That money isn't going to do him much good in the slammer. My bet is that he will be taking a plea but if that happens what are the chances that he will name Martinez if it comes to reducing his sentence?" Carlos asked as he munched on his Media Noche, a delicious Cuban sandwich.

"There's no doubt he will squeal if Martinez is really involved," Raul replied confidently. "He'll save his own ass."

"I don't give a damn about Rivera's ass but Martinez's involvement if it's publicly known could cause a scandal and destroy the company. It's time I made a personal visit to Rivera. His best course is to run if you know what I mean. I may have to use a little friendly persuasion. He might like South America. That's one of the best places to hide or if he refuses to run I'm sure I can still order a hit. I think he'll agree that running is his best option," Carlos said looking at his brother. "How would you like a little extra dough in your pocket?"

Raul frowned, "You have the connections! Get someone else. I'm trying to stay straight, maybe get Emily back in time."

Carlos laughed, "Don't worry, hermano, there are others more skilled at the job and not too hard to find here in Miami. By the way, it's time you came to see my new house on the bay. Everything I always dreamed about when I was rotting away in that cell. Just be sure not to call when Elizabeth is visiting!"

"Hey, Carlos, are you doing her?" Raul asked with enthusiasm.

"I don't want to rush things, Bro, contrary to your coming on to Emily the first time you dated her. But mark my words, it won't be long before it happens. I not only will own her family business but her soul," Carlos said rocking with laughter as he pounded his brother on his back.

CHAPTER 53—2010

As Kaitlin sat glumly considering accepting Bruno Gersbach's generous offer she felt like she was drowning, being pulled rapidly into the river's current pushing her toward calamity. She felt like she was losing hold of her company, started and developed by her ancestors before her. Could she trust Gersbach to keep his hands off the company? Was he really the 'white knight' trying to save the company or did he intend to try to take it over himself? John had been acting so peculiar lately that she didn't know who to trust.

While she was pondering her options, her secretary, Jan Summers rang her up.

"Sorry to bother you but your lawyer Bryon Harrell is here insisting on seeing you right away. I told him you were busy but he won't take no for an answer," she apologized.

"Send him in, Jan. I need to talk to him," Kaitlin answered as she thought, "I can run this by Bryon. He's someone who has always been trustworthy in the past. Maybe he can help me focus. I'm too emotionally involved in this issue."

Bryon noticed immediately that Kaitlin was not her usual, calm self. She appeared to be very upset. He hated to upset her further, but he needed to be honest with her. The worst part is that he couldn't deny that he was having serious personal feelings about her that had nothing to do with business.

"I'm sorry to interrupt you, Kaitlin, but I felt I needed to talk to you about a new issue," he said gently. "You seem to be terribly upset about something. Can I help in any way?"

"First tell me about the new issue. I don't know if I can face another problem. It seems like Pandora's Box has opened these days and one problem after another comes rushing out at me!" she said looking depressed and frustrated.

Bryon went to the bar and asked, "Can I pour you a drink, Kaitlin? What I have to tell you may be a little shocking?"

"I make it a policy to not drink during my working hours, but somehow I think I may need one today so go ahead and pour," she said lighting up a cigarette even though she had given up smoking several years ago.

Bryon poured them both a scotch and then sat down next to Kaitlin on the leather couch. As they sipped their drinks he finally spoke, "I've had some access to the D.A's investigation and it seems like there are new issues concerning the billing of the construction."

Kaitlin gave him a piercing look, "What kind of new issues are you talking about?"

He hesitated before dropping the bomb, "It appears that John Martinez may be actively involved in the overbilling of the construction costs."

Kaitlin turned white and felt faint for a moment. Bryon tenderly held her as she dealt with the blow she had just received. Finally with a quaking voice she asked, "Do you have any facts to support this charge? I just can't believe John would do something like that. He has a very generous compensation package and is a 'company man'. Why would he need to do such a thing? You must be wrong, Bryon."

"I'm so sorry, Kaitlin, but reliable sources are telling me that he was involved in skimming in the Rivera cement job as well as other construction jobs on the boutique hotels in France and Scotland where he received payola for choosing the most expensive bidder on a job and was well paid for it," Bryon frowned.

"Are you saying John was responsible for the terrible accident at the construction site?" she said fearfully.

"No, I don't think he had anything to do with the accident or knew that Rivera would shirk on the job and use inferior products and labor.

I think he just thought he was being paid off for choosing the highest bidder for the job and that was Rivera."

"Who is your source for all this, Bryon? Surely it must be someone jealous of John's position in the company. It sounds like sour grapes," she tried to rationalize. "For God's sake, John is my fiancé! He just moved into our new house. It's our dream home on Old Cutler Road!"

Bryon held her hand and gazed at the huge diamond and then said, "And is his compensation package so generous that he can afford a ring like this and a dream house in one of the most affluent locations in Miami?" he asked Kaitlin.

"Who is your source, Bryon?" she repeated coldly.

"David Wells, Kaitlin. He was also involved in the construction skimming but on a smaller scale than John. However, he tells me that he had never been involved in any of the other payola schemes but was aware that John was and thought he'd get in on the action to quote him."

Kaitlin was now furious and her face was flushed with anger, "Send David Wells in here immediately. I want to hear it from his lips."

Bryon hesitated, "I'm afraid it's too late, Kaitlin. David Wells has gone on the "run". He made his confession to me before leaving. He has apparently been supporting a mistress and also was involved in an expensive divorce case. He's been hiding his payoff in an offshore bank somewhere in the Caribbean. He was afraid he might be charged with the accident and came to me for legal advice. Apparently, some threats were made by Rivera and Wells decided to come clean before he disappeared. I have no idea where he is now. He told me that he didn't want to take all the blame when Martinez was heavily involved."

"How is it possible that all this was going on and I never learned of it? Why wasn't I notified that Wells had left? Have I been off in outer space while this was happening right under my nose?"

Bryon hated to go further but he knew he should reveal all he had learned from David Wells. "Wells also told me that he was the one making the threatening phone calls to you. He was envious of John's position in the company which he felt he deserved and he thought that by making the calls it would cast suspicion on John and perhaps you would fire him and appoint him to John's position."

Kaitlin started to weep softly. Her whole world seemed to be crumbling around her. If this was true her most trusted friend and fiancé had betrayed her in the worst way and her heart was breaking. The General Manager of Domestic Development had also betrayed her and she had not even been aware of all the deceit surrounding her to compound the heartache.

Bryon pulled her up from the couch and put his arms around her. As she raised her beautiful face with tears rolling down her cheeks, he couldn't resist her. He wanted to protect her and take care of her. He held her face up and started kissing away her tears and before he knew it he was kissing her with such love and tenderness that Kaitlin found herself responding to him. The chemistry between them was unexpectedly explosive.

He had to order himself to stop when he realized what he was doing. "This isn't the time to do this and I apologize. I know you are vulnerable and unhappy and I don't want to take advantage of your position, but Kaitlin, I have realized for a long time that I am falling in love with you. I can tell by the way you kissed me that you also have some feelings toward me. I hope that in time when things get back to normal that you will give me a chance to win your heart," he said earnestly.

Kaitlin sighed, "Please leave me alone for now, Bryon. I have too much to sort through. I am so confused and devastated that I am in no position to answer you now. Let's forget what just happened between us. You are my friend and I trust you. That's all I can say to you at this time. I have many problems to deal with including an offer to buy the company. But I can't discuss that now. I am too upset to be rational. I am leaving now to go to my mother's house and try to digest the mess my life has become."

"Just remember, I will be here any time you call or need me," he said kissing her lightly as he turned to leave her office. She watched him walk out the door as she wondered what in the world would happen to heal the wounds and save her beloved company. How could she ever look John in the face again knowing how he had betrayed her trust? One thing she knew for sure though was that any thought of marriage to him was out of the question. She knew instinctively that this was not only the end of their personal relationship but the end of their working relationship. John might be facing jail time when his involvement was revealed. The future looked dark and dismal for all of them. She had never needed her mother more than she did at that moment. She left without saying goodbye and her loyal secretary knew without a doubt that her boss was very upset and she had an idea it had something to do with the very strange disappearance of David Wells.

CHAPTER 54—2010

Carlos knew it was time to put the heat on Johnny Rivera. He didn't want to blow his new cover, so he decided to handle it by a throw-away cell phone where his call couldn't be traced.

As Rivera answered the call, Carlos said, "Hey, Johnnie, I hear that you are rolling in shit these days."

Rivera shouted, "Who in the hell is this and mind your own business?"

"It's Carlos Gonzalez returned from the dead. I hear from my brother that you are indicted and may be heading for the slammer very shortly. Guess they finally caught on to you, old buddy! Has anyone ever told you that crime does not pay?"

Rivera laughed, "You ought to know, Carlos. How many years did you serve and where in the hell are you?"

"Don't concern yourself with that. I have a proposition for you so listen up. You probably have some money stashed away somewhere but you'll never get to use it in jail, and I hear you will have to pay up in the negligence injury case to the tune of several million. I also heard that your insurance company won't cover any of this because of your willful negligence," Carlos said rubbing salt into the wound.

"So what's it to you," Rivera shouted into the phone. "Get to the point."

"I want you to confirm that John Martinez took the big payoff in the deal. If you do that I am prepared to offer you a nice vacation in South America, all expenses paid. You will leave in my private jet tomorrow if you will come clean about Martinez," Carlos said.

"Why do you care about Martinez anyway? What's your interest in this? I have a wife and kids. I can't just pick up and leave like that. Are you crazy?" Rivera asked in a noticeably shaky voice. He knew Carlos' mob connections and reputation for getting his way and he was well aware of the threat in his voice.

"I don't think you'll like the alternative, Johnnie," Carlos said with an intimidating voice. "Broke and rotting in prison isn't going to help your wife and kids. But then I could arrange another alternative if you don't cooperate. I hear the fish are hungry out in the Atlantic Ocean and would love you, you fat slob!"

"Hey, you don't need to get nasty. You just took me by surprise. I still don't know why you want to know about Martinez but I'm guessing a little blackmail so the word doesn't get back to his sexy boss and ruin his gravy train," Rivera said. "You running out of money, old pal?"

"Nice of you to ask, but no I am not running out of money and there is plenty of it available to order a hit in case you are wondering. So what is it, a comfortable life in South America with all those lovely Latinas or a cramped cell in a high security prison?"

"O.K., Carlos. Here's the deal, I put the finger on Martinez and you get me out of the country with no strings attached," Rivera asked in a pleading tone. His former bravado was all gone and he was a broken, scared man.

"I give you my word, Pal. Now give me the goods!" Carlos ordered.

"Yes, you were right. Martinez was on the take and it isn't the first time he has skimmed from a construction company. He made several million dollars on the deal. The middle man was David Wells who also got a big payoff."

"Who in the hell is David Wells?" Carlos asked impatiently.

"He's another asshole, has a big job with the Grand Hotels and a hot mistress on the side who has him by the balls," Rivera explained.

"Was the head woman privy to all this?" Carlos asked with growing curiosity.

"No, she don't know shit. Martinez has pulled the wool over her pretty face and she plans to marry him!"

Carlos thought to himself that it would be easier than he thought to steal the company with such a dumb broad in charge. The information he had just gained would give him the leverage he needed.

"You better have been straight with me or you'll soon be meeting the sharks in the Atlantic Ocean," Carlos threatened.

"My brother Raul will deliver your new passport and identity tomorrow and take you to my private jet. Have a great vacation!" Carlos laughed as he ended the call.

CHAPTER 55—2010

Elizabeth took one look at her daughter and knew that she was truly upset about something. Her hair was disheveled and she had a wild look in her eyes. Liz hugged her and led her to the couch, "I'll make some tea, dear. Just try to relax and then we'll talk. I can tell that something is bothering you. Whatever it is, it probably isn't as bad as you think it is right now."

"Oh, yes, it is, mom," Kaitlin sighed starting to cry again.

When Liz returned with the tea and sat down she turned to her distressed daughter, "Tell me about it, dear. Maybe we can solve it working together."

Between sobs Kaitlin blurted out, "John has betrayed me and our relationship is over. He has been taking payoffs from contactors and accepting the highest bid on jobs so he can put the money in his own pocket. You might say he has been stealing from the company for several years by overbilling. To make matters even worse, one of my most trusted employees, David Wells, was working in concert with him on the Rivera fiasco and now has disappeared off the face of the earth."

Elizabeth looked shocked and said, "How did you find out about this, Kaitlin? Are you positive your source is reliable? I just can't believe that John would do such a thing, and why would he do this? He is very well paid and I'm positive that he is truly in love with you and has been for years. He would be crazy to do such a thing! Surely you must be mistaken."

"Yes, my source is highly reliable. My lawyer, Bryon Harrell, just delivered the bad news. Apparently, David Wells was afraid that Rivera would spill the beans now that he is indicted and that Wells would have to go to jail for his involvement. He went to Bryon for legal advice because he couldn't go to John as he was the chief beneficiary of the skimming. He wanted someone to know that he was the middle-man between John and Rivera. Today when I asked to see Wells I found out he had 'gone missing'."

"This is unbelievable," Elizabeth frowned as she absorbed the seriousness of Kaitlin's predicament. "David Wells has worked for your father for years before you became CEO. He was one of Andy's most trusted employees!"

"He not only was stealing from the company but he also admitted to Bryon that he was the one making the threatening phone calls to me when John was out of town," Kaitlin said as she started to calm down and think more rationally.

Liz looked at her in amazement, "Why? It doesn't make sense."

"Apparently he was hoping I would fire John, and he would be promoted to the position. I always suspected both David Wells and Robert Welch were angry when I took over the company. They felt that they had seniority and should have been appointed to the top positions," she continued as she sipped her tea.

"Don't tell me that Robert Welch was also involved in the scheme?"

"Not to my knowledge. I will never forgive John for his deceit, however. In effect, he was responsible for all our problems. If he hadn't been so selfish and greedy, Rivera Cement would never have won the bid, the building wouldn't have collapsed and poor Peter McInerny wouldn't have been crippled for life." As her fury increased she added, "And we wouldn't have a mountain of legal bills as the construction would have never been halted had he chosen a reliable, honest contractor, the investigation by the Building Department would never have started. I could go on forever. Do you realize that John's dishonesty and greed has nearly destroyed our company?"

"What are you going to do now, Kaitlin?" her mother asked as she shook her head sympathetically.

"I'm going to fire John Martinez for starters both from the company and my life. I'm also going to consider your banker friend's proposal as we need his money if we're going to save the company," she said confidently as her usual composure and leadership started to return. "I need to investigate Mr. Gersbach further and try to see if his intentions are honorable. I am tired of deceit and I feel like a fool for not realizing what was going on right under my nose."

"Don't blame yourself, Kaitlin. Will you charge John with embezzlement for stealing from the company?" Liz asked with concern.

"I haven't decided yet. This bomb just exploded today. I want to hear what possible explanation John will have for what he has done to me and the company. Bryon has subpoenaed his personal bank records and that should tell us part of the story. As you know he has already moved into that expensive estate that was to be our 'dream home' so at least I don't have to kick him out of my apartment. I intend to sell this diamond ring and put the money back in the company."

"At least the company has been dropped from the lawsuit by the injured worker now that Rivera has been indicted," Elizabeth remarked trying to put a positive note on the calamity. "John acted on his own behalf and was not representing the company when he did the skimming. I don't see how the Grand Hotels could be held responsible for his actions when you and the Board of Directors had no knowledge of his activities."

"Let's hope not, mother," Kaitlin sighed wearily. "By the way, are you still seeing Bruno Gersbach?"

"As a matter of fact I have invited him to escort me to a fund raiser for the Opera Guild at the Biltmore Hotel this weekend. It is a black tie event and should be very special. I usually attend these functions alone, so it will be interesting to have an escort. Don't worry, I won't mention anything about John or David Wells. He doesn't need to know that there are new issues. I don't want to say anything that will discourage his help," she said assuring Kaitlin that what she had told her was confidential.

"Thanks, mom, I'm going home now. I'll need to rest before I break the news to John tomorrow. I feel that my relationship with John for the last ten years has been a decade of deceit," she said sadly as she hugged her mother.

CHAPTER 56—2010

Kaitlin had a restless night dreading her confrontation with John planned for the next day. Now here it was! Her initial fury over the betrayal had subsided to some extent but her feeling of loss was tremendous. John had not only been her closest friend and lover for a number of years, but her most valuable working partner to boot. At least that was what she had thought. Now everything had changed in the last 24 hours after she learned the truth.

John came bounding into the office, "Kaitlin, did you have your phone off last night? I tried over and over to reach you. I wanted to fix dinner for you in our new house. I can't wait for you to see some of the improvements I have made. Not that it wasn't already perfect." Suddenly he noticed that Kaitlin was not smiling, but looking at him coldly. He also noticed the diamond was missing from her finger.

"What's going on here, Kaitlin?" he asked taking her left hand. "Where is your engagement ring?"

"My engagement ring will be sold and the money put back in the company. The money you stole," she said pulling her hand out of his grasp.

John turned pale, "What are you talking about, Kaitlin? Have you lost your mind? How can you accuse me of such a thing?"

"I know now that you have been cheating the company by overbilling and taking payoffs from contractors and putting it in your own bank account! I also know now that you chose the highest bidder for each job, not because they were the best, but you would gain the most financially by selecting them. The worst case was the Rivera Cement contract. By skimming money off the deal for yourself you are indirectly responsible for all our problems with the horrible accident, the investigation stalling the renovation which has nearly bankrupted the company, and the mountain of legal bills because of it!"

"You're wrong Kaitlin," he shouted. "Where did you ever get this insane idea? You know I have always put the company first! Rivera is responsible for cheating us by doing a substandard job."

Kaitlin gave a dry laugh, "You can't even be honest now, John. You chose this crook and took a big payoff for giving him the job. His shirking on materials and labor caused the construction to collapse and the lifetime crippling of a worker."

"But Rivera has been indicted for his negligence. How can you blame it on me?"

Kaitlin continued, "And what about the boutiques in Europe and the payoffs there? Luckily no one was injured but you put that money into your own pocket. I want to know why. You have always had a generous salary, bonuses and perks, plus my love and devotion. How could you do this to me and my company?"

"Who told you all this?" he asked with a false bravado masking his fear.

"My lawyer has subpoenaed your personal bank records and he called me early this morning. There were a number of large deposits far exceeding any bonus you might have received. I suppose you know that David Wells has disappeared, but before running he confessed the truth to Bryon Harrell about your involvement in the Rivera affair. As he acted as a middle-man between you and Rivera, he was able to provide the dates of the payoffs, and guess what, they coincided with your large deposits," Kaitlin scowled.

John sat down in complete shock and with a shaking voice he said, "I only did it for us, sweetheart. I wanted you to have the biggest diamond, the most luxurious house. Believe me, I never dreamed that Rivera would shirk and cause a construction accident. What I did didn't hurt anyone. Just taking a little off the top is something everyone in the business does these days."

"Your act was embezzlement from the company, John. You took that money and now it has caused such problems that I may be forced to accept a merger to settle all our legal bills and finish the renovation. I no longer need your services, John. You are fired!"

"You can't do that Kaitlin. I have a contract for another two years," he demanded.

"As you will be fired for 'cause', in your case embezzling from the company, your contract is no longer viable. I want you to gather up your things and get the hell out of here. I never want to see your cheating face again!" Kaitlin shouted.

John pleaded, "You just don't understand. I didn't think I was stealing from the company. I just wanted to give you the best life possible. When I came over from Cuba as a child when we escaped from the Castro regime, I didn't have a dime in my pocket. I longed to have some of the luxuries and wealth that I saw here in Miami. As I worked myself up from poverty and started to earn real money, it got in my blood. I wanted to have more and more. I wanted to share it all with you, Kaitlin. I love you with all my heart and soul."

"Get out, John. You had everything and you blew it! You have turned into a greedy, selfish man and I want you out of my life and out of the company. Don't make me call Security to get you out," she said firmly opening the door to the office and pushing him through.

"Please don't do this, Kaitlin," John said starting to sob. "I still love you."

Kaitlin glared at him, "That's your tough luck. As far as I'm concerned you can spend the rest of your life in a jail cell making amends for your betrayal and deceit. I have no room for you in my life. I hope you enjoy the luxury accommodations in prison. As far as our dream home, we will freeze all your assets and hope to recoup some of the money you stole from the sale of the estate."

John walked back to his office a beaten man as Kaitlin's secretary followed him with her eyes in astonishment. Kaitlin phoned Bryon Harrell, "I have just fired John Martinez. We need to consider charges and freeze his assets as soon as possible."

"I'll be in to see you later today, Kaitlin and update my progress. We need to discuss whether it is the best course to press charges against John or whether we should seek retribution and repayment. Bringing this to light could make your investors nervous seeing John was the Chief Financial Officer. It might also reopen the negligence investigation. The company is off the hook on that now that Rivera was charged and has apparently disappeared. Rumors are he has left the country. Seeing John was CFO they might want to assign blame to the company even though he acted alone on his skimming. Also, we'll discuss the possibility of accepting Bruno Gersbach's investment offer and the legal ramifications."

"Thanks, Bryon. It sure is good to have a friend these days. They are hard to find," Kaitlin sighed hanging up the phone. She was emotionally spent but knew it was time to move on and save the company.

CHAPTER 57—2010

Kaitlin invited all the women in her family over for a coffee klatch on the weekend. It was time to let the family know about her break-up with John. Emily and Autumn arrived together and soon Elizabeth was ringing the doorbell. They all knew something was in the wind. Only Elizabeth was privy to some of the shocking developments.

Autumn and Kaitlin hadn't seen each other for a long time and they warmly hugged each other. Kaitlin had been so tied up with the company's problems and both Autumn and her husband Bill who had completely recovered were busy with newspaper assignments all over the globe.

After serving coffee and pastries, Kaitlin started the conversation, "I so admired the investigative reporting that Bill did after the Haitian earthquake in January. Also, we heard about how he helped with humanitarian aid in Port-au-Prince. His photographs of the tent city and the suffering faces of the people will go down in history."

"I am so proud of Bill," Autumn glowed." All his experience in the war and the suffering he has witnessed has made him so sensitive to poverty and devastation. In addition to the 7.0 magnitude earthquake there were so many aftershocks that followed. Over 316,000 died and millions are homeless."

Emily added, "Miami has played such a significant role in helping those poor people. Only a few days after the tragedy an airlift from Miami delivered over 45,000 pounds of food and emergency supplies to Haiti. We have such a large Haitian population here in Miami the tragedy has really hit home. So many are still trying to locate their relatives."

As Kaitlin filled their coffee cups again Autumn noticed that that huge, sparkling diamond ring was no longer on her left hand, "Kaitlin, what happened to your ring?"

She sat down and looked at the loving women who surrounded her and began, "I guess you suspected that I had a special reason for this get-together." She paused as the women looked at her expectantly, "John and I have broken up. I no longer plan to marry him."

Autumn couldn't hold back her emotion, "Oh, no, Kaitlin. I just can't believe it. You two have been a couple for years. Surely, it can be patched up."

"I'm afraid not," she said sadly. "John has betrayed me and the company in the worst way. I have found out that he was overbilling on our construction jobs and putting the money in his own pocket. He took the highest bids and was well-rewarded for it from hungry contractors. I have fired him and the marriage and our relationship is over."

The women sat in stunned silence, only Elizabeth was not surprised by the revelation since her confidential talk with Kaitlin. Now she said, "We must all support Kaitlin now as she deals with the damage John has done to the company. You and I are board members, Emily, and have significant holdings in the company. As you know we are in desperate financial trouble due to the investigation into the accident and the halting of the construction on the New York project. Now is the time to rally around Kaitlin."

Kaitlin explained, "I already know I can depend on your love and support as we work through this. We have a friendly offer for a merger from a Swiss banker looking to invest. He has proposed putting enough money in the company to get us out of our current financial mess and enable us to finish the renovation project now that Rivera Cement has been found liable and the investigation has been closed. Mr. Gersbach assures me that I will remain as CEO and the chief decision-maker. He will ask to be seated on the Board of Directors where he will give input and infuse cash when needed. The Grand Hotels will retain their name if we agree to the investment."

Emily asked, "What is the alternative? This has been a family business for so many decades going way back to the early 1900's!"

"The alternative is that we declare bankruptcy and our hotels will be sold off to settle our debt," Kaitlin said firmly. "I hate it as much as you do Emily, but this may be our only hope. Otherwise we would be vulnerable for a hostile takeover, and I am convinced that this is not Mr. Gersbach's intention. We need to investigate his offer further and my lawyer, Bryon Harrell, is advising me every step of the way. Also, I am sorry to report that my Director of Domestic Development, David Wells, was also on the take and has mysteriously disappeared. No one can locate him and it is suspected that he has escaped to the Caribbean with his mistress and a pile of money taken from the company."

Elizabeth groaned, "David was a trusted employee for years while Andy was still alive and running the company. Apparently, he never got over being passed over for the top job when Andy died and resented Kaitlin. However, paying for an expensive divorce and a demanding mistress was certainly a factor in his deceit."

"Yes, he was only too happy to serve as middle-man between Rivera and John and was able to cash in on the deal himself," Kaitlin added.

A silence settled over the group as they absorbed the enormity of the matter. Finally they gathered around Kaitlin and each woman hugged her and offered support. Kaitlin felt her strength returning as she felt the power of her family enveloping her in their love and concern. As they left she knew that she would get through this and would figure out a way to preserve the company that had started out as the vision of her ancestors. She was determined not to fail. Now that John was gone, the company was her life and she didn't intend to lose it.

CHAPTER 58—2010

It was the night of the Opera Guild gala at the Biltmore Hotel in Coral Gables and Elizabeth had a beautiful new gown. It fit her like a glove and was a pale gold color that sparkled with sequins. She remembered when her deceased husband, Andy, had invited her to the opening of his first luxury hotel on Miami Beach and how carefully she had chosen her dress for the big occasion. That was long before she and Andy had become engaged and she could remember how excited she was that he had chosen her as his partner for that important moment in his life.

She hadn't had a date for years since his death and she had to admit she was a little nervous as she waited for Bruno Gersbach to pick her up. She hoped that he wouldn't ask about the current status of the Grand Hotels. Kaitlin had asked her to keep John's involvement and his firing confidential until she spoke to her lawyer. She didn't want to place her mother in the middle of the situation.

Carlos had glowed when he received Elizabeth's invitation and realized he was developing important inroads into the family circle. He knew he might be asked questions about his business and was well-prepared. He cut a fine figure in his tuxedo and looked every ounce an important and successful business man.

When Carlos saw Elizabeth dressed in all her finery he had to admit that she was still stunning in her maturity. "You look gorgeous tonight, Elizabeth," he said as he helped her with her wrap. "I bet every man will be envious of me."

Elizabeth was embarrassed when she realized that she was blushing. She felt like a schoolgirl on her first date. "You look elegant yourself, Bruno."

As they drove to the hotel she told him about the Biltmore and of course Carlos pretended that he had never heard it before. He was determined not to blow his cover as he was beginning to enjoy his new lifestyle.

"The Biltmore dates back to 1926 and at one time its swimming pool was the largest in the world and although you probably have never heard of him, the actor who played *Tarzan* in the movies, Johnny Weissmuller, was a swimming instructor. The hotel played host to royalty, both Europe's and Hollywood's. Al Capone and assorted Roosevelt's and Vanderbilt's were frequent guests as well as all the famous movie stars like Judy Garland and Ginger Rogers. President Roosevelt stayed here during his fishing vacations in Miami as well as President Clinton during the present day," she explained.

"That's fascinating! I can't wait to see it," Carlos responded tongue in cheek.

"During World War II the War Department converted the Biltmore into a hospital and it served the wounded and it remained a VA Hospital until 1968. George Merrick, the developer of Coral Gables and the founder of the University of Miami joined forces to help build a great hotel. My grandfather and father also were major builders in Coral Gables. As you know it has strict building codes and has retained its beautiful environment thanks to people like Merrick and my ancestors," she added proudly.

As they drove up to the majestic Mediterranean building, a valet took the car and they walked into the breathtaking reception hall and then walked through the impressive pillars. They could hear voices coming from the courtyard and the sound of a chamber orchestra. Elizabeth explained that cocktails were being served in the outdoor courtyard before they adjourned to the ballroom for the dinner. After dinner there would be dancing to a full orchestra and a performance by some of the divas from the opera.

Carlos noticed that Miami's most prominent and successful persons were gathered together around the fountain in the courtyard. Emily and Autumn came up to greet them. This was the first time Carlos had actually met Emily who had been briefly married to his brother, Raul. He thought that she was much more attractive than Raul had let on. Also, the daughter was a knockout.

The women were aware that he was a possible investor in the Grand Hotels and greeted him warmly. "We are so pleased to finally meet you, Mr. Gersbach," Emily said. "You and Elizabeth will be seated at our table for dinner. Autumn's husband, Bill, will also be joining us so we hope to have a chance for more conversation later. I'm sure Elizabeth will want to introduce you to many new people during the cocktail hour so we'll see you later."

Alfredo Griego, the neighbor who had hosted the neighborhood gathering when he first bought his house came up and handed him a drink, "Hello, Bruno! It's good to see you again. I hear by the grapevine that our hospitality gal is showing you the town!" He pulled Carlos aside as Liz turned to greet some friends, "I thought I might hear from you about investing in my hedge fund. You said you were from Lucerne. Is that where your bank is located?" he asked helping himself to a plateful of appetizers.

Carlos stiffened, "My main business center is in Zug, Switzerland. Have you ever heard of it, Al?"

Griego laughed, "Have I heard of it? That's the town where all the businesses are moving out of the U.S. so they can escape the 30% income tax here. Do you have a lot of American clients, Bruno? I might be interested in getting into the action."

"Haven't you heard, Al? We keep all information about who our clients are confidential. That's why they bank with us in Switzerland," Carlos said roaring with laughter. "But if you'll excuse me, I must find Elizabeth before some of these other men get ideas. She is one attractive lady!"

"She's a fox!" Griego agreed looking at Elizabeth with admiration. "Let's do lunch next week, Bruno, old buddy. There are some great restaurants in Coral Gables and I am not immune to a three hour lunch," he said laughing as Carlos walked away.

They found their table for ten in the elegant ballroom. Bruno was introduced to Autumn's husband, Bill, and some other newspaper executives. They were having a lively political discussion and Carlos was amazed that most of them appeared to be Democrats. He thought that most influential and wealthy people who had money to come to an event like this were Republicans.

Bill who was a humanitarian was raving about President Obama'a Affordable Health Care program being passed into law, "It was only passed by a narrow margin and it's not a perfect bill, but it will enable thousands more to receive health care and help people with high risk existing conditions." He turned to Bruno, "Do you realize the need for health care here? It seems like some Republicans feel that poor people can just go to the emergency room if they don't have insurance and then they sit and spend long hours waiting. People are dying because they can't afford to go to a doctor for preventative help. It's tragic and I hope this bill will help."

"We have a good system in Switzerland I think. For one thing everyone is covered and those who can't afford it get subsidies from the government," Bruno said. He had covered the topic thoroughly when he had his plastic surgery which unfortunately was considered 'cosmetic' and not covered in his case. "People can choose from a broad array of health plans sold by private insurance companies."

"Most European countries are so far ahead of us in providing health care for all their citizens," Emily stated. "Are the people all happy with your system, Bruno?"

Bruno nodded, "I'm afraid some of the politicians think that the subsidies for the poor people are increasing and those are not necessarily the people who will go to the polls to vote for them. Health insurance premiums are not linked to income. So everyone pays the same."

Autumn piped in, "Now that the Republicans have just taken over the House of Representatives, I hope they won't try to repeal the Affordable Health Act. This Tea Party group is very vocal about wanting to get rid of it, and they have many freshmen 'teabaggers' elected in this recent midterm election."

Bill said angrily, "And they want to get rid of all entitlements for the elderly, the poor and the disabled. So far I haven't heard them offer much in return. I still can't believe the Bush Tax Cuts were approved again. That would be a big step in removing the deficit."

Bruno whispered in Elizabeth's ear, "What does Autumn's husband do? He seems very concerned about the downtrodden."

"He is a famous photographer and has captured the faces of poverty both globally and in our own country. I will show you some of his photographs from the Haitian earthquake disaster. You can see the suffering in the faces of the people," she said. "I expect he will win a prize for his work in Haiti."

Luckily the waiters started serving at that time before the discussion got too hot. The dinner was served in four courses with a different wine with every course. By the time they got to dessert everyone at the table was happy and laughing. As the orchestra started to play couples flooded the dance floor. Bruno turned to Elizabeth and asked her if she would like to dance. She smiled as he led her to the dance floor. As the romantic music flooded the room and the lights dimmed she felt a feeling that she hadn't felt for a long time. As Bruno held her close she was starting to have emotions that she thought she'd never have again. She had loved Andy with all her heart and soul, but as Bruno held her closer, she felt warm and protected and wanted. It was a great feeling and when she looked into his eyes she could tell that he had feelings too.

Carlos couldn't believe what was happening. He was starting to remember feelings for Elizabeth that he had buried for many years. She felt so good in his arms and all those years of building hatred toward her started to peel off.

He told himself, "I can't let this happen again. It's not part of my plan." They walked out on the terrace overlooking the gigantic lighted swimming pool and before he knew it he was kissing her and she was responding in a way that gave him hope for the future. "Maybe it was the booze," he thought. "I can't be getting soft. I have too much to lose. I have to keep my head on straight."

But when he looked into her eyes and they sparkled with excitement and happiness he became confused about what he really wanted. His plan was falling apart and he knew he couldn't let this woman ruin him a second time. But why did he feel so good when he held her and kissed her? Why was she so nice and so damned attractive and so sexy? "It wasn't fair," he moaned to himself. He needed to focus on his goals and forget the need for her that was driving him nuts.

When Bruno kissed her Elizabeth felt a familiarity that she couldn't explain. Like she had known Bruno in another time, another place. But she knew that was impossible. She did know that at that moment she felt more alive than she had for years as she looked into his eyes in the Miami moonlight.

CHAPTER 59—2010

Kaitlin was a young woman who had grown up with every advantage. She had a fabulous apartment overlooking Biscayne Bay as well as a huge office in the same building. She had a second vacation home on the ocean. She was a very wealthy woman and ran a huge company, but she was far from happy. The current problem concerning her company rested squarely on her shoulders and she felt the weight of that dilemma. She knew she had to stay calm for the upcoming board meeting. She was waiting to see Bryon Harrell who had an appointment in the next hour.

There would be a board meeting which he would attend and give legal advice and Kaitlin would present the idea of a sizable infusion of cash from Bruno Gersbach's investment bank. Robert Welsh had happily taken over John's duties as Chief Financial Officer. Even though it was an interim position, Kaitlin planned to keep him on in that capacity if he proved himself capable of that much responsibility.

Bruno Gersbach would also be at the meeting to present his proposition. There was no doubt that the company had a serious cash flow problem and Kaitlin was determined not to start to sell off the hotels. That would only be a last ditch solution.

Bryon gave her a hug as he greeted her before the meeting. "How is my favorite CEO today?" he asked.

"Hanging in there," she sighed. "Do you have the paper work ready in case we decide to accept Bruno's offer today at the meeting?"

"I'm totally prepared," he reassured her as they walked to the conference room where everyone was waiting.

The Board Room was enormous and in the center was a round table seating 15 people. She preferred the circular table over the rectangular one as she found discussion easier and more meaningful when she could look into members' eyes and gauge reactions. There were two flat-screened monitors on either side for power point presentations. Only six members were present today at her invitation. She took a fortifying breath before she began. She glanced around the table at the members. Of course John and David Wells were missing. William Petersen who had retired was no longer with them, but he had been replaced by Arthur Hennington, who was a distinguished businessman and had served on several boards of directors for major companies. The banker, Edward Haynes was still on the board as well as family members, Elizabeth and Emily. Robert Welsh, the new interim CFO, was on her left side, Bryon on her right. They greeted her warmly.

She smiled cordially and said, "I have called this meeting for several important reasons today. The good news is that charges from the New York District Attorney's office have been completely dropped. Grand Hotels has also been dropped in the willful negligence suit brought about by the injured workman. Mr. Rivera, the head of the cement job on the New York renovation has been indicted for neglect and use of inferior materials that caused that part of the building to collapse. It also was revealed that cracks were developing and reported to him by his workers and he chose to ignore the warnings."

"Is it true that he has left Miami?" Edward Haynes asked.

"Yes, it is true. No one knows his whereabouts. Now the bad news. I am sorry to report that two of our employees were discovered to be overbilling for construction jobs and skimming money off the top to put into their own pockets. As a result of that I have fired our CFO, John Martinez, and his partner in crime, David Wells who has disappeared along with Johnny Rivera. It is suspected that he is in the Caribbean, but no one knows for sure. I have appointed Robert Welsh as Interim Chief Financial Officer to assume John Martinez' former position." She smiled at him and said, "He has done a splendid job reorganizing the books and I know we can all count on him." Robert Welsh beamed at the compliment.

The members who hadn't heard the news gasped. Those who knew John well found it hard to believe he could be guilty of such an act. "Will he be charged for embezzlement?" Arthur Hennington asked in a stunned tone.

At this point Kaitlin turned the floor over to her lawyer who stood up and addressed the shocked people.

"We have a plan where he can make restitution for the money he has stolen from the company. If he fails to comply, we will be forced to take the matter to the authorities. He has signed an agreement and has made an initial payment to avoid prosecution. He is of course responsible for the missing funds. However, due to the stall in the New York renovation and the associated legal charges the company is having a serious cash flow problem. I will turn the floor back to our CEO who has a proposition to present to you," Bryon said removing a stack of legal papers from his briefcase.

Kaitlin next asked Bryon to bring in Bruno Gersbach who was waiting in the outer lounge to be called. He shook hands around the table and then was seated next to Kaitlin. "Mr. Gersbach comes to us from Switzerland where he runs an investment bank. He is opening a branch here in Coral Gables and is interested in a making a substantial investment in our company. I believe we could call him our 'white knight'." She waited while the group tried to digest this startling news.

"As you know the economy is very depressed and it doesn't seem wise to start selling hotels in this kind of market. It also alerts business that we are vulnerable for a hostile takeover. This would be personally devastating to me and my family. As you know the Donegons have been associated with the hotel business since the 1900's.

Bankruptcy is therefore not an option in my opinion. I previously reported that our cash flow problem was concerning, now it has reached the critical stage. We have delayed paying many of our suppliers and Bob informs me that we won't have the funds to make the next payroll. Also, we have been given permission to continue our renovation in New York by the Building Department but we need more capital to do that. Therefore, it seems plausible to accept Mr. Gersbach's generous offer of cash infusion immediately rather than wait for a catastrophe," Kaitlin stated confidently.

Edward Haynes spoke up with great concern, "Doesn't the SEC require any material change in a company's financial position to be filed within a certain time?"

"Bob, will you answer that please?" Kaitlin said turning to the new CFO.

"Yes, you are correct and we will not file until a decision is reached today. In fact it is a felony not to report and we could be found accessories. We are hopeful that our financial position will be substantially improved after you have heard from our guest. Mr. Gersbach," Welsh said with supreme confidence. He was thriving in his new responsibility. Also, he glowed in the fact that he was well aware of SEC standards and planned to keep everything above board in contrast to John Martinez who tried to 'cook the books'.

She turned to Bruno and asked him to address the group. "Mr. Gersbach, please explain how you plan to help us out of our current financial catastrophe."

Bruno Gersbach rose from his chair and smiled cordially acknowledging each person at the table, "I am prepared to invest 20 million in the company. My intention is to leave the name, Grand Hotels, the same, and I would want Miss Donegon to stay on as CEO. In return I would like a fair percentage of interest on my bailout money and the privilege to buy 500,000 stocks at half the going price. I would also serve on the Board of Directors in a decision-making role. Naturally, I want the best for the company if I invest so much money in its future," he assured the group.

Edward Haynes asked, "What kind of percentage are you thinking of?"

"10% of my cash infusion if I am to save the company's future. So far the market is not aware of the cash flow problem and hasn't reacted and caused the stocks to tank." The members started to whisper to one another. They were still shocked by the prospect of the new proposal, the seriousness of the cash flow problem as well as the dishonesty of trusted employees, especially John Martinez turning out to be a thief.

Kaitlin then encouraged them to think of the alternatives. "We might have to declare bankruptcy if we don't act and I mean act in a hurry. All our obligations are coming due and there is not enough money to cover the debt. Grand Hotels' problems are emblematic of the economic woes facing the country in general. The outlook for growth has darkened and financial issues have gyrated to compound the problem we are facing."

Then Elizabeth rose to her feet and said, "I'd like to personally give my support to Mr. Gersbach. He has bought an estate in our neighborhood in Coral Gables and the association is so pleased to have him join us. I personally appreciate his generous offer to save our company. His is a crucial show of support for our CEO and management team." Bruno smiled a thank you in her direction.

After a brief break where the members had some time to discuss the terms among themselves, a vote was taken without a single dissent. They would accept the proposal and save the company. No one was happy, but it was a decision that had to be made.

There was one person, however, who was elated and that was Bruno Gersbach. At last his dream of taking over the Grand Hotels was turning into reality. He met with Raul for dinner that evening and he was bursting with excitement.

"It's finally coming true, hermano," he said pounding Raul on the back. "I will soon be the head honcho at the Grand Hotels and perhaps even marry into the family!"

"I gotta hand it to you, Carlos!" Raul exclaimed lighting up a cigar. "How did you pull it off? I hope there's a plan for me!"

"Of course," Carlos laughed but he knew that the plan he had for his brother wasn't the one that Raul had in mind. Raul just wouldn't fit in with his new friends and social position. Besides, he had screwed up with Emily and would never be accepted by the family!

CHAPTER 60—2010

Kaitlin agreed to meet Bryon Harrell for drinks that evening. She finally had some sense of relief that the Board's decision would save the company from disaster. She had little time to grieve about John's betrayal and the loss of his friendship with the multitude of problems and decisions she had been facing.

As she dressed for her date with Bryon the phone rang and when she answered it was surprised to hear John's voice, "Kaitlin, can we get together and talk at least? I can't believe you are willing to let go of all we have shared for the past ten years."

Kaitlin caught her breath and replied coldly, "You should have thought about that before you stole money from the company!"

He pleaded, "I know I made a big mistake, but I only did it so I could provide for you in the way you are accustomed. The skimming is a common practice with construction contracts. I guess I just thought that everyone else was doing it and why shouldn't I? I never meant to hurt you. I love you."

"You didn't think embezzling was wrong, John? Come now, you may be a thief but you are intelligent enough to know the difference between right and wrong!" Kaitlin spoke into the receiver sarcastically. "We are giving you the best possible break by letting you pay back what you have taken. We don't want you to go to prison, but if you don't make restitution that is where you will end up!"

"The house is on the market and I am living in a studio apartment and doing everything I can to return the money," he sighed in a discouraged voice. "Please meet me, Kaitlin, so we can talk about it in person. Please try to find it in your heart to forgive me and I promise to spend the rest of my life showing you how much I love you."

"Because of your actions poor Peter McInerny is paralyzed for life and can never work again or support his wife and children. You may not have intended that, but by giving Rivera the contract knowing he was a crook you are responsible. Your actions almost caused our company to go bankrupt because of the halt in construction, the horrible accident and the lawsuit. Robert Welch has been appointed to your position and he has found numerous instances where you 'cooked the books' to hide the fact that you were getting payoffs, not only in the New York job but in the boutique hotels in Europe. Thank God, he is an honest man and is doing everything to meet SEC regulations," she chided him.

John was silent for a long moment as he thought of all he had lost. He was furious that Robert Welsh had taken over his former job and that Kaitlin was holding him responsible for all the company's problems. "Have you ever heard of forgiveness, Kaitlin? I still love you and always will."

Kaitlin grimaced and then said bitterly, "That's your tough luck, John. Get over it! You and I are finished!" She hung up the phone and noticed her hand was shaking. She would never forgive his deceit and betrayal. He was out of her life and dreams.

That evening she and Bryon met at an oceanside bar. It was a beautiful Miami evening with balmy breezes swaying the palm fronds and the crash of waves adding to the atmosphere. They spent time discussing the events at the Board meeting that day and both of them felt good about the outcome.

"Mr. Gersbach has already transferred the money from his Swiss bank account and everything is in order. He signed the contracts this afternoon and Robert Welsh will be working on restoring order to the books all weekend."

He raised his mojito cocktail glass up to hers in a toast. "It looks like the company is on the fast track for being solvent again. The suppliers will be paid off Monday and we will meet all the payrolls at the end of the week."

Kaitlin glowed in the Miami moonlight, "Oh, Bryon, I can hardly believe our good fortune in meeting Bruno Gersbach! He seems to be interested in my mother, too. Believe me that would be something if she fell for him! She has been completely faithful to my father's memory for years and has never shown any interest in dating anyone in all this time."

Bryon led her out to the shore before she went to her car. "Romance is truly in the air," he whispered as they gazed at the huge orange moon hanging over the Atlantic rollers. Before she knew it he was kissing her and again she felt herself responding to him in a way she couldn't explain.

"It was too soon after John to consider a relationship," she thought to herself but then she found herself kissing him again.

"Those mojitos must have been stronger than I thought," she laughed as she rolled down the window of her Mercedes and drove away.

Neither one of them noticed the figure standing in the shadows watching every move they made.

CHAPTER 61—2010

After Kaitlin had so abruptly hung up on him when he had begged her for forgiveness, John was driven crazy by despair and fury. It especially angered him that pompous Robert Welsh had taken his place and apparently was now the fair-haired boy. He looked at is dingy one room studio apartment in a downtrodden part of Miami and wanted to scream. How had he fallen from grace so fast? Was Kaitlin seeing someone else on the sly? He decided to surprise her and drop in at the apartment they had shared in the Grand Biscayne Hotel in Coconut Grove.

He parked his car in the parking garage. He noticed that his name had been removed from his old parking space and Robert Welsh's appeared in bold freshly painted letters. He flushed with fury as he had to go up several levels to find a parking space. As he entered the lobby he saw Kaitlin emerging from her private elevator that whisked her up to her luxury penthouse apartment and the executive offices on the two floors below it. She looked gorgeous as usual he thought angrily. He stepped into the shadows and watched her go toward the parking garage.

John decided not to confront her with all the hotel guests milling in the lobby. He wanted to see where she was going but he would have to move fast to get his car in time because she was on the ground floor close to the exit. He rushed up two flights of stairs and breathlessly gunned up his motor. Luckily for him it was a Friday night and there always was a lot of traffic there in Coconut Grove caused by the TGI crowd who had left work and were headed for all the bars and restaurants that made that area famous. It was bumper-to-bumper traffic and Kaitlin was still waiting to pull onto the street. As he saw her pull out he nearly caused an accident butting in front of a car one space behind her. The driver honked his horn relentlessly but Kaitlin didn't notice as another car was directly behind her.

John had a hard time following her as she turned toward Key Biscayne. He lost sight of her a few times, but finally spotted her just before she went through the toll booth on the way to the causeway that led to the island. The traffic was lighter now and he kept a short distance behind her. Finally he saw her turn off at a popular oceanside restaurant with a tiki bar on the shore. The moon was full and shone on the Atlantic waves as they rolled in with a loud crash.

There were quite a few couples waiting to be seated but the maitre d' quickly spotted Kaitlin and ushered her through the crowd. That really galled him! She always got first class treatment at restaurants and all the head waiters knew her. He got angrier by the minute when he wasn't allowed to break through the crowd of people waiting for tables. He finally edge his way through and managed to find his way to the bar. He found an empty seat way back at the end of the long bar and frantically looked for Kaitlin. She was nowhere in the crowd at the bar.

Then he noticed there were small tables with glowing candles set up on the terrace near the ocean and there was Kaitlin. It was dark except for the flame of the candles but suddenly the full moon came out and shone right on Kaitlin and across from her was Bryon Harrell, the company lawyer.

He ordered a martini and thought to himself, "This could be a business dinner." Just when he was beginning to relax and was on his second drink he saw in the glow of the moonlight that they were holding hands. John's anger now turned to red fury. His heart was pounding as loud as the waves coming in from the open sea. He ordered a third martini as he watched them eating dinner under the stars. He was sure he saw Bryon kiss her hand a few times and they were leaning toward each other and looking into each other's eyes.

He paid his bill and started to stagger over to them when they got up and walked to the edge of the sea. John couldn't believe what he was seeing as they kissed passionately under the moon.

"That little bitch," he slurred. "That's why she fired me! She has been carrying on with Harrell all this time and wearing my engagement ring!" He followed them in the shadows and out to the parking lot and saw Bryon kiss her again when she got in her car. "I'll teach that slut a lesson," he slurred to himself as he staggered over to his car. He got lost several times driving back to the Grand Biscayne where he was determined to confront her and arrived long after Kaitlin had returned to her penthouse and was preparing for sleep with dreams of her pleasant evening and the thought of many of her problems now solved.

He staggered past the night doorman who looked distressed when he saw John's drunken state, but he was oblivious to the fact that John was no longer welcome in Ms. Donegon's penthouse. "Do you need help getting upstairs, Mr. Martinez?" he asked innocently and trying to help.

"There's nothing wrong with me," he snapped. "I know the way." He still had the key to the private penthouse elevator and he lost his balance as it whisked him upwards and he had to grasp the rail on the side of the elevator or he would have fallen on his face.

Staggering up to the door he started to pound on it shouting, "Kaitlin! Let me in! I have to talk to you right now!"

Kaitlin was awakened abruptly and it took her a moment to realize what was happening. "Go away, John," she shouted. "I have nothing to say to you. You sound drunk!" She was quivering with fear as she didn't like what was happening. It was 3 a.m. in the morning and in her half-awakened state she couldn't understand why John was there.

"You bitch, open up," he screamed and continued to pound. "I saw you making out with Harrell tonight, you tramp!" With that he got out his keys and Kaitlin who was trembling in fear thanked God that she had the locks all changed since his departure. Obviously she had forgotten the elevator key.

She lifted the phone and pressed the button for Security. "Come up immediately," she ordered. "Mr. Martinez is trying to break into the penthouse. Please send him away. If he refuses to go, call the authorities."

Only a few moments later she heard John yell, "Take your hands off me! I'll go. Just leave me alone." As she looked out the security opening in her door she saw two burly security men, one on either side of John, leading him toward the elevator.

He screamed back only once to the closed door, "I'll get you for this, Kaitlin! So help me, God!" Kaitlin cried herself to sleep that night after this shocking glimpse into John's true character. To see him like this was truly heartbreaking.

CHAPTER 62—2010

Kaitlin was badly shaken up the next day after John's unwelcome visit in the wee hours. She had slept very little after he was escorted out of the building by her security team. When she walked into the executive offices she was surprised to see Bruno Gersbach waiting in the outer lounge.

"Why, hello Mr. Gersbach. This is a pleasant surprise. Are you waiting for me?" she asked smiling even though she had been in an appalling mood.

"Yes, I am. I wanted to make sure that my transfer of funds came through and I thought I'd like to look over the books with your CFO to see if the amount of my investment was sufficient to plug the hole in the dike," he said pleasantly.

"The morning papers Sunday announced in their Business Section that the Grand Hotels had an investor who was buying up a large share of stocks in the company. I don't know whether you saw it or not. We have kept your name anonymous as you requested. This is sure to boost stocks up this week and I might add a nice gain in your investment as you did get your stocks at half-price," she added.

"Of course, now I have a very vested interest in the success of the company. As I will be checking over the financial status, I would like to propose that you turn over the office space formerly used by that scoundrel David Wells so that I can use it when I meet with various officers of the company," he asked the CEO.

Kaitlin frowned, "I didn't realize that you intended to spend that much time here at the executive offices. I know you have a new company to organize and I realize how much time that can take."

"You must understand that with the size of my investment, I must have a hands-on relationship here, especially knowing that some of your past financial personnel have kept the books to reflect their own interest instead of the company's," he said firmly. "I only require the office space for several days a week as you are right, I have many other responsibilities besides the Grand Hotel."

"Yes, that would be possible, but I must tell you I feel that our new CFO, Mr. Welsh, is extremely competent and trustworthy. He is taking every aspect of his responsibility very seriously. I don't want him to feel that you are constantly looking over his shoulder for possible discrepancies," she advised him.

Bruno shook her hand, "I certainly understand that and you can reassure him that I am only here to help the company back to solvency as well as protect my investment and I am not trying to check up on him. I'm sure he is very capable."

After he left Kaitlin wondered if Mr. Gersbach was going to be a problem in the future. She hoped not as she was tired of calamities and was hoping for some peace of mind. John's nocturnal visit had left her edgy and suspicious of everyone.

Carlos was jubilant at his first effort to infiltrate the company. Having an office on the executive floor would make him privy to important decisions as well as keeping an eye on his investment. His stock deal could well bring him a fortune and the interest alone on his bailout gift could make him one of the richest men in the country if he played his cards right. His next challenge was to undermine Kaitlin so that he in time might sit in the CEO's chair. Being on the Board of Director's would help him meet his goal.

"It was time," he thought slyly, "to steal Elizabeth's heart as well as the company."

When he called her she sounded excited to hear his voice, "Oh, Bruno, I am so grateful to you for investing in the Grand Hotels at this crucial time. I can't believe my good fortune that you moved into my area and were looking for an investment when we needed help so badly!"

Carlos laughed heartily, "Well, you know, Elizabeth, it was a great investment for me and if at the same time I could save the family business, I am pleased."

"I'd like to invite you over for cocktails and dinner so we can share a glass of champagne and toast our mutual satisfaction," Elizabeth said hopefully.

Carlos agreed readily and was at her doorstep the next evening promptly at 8 p.m. He noticed that a table for two with glowing candles and fine china had been set up on the terrace overlooking the water. He opened the champagne and poured some in each of their flutes. She looked lovely in the moonlight. She was wearing an elegant white pant suit trimmed in gold lame. It was hard to believe her age as she still had slim figure and her blonde hair blew in the gentle breeze and her eyes sparkled as they met his.

He found her irresistible at that moment in spite of the hatred for her that had been building for years during his imprisonment. He set down her flute and took her in his arms and before he knew it he was kissing her. She was shocked to feel his male hardness pressing against her and she could hear the excitement in his breathing. She responded to his kiss against her will, but then stepped back before she completely lost control, "Bruno, you are a very kind man and a good friend but I am sure my dinner will overcook if I don't serve it to you now."

She was terribly flustered and couldn't get off the terrace fast enough. She wasn't ready for a romantic relationship or an intimate moment. She still was carrying the weight of the suicide death of her beloved husband. There had never been room for anyone else. He was still with her with every breath she took. Now she was afraid that Bruno might be looking for more from her than she could deliver and she felt guilty about denying him after he had saved the company from disaster.

Bruno was quiet when she returned with the grilled lobster and avocado salad and hot crusty bread. He opened the bottle of fine French wine and they clicked their glasses. Very little conversation took place after that and Elizabeth could sense Bruno's disappointment that she had spurned his advances. Not the romantic music piped out to the terrace or the sound of the gentle waves or moonlight helped his mood.

He left a short time after dinner and shaking her hand thanked her for the dinner. As she stood at the doorway and watched him drive away she was afraid this was the end of their friendship. "Oh, Andy," she moaned to the spirit of her dead husband. "Is it time that I learned to love again, to feel the touch of a man?" She wept softly as she feared that somehow she had just turned away a meaningful relationship. It was hours before she fell asleep as she tossed and turned and wondered how Andy would feel if she loved another.

Carlos was furious as he screeched out of the driveway onto Old Cutler Road. "That damn Andy, the bastard, has won again. First he broke up our engagement and now he's still haunting her. I know she felt something when I kissed her but she is afraid. I'll really teach her what 'afraid' is. No dame is going to get the best of me! Especially Elizabeth! Once was enough!"

But he was feeling very unsettled after holding Elizabeth. Every time he thought of the feel of her soft gentle curves pressing against him he got a 'hard' on. He thought to himself, "It's been too long since I fucked a woman." Alfredo Griego, his effusive neighbor, had passed the number of a high-priced call girl service to him. "The girls are gorgeous and will do anything you want, Bruno. You must get lonely being a bachelor in that big estate."

"To hell with you, Elizabeth Donegon," he said to himself as he dialed the number of the escort service on his cell phone. "You don't know what you are missing, but it won't be long until I have my way with you!"

CHAPTER 63—2010

Raul called Carlos early one morning. Carlos sleepily answered, "Yeah, what is it?"

"In case you haven't read the newspapers this morning a body washed up from Biscayne Bay somewhere around Homestead. So far they haven't identified the corpse but I think it may be Johnny Rivera," Raul said warily waiting for Carlos to explode.

Carlos turned to the voluptuous woman lying nude beside him, "Honey, go to the kitchen and make me some coffee." She yawned and he caressed her breasts which caused her nipples to stand at attention. "Do it now, Baby! You ought to see what caffeine does to me," he said as he stroked his erect penis which was standing straight as a flagpole. She couldn't help but notice and with that quickly left the room.

"What the shit, Raul?" Carlos shouted into the telephone. "I told you to have him pushed out of the plane way out in the Atlantic Ocean. Wasn't he weighted down like I ordered?"

"Wait a minute, Carlos! The pilot wouldn't cooperate with that plan and I was forced to eject him in the bay. I didn't want to worry you but as he was falling I saw the cement block slip off and it hit the water before he did," he tried to explain.

"You, idiot! Are you telling me you did the hit yourself? You should have taken him by boat then and dumped him further out in the ocean. Now look what you have done! Can they trace it to you? Did anyone see you taking off?" Carlos screamed.

"Naw, it was early in the morning and the pilot flew underneath the radar. That's why he didn't want to drop him from a higher altitude. Besides Rivera was acting nervous, very suspicious and tried to back out at the last minute," Raul tried to calm his brother down.

"What do you mean suspicious? When I talked to him I convinced him that if he stayed in Miami he would be facing a long term in jail in addition to going bankrupt," Carlos said arrogantly. "What did he say that made you think he was suspicious?"

"Well, he said some shit about having to leave his wife and children and that he was too old to adjust to living alone in South America without his family," Raul explained.

"So, what did you tell him?" Carlos asked sarcastically.

"Well, I practically had to drag him on the plane as he was ready to turn and bolt. I told him that his wife wouldn't like visiting him in jail and being broke on top of it all," Raul said hesitantly. "I know you didn't authorize it, but I had to promise you would arrange for his wife and children to come to live with him so he finally stepped on the plane even though I had to grab him by the arm and push him inside. As soon as the plane took off he started screaming that he had changed his mind and wanted the pilot to turn around and take him back to Miami. So you see, I had to bump him off a little earlier than planned and consequently I thought I better get rid of him in the bay." He paused and said with some trepidation, "His screaming made me so nervous that I probably didn't secure the cement block properly."

Carlos was furious, "Why in the hell did you wait until now to tell me, Raul? You really botched up the job as I expected. I told you to get someone else to make the hit. All you were supposed to do was meet him at the tarmac and give him the fake new identity.

You were supposed to get someone for the actual hit," Carlos said incredulously as he marveled at his brother's stupidity.

"I know, Carlos," Raul said in an apologetic tone. "I just thought it might be better to keep it in the family. You know with your new identity and all, I just didn't want to involve someone who might later squeal.

The only witness was the pilot. Are you sure he will keep his mouth shut?"

"Don't worry about Pete," Carlos reassured him. "He's one person I know I can trust. I know too much about him. He used to run drugs on a regular basis from Columbia to Miami. I used to use him in the old days before I landed in prison and was able to locate him again when I got back from Switzerland. He's great for staying below the radar." With that he ended the conversation, "Keep your mouth shut! Do you understand?" He hung up the phone just in time.

Bethany came back to the room carrying a tray of steaming coffee and warm croissants. She hadn't bothered to slip on a robe and her round generous breasts were bouncing. Her shiny long chestnut brown hair hung down her back and her long slender legs stretched endlessly. He knew well what treasure they hid and he had paid enough for it. Besides, she was a Cuban girl from his homeland and he could feely communicate with her in Spanish. Since that first night when she was sent over by the Unique Escort Service he had kept her in bed while he fucked her endlessly. All those years in prison had made him horny and dating that frigid bitch Elizabeth hadn't helped to satisfy him.

"Caffeine or me first, Bruno?" she asked.

He turned toward her and she saw how ready he was. Pulling him down on the bed she mounted and rode him until he screamed in pleasure. Feeling her continuous spasms and moans really turned him on. She was one gal who really loved getting fucked even though she cost him a fortune. He might give her a break today, let her sit by the pool and tan her lovely body and sip mojitos while he dropped in at the Grand Hotels executive office.

"I'll take that coffee now, Querida," he whispered in her ear. She looked disappointed when he said he had to go to the office.

She said provocatively, "I'll miss you so much, Bruno. I'll be so hot by the time you get home you'll be sorry you left!'

"I'll look forward to that," he said kissing her and then quickly dressing. He hoped Kaitlin would be pleased to see him. She had seemed a little reluctant when he had asked for office space. He needed to be careful that she didn't get suspicious of his real motives. He also wanted to really check the newspapers for all the information they had on the body that had washed up on the shores of Biscayne Bay not too many miles from the executive offices of the Grand Hotels. He hoped his brother's bumbling mistakes wouldn't somehow compromise his own identity. Getting rid of Rivera was a way of protecting his investment and his eventual takeover of the company. Martinez was gone and so was Wells so it looked like clear sailing ahead and he was determined to reach his goal in the near future.

CHAPTER 64—2010

Bruno entered his new office and looked around and was pleased. It was a corner office and afforded views of Biscayne Bay. He opened his briefcase and pulled out a few of the company's annual reports. After perusing them for awhile he turned to the computer and tried to access the latest financial figures. Unfortunately, he didn't know the password.

He pressed the intercom button and Jan Summers, Kaitlin's efficient secretary answered. "This is Bruno Gersbach and I'm going to need some secretarial service. Put Ms. Donegon on the line," he said in an authoritative tone.

Kaitlin frowned when Jan told her about the request and spoke to him rather abruptly, "We really don't have extra secretarial personnel available for investors. However, I can give you the number of a good temporary office service in case you would like to hire someone on the days you are here."

He snapped back, "Well, if you can't give me secretarial help you need to provide me with the computer password so that I can study the financial records. Surely my 20 million will get me that one small favor."

"I'll ask Robert Welsh to drop by your office and you can discuss your concerns. Our records will be quite transparent from now on so I am sure he will try to answer any questions, especially about your generous loan to the company," she said trying to placate Bruno who she sensed was offended by not being offered his own secretary. She added, "There will be a Board Meeting called for next week on Friday at 10 a.m. so I hope you can attend."

"I'll be there and by the way thanks for making the records available. I'll be waiting to speak to the CFO," Bruno said in a pleasanter tone now that he saw that he was going to be included in the meeting.

Shortly after his conversation with Kaitlin, Robert Welsh knocked on his door. Bruno rose to meet him and greeted him cordially. The CFO gave him access to the password and Bruno was able to study the financial accounts in great detail. Welsh was a meticulous bookkeeper and Bruno could clearly see that his bailout had saved the company from failure. This should give him plenty of leverage with the Board. He printed out the information himself and put it in his briefcase. He would study it at home at his leisure. He chuckled as he saw that Kaitlin and the staff still were looking at him as their friendly 'white knight'.

"It's time to send Bethany home for spell," he thought regretfully. "One more last fuck and then off she goes so I can pay attention to business. Besides, I am getting kind of bored with fucking the same woman time and time again. I'm going to ask for a change of babes next time I call the service."

When he got home he found Bethany sunning out by the pool. She was bare-breasted and her large round breasts looked like ripe melons. He was sure that his gardener had a huge hard on as he saw him trimming a hedge at the side of the pool. Carlos laughed to himself as he came up behind her and reached down to gather the large breasts in his hands. As he caressed them she lazily opened her eyes and saw Carlos standing above her. Between the warm sun shining down and his massage she came quickly and rose to go into the lanai next to pool leading Carlos inside as she almost tore his clothes off.

"Hey, Bethany, slow down, honey. I haven't even had a shower yet," he urged her.

She lay down on the lounge and opened her legs wide to receive him. As usual, he didn't disappoint her. He was always ready for action and he was unusually well-endowed for a male. She was breathing heavily as he teased and massaged her private parts that were crying out to him, "Please, I need you now," she panted. He had only made several thrusts when she cried out in pleasure with continuous spasms as he continued to stretch his entire length inside her and pounded furiously until he also came.

They lay together with arms entwined for a long time until Carlos rose and said, "Pack up your stuff, honey. It's time you left. I have work to do. I can't fuck around like this forever. I've got to work to pay for you, Doll. You don't come cheap!"

The girl looked at him in astonishment, "You don't mean that Bruno! I will even do it for free if you let me stay. I've never met a man that has made me feel like you do. I can't stand to be without it."

"Sorry," he said cruelly, "I may try another broad the next time. You're a nice kid but the honeymoon is over."

Bethany was sobbing as he pushed her out of the door. She pleaded, "Please call me, Bruno. Let's not let it end like this."

Bruno slammed the door and even though she continued to pound on it he turned up the volume on his stereo and wiped out the sound. He was wasting his time fucking call girls. That wasn't going to give him the Grand Hotels. He needed to concentrate on Elizabeth for with her on his side he would have reached his goal, both her inheritance and shares in the company but her ruination, too, when he kicked her darling daughter out of the company!

He was well prepared to plant the first seeds of doubt about Kaitlin at the Board meeting. After all, she had proved to be totally incompetent in recognizing traitorous employees that were stealing from the company right under her nose. Hell, one of them was her own fiancé. She was asleep at the wheel. Under her leadership the whole house of cards was ready to tumble had he not come along and saved the company.

Carlos smiled to himself and thought, "Once I gain Elizabeth's generous share of the company and add it to my recent acquisition of shares plus the shares Raul got out of Emily under his shell company, he would be the majority stockholder and more than eligible to not only warm the CEO's seat but hold the chairmanship of the Board of Directors!"

He reached for the phone as he thought, "It's time to give Elizabeth a ring. Hopefully she will forgive me for hustling out of her place after dinner."

As she answered his call he had his answer as she sounded so excited and relieved to hear from him, "How about dinner at your favorite restaurant tomorrow night?"

"I'd love it, Bruno," she said, "please come to my house for cocktails first. I have missed you."

CHAPTER 65—2010

The next morning Carlos read in the newspaper that they had identified Johnny Rivera by fingerprints even though he was carrying a water soaked passport in a plastic travel folder bearing another identity. They had questioned his wife but all she knew was that he had told her that he was going on a business trip to South America. She told the investigator that her husband never allowed her to ask about his business. She said, "He called it snooping when I tried to find out more details about his business. He told me it wasn't a woman's business and that my job was to keep house and take care of the children." Carlos breathed a sigh of relief and lit a cigarette nervously.

On further questioning she did admit knowing there was a lawsuit regarding some kind of construction accident but she didn't know any details. She said that her husband had appeared worried about something lately but when she asked he had told her to 'shut up'. Carlos silently applauded Rivera for not blabbing everything to his wife.

The article then spelled out the lawsuit and the indictment against him which was public record. The only mention of the Grand Hotel Corporation was citing that the accident occurred at their New York renovation project.

Carlos paced back and forth worrying that his brother's mistakes might lead the authorities to him. "That body should have never surfaced if Raul had taken care of the matter properly!" he swore. He needed to stay on the good side of his brother though until he handed over his shares in the company that he had squeezed out of his former wife, Emily. Of course, Emily had never caught on that she was selling the shares to Raul as at least in this one instance his stupid brother was clever enough to set up a shell company.

That evening when he picked up Elizabeth he was still worried about the Rivera business but he tried not to show it in front of her. She greeted him warmly and they went out to the terrace for cocktails.

"Kaitlin tells me you will be attending the Board Meeting this week. I think it's wonderful that you are taking such an active part in the company," she smiled as she sipped her drink.

Bruno replied, "Well, you know Elizabeth, that is one reason my investment company has done so well. I always try to stay on top of my investments and I am particularly concerned with having a solid management team." He paused for a moment and then said softly, "Do you feel that perhaps Kaitlin needs a vacation?"

Elizabeth looked shocked, "What do you mean, Bruno?"

"Nothing to worry your pretty head about. But with the past revelations about two of her top employees stealing from the company and one of them her fiancé, I just wondered if the whole thing was a little too much for her. She must have been heartbroken to find that her long-term partner had betrayed her. Most women would ask for a break after that!" he said kindly holding her hand.

"I know she was terribly upset, Bruno, but knowing Kaitlin she is putting the company before her own personal needs," Elizabeth said thoughtfully as she passed the plate of appetizers to Bruno.

Bruno took the last sip of his cocktail and changing the subject said, "Now let's decide where we are going for dinner. Your choice, Lovely Lady."

"There are so many wonderful restaurants in downtown Coral Gables. Are you in the mood for French, Italian, Mexican or any other ethnic specialty? They are all there," she said as she turned to take their glasses back to the kitchen.

"The French cooking sounds good to me tonight," he said putting her wrap around her slim shoulders. "Some night we ought to see if they have a good Swiss restaurant in Miami. I sometimes get hungry for the specialties I was brought up on." He laughed to himself as he thought how surprised she would be if she knew that meant roast pork, black beans and rice and plantains!

They discovered an intimate French bistro with candlelight on each table. Soft music was playing in the background and soon Bruno had asked for the wine list. That's one area he had studied religiously as he planned his new lifestyle.

"I will order a different wine with every course, Elizabeth. But first you must decide on the menu," he advised her.

"Why don't you order for us, Bruno," she said almost shyly as the waiter hovered over them.

"If you insist, dear lady," he said turning to the waiter. "We'll start out with escargot with plenty of warm French bread, then French onion soup and our entrees will be the scallops in Beuure Blanc. To start off, we'll have a bottle of merlot with the escargot." The waiter smiled happily when he noticed Bruno had ordered a $300 bottle of wine. It would be a pleasure serving these patrons.

The food was delicious and they savored every bite. Elizabeth felt a little tipsy as they had consumed several bottles of wine by the time their plate of fromage and fruit tarts arrived for dessert. Bruno ordered a dessert wine to go with the last course.

They were both in a jovial mood as they left the restaurant and waited for the valet to bring the car. Elizabeth was giggling like a school girl and hanging on to Bruno for support.

When they reached her doorstep Bruno held her close and kissed her passionately. She found herself responding to him in a way that she had never thought possible since her husband passed away so many years ago.

Bruno stepped back and looked into her deep brown eyes and said, "I can't take advantage of you, Elizabeth, when you are obviously a tiny bit drunk." She looked disappointed and threw her arms around him and kissed him again.

He reluctantly pulled away from her embrace and whispered, "We'll deal with this another time. Sweet dreams of me, my darling."

Later as she began to sober up she realized that she had wanted to have him make love to her in the worst way. She was glad that he had stopped in time. She still wasn't ready to share her bed with another man. Or was she? She slept restlessly wondering how it would feel to be in love and loved again. It was something she had never considered before, but yet tonight she dreaded being alone and her body cried out for Bruno's touch.

CHAPTER 66—2010

Carlos arrived early for the Board Meeting for a reason. He wanted to plant a few more seeds of doubt about Kaitlin's competence in Robert Welsh's ear. By luck he ran into him in the outer office and said in a friendly tone, "Good Morning, Bob. Do you think you might have a few moments to spend with me before the meeting today?"

"I always have time for you, Bruno," he said cordially ushering him into his office. "What can I do for you?"

"After looking through the past financial records it seemed to me that there were many clues that there were discrepancies long before Martinez' skimming was discovered. Tell me, did the CEO not have to sign off on these reports?" he asked dubiously.

"My guess is that she trusted Martinez, that crook, so much that she kind of rubber-stamped his reports without reading them too carefully," he said frowning. "Of course, you realize that I never got a chance to review them in my former position. John was very closed-mouthed about it. He just kept assuring everyone at the meetings that we were on solid ground."

Bruno leaned over Bob's desk and said in a low, confidential voice, "As one businessman to another do you think that the CEO is a little overwhelmed by her responsibility? I understand she inherited her position from her father, but perhaps she needed a little more time learning the business before she took over as head of the company."

Welsh nodded in agreement, "Exactly my thoughts, Bruno. In fact, I felt that she lacked the experience ten years ago when she was first appointed and I'm not convinced that she's learned too much after this recent calamity. I was surprised that David Wells turned out the way he did as he was a very loyal employee while Kaitlin's father, Andrew Donegon was running the show."

Bruno said with concern, "I guess that happens when you have a weak leader. People think they can take advantage and do risky things thinking the leader will never catch on. I'm sure that Wells also realized that she didn't peruse the books too carefully or he never would have tried it. I heard he had an expensive mistress to support and I'm sure that was a factor also."

Bruno paused and then said thoughtfully, "You know Bob, I have a sizeable investment in this company and I believe in a strong management team. I have many responsibilities with my own project, but if it would help return the company to a profitable organization, I could be open to filling in as an Interim CEO until Kaitlin has been mentored in the financial side of her operation."

Welsh stared at him, "Do you mean you would like to replace Kaitlin? It's a family business you know."

"I don't mean to replace her on a permanent basis, Bob. I would never suggest that. But I do believe she is lacking in many essential business skills and actually could profit from some in-service with you. By the way, you are the kind of strong management I am talking about."

"Thanks, Bruno. You do know that she has several relatives on the Board? Her mother, Elizabeth and her sister-in-law, Emily. That might make it impossible to remove her as CEO. I guess it would rest with Edward Haynes and Arthur Hennington. You have my vote, of course. David Wells has still not been replaced and it is possible you could suggest someone for his former position who would join our side," he said with the wheels turning in his brain at a mile a minute.

"Why don't you try to put in a word or two to Haynes and Hennington and get their feeling on the matter?" Bruno said as he rose to leave the office. "I'll see you at the meeting. I'm sure you will have a complete report on the financial status of the company and I look forward to your update." The two men shook hands and exchanged glances of understanding before Bruno walked out of the office leaving Robert Welsh much food for thought.

While the two men were hatching their plans, Kaitlin was preparing for the Board Meeting. She was well-aware that she should have never signed off on all John's reports without thoroughly examining them. But she had trusted him so much and never dreamed that he would take money from the company. She was afraid that she might look incompetent to some of the Board members. She would try doubly hard to impress them at the meeting today.

She wasn't too sure she liked having Bruno Gersbach as a voting member, but that was part of the agreement so she expected to see him at the meeting. Her mother had mentioned something strange that Bruno had said to her. When her mother asked her if maybe she needed a little break from work, perhaps a vacation to help her heal from John's betrayal and nearly losing the company it had startled her. "Why in the world do you ask that mother?" she had asked her.

Elizabeth then told her that Bruno had suggested that when they went out for dinner. This was very upsetting to Kaitlin as to her it implied that Bruno thought she wasn't up to the job or that as a woman she was too emotional and let her personal feelings rule her actions although her mother said that idea was foolish. That he was only thinking of being helpful.

She had to admit that she was feeling a little insecure. There had been serious consequences and the company nearly folded because she had failed to see what John and David Wells were doing. It would take a long time before she recovered from the shock but it only gave her more resolve to stay focused and never operate on trust alone. She kept her emotions in a separate compartment and didn't let them interfere with the job. Now to convince others that she was able to focus on the important things and forget her hurt.

Kaitlin took a fortifying breath as she entered the Board Room. She immediately noticed that Robert Welsh had cornered Edward Haynes and Arthur Hennington and they seemed to be having a serious discussion. She thought they looked a little guilty as they noticed she had entered the room and they quickly took their seats. Bruno Gersbach was already seated and was talking to Elizabeth and Emily.

As she called the meeting to order she wondered if she had a touch of paranoia for it seemed like the members were sizing her up. She told herself that she had to stop feeling so suspicious of everyone. She wondered if she would ever be able to trust again. She mustn't doubt herself. She smiled cordially and greeted each member of the Board individually.

She began speaking in a firm voice even though she felt all shaky inside, "Thank you for your confidence in my leadership during the rough sailing the past six months. I am happy to report the company is now solvent, the renovation project in New York has been restarted and all the construction workers have returned to work and dropped their threats of a strike. As you probably heard, the cement contractor who did the shoddy work has been found dead and his estate will pay off the lawsuit filed by the injured worker. As he was found liable for the accident through willful negligence all charges against our company have been dropped. Again, I would like to thank Mr. Gersbach for his generous investment and we can now confidently resume business on all burners."

She led the group in applause as they all rose to salute their savior, Bruno Gersbach.

Bryon Harrell entered the Board Room at that point apologizing for being late. "Sorry, but I was in court. You will all be happy to know we are officially off the hook on any charges or lawsuits related to the accident in New York. Our stocks have taken a dramatic rise since the news was released that we have a wealthy investor and the New York renovation is back in operation again! I think we owe our CEO some applause for the successful outcome."

Elizabeth and Emily applauded enthusiastically but Bryon couldn't help but notice how slowly the others arose from their seats and how subdued their applause was. He was sure Kaitlin noticed too because she was frowning. He was hoping to have dinner with her that evening and could find out then what he had missed by being late for the first part of the meeting.

Kaitlin sounded discouraged after she and Bryon left the Board Meeting. "Did you notice the hostility was thick in the air, Bryon, especially when you asked them to give me applause?"

"They did seem rather reserved but then we've been through a rough spot and I think most of them are still in shock. Can I take you out for dinner and we'll try to figure it out together?"

"Come to the penthouse and let's send out for a pizza or something. I don't feel like going out tonight. I found the meeting very disturbing. I felt like there might be some sort of movement afoot that I am not privy to."

Bryon looked at her thoughtfully, "Probably your imagination, Kaitlin. And yes, eating in is fine with me as long as we are together."

They finished off several bottles of wine before digging into the pizza and their mood was definitely elevated. Kaitlin looked into Bryon's eyes and said, "I don't think you should drive home tonight. We are both slightly drunk."

Bryon threw his arms around her and kissed her passionately. "I thought you'd never ask," he said as she led him to her bedroom while unbuttoning his shirt at the same time. All negative thoughts were washed away with their passion for one another.

CHAPTER 67—2010

It was early December and Elizabeth and Kaitlin were Christmas shopping. It always seemed a little strange to have warm sunshine and blue skies at holiday time in Miami. There would be no white Christmas unless snow was imported for the children to play in as had been done several years ago just so they could get the feel of throwing a snowball like the children up north.

They were shopping in The Falls in South Miami-Dade County, a unique shopping center with a series of waterfalls and tropical greenery with upscale stores lining both sides of the garden. They liked to go to The Falls at Christmas time because they always had beautiful holiday decorations and colored lights on the waterfalls. It really got them in the holiday spirit even though the temperature was in the low eighties.

Elizabeth was cheerful thinking about her new friend, Bruno. She glowed when she thought about how he had kissed her after their dinner date. She was also happy that this year, for the first time since Andy died ten years ago, she would have an escort for all the Christmas parties she had been invited to. Besides parties given by personal friends there were many charities that she supported that gave lavish black tie events at Christmas time. And then there were many holiday dinner dances at the Coral Gables Country Club where she was a member and of course the Opera Guild gala. She had called Bruno and given him all the dates and he had accepted every invitation.

"Kaitlin," she said excitedly, "I need to get some new cocktail dresses. So let's look while we are here." She turned a bright red when she picked a few sexy gowns and Kaitlin looked at her curiously. "I don't want you to get the wrong idea, Kaitlin, but Bruno will be escorting me to the holiday galas this year. You know I usually don't go to many parties and I have always gone with my lady friends since your father passed away. This year I will need to update my wardrobe a bit since it appears I will be having more of a social life."

Kaitlin was surprised but happy that her mother had decided to get out a bit. She had worried that she had a very limited social life even though she volunteered for many charities and was very active. There just hadn't been a man in her life for so long.

After Elizabeth had picked out several gowns she suggested that she and Kaitlin stop for lunch at one of the many restaurants at The Falls. They chose one that served delicious Italian food and decided to have a glass of wine before lunch.

Kaitlin looked into her mother's eyes and asked, "Did you sense any hostility toward me at the Board Meeting last week? I noticed that even though you and Emily applauded me enthusiastically, the others were strangely reserved. Have you heard anything from Bruno that would indicate that there was trouble afoot?"

Elizabeth frowned, "Well, I told you that Bruno mentioned that maybe you needed a vacation. But I didn't sense he meant it in a negative way. He just seemed concerned with your welfare. Besides, I think you just imagined bad vibes. Everyone stood up and applauded you. Naturally, being your mother, I probably clapped louder than the rest."

Kaitlin sighed picking up the menu, "I hope you are right, mother. Bryon also said he thought I was imagining it."

Elizabeth looked up from the menu, "My goodness! I plan to order the Shrimp Scampi but it's listed at twice the regular price. I do love those huge juicy Gulf of Mexico shrimp that I've had here before. In fact that is one reason I wanted to come here today."

"It's the result of the Gulf of Mexico oil spill, Mom. Not only are shrimp from the Gulf harder to come by at restaurants but they are now very pricey when they are available. This oil spill has not only been hard on the restaurant business including the restaurants at some of our hotels, but it has been hard on tourism. Even though our Miami beaches have managed to escape so far, tourists don't know that and are choosing other places to vacation. It really has hit our Miami hotels hard and just when we are getting back on our feet," Kaitlin moaned.

"It's such a tragedy and it took months to get the well recapped. I feel so sorry for all the wildlife habitats that were destroyed. Did you see the poor pelicans covered with oil on the news? Thank goodness some good Samaritans are trying to nurse them back to health," Liz said with concern.

"Yes, as the Loop Current, which is a surge of warm water that circulates in the eastern Gulf of Mexico, moved north within 30 miles of the spill, scientists have predicted that it would catch the oil and sweep it around the Florida peninsula. If that should happen the oil could contaminate the Everglades National Park along with the mangrove swamps, coral reefs, sea grass and animals and fish that depend on them. Worse our beaches in Miami and along Florida's eastern coast could be tarred," Kaitlin said with a worried expression on her face.

When the waiter came to take their order Elizabeth said, "I'll have the Shrimp Scampi even though I see you've raised your prices."

"Unfortunately, in late November they re-closed the shrimping industry in the Gulf because they found tar balls in the shrimper's nets. We are lucky to get any shrimp but we were forced to raise our prices to meet our costs. We hated to take it off our menu because that is one of our most popular dishes," he explained with regret.

They enjoyed their lunch in spite of the grim after-effects of the Deepwater Horizon tragedy and gathering up all their packages they tried to get back in the Christmas spirit. They knew in their hearts many people were suffering this holiday season after the fall of the fishing business that provided income for so many in the Gulf states as well as sorrow for the families of the eleven workers who were killed in the oil spill accident.

Elizabeth asked Kaitlin to stop at the post office before she dropped her off. They got in a long line of people mailing holiday gifts and buying stamps for their Christmas cards.

As they patiently waited to buy their rolls of stamps Elizabeth glanced at the huge poster on the adjoining wall and turned pale, "Kaitlin, I see a picture of my old fiancé, Carlos Gonzalez. Do you suppose he has been released from prison?"

Kaitlin walked over and read the information under the photo. Returning to her mother she informed her, "It says 'ABSCONDED', or in other words he has run off and is missing."

"My God, Kaitlin, do you mean he escaped from prison," she said trembling and her face white as a sheet.

"No, he didn't escape from prison, but it says he was paroled and never reported to the parole officer after his release. Apparently, he just disappeared!"

"I'm afraid, Kaitlin. Do you suppose he's still somewhere in Miami?" Elizabeth asked breathlessly. "Your father told me that when he was sentenced he was quoted as saying his former fiancé might have turned him in!"

Kaitlin tried to comfort her mother even though now she was worried, "It doesn't make sense that he would hang around Miami where he is well-known. Also, there was a reward offered and my guess is that he has left the country. I'll have Bryon look into it. Maybe he can find out something through his legal channels. In the meantime, try not to worry. Apparently he disappeared over a year ago, and if he wanted retribution I'm sure we would have heard about it. I don't think you have anything to worry about."

Even though she had tried to set her mother's mind at ease, as she dropped her off at her home and saw her entering alone she panicked knowing that the house was secluded with a long driveway and was not visible from the road. The back of the house was accessible from the water. For the first time she felt fearful about her mother living alone. She had a burglar alarm but rarely used it and no security lights. It had never bothered Kaitlin before, but now she had to admit that this former fiancé could be a threat to her beloved mother who was always there to support her with love and encouragement.

When she got home Kaitlin called her mother with concern in her voice, "Mom, be sure you have your burglar alarm on. I know you forget it sometimes. Also, check to make sure all your doors and windows are locked. You may want to get some extra security lights around the front and back of the house."

"Kaitlin, for Heaven's Sake, I have been living alone here for years. You know that the neighborhood association pays for a security patrol that watches all our houses. We have only had a few minor instances in the past ten years," she told her worried daughter.

"With this Carlos Gonzalez on the loose, it wouldn't hurt to tell the security people to come by your house more often than usual. Also, have you considered getting a dog? That might give you a little extra peace of mind. And do you have a panic button for emergencies incorporated into your alarm system?"

"I thought you told me that he had probably left the country and I shouldn't worry and now you are scaring me to death, Kaitlin! Yes, I have a panic button right near my bedside table but I have never had to use it."

Kaitlin replied, "I don't mean to frighten you and Carlos has in all probability left the country but I also want you to be cautious."

After hanging up the phone she reached for her cell phone and quick-dialed Bryon, "Come over to the penthouse as soon as possible. We may have a new problem."

So far they had been very discreet about their budding relationship. This was not the time to erode confidence with the Board of Director's after the John Martinez affair.

Mixing romance with business, especially with another company employee would certainly cause a lot of unnecessary gossip and reflect on her judgment. Better to keep it quiet for now.

CHAPTER 68—2010

Bryon arrived early the next day at his law office and pondered over the new information Kaitlin had given him about Carlos Gonzalez. It was hard to believe that Kaitlin's very elegant and sophisticated mother had once been engaged to a drug lord when she was a young girl. According to Kaitlin he was a happy, energetic medical student at the time they fell in love, and later grew bitter about his friends from his homeland, Cuba, who were imprisoned or killed in the futile Bay of Pigs invasion when John Kennedy was president. Apparently that bitterness caused him to turn to crime with the newly formed Cuban Mafia at which point Elizabeth had broken off the engagement and subsequently married Kaitlin's father, Andrew Donegon.

He planned to go over to the courthouse and examine all the public records about Carlos Gonzalez. He also had a friend who was a correction's officer at the federal prison in Miami-Dade County where Carlos had been held. He had placed a call to the officer and hoped to get more information about the time of the prisoner's release and any other pertinent information. He especially wanted to know if the officer had heard about any threats Carlos may have been heard to make toward other people on the outside.

While he was waiting for a call back he was surprised when his secretary buzzed to tell him that Edward Haynes was in the outer office and hoped he had time to see him.

"Of course," he said walking to the office door to welcome Haynes. He shook hands with the banker and after he was seated Bryon asked,

"What can I do for you, Edward? You look concerned. Is it a company matter or personal?"

"I'm actually here today representing some members of the Board of Directors. Yes, we are concerned about the CEO and her apparent lack of financial skills," he said seriously.

Bryon stiffened, "What do you mean, Edward? I think Kaitlin has done a fabulous job. She was just on the cover of financial magazines last year as 'Entrepreneur of the Year'!"

Haynes frowned, "That's all well and good, but bear in mind the company nearly went bankrupt a short time ago and if it hadn't been for Bruno Gersbach's investment we would have also been in trouble with the SEC for not reporting material changes in our financial picture. Not only that, both she and Martinez could have faced charges had the money not been replaced when it was." He added, "Of course, none of us believe she was in cahoots with Martinez but she shouldn't have signed off on financial statements that were obviously incorrect. In other words, she didn't understand the reports but signed off anyway on John's assurance that the company was solid!"

"So just who do you represent, Edward?" Bryon asked with a worried expression on his face. "Do you have another person in mind for the position of CEO?"

"Well, it could be worse. Mr. Gersbach has again generously offered to serve as Interim CEO for at least a year and has agreed to mentor Kaitlin in the financial side of running a large corporation during that time. I represent Arthur Hennington, Robert Welsh and Mr. Gerbach. That makes four of us and it's possible Elizabeth and Emily will come around when we explain that it is not only for the good of the company, but for Kaitlin's good also," he explained.

"How could this be good for Kaitlin? I don't understand your thinking on this, and what about Mr. Gersbach's own company and his responsibility there?" Bryon asked scowling.

"Don't get me wrong, Bryon. We all think Kaitlin is very strong in innovation. Our idea is to put her in David Well's former position as General Manager of Domestic Development where she can expand on her Boutique concept. Bruno says he has a competent manager to run his new investment house while he is helping us out. Of course, financial matters are his forte and we're lucky to have his offer to step in. As far as her mother and sister-in-law, we are trying to make them understand that this move would strengthen Kaitlin's grasp of all sides of the business and relieve her of some of the recent stress she has been under," he said thoughtfully. "It can easily be explained to shareholders that she has decided to devote more time to innovating the new boutique chain for the next few years."

"So why do you come to me, Edward? I'm not a voting member, only an advisor, but I assure you I would not vote to remove Kaitlin from her position if I did have a vote," he said sarcastically.

"I just wanted to check about the legalities of having a foreigner heading the company, even though it is only temporary," he explained. "He is majority shareholder at this point so he has every right to the Interim position in our opinion."

"How do you figure he's majority shareholder? I thought Kaitlin was," Bryon said in an astonished tone. "And then her mother and sister-in-law own shares. I'm sure they wouldn't vote her out!"

"It was news to us also, but Mr. Gersbach was able to buy up Emily's shares some time ago. Apparently she was having financial problems caused by her expensive divorce and was approached by a company to sell her shares. Bruno heard about it through his financial investment channels and bought up the stock from the company she had sold to. As you know he bought up a giant share of the stocks in the half-priced deal we gave him when he bailed out the company."

Bryon was in a state of shock and asked, "When do you intend to make this move, Edward? It appears you have the majority of votes even if Elizabeth and Emily vote with Kaitlin now that Mr. Gersbach was gifted with voting rights."

"We plan to do this at the Board Meeting the first week in January. We think it would be unkind to do this to Kaitlin just before Christmas," he said kindly. "If there is any problem with Bruno's Swiss nationality please let us know and I guess Robert Welsh would be next in line because of his financial expertise. Seeing it is only an internal matter and we plan for Kaitlin to resume the CEO post when she is more mature, I don't believe it is necessary to hold a meeting with the shareholders for approval."

After he left, Bryon sat alone in stunned silence. He told his secretary to hold his calls and cancel all his appointments. How in the world could he break this news to Kaitlin? The company was her world and it was a family issue for her. She had been right on target when she suggested something was underfoot at the last Board Meeting. It was far from being just her imagination as he had suggested to her.

He had to admit he was falling in love with her and he knew this would break her heart.

CHAPTER 69—2010

It was the week before Christmas and Bryon was determined not to ruin Kaitlin's holiday with the devastating news that had been delivered by Edward Haynes. The two of them had spent many nights together and Bryon was falling more and more in love with Kaitlin. He wanted to shout it from the rooftops and tell it to the world. But she insisted that they keep the relationship secret for the time being and he had agreed to her terms. Unfortunately, that meant that they couldn't attend any Christmas parties that included Board Members or friends of the Board. They were both content to dine and dance in some of the hidden places in Miami.

Deep in the night they would hold each other and dance to jazz with a bluesy lilt in some dark corner bar hidden down narrow, dark alleys where only those in the know could find them. Slightly drunk and in love they would sit for hours listening to the music and looking into each other's eyes. Often well-known musicians played at these small, intimate bars after their regular gigs.

"This is the best Christmas I have ever had," Kaitlin whispered to Bryon. "Just the two of us with no one around to bring us a fresh crop of problems. I wish it could stay like this forever." Bryon kissed her passionately and no one noticed. It was if they were alone in the world of the mellow tenor sax, the candlelight and the dark room.

Unable to control their passion for one another any longer, Bryon paid the bill and they went out on the dark street to the car. "I can't wait until we get home, Bryon," Kaitlin moaned as she started to unbutton his shirt.

They climbed into the back seat and in a minute had undressed each other. Bryon entered her immediately in answer to her frantic demands. They both felt the earth shake as their frantic coupling exploded into a million waves of pleasure.

"I love you, Kaitlin," Brian whispered over and over again.

Kaitlin finally admitted, "I love you, too. With all my heart and soul."

Somehow Bryon could never find the right time to tell her about her planned demotion in January. He loved her too much and he refused to break the spell of magic that they were encased in. He didn't want to be the one to remove the sparkling stars in her eyes that reflected her happiness as she gazed at him. He was a coward and so afraid he would lose her if he revealed the plan which might very well destroy her.

While Bryon and Kaitlin were making love, Elizabeth was snuggled up to Bruno on the dance floor at 'The Holiday Snowflake Ball', an elegant charity, and wishing he was making love to her. The colored lights flashed on the beautiful snowflakes hanging from the ceiling as the full orchestra played romantic Frank Sinatra songs with a singer who sounded just like Frankie. She was wearing a low-cut lavender gown with sequins sparkling like the snowflakes above. As Bruno brushed his hand across her chest she felt him caress her cleavage and she started to tremble.

So far she and Bruno had attended seven Christmas functions and each time he had returned her to her home he had given her a brotherly kiss on both cheeks in the European fashion. He was such a gentleman and each time she left him she felt a hunger for his touch that he never satisfied. She was sorry that she had turned him down so abruptly the first time he had tried, and now he treated her with extreme respect when she was silently crying out for his body.

That evening as they returned to her house he surprised her by kissing her passionately. She felt him unzipping her dress as they stood there on the front porch.

She said nervously, "I think we better go inside, Bruno." Her face was flushed and she reached up and undid his tie and started to unbutton his shirt as he stared at her breasts that were now completely revealed as her gown slipped to the floor. He was amazed at how beautiful her breasts were as Elizabeth was no kid. He carried her up the spiral staircase to her bedroom and placed her gently on the bed. As he pulled off his pants she turned a bright scarlet as she couldn't help but notice his well-endowed male organ which was obviously ready for action.

For the better part of an hour they just kissed, caressed and fondled. Her breath and heart-rate accelerated more with each intimate caress. From the sound of her mouth came a sound that was barely human and she felt like she was passing out. She had been needing this for so long, especially the touches. As they clung together a pounding tropical thunderstorm caused lightning to strike nearby and lit up the sky like a million fireworks and clashes of thunder rattled like the sound of the headboards as Bruno thrust inside her over and over again. She didn't think she could have asked him to stop if the roof of the house had been ripped away. Afterwards she lay there like a trauma victim, shaking and wet with sweat. He regretfully rolled off her and instead of dressing and leaving he spooned his body next to her and held her tenderly.

"That was wonderful, Elizabeth. Why didn't we try this sooner?" he said nuzzling her cheek. She lay there happily in his arms. There was something so familiar about him, about the way he caressed her and made her feel alive again. It was as if she had known and made love to him in another life.

"It has been a long time, ten years, Bruno since I have been loved by a man. I haven't allowed myself to think of it for all that time. You have awakened feelings that I thought were lost forever," she whispered into his ear.

It wasn't long before Bruno held her face in his hands and gave her a long, passionate kiss and a moment later she was ready and begging him to enter her again. She could hardly believe her need for him as he fondled the wet spot between her legs until she thought she would die, aching for the feel of him inside her. This time they came together and then lay there spent while the rain pounded on the windows and they could hear the crash of the waves beyond.

Finally, he got up and announced, "May I use your shower, Elizabeth. You have caused me to work up quite a sweat!"

"Of course, you will find towels and shampoo in the bathroom. Let me know it you need anything," she said lovingly wondering what it would be like to take a shower with him.

As he turned to go into the bathroom, she gazed at his amazing physique, so beautiful for a man his age. And then her world came crumbling down as her eyes alighted on an unusual star birthmark on his left buttocks. She turned pale and gasped. Her heart beat rapidly with fear and disappointment.

"But how could it be? This man didn't look anything like Carlos, her lover of so many years ago although their body stature was similar. But how could someone else have the star birthmark in exactly the same place? She had teased him about it endlessly during their courtship and called him "Her Star-Studded fiancé" good-naturedly.

She was trembling now and frantic. She would test him out. She had to find out for sure. As she heard him turn off the shower she called to him, "Carlos!"

"Si, Querida," he said as he toweled himself off and then suddenly realized his mistake. He tried to cover up by saying, "You really are funny, Elizabeth. I thought I heard you call me Carlos and thought you had me mixed up with one of your other guys so I answered in Spanish!"

She wasn't laughing. "You answered to Carlos because that's who you are. You must have had plastic surgery, but you forgot one thing. You forgot to ask them remove the star birthmark. Don't forget I have seen it many times in the past and don't tell me that every man has one. It is extremely unique. No wonder I felt like I had met you before. How could you do this to me, Carlos?"

He was no longer stunned but was red with fury. His eyes threw daggers at her and he grabbed her by the arm so forcibly that she nearly fell backwards and hit the wall. "How could I do this to you, Bitch, when you sent me to prison for years? I have waited all this time to get even with you for what you and your bastard husband did to me!"

"Would it surprise you to know that neither Andy nor I turned you in? We had nothing to do with it. You were sent to prison because you were a criminal and it doesn't appear that you have changed!" she said shaking a fist at him.

He lunged at her and roughly threw her on the bed knocking the wind out of her and put his strong hands around her throat. He was squeezing the life out of her as he choked her. She knew at that moment she was about to die as she gasped for breath.

As his hold tightened she prayed to her dead husband, Andy. "Help me, Andy," she cried silently unable to speak. "Show me the way."

She could hardly breathe and saw the bright light as the specter of death approached but then as if Andy's spirit was guiding her she somehow found the strength left in her limp body to reach for the bedside panic button and press it. Immediately loud sirens screamed out in the night and the phone started ringing. He looked at her with panic and loosened his grip on her neck and she gasped and took a frantic breath of air. Carlos ran down the stairs and within moments even in her semi-comatose state she heard the screech of his tires as he sped out of her driveway.

The police and paramedics found her lying there in the bed gasping for breath but still alive. They rushed her in the ambulance to the hospital.

Carlos had long prepared for this day even though he was confident that he would never be discovered. He had carefully orchestrated his escape plan should the worse happen.

His life had been ruined again by the same bitch. How could he have let that happen? Why hadn't he remembered that damn star on his buttocks? But as he asked himself all these questions he reached for his cell phone and initiated Plan B. His pilot sleepily answered the phone.

"Have the plane ready for take-off in 30 minutes. I will meet you on the tarmac. We are going to South America tonight. File a flight plan for Chile, but we are going to Brazil," he ordered. He paid the pilot big bucks just to sit on his ass and wait for this call which he had hoped he would never have to make.

He tried to keep close to the speed limit so he wouldn't be picked up as he drove to his tiny secret house in Coconut Grove which he rented. No one knew about it except his brother with whom he had discussed Plan B in great detail many months ago. It was set back, hidden by lush tropical foliage. He quickly grabbed his suitcase which had been packed and ready for months in the event he might somehow be discovered.

He picked up his new identity papers and passport of which he had several choices. He next rushed to another car which had stolen license plates and was hidden in a secluded carport and headed for the regional airport. On the way, he used his cell phone to transfer his millions in his Swiss bank electronically to an account he already had set up in Brazil in expectation of the worse scenario. As an afterthought, he rang his brother who sounded drunk. "Plan B, Asshole. I will let you know when I get settled in my new hacienda."

An hour later he was airborne and as he flew over the lights of Miami he saluted and shouted, "Goodbye, all you stupid bastards, until we meet again!" He laughed as he opened a bottle of champagne and settled back in the comfortable expensive leather seat of his corporate jet. As he became very drunk he dreamed of his new life. He would buy a huge villa overlooking the sea on one of the remote and beautiful beaches in Brazil. It would be like the beaches of Cuba, his homeland. He pictured himself sunning on the beach while two sexy Latina beauties made love to him. One of them would bring him a margarita and then they would swim nude in the sea. He would grow a beard and let his hair grow. Maybe wear a pony tail. He smiled as he thought about the millions of dollars being transferred to his new account. Life was good! His future looked bright! No one would ever find him!

EPILOGUE—
ONE YEAR LATER

The police located Carlos' car where he had left it in the Coconut Grove carport after the owner of the house reported that he had disappeared without settling the bill for the rent. On entering the house in Coconut Grove the police found a sardonic note that said, "Why did it take you so long, Assholes? Sorry, I got tired of waiting for you! Your friend, Carlos Gonzalez." So far there was no trace of Carlos. He had disappeared again.

Elizabeth Donegon was in therapy after her brush with death. Autumn's husband, Bill Pierce, who had suffered post-traumatic stress in the war, was a great help to her in dealing with the aftermath of the life-altering event. She never dated again or had any desire to have a man in her life after her experience with Carlos Gonzalez. Emily was equally turned off from dating after her experience with the other Gonzalez brother. Through Bryon's investigation of Carlos, it was discovered that Emily's former husband, Raul, was the brother of Carlos Gonzalez. Elizabeth and Emily were shocked at that revelation and could see it was all a plot from the beginning when Emily first met Raul. They both hoped that there would never be a Gonzalez to cloud their lives again. Autumn and Bill had another child, a girl this time named Spring as she was born in April. Elizabeth and Emily took turns doting over Billie and Spring.

Kaitlin Donegon retained her CEO position and never learned about the impending mutiny plans of the male Board members. She had appointed a young, enthusiastic and bright executive with experience with another competing hotel chain to the position formerly held by David Wells. He had great plans for expanding their chain of boutique hotels. Edward Haynes, Arthur Hennington and Robert Welsh were terribly embarrassed by their poor judgment in almost positioning a former drug kingpin in the company's top position. It was a long time before they could look Kaitlin in the eye even though she was unaware of their planned rebellion. They were relieved when Bryon Harrell revealed that he had never told Kaitlin about their planned uprising.

She went over every report handed to her by Robert Welsh and they went over each item with a fine-toothed comb. She was determined to never lose her focus again and in time she and Robert developed mutual respect for one another. She had recognized her part in rubber-stamping John Martinez' reports without being told and was determined she would never get caught asleep at the wheel again.

John Martinez finally was hired by a small advertising agency in Miami and was making his restitution payments each month. He and Kaitlin never spoke again.

Bryon Harrell became a partner in his law firm and another associate was now representing the Grand Hotels when Bryon resigned. Kaitlin and Bryon no longer had a conflict of interest and openly started dating. They were very much in love.

Kaitlin Donegon and Bryon Harrell married in December at a small civil ceremony at the courthouse. Only immediate family attended. Bryon who was not at all intimidated by the family secret couldn't wait to have a child and Kaitlin felt the same way. In the meantime, they were having fun trying! Kaitlin was sure she would only miss a short time at the office when the baby was born. She was sure she could juggle business with motherhood.

Even though the bad economic times continued, the New York renovation had been completed and was fully booked and the other Grand Hotels, both the major and the boutique chains were doing well considering tourism was down nationwide. As there was no more Bruno Gersbach, they had no reason to pay back his loan or distribute to him the interest promised him. The company was solvent and Kaitlin could imagine her forbearers smiling and patting her on the back. Life was good!